WOLF IN THE HENHOUSE

Colin Mardell

APS BOOKS
Yorkshire

Also by Colin Mardell

Keep Her Safe
Fetch Them Home
Revenge Ain't Sweet
Into Africa

APS Books,
The Stables Field Lane,
Aberford,
West Yorkshire,
LS25 3AE

APS Books is a subsidiary of the APS Publications imprint

www.andrewsparke.com

First published worldwide by APS Books in 2023

A catalogue record for this book is available from the British Library

WOLF IN THE HENHOUSE

Chapter 1

June 2021 - Dunn Loring, Virginia

The local radio station had been left to play in the background after the breakfast news.

"They're playing your song Mom," Ben called from the kitchen.

Saffron Price, shook her head, smiled, and called back from the huge study she shared with her husband when he was at home, "I keep telling you, it's not my song."

"Grandad Walden used to say it was."

"You couldn't take anything Grandad said seriously, he just thought it would be a great joke to name me after a town in the UK that neither he nor anybody he knew had ever been to."

"Why did he do that again Mom?" Ben asked, joining his mom in one hand clutching a bottle of flavored water and a bag of fruit chips in the other.

"He was a big fan of music from the sixties, and *Mellow Yellow* was one of his favorite songs. If you'd listened, there's a line in it that goes something about being mad about Saffron He told me that he thought it was a great name and he thought if he ever had a daughter he'd call her Saffron, but it was when he heard about the English town called Saffron Walden that clinched it. When I came along, Saffron it was. If he'd told my mom at the time, she'd never have agreed."

"Did she ever find out?"

"She didn't until I was about six when in an unguarded moment at a Christmas Party he mentioned that two members of his favorite sixties band, *Pink Floyd* came from near there. Mom went absolutely apeshit."

"Mom, you always tell me off for swearing."

"Yeah, sorry."

"What would he have called you if you were a boy then?"

"Without a doubt I'd have been called Dylan, after Bob Dylan. Nuts about fifties and sixties music he was. I don't know why, but by the time he was old enough to appreciate popular music, most of that stuff would have been old hat. He used to drag my mom out to jive dance classes; I think she only went along to keep him quiet."

"What about you and Dad, did you used to go dancing?"

"Your dad isn't one for dancing, but in my early teens I used to go with my mom and dad sometimes."

"When will Dad be coming home, it's been nearly four months now?"

"I know sweetheart, I spoke to Felix last week, he said that they're hoping to tie it all up by next month."

"Is he okay? He hasn't phoned for nearly three weeks, he normally calls at least once a week."

"I'm sure he's fine, they're six hours ahead of us in Germany. Sometimes it's difficult for him to interrupt meetings to make personal calls."

"Did you ever have to go away for this long, when you were a company field rep Mom?"

"Rarely, Benji. Most of my overseas work was for just a few weeks, a month at most."

"I wish you wouldn't call me Benji; it's a baby name. I'm eight now, I'm too big for that."

"Sorry sweetheart, it's hard for moMs. to get used to their kids getting bigger. I'll try to remember to just call you Ben from now on," Saffron told him. "Did you have a good time with Josh this morning?"

"Yeah it was good. We shot hoops for an hour, then his dad took us to Murphy Field and we played soccer. Then we went to Burger 7 for lunch but his dad got a phone call and had to shoot off before we finished eating because of some kind of emergency at work."

"So that's why Josh's mom dropped you off early. I don't suppose his dad said what the emergency was did he?"

"No, but he looked really worried."

Josh's dad worked out of the same building as she and Brett, her husband.

"What're you working on at the moment?" He said glancing over her shoulder.

Closing the laptop she turned to him, "Nothing very interesting darling. Analysing gas and oil security arrangements in Dusseldorf. I guess you're hungry if you didn't get to finish your lunch. What shall we have for dinner?"

"How about pizza?"

"We had that two nights ago, and you had burger for lunch. How about my vegetarian Mexican Lasagna?"

"That was nice when you did that last time. You've got a bruise on your cheek."

"I know, tough session at the dojo last night."

"Is it okay if I play Call of Duty while you make dinner?"

"I guess, but that's it for gaming today, I don't want you turning into one of those nerds that can't think of anything else."

"Okay Mom."

Later, in spite of herself, she relented and granted another hour of Xbox time before his bedtime at nine o'clock. She looked in on him half an hour later and smiled at him sleeping peacefully, took his eReader from his hand, put it on the nightstand, and turned off his bedside lamp.

Pouring a modest amount of red wine into a large balloon wine glass she went to the lounge to catch up on the news before going up to bed herself. Despite what she'd said to her son, she was concerned about Brett. He wasn't in Germany; he was in the Ukraine, and he'd missed two of his planned home calls. Missing one wasn't that unusual, but two in a row had only happened once before.

She took a long draught from the wine glass and determined that if she hadn't heard in the next twenty-four hours, she'd call Felix Carter, her company family liaison contact, and start making a noise.

Her eyelids were beginning to droop when her cell phone vibrated beside her. Lifting the device, a glance at the screen told her to answer straightaway. "Felix?! What's wrong?"

"I'm outside, can I come in? I don't want to wake Ben."

Hurrying to operate the electric gates Saffie waited at the open door for her work colleague to drive through.

"What's wrong Felix, what's happened?"

"Let me come in, and I'll try to put you in the picture."

"Is Brett alright?" She was beginning to panic now.

"We're not sure what's happening. He's missed several check ins and we can't locate him at the moment."

"You can't locate him!? What the fuck Felix, you've allowed one of our most experienced field agents to go missing. What have you done about it? It's nearly three weeks since I spoke to him. Have you done anything? Who's running this op? Is it still Radwell?"

"Karl's been tearing his hair out, but because the op is so crucial, he didn't want to blow Brett's cover. The DDO authorised a discreet contact when nothing was heard by midday local time, but he's not responded."

"Dear God, what are they doing about it?"

"We escalated the agent alert to Level Two and gave that twelve hours before we did more. The DDO has ordered in two more agents, one from Poland and one from Belarus. They'll be in theatre by the morning."

"Jesus, Felix; doesn't anyone have any idea where he is?"

"It may be that he's just decided to go dark for a while. We can't risk doing more to blow his cover if that's the case; he was on the brink of something really crucial."

"What are you doing here then? Shouldn't you be at your desk throwing resources at this?"

"The whole team is doing everything they can, Brett is too important to us for this not to be given top priority. Rest assured the DDO is on top of this. He wanted to delay telling you until tomorrow but I insisted you should know and it should be me that tells you."

"Okay, thanks, I think. When did you last hear?"

"I can't stay long; I've got to get back."

"Don't fuck me about Felix, when?"

"He missed a scheduled contact sixteen days ago."

"How many routine contacts has he missed?"

"Three now."

"Three! What's Radwell been doing? Did anyone else know about this?"

"He kept it under his hat for five days. Says that's the way Brett would want it."

"That's crap and you know it. So when I spoke to you last week you had no idea where he was and you just fed me a load of garbage. That timeline you just gave me sounds like another pile of horseshit."

"I'm sorry Saff but Mark said that the DDO had put a blanket ban on any mention of it by anybody to anyone else."

"Well fuck you very much, and the DDO."

"We're doing everything we can."

"No you're not, you've sat on your asses for more than a fortnight while one of your top agents is missing and kept it a secret from his family. Fuck off, Felix. Just go and do your job. And remember this, if I discover that you've just reeled off another load of lies to cover your asses and something's happened to Brett, I'll rip your balls off and ram them down your throat."

Pouring the rest of the bottle into her glass, she couldn't decide whether she was more scared or angry. Brett would never miss more than one scheduled contact unless something was seriously wrong, and his handler Karl Radwell should have been alarmed after the first one and all over it after the second.

Thirty-eight-year-old Brett Price was a CIA field agent, he'd worked in the European sections of the agency for fifteen years. Regarded by colleagues at all levels as a professional at the top of his game, Brett was a holder of the Distinguished Intelligence Medal, and he'd both led and taken part in numerous successful operations.

Saffron's outward appearance would fool most people who didn't know her well. She was thirty-five, an attractive, cheerful, and even-tempered work at home mom, with a modern outlook on life. She would never have been regarded as a domestic goddess by anyone. She hired a cleaner to do the worst of the housework, avoided cooking where possible, and had a gardener to do the yardwork, allowing her to devote more time to her son and her work. Without being reclusive, Saffron wasn't exactly gregarious either but with her friendly disposition most people found her a pleasant acquaintance.

With a strong aversion to injustice, what most people didn't see was that if she or her family were threatened, she could become extremely dangerous. Having once been a CIA field agent herself, she understood how the agency worked and knew exactly what the protocols were for dealing with these situations. She'd worked alongside Brett on a number of missions in the first year of her career but after their relationship became something more than colleagues and been exposed to their bosses, she'd been forced to move. With her degree in Slavic languages she was snapped up by the Russia and Eastern European Section where she worked predominantly in Poland, Lithuania, Belarus, and Ukraine, only seeing Brett when they were able to arrange leave to coincide with each other.

In her four years on the frontline in clandestine operations, she gained a reputation among her colleagues for being physically tough, level-headed, intuitive, instinctively clever, and ingenuously resourceful. Her razor sharp analytical skills constantly contributed to her success.

Then when Saffie unexpectedly fell pregnant with Ben, she stepped down from field missions altogether but remained with the agency. They married and since the birth, she worked flexible hours and predominantly from home as an analyst for the Russian Section.

When she finally retired to bed that evening it was nearly midnight, and although she hadn't finished all the wine, she'd drunk far more than she normally would have, and anticipated waking with a headache.

Chapter 2

Saffie, as she preferred to be called, had always been a shallow sleeper, and with all that was on her mind even the wine hadn't affected that. At three o'clock something woke her. Instantly alert, she opened her eyes and listened. At first nothing, then a shuffling noise and a stifled groan from Ben's room. She crept out of bed and silently opened the drawer of her nightstand, took out her handgun, pressed the safety catch off and cocked it as silently as possible.

Tiptoeing barefoot across the floor she peered around her half-open door. The dim glow of the landing nightlight was enough for her to see an armed man in black clothing and wearing a ski-mask staring furtively into her son's room. She pressed the panic button on the wall by the light switch to alert the police.

"Hold it right there asshole," she shouted. "Drop the gun."

The man spun in her direction just as a second masked man appeared in the doorway with one hand over her terrified son's mouth and holding a gun in his other.

"No bitch, drop your gun or..." The first man started to demand.

A 9mm soft-nosed bullet passed through his head before he got to finish the sentence.

Using Ben as a shield, the second man dragged him over the body and backed toward the head of the stairs. "You stupid whore if you'd done what you were told nobody needed to get hurt. Now drop the gun or I'll kill the kid here and now."

As he spoke they both heard the sound of approaching police sirens.

"We've got company now asshole," she told him, dropping her gun. "Your move."

He continued shuffling back toward the stairs, still holding her son. "What the fuck Fly, is that the cops? I thought that wasn't supposed to happen."

A third man wearing a rubber Donald Trump mask appeared from behind him on the stairs, and stepped in front of the man holding Ben to keep her covered. "Just get the kid out of here you useless cunt. And you bitch, if you want your kid back alive, you'd better stay the fuck where you are."

He slowly backed down the stairs after the man holding Ben, and she followed him to the head of the staircase.

"If you come any closer you're dead meat," Trump threatened.

Saffie watched the man holding Ben, roughly manhandle him out the front door.

"Mom..." She heard her son plead, and he was gone.

Trump kept his gun trained on her and stayed at the open door until she heard a car door slam followed by a shout, "Get in Fly, quick!"

As Trump turned and ran out the door, she picked up her gun, ran down to the door, and fired at him as he threw himself into the passenger door of a black GMC Yukon. He screamed and dropped the gun as her shot hit him in the hip. The car door slammed as the car accelerated toward the gate, its wheels spinning on the gravel. Bare feet on the gravel prevented her moving fast, but she fired two more shots, attempting to hit the tires, but wary of hitting the fuel tank she was forced to hold her fire, and watch the big vehicle race through the open gate.

Overwhelmed by despair she sank to her knees on the grass at the side of the drive and wept. She was still there when moments later, first one police patrol cars swept into the gate shortly followed by another.

"They've taken my son. You need to get after them now!" she yelled at the first cop.

"Throw the weapon away, move back from it," The first officer ordered.

She did as she was told, knowing that resistance would have deadly consequences. "Now lie face down on the floor, put your hands on your head, lace your fingers, and cross your ankles."

She obeyed and said nothing until he'd retrieved her gun, "Are you going to get after those bastards or not? Black Yukon, Ohio plate HTM 9198, turned into Gallows Road, heading North towards I-495. Looked like three men in the car, one's got a gunshot wound in his right hip. Are you gonna do something or just stand around with your thumbs up your asses."

One cop handcuffed her and allowed her to stand, "Just calm down Ma'am and tell me what happened."

"I heard a noise, grabbed my gun, and went to investigate. There was a guy on the landing with a gun, I told him to drop it, but a second armed guy came out of my son's bedroom holding him around the mouth, so I shot the first guy."

"You shot him?!"

"Yeah I figured one less guy to deal with wouldn't hurt."

"Is he still in there?"

"Yes."

"Miguel, you and George get in there and see if we need an ambulance."

"I shouldn't bother. Few people walk away from a 9mm round through the head. A third guy came up the stairs, told me to drop the gun or they'd kill Ben. I did, and he kept me covered until the second guy had taken Ben outside. Someone called him from the car, he ran, I grabbed my gun again and got to the door before they'd driven away. I shot him in the hip as he got in the car and he dropped his gun, that's it over there. When they pulled away, I fired two shots at their tires, I don't know if I hit them, but I doubt it."

"Took a bit of a chance, firing at a car with your son inside didn't you?"

"I know how to use a gun; better than you I suspect. My son could be heading anywhere in the USA by now; are you going to do anything or not?"

"My colleague has asked for a BOLO for the car you mentioned."

Another patrol car pulled up outside the gate and a uniformed sergeant got out, "What the fuck's going on, Mitchell?"

"This lady alleges her son has been kidnapped at gunpoint Sarge."

"Have you identified the lady?"

"Just about to Sarge."

"What's your name, Ma'am?" the sergeant asked.

"Saffron Price, and this is my house."

"How can we quickly identify you?"

"You could grab my purse from the table in the hallway, my ID is in there. Also if you could grab me some clothes, I'm getting a bit pissed off standing here in a t-shirt and panties so your pals can check out my ass."

He sent one of the patrolmen to fetch her purse.

"You seem very calm, considering you say your son has been kidnapped Ma'am."

"I'm not calm, I'm fucking furious, but there's nothing I can do about it until you Keystone Cops start taking me seriously. And I'm not just *saying* it, I'm telling you. Meanwhile my son is probably halfway to San Francisco by now."

The patrolman returned. "She's who she says Sarge; and she's a spook."

"Oh shit."

"Oh shit, is fucking right sergeant. Yes I'm a spook, so get these frigging cuffs off me now, so I can get the feds onto this, someone who knows what the fuck they're doing."

The senior cop nodded to the other one who immediately released her from the restraints, "This isn't a federal case yet until it's established that they've crossed a state line," he told her.

"Give me strength Sergeant, were you born this dumb or did you have to work at it. I'm with the agency, do you seriously think for one second that when an agent's child is kidnapped at gunpoint they'll give two fucks whether he's crossed state lines or not. Let me get to my phone."

"Where is it?"

"By my bed."

"I can't allow you upstairs just yet Ma'am, it's a crime scene."

"Then get one of your guys to fetch it for me; and get me some fucking pants." She was yelling by this time.

The phone arrived with the pants she'd been wearing the day before. She speed-dialed Felix and he picked up on the second ring.

"We've heard nothing more Saff, I'll tell you..."

"Shut up for two seconds. Ben's been kidnapped."

Chapter 3

Within forty minutes Felix and Radwell had arrived and ushered all but two Fairfax PD detectives, and the CSI out of the house.

The open plan layout of the house didn't lend itself to privacy but having beaten the cops into submission they agreed to restrict their interests to the first floor for the time being, she led the two CIA agents into the big study.

"Are you going to tell me what the fuck is going on Radwell?" she demanded, "Or am I going to have to march down the drive and talk to one of those TV reporters that just turned up? I'm sure they'll be fascinated to learn that the CIA have mislaid a senior agent close to the Russian border. Then decided to keep it secret from his wife until his son's been abducted, thereby exposing him to blackmail."

"Hey first of all knowingly divulging the identity of anyone working undercover for the Central Intelligence Agency would be a felony," Radwell belligerently responded. "Secondly we don't know if there's any connection between Brett's apparent disappearance and your son's abduction, there could be any number of reasons for that."

"Name one. This wasn't a burglary gone wrong; there were four of them, all armed. This wasn't a paedophile kidnapping, and it wasn't a home invasion. These guys came prepared, and they came for Ben, not for me. There's no logical motive other than some sort of hostage/blackmail scenari.o. What they wouldn't have bargained for was one of them being killed, and another with a serious wound."

"Yeah okay, but who're they planning to blackmail, you or Brett?"

"How the Hell did you get to be an SOO, Radwell? Brett of course, if they wanted what I know, they'd have taken me as well. Whoever's holding Brett clearly wants something from him and he's refusing to provide it and they need Ben for leverage."

"So why not take you too?"

"They may well have wanted to, but after I'd shot one of them and they could hear the cops coming they probably changed their minds."

"What do you mean they could hear the cops were coming?"

"They heard the sirens."

"How would the cops have even known that there was a problem; you didn't say you'd called them?" Felix asked.

"Because I hit the silent panic button in my bedroom; it goes straight through to the cops."

"Let me have a word with the cops. This still doesn't explain how they got here that quickly." Felix went up the stairs two at a time.

"Saffron, while Carter is upstairs. How much has Brett told you about this op?"

"Not a lot. It would be a severe breach of protocol to pass on detail to me; we're both aware of that," she lied. Brett always told her where he was working even if he didn't say exactly what he was working on. "All I know is that he's somewhere in Europe. What more are you prepared to tell me now?"

"Not a lot, he was supposed to be Kyiv, but he hasn't been seen there for more than two weeks."

"What was he doing?"

"Trying to gather intelligence on the buildup of Russian forces on the border."

"That makes no sense, Kyiv is miles from the border, and Brett's not an expert in military intelligence. Why send him to gather that sort of intel; it's outside his area of expertise."

"I can't say anymore, I'm sure you understand."

"No I don't understand. Brett hasn't been involved in Russian ops for more than ten years, so he wouldn't be up to speed with everything that's happening in that area lately, nor have a working relationship with all the players. What's more he doesn't speak Ukrainian and his Russian language was never brilliant; he'd have been rusty. Eastern Europe and the Black Sea was more my area. I don't understand why he was even on the op in the first place."

Before Radwell could reply, Felix came back into the room, "The Detective Sergeant says they didn't get an alert from your panic button at all; the only reason the patrol cars got here so quickly, was because they were the second car on a nearby domestic disturbance and they were diverted here after your neighbor called in to report suspicious activity on your property. When a shot was heard whilst she was on the call they doubled the attendance."

"So why didn't they get the panic alert?"

"He says the line must have been tampered with. That could only have been done by someone with advanced knowledge and skills in security alarm systems. He'll look into it."

"They'd have needed detailed knowledge of our security system to do that. This must have been planned over several days, more evidence that this was a targeted incident," Saffie told them. "I need to review our security arrangements ASAP. In the meantime what the Hell is happening about Ben?"

"The FBI will be here any minute I expect," Radwell explained. "With the security implications, they'll take over the investigations into the kidnap from the cops. I'll leave you alone when they get here. Please be assured that we're doing everything we can, from our side of things, and if there's anything we can do for you, Felix will be on hand."

"Hearing you say that you're doing everything you can doesn't assure me of anything after your last few weeks' performance I'm afraid. What does that even mean?"

"I can't go into detail I'm afraid."

"I thought not."

She heard a car pull onto the drive, and a few minutes later a man and woman appeared at the wide opening to the study area. They introduced themselves as Special Agent Sofia Ramirez and her partner James Burns.

Radwell offered his hand to Burns and introduced the three of them.

"Yeah thanks, if you leave us your cards, we've got it from here. If we need anything from you spooks we'll be in touch," Ramirez told him. "James, if you can find the lead cop and have him put you in the picture. Ms. Price and I will have a preliminary chat."

Radwell looked furious at the rebuff but handed over the card as she'd asked and said goodbye.

"I'll stick around if you want Saffie." Felix offered.

"Don't bother, I doubt there's anything you can do here. I'll give you a call if I want anything. Maybe call me in the morning."

"Okay Ms. Price, talk me through the events of the last twenty-four hours," Ramirez said. She placed her phone on the coffee table in front of them. "If it's okay with you I'll record this to save making notes."

Saffron didn't object and proceeded to give a detailed account of all that had happened.

She spoke for nearly fifteen minutes with few interruptions, and when she'd finished Ramirez asked, "I understand that you and your husband are CIA agents, so I'd imagine you take security seriously. Tell me what precautions you take."

"While I was once a field agent like my husband, these days I'm just an analyst. Our electronic alarm is a fully integrated security system, including intrusion alarm, internal and external video surveillance with video recording, PIR lighting in the grounds, and a panic alert to the local PD."

"Is the system monitored by the alarm company?"

"No. For obvious reasons we don't want our day-to-day affairs monitored by strangers. The video is saved to the cloud as well as the control box hard drive."

"So what went wrong last night?"

"That's what I want to know. I've just been informed that the panic alert didn't work."

"Have you checked the system?"

"Since it happened less than an hour ago, I've been cuffed and questioned by uniformed cops, then interrogated by CIA agents, and now by you, so checking my security system hasn't been an option, especially as no-one has asked me to. We can look at the video now if you want, but I doubt that it will tell us much more than I've already told you."

"Where's your controller?"

"We can do it from my iPad, it's over there on my desk."

Ramirez collected the tablet and handed it to her just as Burns and a detective came into the room.

"This is Detective Sergeant Jan Wolski, Fairfax County PD," Burns said. "He's been helping us with the enquiry until now."

Wolski didn't look happy at being relegated to a subordinate role.

"Good morning Sergeant, what have you managed to discover so far?" Saffie asked.

"Nothing other than that it was pretty good shooting for anyone given the dim lighting and the stressful situation, Ma'am."

"You'll have gathered by now that this isn't a run of the mill domestic household. I've had advanced weapons training with my employment, and I regularly attend the range."

The cop began writing in his notebook.

"We were just going to review video footage from Ms. Price's security cameras," Ramirez told the newcomers.

Saffie interrupted, "Give me a moment or two and I'll see if I can have it play on the big screen over there in the corner so we can all see."

Two minutes later they were watching the gate open for Felix.

"Why was Agent Carter visiting that late at night." Ramirez asked, "Do you have an intimate relationship?"

"No we don't; he came to deliver some distressing news about my husband."

"And what was that?"

"He's missing."

"Is there any way it could be connected with your son's kidnapping?"

"I'd be astonished if it weren't."

They fast forwarded the video through to where, in the light from a streetlamp, they saw a man climb the perimeter wall, interfere with the electric gate controls, and open them to allow the SUV to reverse through. Halfway up the drive the PIR lighting kicked in and the grounds were lit up like daytime.

"The guy climbing the wall, that's what the neighbor spotted." The detective said. "She couldn't sleep and decided to take the dog for a walk. She saw the guy and called it in from her cell phone."

They allowed the video to continue, occasionally pausing or shifting between camera views and sometimes watching the same activity from more than one angle. The man who'd climbed the wall, ran alongside the reversing Yukon which stopped close to the front door and began picking the front door lock. Three men from the car got out and waited until the door was open, while the fourth man waited in the driving seat. As soon as the lock guy was finished he ran off back down the drive and disappeared out of the gate.

"Sergeant, it's going to take some time for us to rustle up a team from Richmond. Will you get someone to speak to that neighbor again and find out if she saw how that guy got here and how he got away?" Ramirez asked, "And get a door to door started to see if anybody else saw or heard anything and if there's any private camera footage.

"My partner should be with the neighbor right now. And for your information Agent Ramirez, this ain't my first day on the job; all those things are already in hand." He went out and quickly spoke to his partner on his radio.

They continued to watch the video and it was obvious that things had happened exactly as Saffron had described.

"Thanks for that Ms. Price. That leaves us with the $64,000 question why didn't the panic alarm go off?"

Wolski came back in the room, "I think I can answer that. Your neighbor, Mrs. Hamilton, recognised the guy who climbed the wall before he pulled his balaclava down. She doesn't know his name, but he came to her house once to service her alarm. What company do you use Ms. Price?"

"Safepoint Security."

"Same company. I'll get someone down there first thing."

"Thank you sergeant. Sorry about earlier, you're right. Is the house to house started underway yet? Some people down a street like this must have cameras who might have caught this guy."

"As I said agent Ramirez, we're already on it. The SUV has been found abandoned in a school car park in Oakton with a bullet hole in one of its rear tires. I've asked for it to be impounded and given a complete examination by our forensics team. We're looking for any cameras that might have recorded the car swap."

"I'm curious though Ms. Price," Burns asked. "How come you didn't wake up when the garden lit up like New Years in Times Square?"

"I have blackout curtains, Agent Burns. Not only that but I was tired. I'd been concentrating hard all day finishing a report I've been working on for weeks, I was stressed from the news about my husband, and I'd consumed the best part of a bottle of wine."

"And yet you were still able to shoot an intruder in the center of his head and the tire of a moving vehicle from what, ten yards?"

"Have you ever heard of adrenalin, Agent? A wonderfully efficient sobering substance."

"Still, it was quite a feat."

"Where are you going with this; that I was somehow involved or colluded in the kidnap of my own son? If you've any intention of trying to find him I suggest you restrict your questions to realistically relevant subjects."

"What are your thoughts Ms. Price?" Ramirez asked.

"That whoever took Ben, did so on behalf of those who're holding my husband. And that a person or group wants leverage to force Brett to do something or reveal something that he's been refusing to do until now. That being the case it appears that they're now getting desperate. The people holding Ben have been hired-in to do it. They obviously didn't know what the fuck they were doing. I suspect they're common criminals, low rent gangbangers who put the op together at short notice."

"Could they be agents of a foreign government?"

"It's possible, but unlikely - too many mistakes."

"Such as?"

"They hired that alarm engineer to do something without making sure he couldn't be recognised. They made their move while there was a witness on the street. Once they'd made their entry, they should have secured Ben and me at the same time, even if they didn't want to take me. Then, why was the first guy waiting at Ben's door not mine? Finally, they allowed me to retrieve my own gun, which gave me the opportunity to shoot after them."

"So you think they should be easily identifiable then?"

"If the alarm guy is still alive, it will give you a shot. I notice that you haven't mentioned whether you've identified the asshole contaminating my second-floor landing yet, Sergeant Wolski. Anything known?"

"Yeah, his prints are on file. His name was Jasper Ingram, AKA Scratchy, a low-level member of a low level gang that call themselves the Five Trey Bloods operating out of Richmond. The local PD say they're a break-off from another gang and they barely register in the gang squad activities. It's generally thought that they'll soon be subsumed back into the main group or be killed by them. It's thought that this is the first time they've attempted something like this."

"Richmond PD will be picking up other members of the gang before the day is out, if they haven't disappeared into the woodwork," Burns promised.

Ramirez jumped in, "You can rest assured that we're treating this as a national security matter and giving it top priority Ms. Price,"

It was nearly six a.m. when they finally finished questioning her.

"One last thing before we go Ms. Price. We'd like to leave someone here, to make sure you're okay and to monitor incoming calls on your landline."

"Two things about that, Agent Ramirez. First, I think I've demonstrated that I am quite capable of looking after myself; and second, your organization is more than capable of monitoring my landline and cell phone remotely. If you want me to sign something to say that's okay I'm happy with that."

"PD will leave a cruiser outside the gate for the time being anyway."

By the time they eventually left her alone, the CSI guys had finished too, leaving her with a blood-stained floor and a bullet hole in the wall.

Chapter 4

She watched Ramirez's SUV and the PD sedan drive out through gates that would no longer close behind them. Then she went straight back to the study, opened the bottom drawer of the desk and took out one of several brand-new burner phones that they kept for making under the radar calls. Then, having looked up a number she hadn't used for many years she dialed hoping that the number's owner was, A. still alive, and B. still using the number.

"Hello."

"Who's this?"

"Essex Girl."

"Wind velocity?"

"Nil."

"Text me from a new number. I'll call you back."

With yet another new phone she sent a short text that just read, '*New number*', and waited. Two minutes later the phone rang from a different number.

"Lemon tree, long time no see. Are you back in the game?"

"Thanks for calling back Pearmain, and no, not exactly. I'm still working for the company but now just as an analyst."

"I'm not going to be much use to you as a source. The River House wouldn't like it."

"I know that, and it isn't the reason for my call, and this conversation isn't sanctioned by my department head."

"Okay, tell me and I'll see if I can help."

Pearmain stayed silent as she brought him up to date with her current status as wife and mother. Then she dropped the hammer about Brett's disappearance and Ben's abduction.

"I've been hearing a lot of whispers over the last few days about people being picked up and given the hard arm about a missing person. Where was Rider - Brett's code name - *operating, and what was his brief; am I allowed to know?"*

"I'm being told that he was in Kyiv, and they're telling me he was supposed to be gathering intel about Russian troop movements on the border."

"All or part of that is bollocks. Kyiv is too far away from the border to get anything useful that they couldn't learn by other means including satellite. What's more, that's not the area where your guys have been searching. The scuttlebutt I've been getting is all about the Donetsk region, in particular an area north of Mariupol. Separatist groups are particularly active in that area."

"That's what I thought, and I don't understand what they would want from Rider; he's a field agent, he gathers information and reports back; he doesn't promulgate it and doesn't hold secrets. Even if he did he'd be a conduit and it would be in the form of a message. Any messages he may have had would be redundant now he's been missing for this length of time; no agency would allow themselves to be held to ransom by the lives of a single agent and his family."

"Precisely my thoughts. If they'd killed him it would make more sense, but from what you say that doesn't sound likely, at least not yet. There's something else going on here."

"Exactly, although I can't spend too much time looking into it - my priority has to be my son at the moment."

"Look Lemon, I can't get directly involved, my friends on the riverbank would string me up, but I'll put out as many feelers as I can."

"Thanks Pearmain, I owe you one."

"Any clues who the lucky Rider is, do I know him?"

"I don't believe you've met, and you know I wouldn't say even if you had?" she replied with a smile.

"Touché. Keep that mobile charged and close to hand."

She ended the call with a momentary smile at the British name for a cell phone. Pearmain was an English agent working for MI6 or the British Secret Intelligence Service, as it was now formally known. He'd been working undercover gathering intelligence for them throughout Central and Eastern Europe since before she was recruited by the Agency. They'd worked closely together during her first field op in Germany, and before she met Brett, they'd even started a brief affair which was quickly quashed by their parent organizations. She prayed that he'd manage to dig something up, because she didn't trust Radwell; his handling so far had been so incompetent it bordered on neglect.

Next she called Felix. He picked up straight away.

"Felix, I know you're not involved in the investigation into Ben's abduction, but I'm certain that you're monitoring it. What have they got so far?"

"Christ, Saffie they've hardly had time to get up to full speed yet."

"I didn't ask that."

"All I know is that the alarm engineer is missing, and they've picked up three gang members. None of them are talking, but that's no surprise, they're not the ones involved in the raid though. Richmond PD are going to start piling on the pressure by interrupting drug dealing operations in the area, in the hope it might loosen some tongues."

"Tell me about this alarm guy."

"His name is William Ross, goes by Billy. He's 34 and he's worked for Safepoint Security for seven months, he's got a drug habit and he's in debt."

"What's his drug of choice?"

"Fentanyl.

"What about the dead guy, Ingram?"

"Jesus Saffie, you're not think of going after these guys yourself I hope."

"You don't need to know. Just tell me."

"He rented a room in a beat up house in Weber Street, Richmond, number 2510."

"Keep me up to date with whatever you hear; and by that I mean both ends of this." She ended the call before he could reply."

She needed to get herself ready to go out. At the top of the stairs she hesitated at the sight of the now dried blood stains on the floor and wall, but only for a moment. Glancing into Ben's room brought a lump to her throat and her eyes began to fill up. She shook her head, reminded herself that there was no time for sentiment, shrugged it off and let the ball of hatred and fury that had been building inside her take over.

Calling her supervising agent she left a message to say that she needed to take some sick leave. This was only the second time in twelve years she'd done that, so she didn't anticipate a problem.

After a shower, she dressed in a tired looking olive drab t-shirt, with the well-worn combat pants and matching jacket that she wore for their family wilderness vacations. Then she went to the garage and the concealed gun safe and took out her husband's spare handgun, a Heckler and Koch HK45 semi-automatic pistol. She also took three magazines, a suppressor, a combat belt, hunting knife, and a Mossberg 590 9-shot pump action shotgun fully loaded. She put it all in the gun safe in the trunk of Brett's Jeep Wrangler alongside a number of other things she'd bought from the house.

The FBI and the cops had kept a lid on information about the nature of the incident, and in the end the TV vans and reporters had given up and left to attend a bank heist in Oakton. After securing the house as well as she could, she got into the Jeep and headed down the drive and waved to the cops in their car as she passed. She hoped that when the events of the night found their way into the press her name wouldn't be connected.

Her first stop was the garage where they had their vehicles serviced.

"Hey Mrs. Price, how you doin'? The owner greeted her in a passable Joey Tribbiani impression.

"I'm good thanks Toni."

"The Wrangler giving you problems?"

"No, it's fine thanks, but I was hoping you could do me a small favor."

"If I can, I will."

"It's a bit unusual, so if you want to say no I'll understand."

"Just ask. You and Mr. Price are good clients so I'm happy to help if I can."

"When I was here last time, I spotted some license plates on the wall of your workshop. I was wondering if I could buy a pair. I need to disguise the Jeep for a day or two."

"No problem, Mrs. R, but none of those on the wall would be a good idea. They all come from scrapped vehicles long since deregistered and the cops would pick that up in a heartbeat if you were stopped. How about I let you have the plates from a Wrangler that I'm breaking for parts? It's a different model than yours but, unless they're being really thorough, I doubt the cops would spot that. It's registered to Dr. Hislop. She hit a tree with it, she's 83 and has decided to hand in her license. I offered her what the insurance company would pay and she accepted."

"That's more luck than I deserve, but is she okay?"

"A few minor bruises that's all."

"I don't suppose you could change them for me now could you."

"How about I stick the phony ones over your original ones with Velcro, then you can switch back whenever you want?"

"Genius. Probably best not to ask how you came up with that on the spur of the moment eh?"

He smiled, "Probably best, same as me not needing to know why you need to do it."

Fifteen minutes later she was driving out of his yard having set the GPS for Weber Street Richmond and after handing over a $100 bill. He'd only asked for $20, but she insisted.

Chapter 5

It was ten-fifteen when she pulled off I-95 at Exit 73 for Richmond, stopped, and Googled somewhere to eat. Disgusted to find the only option available before eleven-thirty was McDonalds, she resigned herself to a gastronomic abuse she'd once sworn never to do again. What happened to all the old-fashioned American truck stops and diners, she wondered.

Whoever was providing Ingram with a room was most likely either still answering questions at the cop station or making himself scarce, but she hoped that a few of the neighbors might be around for a chat. So, having fueled herself with far too many carbohydrates, she got back in her car and drove to find the house only to discover that the street was much more up.m. arket than she'd expected. It was never going to find itself on America's most desirable districts, but most of the properties were well maintained with tidy front yards. The same couldn't be said for Ingram's home. It was a single story, timber-framed house that hadn't seen a lick of paint in decades. There was a police cruiser parked out front with two cops inside.

She drove past and parked a hundred yards away, close to where an old guy was tending a small flower bed in his front yard.

Jumping out of the car she walked over to him. "Excuse me Sir, sorry to bother you. Do you know what's happening along the street there with the police? I was supposed to be delivering a package there, but I don't want to be spending hours talking to cops."

"Who's the package for; George, or that piece of shit grandson of his?"

"George I guess; the label just says Mr. Ingram. It's a comfort parcel from the church. I'm just helping out doing deliveries because my mom had a fall."

"The police raided the house first thing and tore the place apart. His neighbor just told me that his grandson got himself killed doing a home invasion somewhere North of here, couldn't have happened to a better person. George had a panic attack when they told him and they took him to the hospital."

"What's the grandson mixed up in, do you know?"

"Drugs from what George said. He's done everything he could to help that boy; took him in when his own folks threw him out, even settled his debts and bailed him out twice."

"His parents live nearby?"

"Yeah, couple of streets over; Wright Street. I don't know the number. Why do want to know?"

"I thought maybe the church might want to send condolences, but thank you, Sir, you were real helpful."

A quick search found the telephone number of a Mr. and Mrs. Ingram of Wright Street, along with the number of their house.

The houses in Wright Street were similar to Weber and the Ingram house was a tidy example.

A smart woman in her mid-sixties answered after her first knock. "Can I help you?" she asked in a Southern drawl.

"I hope so Ma'am. My name's Cissy Hanrahan; I'm with the FBI, currently on secondment to the DEA." She held out a wallet with a fake ID provided for her by the agency for her final op over eight years before, "I was hoping that you and Mr. Ingram could spare me some time."

"If it's about our son, we already spoke to your colleagues this morning. We haven't had anything to do with him for five years."

"I know that Ma'am. I'd just like to clarify a few things. I hope it won't take long."

"Very well, come inside."

She led the way through to a living room, where a man sat in an overstuffed chair clutching the handle of a walking stick. "It's the FBI again, William."

"Good morning, Sir. Cissy Hanrahan FBI but currently attached to the DEA, Arlington office."

"We told you all we know about Jasper's activities this morning."

"I know that, Sir, and I'm sorry for your loss. I'm just trying to learn a bit more about how he got mixed up with the gang in the first place. It seems to me that you're decent folks and must have been heartbroken about him ending up like this."

"He was a good kid until he flunked out of college. From then on it all went downhill. He got a job as a tire fitter, but the pay was crap and one of the other guys talked him into getting involved in robbing a bodega. He got caught and went to jail for a year and when he got out he was hooked on drugs. That was all it took for the Bloods to get their hooks into him. It's mostly been low-level crime until now, leastwise that's all he's been caught for, but the drugs had him and the bastards in the gang kept wanting more and more from him to provide the shit. We stopped giving him money after he stole my wife's jewelry. The last straw was when he stole my dad's war medals. We threw him out but Dad still gave him a home."

"What was the name of this guy at the tire-fitting shop, can you remember?"

"Unlikely to forget. Jose Hernandez."

"Is he still around do you know?"

"Got out of prison last week again I think."

"Do you know where he lives?"

"Sure, right down the street; number 2409."

"You've been real helpful, thanks a lot."

"Do you want to leave a card?"

"Sorry, I'm fresh out of them. Been handing them out all morning."

When she was back in the car she checked her phone, and there were two missed calls from Felix. She called him back.

"Where are you?"

"Out and about, why do you need to know?"

"There have been two calls to your landline."

"Who from?"

"They hung up when you didn't answer."

"Where were they made from?"

"Pay phones in Richmond. One was outside McDonalds on Hull Street, the second on the Broad Rock Industrial Estate. Look, I can tell you're in Richmond, you can't tackle these people on your own. What happens if these people are calling with a ransom demand?"

"These people don't want ransom, and even if they did it would only be to boost whatever they're getting from whoever put them up to it. Thanks

Felix. I'll be in touch." She ended the call, turned the phone off and removed the SIM card.

'Next stop Mr. Hernandez,' she said to herself as she put the car in drive.

Stopping three doors away from the house, she lifted the combat belt complete with knife and strapped it around her waist under the hunting jacket that came down to her butt. Then put spare magazines for the handgun in the thigh pockets of her pants, checked the gun, fitted the suppressor, and tucked it into her belt behind her.

Casually pulling her peaked forage cap down she strolled to the front door of the house and knocked. Whoever came to the door just shouted, "What do you want?"

"Jasper ain't around. I was told you might be able to help a girl out."

"Fuck off. I don't know you."

"Course you don't, I been getting my shit from Jasper."

"Fuck off; I don't do that shit no more."

"That ain't what Jasper's been saying. He told me you were cool and when you're out, you'd be the go to guy for all sorts of shit."

"How do I know you're not a cop."

"How about I show you my tits; a cop wouldn't do that would she?"

The door opened. "Okay then bitch you'd better not be shitting me or I'll fuck you into next week."

"There's no need to be an asshole, I'm just a customer."

He closed the door behind her and she saw that he was holding a gun, "Okay then bitch, let's see your rack."

"Just a minute, I need to take this jacket off first." She slipped it off her right shoulder and when her hand was behind her she quickly stepped toward him, pulled her gun, and thrust it under his chin. "Drop the gun. One chance, do it now or I'll blow your brains all over this shithole and be gone before anyone knows I was here."

He dropped the gun and tried to put on a show of bravado, "You're dead bitch; you may be breathin' but you is as good as dead. When the bros find you they'll pass you around like a bogie until your pussy is like a wet donner kebab."

"Brave words for someone who's not going to have genitals if he doesn't shut the fuck up. Walk to the middle of the room and get on your knees, NOW!"

He did as he was instructed and within a few minutes he was lying on his face with his wrists and ankles restrained with zip ties.

"Okay Jose, this the bit where you get to find out if you'll live the rest of your pathetic life with or without balls."

"What you want bitch?"

"During the night, your good friend Jasper and some of his pals abducted an eight-year-old boy from his home in Dunn Loring. I want to know who it was, and I want to know where they're holding him. Your turn to speak now, go."

"I got nothin' to do with that."

"We'll start with who then."

"How should I know?"

"Because nothing like this happens in your pathetic little boys' clubs without everybody knowing at least something about it."

"I'm not in the gang anymore; I quit."

"I see, so you get out of prison realizing that you've been a silly boy all these years and decide from now on you're going to be a model of propriety and work for the good of the community; then the bros say, 'Hey, Jose, it was good while it lasted, have a nice life.' Is that how it went?"

He attempted to explain that he'd paid his dues, and they let him go, until he felt her cutting his belt.

"What're you doin'?"

"Just getting these clothes out of the way so I can see what I'm cutting, keep still." The knife sliced through the belt, underwear, and pants right down his legs as far as the zip tie. The razor sharp weapon separated the fabric as if it were gossamer.

"Look I'd tell you if I knew."

"Seeing as you're on your front, I'll leave your balls for the minute and just cut your sphincter muscles? That way you'll still be able to get it up, you'll just be permanently incontinent and you'll be wearing diapers for the rest of your life." She pressed the point of the blade between his buttocks.

"Alright I'll tell you what I know, but it ain't much."

"I'm listening."

"It's a guy called Junior Fly and his homeys. Some dude give them ten d-notes to do the snatch. The boss don't know nothin' about it. Fly's history if he finds out."

"What about the other guys?"

"A guy called Scratchy and Fly's two homeys, Blue Boy and Rack."

"Where will I find them?"

"They got a place on East Tenth Street, corner of Everett."

"What's the boss's name? I ain't gonna tell him that you talked, I just need to know his name."

"Sab, short for Sabotage."

"I hope you're telling me the truth Jose, because I'm going to leave you like this and if I have to come back things are going to get very messy. Are we clear?"

"It's all I know, I promise. Please don't tell them you got it from me; they'll fucking kill me."

She zip tied remnants of his underwear in his mouth and left him to his thoughts.

Chapter 6

Setting the GPS for Everett Street she saw it was only minutes away. Leaving the car thirty yards away in East Tenth, she walked around the block to get an idea of the layout. At the front of the small single story building the windows were boarded, giving it the outward appearance of being abandoned.

Surrounded by a broken row of mature trees and wild shrubs, it was the only remaining structure on a rectangular plot that was ripe for develop.m. ent. The building didn't appear as if it had been designed to be lived in, but maybe as a small office. It looked isolated and incongruous in the predominantly residential neighborhood. She saw that even in daylight it was possible to approach the side of the building without being seen from inside. The quiet area had very light traffic and there were no pedestrians in sight.

If Ben were inside, leaving it until nightfall meant prolonging his ordeal or worse, risking him injury if he hadn't been hurt already. Calling the cops or the FBI meant waiting for them to faff around applying for a warrant, with no guarantee one would be granted just on the strength of a phone call from her.

Decision made and hoping that nobody in the few houses within sight were watching, she dodged into the cover of the trees and pulled on a pair of nitrile gloves.

What remained of a fence lay flat on the ground. She stepped across it and up to the back door then tapped on it with her gun's suppressor.

She heard the sound of people hurriedly moving around, then tapped again.

"Who is it?"

"Cissy."

"Who's that, what you want?"

"I've got a message from Jose."

"What the fuck does he want?"

"He told me to warn you that Sab knows about the kid. I don't know what it means."

There was an immediate scrabble of activity.

"Fuck!" someone shouted.

"You stupid bastard Fly; I told you he'd find out."

"How the fuck can he know? Get her in here now."

The door opened, the right arm and shoulder of a man appeared in the gap between the door and frame. Before the man had a chance to utter his first word, Saffron shot him in the elbow and charged the door.

The man screamed, dropped the gun he'd been holding and fell backwards. Saffie rolled and shot a second man in the knee as he tried to bring his gun to bear on the space where she'd been fractions of a second earlier. A third man sitting in a chair tried to reach for a gun on a small nearby table but only succeeded in knocking it to the floor.

After standing up, she gathered the weapons and ordered them to move together. They struggled to move toward the man in the chair.

"One chance to answer before I start shooting again. Where is he?"

"Fuck of..." The man in the chair began to say before Saffie shot him in the opposite hip to where she'd shot him at three in the morning.

"Anybody gonna tell me?"

"Through there on the left," Elbow man said through clenched teeth.

"Now, which one of you is going to tell me who paid you to do this? Fly, you're in charge here aren't you? If you don't want a bullet in your balls start talking."

"He said his name was Lopez."

"What did he look like?"

"I never saw him, he gave Scratchy ten grand and said we'd get another ten if we kept him for two weeks."

Saffie picked up the guns and walked through to the bedroom and her son was lying on a filthy bed. His wrists and ankles were duct taped and so were his mouth and eyes. She told him not to speak, quickly cut him free and gently removed the tape from his eyes and mouth.

The remnants of the reel of duct tape they'd used to restrain Ben was on a nightstand, so she grabbed it.

"Wait there. I'll be back in a second."

Using the tape, it took her very few minutes to completely immobilize the gangsters. She wasn't worried that the soft nosed bullets would tie Brett's gun to the scene but she picked up her shell casings and collected the three wounded men's cell phones, knives, and wallets. There was more than three thousand dollars in Fly's wallet. Assuming it was part of the payment for Ben's abduction, she took it. In the kitchen she found a strong plastic bag, put the money, weapons, and phones in it and returned to her son.

"Okay sweetheart, you're safe now. I'm going to lead you out the door to our car. Don't speak and I want you to keep your eyes closed until we're outside. Are you ready?"

"But I need to use the toilet Mom; I might wet myself," he whispered.

"Okay, go ahead, in the corner there. I won't look, just don't say anymore until I tell you."

"Ready now?" she asked when he was done. He nodded. "Close your eyes."

The three men groaned and sobbed as they passed through the room and out the door.

Outside she turned to her son, "Okay sweetheart you can open your eyes again, and you can talk if you need to, but we'll talk properly in a minute, okay?"

In the car she set the GPS for an address in Harrisonburg that she hadn't visited for eight years. She drove silently for an hour, during which Ben stayed similarly quiet. Turning off I-64 at Zion Crossroads, she found an I-Hop diner and pulled into the lot. She shut the engine off and turned to Ben.

"How are you my darling?"

"Okay I guess."

"Are you hurt?"

"No."

"Then tell me how you are, and just so you know, only saying, 'Okay I guess', isn't good enough."

"I was so scared, Mom." He began to cry.

"You had every right to be, Ben. It would have been terrifying for anybody. I was frightened too, for both of us."

"But you didn't look scared, not last night when you shot that man, or today when you came in there by yourself and shot the rest of them."

"I may not have looked scared but believe me I was as terrified as you were. Anybody that tells you they're not scared in a situation like that is a liar. I should tell you something about me that I've not told you before, I've been trained to deal with situations like that."

"You have?"

"You know that your dad and I work for the company yes?"

"Yes."

"And you know what the company is, don't you?"

"It's an international import and export company isn't it?"

"That's what we tell people, but 'the company' is a euphemism for the CIA."

"Dad's a spy!?"

"Sort of, and so am I. These days I'm mostly just an analyst but when we met I was a field agent just like Dad. We were sure you would have worked it out after we made such a big deal about you not talking to anybody about the work we do."

"Josh told me his dad was a spy. I didn't believe him."

"Bridger works at the George Bush Center where your dad and I are based, but he's not exactly a spy anymore; he's a Director of Logistics. It's still a very important job though."

"Where is Dad?"

"At the moment we're not sure, but the agency is throwing everything into finding him and bringing him home," she told him with a confidence she didn't feel. "I need you to trust me, because I'm going to help do that."

"What are you going to do?" The trepidation in his voice was obvious.

"I can't tell you the detail, but first I'm going to take you to stay with a friend of mine. She'll look after you and keep you safe while I'm away. Do you understand?"

"I guess."

"Good boy. Are you hungry?"

"Starving."

"Okay then, let's go inside and fill up."

Chapter 7

Once they'd finished eating Saffie rescued the gangsters' cell phones from the trunk while Ben climbed back in the car. She looked through the contact lists until she found one that showed 'Sab' and called.

"Fly, what the fuck you want?"

"Fly can't come to the phone right now."

"Who's this?"

"This is Cissy. I thought you'd like to know that Fly and his two homeys, Blue Boy and Rack have been working on a little free enterprise and got themselves all tied up and hurt. Perhaps you can get them some help. It's too late for Jasper, he's taken his last hit of whatever pharmaceutical you've been selling him."

"Listen bitch, I don't know who you are yet, but when I find out, you'll..."

"No you listen asshole. You want to know why you're getting heat from the feds, ask Fly. I've been doing you a favor." She ended the call and threw the three cheap phones in a nearby trash can and got back in the car.

"Just one more call to make and we can be on our way," she told her son.

Using the burner phone that she'd used to return Pearmain's call, she called Directory, asked for a number, and called it. The number was a landline and she hoped that the owner was at home.

"Hello?"

"Is that the candy store?" Candy store was a game they used to play when they were kids.

"Saffie?!"

"Mary how are you?"

"I'm great thanks. It's so good to hear your voice. When are we ever going to meet up like we promised?"

"In about two hours if it's okay with you."

"You're visiting? That's fantastic!"

"You may not say that when I tell you why. I need a favor, a huge favor."

"Just say; if I can, I will, you know that."

Saffie started to explain but Mary interrupted, "*Just come, Ben can stay as long as he needs to.*"

"Thank you so much Mary." She ended the call and pushed the car into drive.

"Where are we going?"

"To see your Aunt Mary. She has a little farm just outside Harrisonburg where I spent a lot of time as a girl."

"Is it the Aunt Mary that sends me presents for birthday and Christmas?"

"That's right, you'll love her."

A little over ninety minutes later they were pulling into a farmyard to be greeted by a furiously barking border collie, and chickens that scattered out their way as she stopped.

The front door of a large, recently built farmhouse opened and a small woman in jeans and plaid shirt came out wiping her hands on a tea towel. The smile on her face demonstrated the pleasure she felt at her visitors' arrival. Saffie got out of the car to meet her, and the two women hugged as Ben shyly held back. The dog fussed around the visitors panting and competing for attention.

"Ben, this is your godmother, Aunt Mary."

"My, my Ben, I haven't seen you since your Christening, what is it, eight years ago? What a handsome young man you're growing into," she said, holding him by the shoulders. "Come inside the pair of you and tell me what's going on. This is Gwyneth by the way; completely harmless." She patted the dog.

Mary led them into the house and into a huge traditional style kitchen.

"Where did this house appear from Mary? All this time I've been envisaging you in the old one."

"Mom and Pop had it built so that me and my husband could move in and make a house full of grandkids."

"Husband?"

"They were convinced that Albie and I were going to get hitched."

"Albie, but he's..."

"Gay? Yeah but they didn't believe it and went ahead and had this place built about three years ago."

"Where are they? In the old house?"

"Pop died soon after this was finished and Mom went soon after."

"Oh God Mary, I'm so sorry. I'd have come if I'd known."

"I'm surprised your dad didn't mention it."

"His memory wasn't so good anymore. He had early onset dementia and he passed about nine months ago too. He'd looked after Mom all those years, but he went downhill fast after she died. You know he was in assisted living didn't you?"

"I remember you saying. It's sad, your folks were so much younger than mine too.

"Surely you don't run this place on your own now."

"Heavens no. I got several hands working for me and Rusty the foreman to keep an eye on things. I bought the Sanders place across from here when the old man passed on. The kids, Eliot and Lacey weren't interested in taking it on, but they're still there."

"What about your love life?"

"There's no-one special but I do alright. Coffee?"

"That would be great."

"What about you, young man? Milk or soda?"

"Soda please."

"Why don't you help yourself from the fridge over there and grab a couple of these flapjacks if you're hungry. They might still be a bit hot so be careful. You can have a look around while I catch up with your mom if you want. It's quite safe. Just don't go into the field at the back of the house; Old Fred the bull is a bit frisky at the moment."

Ben went outside again with a can of Mountain Dew in one hand and a flapjack in the other followed by Gwyneth.

"He's a bit quiet, is he just shy?"

"After what he's been through in the last fourteen hours it's not surprising."

"Okay then Saffie, tell me all about it."

Recounting all she could without breaking too many federal laws, Saffie explained all that had happened, omitting the finer detail of her treatment of the gangsters.

"You always were the daring one out of the two of us, and I knew there had to be more to that import and export business than you were letting on, but I never guessed you were a spook."

"Yeah well, it's not something you put on your business card. It's why I could never be relied upon to turn up for visits."

"So what happens now?"

Saffie frowned, "As soon as I can, I'm going to catch a flight to Ukraine and find out what the fuck is going on for myself."

"What can you do that the people on the ground aren't already doing?"

"Maybe nothing, but I don't trust the information I'm getting. Someone isn't telling me the truth, I'm pretty sure I know who it is but I can't prove it from here. At the moment, I'm completely off the grid, and I'm hoping I can be in Donetsk before they even know I'm out of the country."

"Jesus, Saffie, what if something happens to you?"

"If neither of us come back then the conditions of our wills will kick in. Are you still okay with that?"

"Of course. I just never expected to get advance notice is all."

"I'm sorry about this, but I could never forgive myself if something happened to Brett when I could have done something to stop it. Having said all that, I'm not anticipating it being especially dangerous. As soon as I find out who's holding him I'll get someone I know to mobilize the Ukrainian authorities."

Even as she explained it to her friend, she was pretty sure that it might not be true. The likelihood of things going Western was quite high if the situation was as she imagined it might be.

"What if it's the Russians?"

"I'm ninety percent sure that it won't be."

"I'll take your word for that. Fried chicken, mash, and okra alright for dinner tonight?"

"That sounds lovely."

Saffie was about to say something else when the burner she'd been using to speak to Pearmain buzzed. "Hi." The signal was weak so she put it on speaker.

"Lemon tree, what's happening at your end?"

"My son's free and in a safe place. Company HQ weren't involved in achieving that and haven't been notified. Any news from your end?"

"I'm pretty certain that Rider's hijack hasn't been sanctioned by any of the usual suspects. Your colleagues have been upsetting a lot of people though by overturning stones that would have been well left unturned. It crossed my mind if that might be a possible motive behind this; although I doubt it, I suspect the real reason may be closer to home.

"Me too. Anything else?"

"Depends on what you propose doing about it."

"I'm getting the first flight out there tomorrow or the day after."

"Where to?"

"Kryvyi Rih."

"Good choice. Let me know your flight number before you take off and I'll meet you. Travel light."

Travel light was intelligence community speak for, 'resources will be provided'.

"Thanks, I can't tell you how much I appreciate that."

"I need this cleared up nearly as much as you do. All these Yankee spooks running around is making too many people uncomfortable. Did you know that a Dutch Uncle had been out here three weeks ago?" Pearmain's code meant a Langley supervisor.

"No I didn't."

"Neither did my own company rep until he'd gone home. Thought you should know."

"Thanks, that's interesting. I'll be in touch." She ended the call.

"Lemon Tree?" Mary said.

"Long story, best not to ask." Saffie replied, "Mary, I only have the clothes that I'm travelling in, likewise Ben. I couldn't trouble you to lend me a couple of pairs of pants, shirts, panties, and a bra could I? It looks like we're still about the same size. Something to carry them in would be good too."

"No problem, I'll sort them out after we've eaten. What about Ben?"

"I was kinda hoping you could run him into town and get him a few things. I'll leave you some money."

"Where are you flying from?"

"My plan, if I can put it together, is to fly Charlottesville to Baltimore first, then to Ukraine from there."

"How about I drive you to the airport and then I take my godson shopping while we're there?"

"That would be amazing, Mary. Thanks so much."

"It will be a good opportunity for me and Ben to spend some quality time together."

Their host set about preparing their evening meal while they exchanged tales of what they'd been up to over the intervening years.

"I wonder where Ben is," Saffie said.

"He won't be far. Give him a call, dinner won't be long."

She went out into the yard just in time to see a huge tractor drive from behind the barn with Ben sitting on the driver's lap and steering. The grin on his face was a delight to see. The vehicle stopped beside her, the driver climbed down and helped Ben jump down beside him.

"You must be Ben's mom, I'm Rusty. Pleased to meet you," he said offering his hand.

"Saffron, good to meet you too. Has Ben been getting in your way?"

"No, Ma'am, I offered him a ride when I took some feed to the milking shed over yonder. Turns out he's a dab hand at steering."

"This tractor is awesome Mom! It does tons of things."

Mary appeared on the stoop. "We're about to eat Rusty. You hungry?"

"Thanks a lot Mary, but I'm out tonight. Just gotta put this little baby to bed."

"I might be out most of the day tomorrow," Mary told him. "Have a good night; we can catch up when I get back."

"Bit of a hunk there Mary," Saffie remarked with a grin. "Any chance?"

"I confess to a dabble every now and then, but he likes to play the field a bit too much to my taste."

"That tractor's a bit of a beast isn't it?"

"Came with the Sanders' spread. They were more into crops than we'd been, and we're keeping that up. It allows me to spread the risk of good and bad years in the different sectors."

After dinner, when Ben was in bed, Mary took Saffie upstairs and between them they sorted out a bag and some clothes for her to borrow.

"I'll put Ben's clothes in the washer now and have them dry by the morning. Worst comes to the worst he can go commando tomorrow until I can get him some underwear."

Chapter 8

Saffie was awake at 6am. She showered, dressed, and collected Ben's clothes from the dryer before finding that Mary was already up and about.

"Just been letting the chickens out and collecting the eggs."

"I think I just saw Randy saying goodbye to a lady friend outside the old house," Saffie commented. "She walked off down the track."

"That'll be Lacey Sanders."

"That's never little Lacey? She was only about six last time I saw her."

"She's at UVA now, studying aerospace engineering. Doing well too from what I hear."

"I feel old now."

"Eggs, bacon, and hash browns be okay for breakfast? You've got a long day ahead of you."

"Sounds great, thanks. I'll chase Ben out of bed."

Her son was already awake when she poked her head in the door and handed him his clothes.

"I'm so sorry I've got to leave you sweetheart. I know you're worried about your dad, as am I, but I hope to have some news in a few days."

"I understand Mom, but I'm worried about you as well you know."

"I promise I won't take any unnecessary risks," she said, silently hoping it was a promise she could keep.

"These eggs are really yellow, Aunt Mary," Ben remarked over breakfast.

"That's because they're fresh, only dropped out of the chicken's bum this morning. And it's just Mary."

He giggled.

"If you leave the keys to your car, I'll get Rusty to put it in the old hay barn, it's half empty at the moment."

The drive to Charlottesville airport was straightforward, taking little more than an hour and they arrived in time for Saffie to catch the early Baltimore flight. Ben's farewell was tearful and did nothing to put Saffie's mind at ease. As she thought about it, her own eyes were more than a little watery throughout the short flight to the international airport that also served the country's capital.

Not entirely confident that the Cecelia Hanrahan ID would get her through the various identity checks, even though the passport and visa both still had fifteen months to run she was a little on edge. Travelling on her own ID wouldn't be illegal, she hadn't committed any crimes, or none that they knew about, but she didn't want either of the agencies to know where she was. She wouldn't put it past the CIA getting her bumped off the plane. Getting a visa on her own ID would have been too time consuming, and if it were flagged, both the FBI and CIA would get an alert.

Saffie had a little over $10,000 in her 'Hanrahan' account, and with the money she'd taken from Fly, she hoped that would be enough to pay for everything without transferring any from one of her other accounts.

The Ukrainian city of Kryvyi Rih wasn't a popular destination and she hadn't booked a seat. She was deliberately leaving it until the last minute to reduce the chances of an intervention, gambling that there would be at least one free seat.

Whiling away the time, she was glad that she hadn't relied on the airport shops to provide suitable clothes for what she imagined she'd be doing. The sensible working clothes that Mary had given her would be perfect. However, she did find a shoulder purse that would be far more practical than carrying everything in the weekender that Mary had loaned her. She transferred her papers and wallet into it and loitered around to kill time. There were still more than three hours to wait before she thought it a good time to approach the United Airlines desk, so she bought a book to read on the plane and grabbed a sandwich to tide her over until she was on the plane.

Unfortunately her gamble didn't pay off, the clerk had sold the last remaining seat an hour earlier, and the best he could offer her was a seat on the same flight the following day which she had no choice but to accept. She was furious with herself.

Saffie had almost resigned herself to yet more airport lurking until the same time the following day when a travel bureau eventually found her a room at a cheap two star hotel called the Roadside Hostel just off the airport approach. She had no idea what to expect, and for $65 a night she hadn't been anticipating the Hilton, and she was proven right not to. The photos on the net that the guy had shown her made it look clean and spacious, whereas what she found was a tired and scruffy building long overdue for a complete refurbishment.

The morose desk clerk looked as though he wanted to be there even less than she did and went through the motions like an automaton. "You're in room number twenty-two, second floor front." He handed her a key attached by a cable tie to a piece of wood about the size of a cellphone. "There's no phone in the room, but there's free Wi-Fi if you need it; the access code is written on the key fob. Breakfast is ten dollars served in the dining room between seven and ten-thirty. No smoking in the room and no loud music. Checkout is at ten. If you want to stay longer, please inform me as early as possible. Fifty dollar charge if the key isn't returned. Have a nice stay," he reeled off practically without taking a breath.

"Is there somewhere close to eat?"

"There are bars, cafes, diners, and restaurants in the town, and there are info handouts about some of them in the room. We don't give recommendations. If you order takeout, you'll have to meet the delivery guy in the lobby. We don't allow deliveries to the rooms. Spillages and obnoxious smells will attract surcharges."

The room smelled damp, and the linen looked laundered almost to the point of being threadbare, but it was somewhere to grab a few hours' sleep.

Leaving her bag in the room but taking everything of value with her, she went in search of something to eat. The sleazy sports bar and grill at the back of the hotel was closest. It wasn't a night for haute cuisine; she'd settle for anything just to keep her going.

The bar was a big saloon with poor lighting, the kind of place she'd normally actively avoid, but with a mental shrug she pulled up a stool. A barman spotted her and nudging one of the other servers out of the way, rested his elbows on the counter and gave a wide smile. "What can I get you sweetheart?"

He was wearing a too small t-shirt that had obviously been chosen to exhibit his physique to best advantage. He'd clearly been working out.

"Just a light beer and the menu please."

"Menu? It's a grill, the menu is whatever you normally get in a grill in America."

"In that case I'll have a grilled cheese with a slice of apple pie and cream to follow."

He took a Bud Lite from the cooler, flipped the top and popped it on the bar.

"You got a glass for that?" she asked.

"Look around you, sweetheart. Does this look like the sort of place that serves a light beer in a glass? But I guess for a pretty little lady like yourself I can make an exception," he said with a lascivious leer.

"I just want the drink and something to eat, so if you could just arrange that, it would be great."

He poured the drink and left her alone while he served a group of four men that had just walked in."

There were more than forty people in the bar either watching or completely ignoring the four large screen TVs all showing different sporting events. She sipped her beer and waited. Eventually the barman appeared with her sandwich.

"Here you are darling, I made it myself."

"Very talented. Are you going to fetch my apple pie now?"

"Sure, why not."

A few minutes later he returned with the pie and a plate for himself. "I'm just about to go off duty. I thought I might join you. Is that okay?" He said, pulling up a stool.

"No. I don't want company; I just want to be left alone to eat my food thanks."

"Come on sweetheart," he said, placing his hand on her knee.

"If that hand isn't off my knee in three seconds, I'll hurt you."

He moved his hand further up her leg to within an inch of her crotch. "I'm only being friendly."

She put her half-eaten toasted sandwich back on her plate, stood and kicked the stool from under him.

"You fucking bitch, you'll regret that."

She didn't reply; just kicked him squarely in the balls as he tried to get up. He screamed loudly and the hubbub of conversation stopped and apart from the unintelligible clamor of several different TV commentaries the place was silent.

"I don't take kindly to sexual assault buddy and you were warned. You say you're off duty now. That's good so you can fuck off and leave me to finish my meal in peace."

"Got beaten up by chick then Jeb eh; those protein pills must be wearing off then?" somebody shouted, provoking a chorus of cat calls and laughter.

He struggled to his feet and waddled out.

Saffie picked up the stool and went back to her meal.

"Would you like another beer to go with that? On the house," a girl behind the bar said.

"That's kind, but this one will be enough, thank you."

"I've wanted to do something like that for months."

She finished the food and took the last mouthful of her beer before putting a twenty on the bar and walking out.

As soon as she stepped from the projecting doorway, a figure stepped up behind her, a muscular arm gripped her around the neck, and a hand tightly grabbed her breast.

Saffie knew who it was and had almost expected the amateurish attack. She lifted one foot and scraped the heel down the shin of one of his legs as hard as she could. Even through the fabric of his pants the hard soled combat sneakers designed to look like fashion shoes that she was wearing, removed a layer of skin. He cried out in pain and loosened his grip enough for her to slip out of his grasp. She spun and hit him in one eye with a straight fingered punch. His hands went to his face, and she released yet another vicious kick to his balls.

The pain was clearly so great he'd lost consciousness. Saffie would be surprised if his testicles survived rupture, and he might have lost sight in one eye. Popping her head back through the bar door, she called to the bar girl, "Your pal Jeb seems to have hurt himself out here, you might want to get him some help."

She walked away, back to the hotel.

Chapter 9

Showered and dressed the following morning, she took her bag and looked in the dining room at what was on offer for breakfast and decided against it. Most other guests appeared to have made the same decision. She settled the bill and called for a cab from the company that had brought her from the airport the previous night and waited outside for it to arrive.

The driver was Asian with very poor English, but she managed to make him understand that she wanted to go somewhere to eat, and close to some shops.

He smiled and nodded and drove her to a Turkish coffee shop on a strip mall in a poor part of the city. She decided it would have to do, paid him, and went inside. The family run café was welcoming and served her with an egg-based dish call menemen, and a coffee that was so strong she didn't think she'd sleep for a week.

In spite of herself she ordered a second coffee and thought about what was next. She was frustrated about the wasted day and the delay to her plans caused by her own futile attempt to remain below the radar until the last moment. Realistically, it was doubtful that anybody would be expecting her to travel to Ukraine, and unlikely there would be a flag on the fake identity she was using, but in her profession, caution was something that became second nature. Her ID had presented no difficulties when buying the ticket, but the real test would be passport control later that day.

After a third coffee she was restless from the caffeine buzz. It wasn't something she was used to and she decided to try and walk it off.

Walking through downtown Baltimore unaccompanied wasn't a recommended pastime for an attractive white woman, but it was no worse than in some other countries. She'd been in much riskier situations in the past and might do again in the coming days.

This was one of the most populous cities in America, and yet also one of the poorest in spite of its close proximity to the nation's capital. Its high crime rate and reputation as the murder capital of the USA did nothing to attract investment, therefore much of the city remained rundown. Despite its reputation and deprivation, she wasn't feeling threatened, although it was obvious she was a curiosity. Three times she was asked if she was lost; the third time by an elderly Hispanic lady. Saffie explained that she was looking for a shop that sold ladies underwear. The lady gave her directions and offered to take her in her car, Saffie politely refused and told her she'd prefer to walk because she needed the exercise.

The route the woman had recommended took her through a rundown area of mostly boarded up small trading warehouses and industrial units, most showing no sign of recent occupation. One of the few showing any indication of activity was a unit selling military surplus clothing and accessories. She went inside to look around and ended up buying a pair of black combat pants, two black t-shirts and a black ski-mask.

"Watch yer planning girl, bank raid or an attack on the Pentagon?" the checkout guy asked.

"Neither, just invading a foreign country," she replied with a smile.

"You can invade my country anytime you want, girl. I won't put up no resistance."

"You'll have to wait; I've got South America to do first."

He was still belly laughing as she walked out of the door.

A hundred yards further down the street a Mercedes sedan pulled up beside her, the passenger window rolled down, and the driver leaned over.

'Here we go,' she thought, and pressed the voice recorder icon on the phone she'd been holding.

"Can I drop you off somewhere sweetheart?" It was a man she'd seen in the military surplus store, a white guy about her own age.

"No thanks." She carried on walking, but the car kept pace with her.

"I can make it worth your while."

She stopped, "Oh yeah, how would you do that?"

"Money, what do you think?"

"So, you're proposing to pay me for the privilege of giving me a ride. That's an unusual arrangement."

"Oh come on, you know what I mean."

"I think I can guess, but I haven't seen you before. How would I know if I can trust you?"

"Well there has to be a first time for every regular doesn't there?"

"I guess, how much do you normally pay girls to be allowed to give them a ride?"

"About a hundred bucks."

"That's not much, it looks like a seller's market around here, I can't see a lot of competition."

"Okay then, how about two hundred?"

"I might think about it for two fifty, but I'd need to see the color of your money first."

He fished his wallet out of his pocket and opened it to reveal a wad of notes although she couldn't see the denominations.

"They could be singles for all I know. I don't want a purse full of one dollar bills." She was enjoying herself now.

"If you get in, I'll let you count them."

"You could just drive off without paying, then you'd get to give me a ride for nothing."

"What if I get out and pay you and then we could go for a ride?"

"Okay, that sounds like it could work. What's your name?"

"Shall we say Jack, What's yours?" he said getting out of the car and walking around the hood.

"I'm Cecilia, but you can just call me Cissy. My you're very tall."

"And you're very horny."

"Thank you, are you going to let me see your wallet again?"

He handed it over, "I hope you're not fucking me around Cecilia. We don't see too many white chicks around here and if one got hurt, nobody would be too surprised."

"No, I'm just being cautious."

She took the wallet and opened it, "You're not being honest with me are you, it says here that you're Ryland Earl Simmonds, a high school principal.

"And like your real name is Cissy."

"Cissy is my real name; look I'll show you my ID," she took out the FBI ID she was using and opened it. "There, see."

"Oh fuck."

"Oh fuck indeed."

"What happens now?"

"As I see it we have two options. The first is we get in your car and drive to a police station and I fill in a report about you soliciting prostitution. Of course that could have quite a few significant consequences for you because these things rarely stay out of the press."

"What's the second option?"

"Where you pay a fine roughly equivalent to that a court might impose, I take a ride in your car to the shop I was on my way to and we say no more about it."

"That's blackmail."

"Yeah, it is, isn't it. So what's it gonna be?"

"How much is the fine?"

"Let's call it two thousand dollars."

"You're a fucking crook."

"Report me."

"You don't have any proof that I did anything."

"Other than this recording I made on my phone you mean?"

"Bitch."

"Careful, I might have to recalculate that fine," she held out her hand and waited while he counted twenty $100 bills into it. "Now hand me your car key."

"What?"

"You didn't think that I'd let you drive did you? Not when you just made unwanted sexual advances and threatened me."

He handed her the key and she pressed the button to lock the car. I'm going to a nearby strip mall, I'll leave the car there with the key in the glove box. I shouldn't waste time getting there, I believe the crime rate in these parts is quite high."

"Which strip mall?"

"Not sure, there can't be many. Have a nice walk."

After walking round to the driver's door she unlocked it, got in and locked the doors again. She adjusted the seat then drove away and watched Simmonds in the rearview as he started walking hurriedly after her.

She found the mall that the Hispanic lady had told her about less than a mile away. After parking, she put the key in the glove box, got out and walked away.

It didn't take long to buy the underwear she needed and as she came out of the shop she saw Simmonds rushing to his car panting and sweating as if he'd run a marathon. She stood and watched as he searched for the key and relax when he'd found it.

He started the car and when he looked up, he saw Saffie wave and smile pleasantly. When he tried to hurriedly pull away, there was a screech of brakes and the crunch of two cars colliding. It wasn't serious although the ensuing argument could have been, but Saffie didn't wait to find out. A hundred yards further down the street a cab discharged its passenger, she climbed in and asked to be taken to a good restaurant.

The cab driver's idea of a good restaurant wasn't the same as hers, but it was good enough to fuel herself through the next few hours until catching another cab to the airport.

After her meal she stepped into a charity gift shop and handed over half of the cash she'd bullied out of Simmonds.

She spent the remainder of the day wandering around just to eat up the hours. It was tedious and tiring. Mid-afternoon she found herself in a modern mall, one of the ubiquitous, concrete, and marble monstrosities that once inside you could be in almost any city in the western world. She hated places like that but they'd somehow become a necessity for many people. There was nothing there that would make life any easier in Ukraine so she bought a coffee and Danish in the food hall and left by the same pedestrian doors she'd entered by.

As she stepped onto the street and continued in the direction she'd been heading, she spotted a moped fifty yards along the street start up and head toward her on the wrong side of the road. With its two helmeted riders It was so obviously going to be a bag snatch they might have just as well held up a sign. The only question was, who was the intended victim, was it her or the woman approaching from the opposite direction?

The bag that Mary had loaned her was a tough leather weekender with a shoulder strap and strong handles. She gripped the handles tight and waited to see what would happen. The other woman stepped away from the curb to allow Saffie to pass on the traffic side, leaving her as the bikers' only viable victim. At the last moment she grabbed the bag handles with her inside hand and whipped it away from the bike passenger's grasping hand. The scooter momentarily wobbled, accelerated, swerved to avoid hitting an approaching car, then ran into the back of a parked truck.

Saffie waited to see what happened next, and when neither of the riders moved, she turned on the burner on which she'd originally called Mary and dialed 911. But by the time she'd finished the call, the passenger was struggling to his feet. The driver though remained motionless, as people had begun to gather round. Saffie decided not to wait any longer.

'For fucks sake,' she thought. 'In less than twenty-four hours I've been sexually assaulted, propositioned, and nearly mugged. No wonder Baltimore doesn't get much tourist trade, I'd have been safer in Kyiv.'

At her next opportunity she grabbed a cab for the airport. She was about to turn the phone off when it buzzed with an incoming text, opening it up it read, '*Saffie, if you get this, can you call me as soon as you can? Mary xx.*'

The incoming call had been from a cellphone, but even if she'd ever known Mary's cell number, she was doubtful that she'd have recognized it, so she wasn't convinced it really was her friend. It was quite possible it was some sort of ruse to get her to reveal her whereabouts. She asked the driver to stop at a shop where she could buy another burner, but she was out of luck, he'd already turned onto the I-95 airport approach road.

At the airport departures entrance she hurriedly thrust a fifty dollar bill in his hand, grabbed her purse and bag, rushed inside, and searched for somewhere to buy a new burner. A news and bookstore provided one at an inflated price, but she was in no position to complain. Outside the store she tore it out of its packaging and turned it on. As soon as the device had finished booting up she went into the settings and turned the locations to off.

She looked for a quiet corner to make the call and looked up the number from the other burner and dialed. Mary picked-up very quickly.

"Mary, what's wrong?"

"Oh Saffie thank God you're okay. We've been going out of our minds."

"What's happened?"

"It was on the news earlier that the FBI were searching for the mother of a recently abducted eight-year-old boy. They said that the woman was the wife of a government intelligence agent who was also missing and there were fears for all their safety. Ben's been really scared."

"For fucks sake. Sounds like they're trying to flush me out. I'm fine, I'm not even out of the country yet, although I will be in a few hours. If that's all they said, it's not a genuine appeal for information. If it were, they'd have named us and provided descriptions. Let me talk to Ben."

"Mom, are you really okay?"

"Sure I am, I've been a bit busy. I'm sorry they worried you like that, but you've no need to be concerned, I just need to stay under the radar for a few days that's all."

"Are you still at the airport?" He could hear the background noise.

"That's right, I'm taking off in about three hours. Are you enjoying it at the farm?"

"It's great, Rusty's been teaching me loads."

"Make the most of Mary's fantastic cooking because you know I'll never be that good. I love you sweetheart."

"I love you too Mom."

Mary came back on the line.

"Please stay safe, Saff."

"I will. I'll get a message to the FBI to let them know that I'm okay, but I'm going to let them sweat about Ben. I don't want that investigation to go cold."

They said goodbye then went back to the news shop and bought a lunchtime edition of a paper with a small piece about the missing wife and son of a CIA agent at the bottom of the front page.

Saffie looked around her for an honest looking person to take her photo with the phone whilst holding the paper. A young mother and her daughter walking by fitted the bill and obliged. She thanked them and sat down to read the article which only amounted to a few lines.

Wife and son of US Intelligence Agent in Kidnap Mystery

In the early hours of Monday morning the son of a CIA agent currently operating overseas was kidnapped at gunpoint. One of the kidnappers was killed in the incident, and for understandable reasons investigators have been keeping the details under wraps but our sources are now hearing that the boy's mother has now also disappeared, and there are fears for the father's safety. The FBI are giving little detail but have asked if anybody with information about these incidents should contact them on the following number. 540-662-3531.

Saffie saw through it right away. This had Ramirez written all over it. She called the number, which turned out to be their Winchester office. She just asked for an email address where she could forward information about a federal crime. Having talked her way out of speaking to an agent she was eventually given the email address.

Next she used the airport Wi-Fi and logged on using the number of the burner phone number as her ID. Then, using an anonymous email account, that she hadn't used for nearly a year she sent the photo for the attention of Special Agent Sofia Ramirez with the message, '*I'm fine. No need to worry.*'

She knew that given time, the Feebies had the means to trace that email back to the Airport IP address, but she doubted they'd bother, and even if they did, by that time she'd be out of the country.

Chapter 10

Standing in the queue for passport control, her doubts about the Hanrahan ID returned. In the end she needn't have worried, she was waved through with the respectful nod she'd come to expect in the USA whenever she passed through with a federal ID. Her bag passed through baggage check without incident and she made her way to the gate twenty minutes before boarding began.

Waiting to board with the other economy class passengers, she was still marginally uneasy that she'd be stopped and she'd stay that way until the aircraft lifted off. In theory, either agency could have the plane turn around midflight, but without evidence of a serious crime, she knew they wouldn't do that.

Finally, her bag was in the head locker, and she was in her seat by the window with the belt tight around her. She was beginning to relax when a flight attendant leaned across her fellow passengers.

"Excuse me, Ms. Hanrahan?"

Her heart sank, "Yes."

"One of our First Class passengers has failed to check in. The Captain asked if you would like to upgrade."

"Oh, yes thank you very much."

The two passengers who were forced to make way for her didn't look happy about it, but neither complained. Sinking into the new luxurious seat, minutes before takeoff, she couldn't have been more grateful for the uplift. One of the few and very rare advantages of being a law enforcement officer and travelling by air in the USA was if upgrades were available they were generally offered to them first.

She was already tired from the tensions and events of the previous days, and it was a ten hour flight to be followed by a minimum six hour drive to the area where she suspected Brett was being held. As things stood she still had no idea how she was going to get there - bus, train or hire car - nor what she'd be able to do once she arrived.

Three hours into the flight she finally fell asleep, the book she'd bought open on her lap,and even under torture she couldn't have told anybody anything about the plot. Four hours later an attendant woke her to ask if she wanted something to eat. She accepted, if only for the practical reason that she knew she needed something inside her.

Apart from a visit to the bathroom she sat quietly awake for the remainder of the flight. Before takeoff, she'd texted her flight number to Pearmain but he hadn't replied. She'd charged the burner phone at Mary's house and again in the hotel but then kept it turned off to save battery. She hoped Pearmain got the message.

The landing was as smooth as any she'd had as an experienced flyer, and she was thankful that at last she'd be able to get on with her self-imposed task. Along with most of her fellow passengers, she turned the phone on as the plane taxied to the terminal and it immediately began to beep, adding to the chorus from the other phones. The message read, '*Catch a cab to Raziotel Hotel, Magistralna St, Room 223.*' She sighed with relief, but didn't send a reply, confident he wouldn't expect one.

After removing her bag from the locker, she joined the short queue to disembark. Smiling she thanked the flight attendants and stepped onto the jet bridge before making her way to immigration ahead of most of her fellow travelers. Walking fast she arrived at the row of passport control booths to be only second in a queue.

The uniformed immigration guy waved her forward, she handed him her passport, he studiously looked it over and looked at her face, and in English asked, "Would you mind waiting for a minute Miss Hanrahan?" His hand disappeared beneath his desk, no doubt to press a button.

"Of course," she replied. The thought that her plans were about to go toes up crossed her mind, but she attempted to maintain a nonchalant visage."

A uniformed policewoman and a man in plain clothes appeared through a side door.

"Would you come with me please Miss Hanrahan," the man said in heavily accented English.

They led her along a narrow corridor past a number of small, mostly empty, interview rooms with clear glass windows before showing her into the final one.

"Have seat, Miss Hanrahan. My name is Captain Chornyi. Wait here few minute, I be back soon."

Seated on the uncomfortable plastic chair, all the time under the dispassionate gaze of the policewoman and probably a camera, she wondered if this was a tactic to make her feel vulnerable or if he really was making some sort of enquiries. In the end it was close to forty minutes before he returned.

"I sorry make you wait," he said without an explanation.

"I'm happy to talk in Ukrainian if you find it easier. It's been a few years but I think I'll cope." She knew she had an accent of her own. Her diction had always impressed her uni tutors but any Ukrainian would immediately recognize she wasn't native in spite of her excellent vocabulary and grammar.

He switched to his native tongue. "Thank you Miss Hanrahan that's very helpful."

"Is there a problem?"

"I hope not. Could you tell me the purpose of your visit."

"I have some leave and I was hoping to look up some people I became acquainted with when I visited here nine years ago."

"You work for the Federal Bureau of Investigation, the famous FBI, is that right?"

"That's right. For the time being that is."

"How do you mean?"

"I'm currently serving out my notice, and on leave and I thought I'd use some of the time left on my Ukrainian visa to renew my friendships here."

"You could apply for another visa."

"If you'll forgive me for saying so, a major conflict with Russia is looking increasingly likely. If that happens I imagine it will be some time before Ukraine will be issuing visas to non-essential travelers like me. What's more I'm pregnant and I doubt I'll be travelling with my newborn child for a year or so."

"So you're not here in any law enforcement capacity then, Miss Hanrahan?"

"Certainly not."

"That's good because your credentials, impressive as they are, hold no sway in this country."

"I'm well aware of that Captain."

"Your Ukrainian is very good by the way. Where did you learn?"

"Thank you. I studied Slavic languages at university."

"Is that not unusual?"

"I had thought of a career in the US State Department but somehow got side-tracked into the FBI."

"What was the purpose of your previous visit to Ukraine?"

"No doubt your records show that I was here to escort an embassy staff member back to America because she was suspected of a crime."

"Very well then, Miss Hanrahan, I wish you a safe onward journey, a pleasant stay in Ukraine, and good luck with your baby."

"Very kind, Captain."

They shook hands and the expressionless policewoman showed her out.

Five minutes later she was in the taxi and on her way to the address Pearmain had texted her, relieved to discover the driver accepted payment in dollar; as yet she hadn't acquired any local currency. The bureau de change at Baltimore/Washington airport hadn't held Ukrainian Hryvnia and there certainly wasn't time for her stop and try to get some now, so she was relying on the power of the almighty dollar to see her through.

Chapter 11

It was after 8am when she arrived at the hotel. There was nobody at the desk so she went straight to the room and knocked.

Pearmain opened the door, "Were you followed?"

"I don't think so, but as a passenger in a cab, I can't be certain."

"Hand me your bag."

She did as he asked and he ran a scanner over both it and her before handing back the bag. "You're clean."

"That's good," she said, although she hadn't expected otherwise.

"What kept you? The flight landed ages ago."

"Sorry, but the immigration cops insisted on an interview."

"Did they say why?"

"Do they ever? No, the questioning was superficial in the end. They asked the purpose of my visit. I'm using the fake ID I used when I was last here. It threw up that I'm supposed to be an FBI agent, but I had no choice at such short notice. The passport and visa fortunately still have over a year left to run."

"Do you think they knew who you really are?"

"I doubt it. They may suspect that my presence in the country has something to do with Brett's disappearance, although there's no evidence of that. It's my guess that they were just putting me on notice that law enforcement is their job not mine."

"I've been monitoring the activities of your countrymen; from what I can tell they've got the Russians and Russian-backed dissidents all as confused as each other. None of them have a clue who's got him, or in most cases who it is they've got, although it would be my guess they're just as anxious to get their hands on him as your guys are for their own reasons."

"If you had to guess, who would you plumb for?"

"Neither of the above. There are one or two small-time gangs popping up and trying to make a name for themselves and my guess is it would be one of them, in particular some new kids on the block, a group of Belarussians who call themselves New Minsk, and they're based in Slovyansk. The leader is a guy called Novak Hevil.'"

"What do you know about him?"

"He's only twemty-six, been locked up three times for offences involving violence. His gang, if you can call it that, consists of two former cell mates, five local crims who haven't yet graduated to the big time, and three guys he went to school with. Mostly they're involved in street muggings, blackmail, prostitution, kidnappings, which to my mind is what puts them in the frame for this. They're even suspected of a couple of murders for hire. Nobody's been taking them seriously until now, but if it does turn out to be them, they might find they've overstepped their mark, and some of the big boys will take them out."

"Do you know where I can find him?"

"Hevil lives in Hadishya Street in Slovyansk but I doubt they'd be holding Rider there. There's a rundown building on Kharkivska Street, junction of Prestyzhnyi Lane where they hang out; that's a possibility,. That's all I've got for you at the moment, but I wouldn't waste too much time doing whatever it is you intend to do. When the big players get pissed off with all the extra attention, they'll make a move against them themselves."

"Thanks, that's good advice."

"There's a red three-year-old Audi A3 in the car park. Here's the key. It's got GPS but I don't know which language. Nobody's looking for it; it's completely clean. You can use it for as long as you need, when you've finished with it just leave it wherever." He handed her an envelope. "Here's some Ukrainian currency, I haven't counted it but I'm told there's about a thousand US dollars' worth. Do you need a gun?"

"It might come in useful."

He handed over a pistol with a suppressor attached. She recognised it immediately - a 9mm Makarov. A Russian handgun that had been in use since the early days of the Cold War, but this was a recently modified version that accepted a bigger 12 round clip.

"I haven't got a spare mag for it, so don't go getting yourself in a protracted gunfight."

"Do you need reimbursing for all this stuff?"

"No, forget it. It all came from the same dead minor Russian mobster and nobody's looking for it."

"I can't thank you enough for all this."

"Don't worry about it, it's not as if you didn't do enough for me back in the day. Last of all, before I let you go, here's another mobile phone. Use it for anything except calling me. Once again it was the gangster's but I've taken it back to factory settings, put in a new SIM with about a hundred bucks on it. There's no password needed. Oh, and there's a recent picture of Hevil in the glove box."

"You're a true friend, Pearmain."

"Good luck, try not to need me if you can. Wait here for ten minutes before you leave. The breakfast here is supposed to be good and the room was booked in the name of Nastya Mazur if you want to partake."

He opened the door and left, leaving her to bless her good fortune for having worked with him all those years before.

After taking advantage of the breakfast, which wasn't quite as good as Pearmain had suggested, she went out to the car park, pressed the remote button on the key and watched for lights to flash.

The outside of the car was dirty with road grime although not excessively, so it wouldn't stand out. She searched it for any remaining incriminating evidence of its previous owner including the trunk and the glove box and found nothing other than the photo of Hevil. After taking a few moments to familiarize herself with it, she turned on the ignition. It turned out that the GPS was in German, which was good because although she was fine with spoken Ukrainian she wasn't so hot with the Cyrillic script when in a hurry. The tank was full, so she set her destination for Slovyansk, and the GPS confirmed that it was over six hours away.

Saffie had been recruited into the CIA as her first job after university with a degree in European Languages, and a Masters in Russian, Polish, and Ukrainian. That, coupled with her cool head, love of martial arts, and first class analytical skills had made her a shoo-in for field agent, and she'd found herself in Poland within months of completing her training. Although young compared with most of her colleagues she quickly gained their respect. It was during a brief spell in Cologne that she met Brett on an op to catch a Russian agent and turn him to work for the CIA.

As she drove through mile after mile of sweeping agricultural landscape, she thought about those few months together professionally. They'd developed a rapport almost immediately and the successful outcome of their work earned them a month of down time during which their relationship grew into something more. After that they both did everything they could to coordinate their homeland time. Since their son Ben's birth they still had to spend a lot of time apart, but they cherished their time together all the more because of it. She couldn't bear the thought of losing him.

After stopping for a meal in Dnipro approximately halfway, she arrived in the center of Slovyansk and found a Hotel with a free room called the 'Hotel de Paris' near the center of the city. She checked in, brought a map of the city, then found her way to her room. It was too early in the day to go looking for her prey so she laid on the bed thinking through her plan of action.

In many ways it felt like the beginning of every solo field op she'd been on in the past; she was lonely, and with a heavy onus of responsibility on her shoulders, and just like then there was no time to dwell on it. This was different to an authorized op though, because this time she had a huge personal stake in the outcome, and worse she was isolated with no hope of backup if she was forced to go in hard. She might be able to get logistical support from Pearmain, but it wouldn't be on tap.

At seven o'clock, she decided to try out the hotel restaurant. The dining room was dull and utilitarian and having taken her seat, she was offered a menu by a young waitress. The food clearly wasn't going to attract a Michelin Star any time soon, but Spaghetti Bolognese was there and she didn't think they could go far wrong with that. Accompanied by a small light beer the meal was acceptable at best, but there was plenty of it and she wasn't there to enjoy herself.

While she ate, a man came into the restaurant and was shown to a nearby table. She wasn't paying particular attention to him, but every time she glanced in his direction she saw that he'd been looking at her. She was unlikely to be interested in the attentions of a man at the best of times, and certainly not from a horny middle-aged traveling lothario in a cheap hotel, still less on this trip. Not wanting to encourage him, she finished her meal and went to the bar. She asked for a straight scotch, and after watching the barman pour a generous tot in a glass, she took it and sat near the window to watch the early evening activity in the square outside.

"Mind if I join you?" a voice said in an English accent.

She turned to see the man from the restaurant taking the seat opposite and placing two glasses on the table between them.

"Bought you a top up," he said pushing a glass toward her."

"Thank you, but I wasn't looking for company."

"My name's Nigel Jenkins. Surely a little friendship among those far from home can't harm, can it?"

"Probably not, but as I said I'm not looking for company, and I'd prefer to drink alone."

"Oh come on sweetheart..."

"I obviously didn't make myself clear. I'll try again. Fuck off. Is that easier to understand."

"Bitch." He stood up, poured his own drink down his throat in a single draught and turned toward the bar.

"Don't forget your second glass," she told him.

He ignored her and took a stool at the bar.

Several times she noticed him watching her in the mirror behind the bar. When she'd finished her drink she took the one left by Jenkins, handed it to the barman, and said loud enough for the would-be nighttime companion to hear, "You'd best pour that away, I think it may have been tampered with."

In her room she prepared herself for the evening. It was simple enough; cargo pants with a broad webbing belt, t-shirt, her combat sneakers, and her hunting jacket. Not an outfit that your run of the mill girl about town would wear, but not entirely out of place for a woman in a poor city in an impoverished part of the country.

She left the gun in her shoulder purse for the time being but distributed most of its other contents into the various pockets of her pants. She looked around the room to see that everything was as she wanted, and the last thing she did was tuck a loosely folded piece of toilet tissue under the door so that only the tiniest corner was exposed after it was closed. On her way out of the hotel she passed the barroom and spotted Jenkins still propping up the bar.

In the car she set the GPS for Hevil's address which wasn't far so she was there in a few minutes. Parking a hundred yards from his home, she left the vehicle and walked around the block to get a feel of the area, leaving his home to the end of her circular route. Although it was more than an hour before sunset, the mainly residential streets felt dark and uninviting. There were a few cars parked, but she only saw two other people walking.

Hevil's house was barely distinguishable from those around it except it was detached, whilst most others were in terraces. She didn't dare use the side alley to take a look at the rear so she continued to her car, but as she got back in the vehicle she looked back and saw Hevil and another very big man, probably a bodyguard, come out of his front door and get into an Audi A5 parked outside. She watched from her driving seat as it pulled away and drove past her with the big man driving. She waited until it turned at the end of the street before making a three-point turn and following it.

It wasn't yet dark and tailing a car in light traffic without the luxury of a tracking device was risky, but she felt she had little choice. Staying well back she managed to keep it in sight as it drove right across town and pulled into the yard of a small farmhouse on the outskirts of the city. She stopped short of where it had turned and pulled into a side road of houses that were considerably further up.m. arket than Hevil's own.

Sitting in the car, she was torn between waiting for Hevil to leave to take a closer look at the place or coming back later. In the end her mind was made up for her when the occupier of the house she was parked outside, opened his door, and pointedly stared at her. She indicated her phone, smiled at him, waved, and drove away.

Chapter 12

'Next stop Prestyzhnyi Lane,' she thought. When she got there, she discovered that 'lane' must mean something entirely different in Slovyansk than it did in the English-speaking world. The street was even more depressing than Hevil's road. The housing was pretty much the same but generally in a much worse state of repair. The building that Pearmain had suggested might be some sort of hang out, must at one time have been a vehicle workshop or something similar. There were tall, wide, sliding, timber doors across much of the front with a wicket door set into one, and to one side was a window to what may have been an office.

She made a circular reconnaissance of the block in the same way that she had with Hevil's home. There was a Russian built Kamaz all-wheel drive SUV parked on the broken ground behind the building about twenty feet away. Whatever had once been behind the building had been demolished leaving the rear easily accessible. There was a rear door and to one side, clear glass windows from about five feet up. The lights were on which ought to make whatever went on inside easily observable.

If this were their 'headquarters', Saffie knew that the likelihood of Brett being held there was slim, but she decided to try to see what she could learn by looking inside. The darkness was almost complete by this time, and looking around she could see nobody about, so she crept across the uneven ground to the workshop rear window.

Although the glass was filthy, on tiptoe she could see two men inside who appeared to be arguing, but there was music playing and she couldn't make out what they were saying. She looked around for something to stand on to give her a better view and get her closer to the glass to hear more. Behind the car she found a block of bricks still cemented together, probably debris from the demolition. She rolled it against the wall and stepped up.

"... should just kill him now."

"If we did that Novak says we lose the second half of the money."

"How much is that though?"

"Ten thousand dollars; that's thirty-five-thousand Ukrainian hryvnia."

"We can't even be sure that they will pay up, especially after you shot the American."

"Novak..."

"It's not polite to listen to other people's private conversations bitch," someone said as he grabbed her around the neck with one arm and viciously punched her in the kidney with the other. In all normal circumstances the unpredicted blow would have crippled her. What the guy hadn't accounted for was the handgun in her belt, and the power of his blow resulted in him breaking bones in his hand.

The pain caused him to loosen his grip around Saffie's neck allowing her to grab the wrist with both hands and swing under both their arms until she faced him. She released his wrist with her right hand and hit him in the throat with a powerful punch of her own. When the man dropped to his knees struggling to get air into his lungs she punched him again, this time in the temple, knocking him unconscious, or possibly dying.

The fight was over in seconds but leaving her little time to decide what to do next. Walking away was clearly no longer an option, so she knocked loudly on the door and shouted, "Quick, call an ambulance!"

She waited and after a long pause, she knocked again, "Hurry, there's a seriously hurt man out here, I think he's been attacked!"

Eventually the door opened outward a crack, "Who are you?"

"Me? I'm nobody, I was walking past and I saw this man lying here. You need to hurry he's having trouble breathing."

He pushed the door further open and pointed a gun at her. "Move back."

"Hey, there's no need for a gun, I was only trying to help."

The man spotted the injured man and knelt beside him. "It's Dmiytro, I think he's dead," he called to the guys inside.

She could see the second man inside standing away from the door and also holding a gun.

"No, I can see his chest move, he's still alive, look," she said, feigning concern.

"Get in here you nosey bitch," the second man said, menacingly pointing the gun at her.

"Why, what have I done. I was only trying to get the guy some help. Is he a friend of yours?"

"Just shut the fuck up and get in here."

"What're you going to do?"

"I haven't decided yet, just get in here."

Demonstrating a level of fear that wasn't entirely false, she stepped through the door and pushed her hands as high in the air as possible, like a kid playing cops and robbers. A third man that she hadn't seen stepped up behind her, grabbed her breasts and pulled her against him.

"She's got a..."

His speech was interrupted by her head slamming backward into his. Barely able to see, and with blood pouring from his nose, he let her go. She pulled her gun and before he had time to react, she shot the man in front of her in the chest, and with a second shot in the head he died without making another sound.

Spinning to confront the gangster who'd been tending the man outside, she ordered, "Drop the gun or you're next."

The confused guy didn't even have time to raise his gun. His jaw dropped at the swift sequence of actions by the seemingly harmless woman, but his gun fell to the ground.

"Drag your buddy inside." He hesitated, so she fired a shot between his feet, "NOW! And close the door behind you."

The man wasted no more time and did as she'd demanded. By this time it was obvious to all of them that Dmiytro was dead, and his friend looked terrified that the same fate awaited him.

"You," she said, pointing her gun at broken-nose man, "Are you armed?"

He nodded, still holding his nose with one hand.

"What have you got; gun, knife?" He nodded again, "Throw them over here."

A gun and a switchblade were thrown at her feet.

"What about you asshole, have you got anything else?" she said to the man who'd come outside to help.

He shook his head.

Then, standing away from them she took a quick look around. The place reeked of cannabis, and she suspected they were all stoned which would account for their pathetic responses to her attack.

A workbench ran the length of the back wall, covered with junk including empty pizza boxes and other fast food containers, but amongst the detritus was the kidnappers' favorite accessory, a roll of duct tape.

"Anybody else in here?" she asked.

The man with the broken nose shook his head. "No," he said with difficulty.

Almost as soon as he'd said it, she heard a toilet flush. Moments later another man stepped out from the accommodation area. As he took in what was happening he made a grab for the gun tucked into his belt. The headshot from Saffie's gun killed him before his fingers closed around the grip.

She spun back to the two men still standing, "You, what's your name?" she asked the man she'd first seen at the door.

"Marko."

"Okay then Marko, I want you to take that reel of tape and use it to tape up the other guy's hands behind his back and put some over his mouth. And make a good job of it or you'll get the same treatment as your buddies. What's his name?"

"Mykolo."

It wasn't long before Mykolo was sitting on the floor, his hands taped behind him and blowing bubbles of blood from his nostrils.

Saffron used the switchblade to make a small hole in the tape over Mykolo's mouth to help him breathe.

"Okay then Marko now you and I get to have a chat. Sit down while I tell you the rules. First, I ask a question, then you give me the answer, the full answer, leaving nothing out. If I'm satisfied with what you tell me I won't hurt you. When I say hurt, I mean seriously, and permanently. If at the end I am not convinced that what you've told me is the truth I'll kill you. Do you understand?"

"Who're you?" he asked barely able to conceal his fear.

"Someone with a lot of rage, and without a lot of time or patience. Easy ones first. What's his name?" She indicated the first man she'd shot.

"Vasyl."

"And the other one?"

"Josip."

"Very good. Now, to save time, let me tell you what I already know. I know that you hang around with Novak Hevil, I know that you've kidnapped an American and you did it because you were paid to, by another American. I want to know who it was that paid you and where the hostage is being held. Also I overheard one of you saying that he'd been shot. I want to know how he was wounded, and how bad he is. Your turn."

"I can't tell you; Novak will kill me?"

Saffron shot him in the arm and he screamed for a while.

"Are you getting the idea yet?"

Marko grunted his reply through clenched teeth, "The man was called Lopez; I think he was American."

"What did he look like?"

"I didn't see him; Novak did the deal."

"What was the deal?"

"Lopez paid us $10,000 and we were to hold him until he told us to let him go, then he would us another $10,000."

"How did he get wounded?"

"When we grabbed him, he wouldn't cooperate so Vasyl shot him in the leg?"

"How is e now?"

"He has a fever and keeps going unconscious."

"Where is he?"

"At a farmhouse in Vulytsya Myru." He pronounced it *Vulture Miru*. "It's on the other side of town." It was where she'd followed Hevil earlier.

"Who's guarding him?"

"Boyko and Petro; maybe Andriy too unless he's with Novak."

"Is Andriy his bodyguard?"

"Yes, when Vasyl isn't doing it."

"Who's in charge when Novak isn't here; tonight for example?"

"Mykolo tonight. If not him then Vasyl."

"Do you change guards very often?"

"Josip and I are supposed to take over at two o'clock until eight. Novak will come looking if we don't turn up."

"Do you all have cell phones?"

"Yes."

"Have any of you got a car nearby?"

"Mykolo's car is outside."

"Get Mykolo's car keys and phone and give them to me. Then fetch all the other phones and leave them next to Vasyl."

He moved to stand up. "No on your knees."

With the wound in his arm it was a struggle but he succeeded.

"Where's Novak now?"

"At the Karaoke nightclub in the city I expect. He goes there every night."

"How will he know if you haven't relieved the others on guard duty?"

"Boyko will call him."

"Okay Marko, this is where you and I go for a little walk. We're going outside, I'm going to unlock Mykolo's car and you're going to sit in the passenger seat. Then, and this is the important bit, you're going to do exactly as I tell you and nothing else. Any deviation and I'll kill you. Do you understand what I say?"

"Yes."

"Do you believe me?"

"Yes."

She picked up the roll of tape. "Very good, stand up and slowly open the door. Now step outside and stay well clear of the gun you dropped earlier."

She pressed the remote on the key fob, the car lights flashed, and he opened the door climbing in awkwardly holding his injured arm. Saffie got in the back seat behind him, then pulled three feet off the reel of tape and said, "Hold that."

No sooner had he cautiously taken the loose end of the tape from her, than she wrapped it around both his head and the headrest, inadvertently catching his hand in the web of tape she continued to create enclosing both him and the car seat.

"That should do it. Now you be a quiet boy, and I'll be back in a minute."

She picked up Marko's gun and went back inside where Mykolo was trying to crawl to the discarded switchblade.

"Naughty, naughty, Mykolo. I didn't say you could move, did I? However, seeing as you're in such a hurry I'll let you stand up."

With his hands taped behind him, he struggled to get to his feet. Then she walked him outside, forced him to climb in the trunk of his own car and pulled the tape from his mouth to let him breath.

She closed the lid, ignoring Mykolo's muffled curses and went back to the workshop, where she removed the magazines from the guns. Two of them were compatible with the one she was using so she pocketed them along with the switchblade.

Leaving the door unlocked she got in the driving seat of the Kamaz, and moved it a few streets away next to an empty building lot.

"I expect somebody will find you in the next few hours. Have a nice life." She got out of the car, closed the door, and threw the keys into the distance.

Chapter 13

She speed-walked back to the workshop and began making preparations for the next stage of the plan that she was still making up as she went along. She anticipated that the harbinger that things were about to kick off again would be when Mykolo's phone began to ring. It was nearly one-thirty so she didn't expect to wait long. In the end, it was nearly an hour before a phone began to vibrate beside her. She lifted it and saw Novak's name on the screen.

"Novak, nice of you to call."

"Who's that, where is Mykolo?"

"I'm sorry Mykolo is a bit tied up at the moment and can't come to the phone." Then she ended the call.

Another thirty minutes was all it took for them to arrive. Saffie watched from some boards fixed across the open steel roof joists to carry a water tank and provide storage.

Getting up there without a ladder had been a major exercise. It had involved a lot of energy and no small amount of ingenuity. A motorized chain engine hoist hung from a sliding track attached to the underside of the joists. She slid it along the track until it was roughly alongside the boards; then she fashioned a stirrup from a piece of steel and some electrical cable. Attaching it to the chain was the most time-consuming part of the exercise, but in the end it still gave her time to hoist herself toward the roof and clamber the last three feet onto the boards.

Once she'd settled herself where she could see both entrances, she lay on the dusty ledge, praying that the chains would have stopped swinging by the time they arrived. As it happened they were still moving a little but it went unnoticed.

Predictably, Andriy had been given the job of making the first sortie. His entry, when it happened, under most circumstances would have been a gigantic tactical mistake. The rear door was suddenly thrown open, the big man appearing in the doorway gripping his gun two-handed and exposing himself to fire from anybody inside. On this occasion it suited Saffie to leave him unchallenged.

At first he ignored the three bodies, and his gun followed his eyes as they swept around the room. If he'd looked up at that moment he might easily have spotted Saffie, but the untrained mobster wasn't thinking in three dimensions and he went through to clear the toilet, kitchen, and office.

As he emerged back into the workshop, Saffie heard him speak into his phone, "There's no-one here, except Dmiytro, Josip and Vasyl and they're all dead."

The wicket gate burst open and Hevil stormed in. "Where the fuck are Mykolo and Marko?"

At that point Saffie used Mykolo's phone to call Hevil.

"Mykolo, what the fuck's happening?" he said as he answered.

Saffie immediately called Vasyl's phone from Marko's, causing both men to turn towards the vibrating phone on the bench and shot Hevil in his lower spine. He screamed, his legs gave way and he dropped to the floor, crippled.

Andriy spun around without knowing where the silenced shot had come from, and before it occurred to him to look up he'd taken a bullet in the upper thigh.

"Throw your gun away or the next one is in your head," Saffie ordered.

With difficulty the man obeyed.

"Now take Hevil's gun from him and throw that away as well; then sit against the bench."

Hevil was groaning loudly and struggling to move, in no condition to object as his minder took the gun from his hand. However, instead of throwing the weapon out of reach, Andriy flipped onto his back and began firing wildly into the roof space. Saffie took careful aim and shot him, but not before she felt something very painful hit her.

"Shit!" she loudly exclaimed, thinking at first that she'd been shot, but she looked down to see a long sliver of wood embedded in her leg. She pulled it out and found it was about four inches long, an inch wide, and a quarter inch thick at one end tapering to a fine sliver at its tip. The wood had sunk almost three inches into her thigh, penetrating her tensor fascia muscle along the side of her leg, maybe even passing right through.

It was some consolation that it hadn't been a bullet, but it was nonetheless still extremely painful and would restrict how she handled the next stage of her plans. It must have missed her femoral artery because it didn't appear to be bleeding profusely. Nonetheless she'd still need to put some sort of dressing on it.

After using the hoist to lower herself to the floor, she searched for something to treat the wound and found a depleted first aid kit in what had once been an office. An old-fashioned gauze field dressing with damaged packaging was the best she could do, but there were no painkillers. Stripping her pants to her knees she examined the wound, it looked relatively innocuous but the blood was still flowing steadily, and it hurt like hell. With nothing to clean it with, she spread the remainder of a tube of antiseptic cream into and around the mouth of the wound and tightly tied the dressing around her leg.

Back in the workshop she kicked Hevil and he stirred.

"Okay asshole I know your chums are holding an American hostage, I know who's guarding him, and I know where. I also know that you were paid to take him by a guy you know as Lopez. I need you to tell me everything else you know about him. You're alive at the moment, but if you can't tell me anything else useful you won't be when I leave. Okay?"

"Who are you?" he managed to ask through clenched teeth.

"I work for the Donetsk People's Militia; we'll be taking over this little operation."

The threat of involvement by the ruthless Russian separatist group convinced him that silence wasn't an option. "I'll tell you, but I don't know much. I think that Lopez is American, he offered me twenty thousand dollars to take the man. I agreed after he gave me ten thousand advance. We were only supposed to hold him for four days but it's been nearly three weeks and now he won't answer my calls."

"What does Lopez look like?"

"He's white, but he was wearing glasses, a wig, and a covid facemask when we met." Hevil struggled to get the words out through the pain, but it was clear he wanted to appear helpful, "He was about one point eight metres tall and he looked overweight, but I think that might have been padding because his face was thin. He kept coughing; it was weird like a squeak. I thought he might have Covid."

"How did he contact you?"

"Another man, an American I think, came up to me in a nightclub and told me that a man outside had a business deal for me. Lopez told me the guy we were to take was his business partner who'd screwed him for a load of money."

"How have you been trying to contact him?"

"With the phone he gave me, it's in my top pocket. There's only one number in there."

She took both the phone, a burner, and his personal cellphone after forcing him to give her the passcode, and while she was at it she emptied his wallet of cash, much of which was in US dollars.

"Okay, anything else I need to know?" she asked.

"He had very good Ukrainian, like you. I promise there's nothing else."

"Okay I'll let you live for now."

"Call me an ambulance or a doctor, please."

"Like you have for your hostage you mean? I don't think so."

After taking the clips from the other gangsters' guns, Saffie left via the rear door and threw them into the distance. She was aware that her prints and DNA were all over the scene but there was nothing she could do about that without setting fire to the place. Banking on the Ukrainian cops being only too pleased to have the gang permanently shut down and too busy with the impending crisis on the border, she abandoned the building. Once they'd found she wasn't on their own records, she doubted that they'd institute an expensive international records search.

She brushed the dust from her clothes, got back in the A3, and drove away.

Chapter 14

The drive to Vulytsya Myru was uneventful but it was past four a.m. when she parked up a hundred yards from the farmhouse where she could watch the open gate. Then taking Hevil's personal phone and activating it with his passcode, she looked through the list of recent calls, found a two minute incoming call from Boyko and called it back.

The gangster answered almost immediately. "*Novak, what's happening?*"

"Novak is dead, and so is Andriy. In case you're wondering Dmiytro, Mykolo, Marko, Vasyl, and Josip are also with the angels, so you and Petro are now the only surviving members of your little band of brothers. They were stupid and resisted, will you?"

"Who are you?"

"As I explained to Novak before he died, I work for the Donetsk People's Militia. They're not happy with you snatching that American in their territory without clearing it with them first so they're taking over the operation. We're watching the farmhouse, and I'm suggesting you leave in the next five minutes to save us the trouble of coming in there and killing you two as well."

"How do we know you're not lying?"

"You don't, but as of now you won't be able to contact any of your buddies because they're dead. Are you willing to take the chance?"

"Okay we'll go. What shall we do with the Yankee?"

"Is he still alive?"

"Yes."

"Then make sure he stays that way. Remember, we know who you are, so if he's dead when we go in, we'll know who's to blame." She ended the call, put a new magazine in her gun and watched while she waited.

Four minutes passed before a battered VW sedan came out of the farm gate like a rally car. She watched until it was out of sight and then drove her own car through the same entrance.

With her gun drawn she warily approached the open front door and cautiously crept inside. Moving silently from room to room, she ignored the pain in her leg as she made certain there were no more of Hevil's accomplices left to cause problems Once she was convinced the first floor was clear, she climbed the stairs one at a time, as much because of her wound as for stealth.

She found Brett handcuffed to the headboard of a rancidly filthy bed in the rear bedroom, he was hovering on the brink of unconsciousness. He had something wrapped around his leg that may have once been a sheet. His blood had soaked through and dried. He'd lost a lot of weight; he was unshaven, and he stank.

"Brett darling, it's me Saffron."

"Saffie?" he mumbled.

"How are you my love?"

"Hot, cold, pain. Why are you here?" His hesitant words were barely audible, and his eyes kept drooping.

"Don't worry about that for the minute, are you well enough to answer a few questions?"

"Is it really you? I must be delirious, am I hallucinating."

"Remember our special kiss?" she asked. Then, ignoring his foul breath she kissed him using her tongue in a way that she knew he particularly liked. Then she gave him some water from a bottle near the bed.

He became lucid for a few minutes. "You shouldn't be here; the company will go crazy."

"Like I give a fuck. What did these bastards want?"

"I don't know."

"Haven't they questioned you?"

"No, they'd only say they'd let me go when they got word." He drifted away again for a minute or two and she decided against trying to get more from him.

When he woke again she told him, "I'm going to get you out of here soon darling, very soon, I promise, but I can't be here when the cops arrive, you understand that don't you?"

"Just go my lovely, I'll be okay."

"I've missed you so much, Ben and I can't wait to have you home again, but you'll need to get better first." She kissed his cheek and went out the door already phoning the US embassy in Kyiv, using Hevil's phone.

"The missing American agent you've been searching for is in a farmhouse in Slovyansk on a road called Vulytsya Myru. He's handcuffed to a bed; he's been shot and needs urgent medical attention. Have you got all of that?"

"Who's speaking Ma'am."

"Never mind that, just do something quickly." She ended the call confident that it would have been recorded. Then, hurrying to her car she took a moment to gather her thoughts before moving the vehicle close to where she'd parked earlier to watch what happened next.

It was twenty minutes before the first two police cars arrived, followed shortly after by an ambulance and several other vehicles. When there were far too many people there for it to be swept under the carpet without action, she turned Hevil's phone off and removed the SIM, and did the same with his burner, putting them in her purse.

It was six-fifteen in the morning and daylight when she limped into the lobby of her hotel. She was exhausted, in a lot of pain, and what she wanted more than anything were a shower and some sleep. She doubted sleep would be on the menu in the near future though.

"Madam, are you okay? You're bleeding," the desk clerk said as she limped into the hotel lobby.

"I was mugged, and the bastards stabbed me in the leg?"

"Would you like me to call the police?" he offered.

"No thank you. My trip to Slovyansk has been a waste of time and a disaster from start to finish. I'm going to change my clothes, pack my bag and go home to the States. If you've got a good first aid box it would be helpful."

"The deputy manager is a trained first aider, shall I ask her to come to your room when she gets in? She won't be long."

"That would be kind, thank you."

Grateful for the elevator she made her way to her room. As she put the key card in the reader she noticed that the telltale piece of toilet tissue she'd put under the door was no longer there. There wouldn't have been a cleaner in the room overnight, so somebody must have acquired a key card of their own or bribed someone to let them in. The rudimentary precaution that she'd hurriedly put there would have been spotted by a professional and replaced when they left, so whoever was responsible was either still there lying in wait, an amateur, or both. Either way she wasn't about to take any chances.

Taking her gun from her bag, she opened the door as quietly as she could and placed her bag on the floor. Two steps into the room revealed a sleeping man on the bed wearing only a t-shirt and boxer shorts. She closed the door, checked the bathroom, and approached.

"Can I help you Mr. Jenkins?" she said, standing over him, but without revealing the gun.

"Wha... Sorry I fell asleep. I was hoping that you could spare me some time when you'd finished with your other clients. I've got plenty of money, I'll pay whatever you want."

"Clients?"

"You know what I mean."

"No, I'm afraid I don't. Enlighten me."

"Look if I've got this wrong I'm sorry, but I thought you were a...you know."

"No, I don't know, that's why I asked you to explain. Perhaps this will help you find the right words." She pressed the muzzle of the gun into his crotch."

"Oh my God!"

"Explain, now."

"I thought you were a high-class working girl."

"Oh I get it now. You broke into my room because you assumed that only a prostitute could be staying in a cheap hotel on her own. Is that right?"

"Yes I'm sorry."

"Okay then, if that's what you want and you're prepared to pay, let's get at it. Take your clothes off."

"But..."

"I said strip, NOW."

Awkwardly he removed his last two items of clothing, all the time nervously watching her casually toying with the gun.

"Are they the rest of your things?" she asked indicating the pile of clothes on a chair.

"Y-yes." the naked man replied.

"Okay, stay there," she told him.

She rested the gun on the small dressing table and went through his pockets removing everything, wallet, keys, and passport. In the wallet there was a great deal of money in three different currencies, she took it and put it in her purse without bothering to count it. "That should be enough."

"But I can't afford all that."

"I'm a very expensive date, Mr. Jenkins." Then she used the switchblade to shred his passport before opening the window and throwing all his clothes into the void.

"Right then Mr. Jenkins, how do you want to go about this? Shall we go with me straddling your chest with my gun in your mouth while we see what comes up, or would you prefer I press this little knife into your testicles while you masturbate?"

"No, nothing it's alright."

"Are you sure? I don't do refunds." She prodded his balls with the knife.

"Just let me go, please."

"Okay, if that's what you want. The door is there, help yourself."

The middle-aged man scrambled off the bed and made for the exit. "You make sure you have a good day, Mr. Jenkins," she told him and closed the door.

After flushing the remnants of Jenkins' passport down the toilet, she put the gun in her bag, stripped to her underwear and waited for the first aider to arrive.

In spite of the pain, she was nodding off by the time someone knocked.

The woman at the door identified herself as Irina, the deputy manager, and Saffie let her in.

Irina was clearly very good at what she was doing and extremely critical of 'whoever' had previously dressed the wound. Most of the bleeding had stopped by that time so Irina just cleaned the wound, put butterfly stitches on it and put a large waterproof dressing on top.

"There was a naked man wandering the halls a few minutes ago, Irina. He accused me of being a prostitute and taking all his money. I think he was a bit mad."

"Really? I'll get security to have a look around. Where were you mugged?"

"Somewhere in the Northeast of the city."

"What on earth were you doing up there?"

"Searching for an old friend. I went to where she used to live and the people there didn't know who I was talking about, but I found her parents' house. Her mother told me that my friend had moved to Poland without telling me. She kept me talking for hours, drinking vodka, then I fell asleep. I was just walking back to my car when two men tried to grab my bag. I fought them off but one had a knife. It might have been worse but someone came out of their house and chased them off. He helped me put that dressing on."

"I think you should tell the police."

"I really don't want to wait around any longer. I need to get home and put all this behind me."

"You'll have a rest and take some breakfast before you go, surely? The dining room will open at seven-thirty."

"Maybe, but I need to see what time I can get a flight." She thanked the woman, took a shower, dressed, and packed her bag. Without a laptop or a smartphone with legitimate credentials she couldn't search and pay for a ticket online, so she needed to get to the airport as early as possible to be sure of a seat out of the country in case the police began a search for her.

She waited until the dining room opened and made sure to have the biggest breakfast practicable, knowing that she still had a six hour journey back to Kryvyi Rih.

After settling the bill, on her way to the car, she dropped Jenkins' keys and credit cards down a drain and began the long drive to the airport.

Chapter 15

Tiredness dictated another stop at Dnipro, and added at least another hour to her trip, but after a meal she felt slightly refreshed and she managed to dispose of the last spare ammo clips in a parking lot dumpster.

During the second half of the drive to Kryvyi Rih, Saffie struggled to stay awake. Several times she found her eyelids drooping; and once she was shaken awake as her nearside wheel mounted the grass at the side of the road. When she finally arrived in the center of Kryvyi Rih, she found a place in a car park, rested for a moment, and inadvertently fell asleep.

She calculated that she could only have been asleep for an hour when somebody bumped into her mirror squeezing between cars. Steeling herself to continue she stripped the gun to its component parts, and after double checking there was nothing in the vehicle to link it to her or to any of her activities, she abandoned it, leaving the key in the ignition.

Limping through the busiest part of town she dropped the knife and gun parts in different trash cans along the route. In a drug store she bought packets of both Tylenol and Tylex before continuing until she found a waiting cab. On the way to the airport, she tore open the packet of Tylenol and swallowed four.

Inside the airport terminal the departure board showed that there were two flights to Germany that evening. A ticket bureau that served several airlines, was able to get her on a Turkish Airlines flight to Berlin at nineteen-forty. It surprised the clerk when she asked to pay with cash. It was clearly not something that happened very often but he agreed there was no reason not to. She counted out the notes from what she'd recovered from Hevil's wallet as he watched, and she waited while he painstakingly repeated the exercise.

The painkillers that Irina had given her had completely worn off by the time she'd arrived in the town and the Tylenol she'd swallowed in the taxi still hadn't taken full effect. She knew they'd be barely adequate when they did. The Tylex would be much more effective but she was wary of taking them before the flight because their soporific effect would make her sleepier than she already was. Hoping that the excessive dose wouldn't have any lasting effect she swallowed two more Tylenol, hoping that they'd help take the edge off. It was too early to check in and go through to the departure lounge so she took a seat clutching her bag to her chest, knowing that she'd inevitably fall asleep.

The next thing she knew was when someone bumped her injured leg with their suitcase. She cried out in pain, but the offender barely acknowledged what he'd done. The pain that the knock had triggered was excruciating and it took several minutes before the waves of pain subsided enough for her to think about looking at the time.

'Fuck!' she swore to herself. The departure board was displaying that her flight was only forty minutes until take off.

She hobbled to the check in desk, who reminded her she had limited time to get to the gate. Thankfully, the passport control and baggage checking arrangements weren't crowded and she managed to hurry through without any delays. It was only minutes before they closed when she reached the gate, and by that time the pain was almost unbearable.

Her economy seat on the Airbus 319 was a far cry from the luxurious wide leather one she'd been given thirty-six hours earlier. It was on the aisle and the two others sharing the row were a mother and her five-year-old son. She put her bag in the overhead locker and her shoulder purse under her seat, but not before taking three Tylex.

Once again she felt relief when the plane was in the air. The flight was only a little over two hours, but the boy had insisted on using the bathroom twice in that time forcing Saffie to stand up once on their way out and again on the way back. She was blissfully grateful when the wheels touched the tarmac, but the deplaning exercise was just as painful.

By the time she was through immigration and customs it was gone ten p.m. The little sleep she'd had seemed to have had no effect; she was exhausted, and the painkillers were wearing off. She steeled herself to find a flight home as early as possible.

The clerk at the ticket bureau did his best, but there were no direct flights from Berlin to any East Coast airport in the DC area. The best he could offer was a first class seat on a Lufthansa flight to Dulles via Frankfurt leaving at 08:45. To add insult to injury he couldn't find her a room to spend the night, condemning her to a whole night on airport furniture.

She called Mary's landline, using the burner phone that she'd used to call her from Baltimore on, "Hi, is that Miss Mary Campbell-Adams?" It seemed safest to use Mary's mother's maiden name.

"Eh? Oh, yes, yes it is. Can I help you?"

"This is Serena Perry; I was calling to find out if that package I left with you is working out okay."

"Oh yes, it took a few hours to get to full working temperature, but after a little bump in the road it's been okay. It's completely operational now and appears to be settling into our use very nicely."

"I'm relieved to hear that. I'm hoping to be around that way again in the next day or two, so I'll stop by to see it in action."

"Did you ever manage to locate that missing package that you were so concerned about?"

"Yes I did. It was a little damaged but I think it'll be okay after a short while in the shop."

"We'll be glad to see you when you come back. In the meantime take care of yourself."

"Sure thing, Miss Campbell-Adams. Bye for now." She hung up.

She looked for a bureau de change and converted her remaining Ukrainian Currency and Jenkins's English pounds into US dollars. After searching for somewhere in the terminal still open to eat, there was nothing. She ended up with sandwiches and bottled water from a vending machine, huddled on an airport bench clutching her bags, and frequently woken by floor polishing machines, background airport noise, discomfort and pain. The next seven hours seemed interminable.

Saffron could also have done without the short one hour hop to Frankfurt and the three hour stopover before reboarding the plane to Dulles. It was exhausting. Back in the day, long haul journeys for her had been just an inconvenience that had to be endured so she could do her job. Now though with the stress of Ben's abduction, Brett being taken hostage, his injury, her own; and all the events in between, it was unlike any field operation she'd ever been involved in. What worried her now was that she knew it wasn't over.

She slept deeply during the nine hour flight to Washington but when she woke she was sweating profusely. She had a temperature and possibly a fever. The wound felt hot even through the dressing and her pants, and the pain had spread to her groin. To retrieve her true ID to get treatment for it on her insurance she'd need to get home, but that would take time she didn't have to waste. So, after enduring the formalities at the airport she asked the cab to take her to a hospital, where they allowed her to pay cash for her treatment.

They stitched and redressed the wound after retrieving a large splinter still lodged inside it, gave her more painkillers, an antibiotic injection, and some pills to follow it up.

It was seven p.m. when she stepped through the door of her home having torn down the crime scene tape and broken the seal that they'd put around the door that indicated either the police, FBI or both had returned to the house after she'd left. She made a pot of coffee then put the SIM back in her own smartphone. As soon as it latched onto a mast it began to beep like crazy. She left it to finish playing with itself and waited. She didn't have to wait long, six minutes to be precise, before it rang. She looked at the screen and answered. "Felix, what's happening?"

"Saffie, where the fuck have you been?"

"Busy."

"Doing what?"

"None of your concern."

"Haven't you been worried about Ben?"

"No."

"Why not?"

"Because he's safe and that's all you need to know."

"Was it you that shot up those gangsters in Richmond?"

"Which gangsters were they?"

"You know who I'm talking about."

"Did they have anything to do with Ben's abduction?"

"Yes, his DNA was all over one of the rooms in the house."

"And they got shot up?"

"That's right and killed."

"So what's the problem?" She was losing her patience now. "Listen Felix, stop fucking around talking about a problem that's been solved and tell me what's happening about my missing husband."

"He's been found."

"He has? That's fantastic! Where is he?"

"He's still in Ukraine, but he's got an injury."

"What sort of injury?"

"A bullet wound in his thigh."

"Shit, will he be okay?"

"Apparently the docs thinks so, but he's got a bit of a fever at the moment, and they're concerned about the infection. The agency will fly him home as soon as he's well enough to travel."

"Can I speak to him?"

"I'll try to sort something out."

"Great I've got to go now. I need some sleep, speak soon." She ended the call without giving him time to protest.

She quickly scrolled through the other calls and messages and decided there was nothing that needed her immediate attention and went to bed.

Chapter 16

She was woken at ten a.m. by her phone ringing and someone banging on her front door. The pain in her leg was almost as bad as it had been before being treated, so getting out of bed was difficult. Grabbing a bathrobe she limped down the stairs and looked through the peephole to see Special Agents Ramirez and Burns. She opened the door to them and asked them to wait while she answered her phone, but it stopped ringing.

"Don't bother, it was me," Burns said.

"What do you want?"

"We need to speak to you Ms. Price," Ramirez told her.

"Okay, go through to the kitchen. I need to use the bathroom."

"Why are you limping?"

"I fell off a horse."

"Why were you on a horse?" Burns asked.

"Does it matter?"

"Seems strange that you went away on vacation, given that your husband and child were both missing."

"Are we going to stand here talking about things that 'seem strange' until I piss myself, or are you going to let me use the john? I'm sure there's something in the constitution about cruel and unusual punishment."

Using the bathroom involved bending the leg that didn't want to be bent, but she did what she had to and joined them in the kitchen after retrieving the painkillers and antibiotics from her purse. She poured a glass of water and began taking the pills while she waited for the agents to start asking questions.

"Antibiotics Ms. Price?"

"That's right, Agent Burns."

"I thought you said you fell from a horse."

"That's right, I did."

"How does that result in needing antibiotics. Are you sure you don't have a bullet wound?"

"What, you think I've been involved in a horseback gunfight, Agent? This is twenty-first century Virginia, Agent Burns, not the wild west?"

"This no time to be facetious Ms. Price." Burns tetchily replied.

"Oh really? Please let me know when it is."

"Why don't you just answer the question?"

"I fell on to a sharp piece of wood and got a nasty stick injury okay? Now are you going to get on with why you're here?"

"Your son was kidnapped, Ms. Price."

"That's right, and as I'm sure you've been told by now, he's been found and is in a place of safety."

"How can we be sure of that?"

"Because I told you."

"I want to know where he is, to satisfy myself that he's not still in danger."

"I'm not prepared to say at the moment."

"Why not?"

"My son is now safe and so is my husband, but why they were taken is still unclear. There are other things at play, and until I know what they are and who's responsible, my son is staying where he is and I'm saying no more."

"We have a duty to conduct a full investigation, Ma'am." Burns told her.

"You'll have been the people that discovered where my son was being held then."

"No but..."

"Then whoever it was, was clearly better informed and more efficient than you've been."

"Where have you been the last few days, Ms. Price?" Ramirez asked.

"Away."

"Have you been out of the country?"

"Why do you ask?"

"You sent me an email with a photograph of you at an airport."

"I was meeting someone, and before you ask, it had nothing to do with my son's abduction."

"You're not above the law, Ms. Price," Ramirez told her. "Your association with the CIA gives you no authority in this country. We'll continue this investigation, and if we discover that you broke any laws while securing your son's release, we will bring charges."

"I'd expect nothing less. If that's all, I'd like to get on with my day."

"I'm sure we'll be back, perhaps with another warrant," Burns told her.

"Help yourself, although I've no idea what you'd be searching for that you haven't already found, perhaps on the visit you made after I left."

They both looked puzzled but didn't respond. She watched them drive away and closed the door.

After a shower, she made herself something to eat, and once the painkillers had kicked in she felt a lot better. In her office she opened her laptop, certain that her CIA colleagues had cloned the hard drive and turned everything over, looking for any small misdemeanor to nail her with, should it become expedient. They'd have done exactly the same with Brett's things while they were about it. There was nothing to find of course unless they'd put it there themselves, but like most efficient intelligence agents, she and Brett had introduced safeguards against that.

She couldn't have explained why she chose that moment to do it, but she quickly read through the report that she'd been putting the finishing touches to when everything kicked off a few days earlier, decided it was fine as it was and forwarded it to Meredith, her supervisor.

She was making herself a coffee when the burner she'd used to contact Pearmain buzzed.

"Wind velocity?"

"Nil."

"I'll call you back."

Seconds later the burner he'd given her in the hotel buzzed.

"Jesus wept Lemon Tree, have you evolved into some sort of avenging ninja?"

"They shouldn't have fucked with my family."

"The cops are going mental over here."

"I don't know what they're so concerned about. I did them a favor; everybody else whose job it was had done fuck all."

"It'll settle down soon I guess, but people on Twitter over here are calling you a hero. The authorities have too much else on their plate at the moment, but I wouldn't be planning on any return trips to Ukraine in the near future just in case."

"I won't, thanks for everything once again."

"No problem, good luck with the rest of it though, and destroy this phone."

"I will, thanks." He was gone.

She removed the SIM from Pearmain's phone and flushed it down the toilet, then she snapped the cheap folding device in half and put it in the trash.

She was contemplating trying to deal with the blood stain on the landing floor when her personal cellphone rang from an unknown number.

"Hello."

"It's me sweetheart."

"Brett darling, how are you?"

"Improved a bit, but I feel like shit. It looks like they've managed to halt the infection before it did any permanent damage, so that's good, but it may be a while before I'm fully mobile."

"There's no hurry. I'm a bit damaged myself at the moment; I fell off a horse."

"Fell off, that's unusual for you. Not serious I hope." She could hear in his voice that he was trying to read between the lines.

"No, I'll be okay in a week or so."

"What's this I hear about Ben being kidnapped?"

"That's right, somebody made them release him a few hours later."

"Thank God for that! Well done, whoever that was. How is he?"

She could tell that he'd read between those lines. "He was a bit shaken up, but he's okay. I've sent him away for a bit of a holiday while we try to put this behind us.

"What about the bastards who took him?"

"I gather they've permanently retired from the hostage-taking trade. When are you coming back?"

"Maybe tomorrow or the day after. I'll call you."

"What have they told you about the people who took you?"

"Only that they were a bunch of small-time gangsters. Most of them are dead, and the ones they caught that are still alive won't say anything except that they were paid; they're all in hospital. I'd better go, the docs are here."

"Can I get you on this number?"

"Yes, it's a burner, but there should be enough money on it for the next couple of days. Goodbye sweetheart."

"Take care darling."

With the wound in her thigh she couldn't bring herself to try getting onto her knees to clean the blood stain so she looked for the number of a crime scene cleaner whose name she recognised and they agreed to send someone that afternoon.

With nothing to do she was soon bored and decided that the office/study was long overdue for a do over, especially after the police, FBI, and CIA had been through it more than once. After a quick look around, it occurred to her that they'd left it suspiciously tidy.

The garage was normally Brett's domain. She usually only went in there during the winter months after parking her car inside. From the gadget cabinet above the workbench she grabbed the bug detector.

It took her less than a minute to find listening devices under both desks. The weird thing was that they weren't the same as each other, suggesting that they'd been planted by different people. This started her thinking that there might be others, so she began a methodical search and found others in the living room and kitchen. Some of the equip.m. ent looked quite modern so she couldn't be certain that either her or her detector were good enough to have found everything. She needed a professional.

After looking up the number of a woman she hadn't spoken to for five years, and taking the burner she'd been using to contact Mary when she and Ben were on her way to Harrisonburg, she went outside.

"Linda, it's Saffie."

"Saff, how the Hell are you? I haven't seen you since Rhianna's funeral."

"I'm okay I guess, but I need your professional help. It's hyper confidential so I'd be grateful if you could handle it yourself."

"No problem, but the earliest I can come is tomorrow morning, is that okay?"

"That'll be great. We're still in the same place, thank you."

"Be there about ten."

She left the listening devices where they were and continued straightening the room. Her own desk was simple; she always worked clutter free, and any extraneous paperwork was always shredded, while anything essential was stored in her paper-free system.

Brett was more of a traditionalist and he supplemented cloud storage with a conventional filing cabinet. She went to it and found the lock had been forced, although she couldn't tell what, if anything, had been interfered with. His desk was relatively tidy, and she left it for him to sort out when he was ready.

The rest of the tasks were simply housework and she left most of that to the lady she paid to come in once a month.

The crime scene cleaner arrived midafternoon but in spite of working at the stains for over two hours, it was still possible to see where the ones on the floor had been if you knew where to look, and the wall would need a coat of paint where he'd filled the bullet hole.

By the evening, with the help of the analgesia, the pain in her leg had receded enough to sit and relax a little. She was used to her own company in the evening after Ben had gone to bed, but the house felt empty knowing he wasn't there.

It occurred to her that the police still had her gun, and Brett's spare was in the Wrangler in Mary's barn. The only firearms that were still in the house were a double-barreled skeet gun and an Armalite AR-18 automatic assault rifle. Both had belonged to Brett's father, and both were practically useless for self-defense at close quarters. This was a situation she needed to remedy, although it was too late to do it then. She also needed to find a new company to rectify the alarm; the last one had disqualified themselves by failing to properly screen their staff.

It was nine p.m. when the doorbell rang. She quickly grabbed a knife from the block in the kitchen and looked through the peephole. 'Felix. What does he want at this time of night?'

She opened the door.

"What's with the knife?" he asked.

"The cops have still got my gun. What the Hell do you want?"

"Hey what's with the hostility? I'm on your side you know."

"Are you?"

"What's that supposed to mean?"

"Brett was missing for nearly three weeks before any of you lot decided to get off your asses to do anything about it or even bother to inform me. In the end it wasn't even your guys that found him - it was some unidentified do-gooder."

"I told you, Radwell gave orders to sit on it while we made discreet enquiries; my hands were tied."

"Well it isn't good enough; unless I get answers soon, I'll be asking to see the DDO about this. Brett's been one of your top European agents for years and it looks like you were ready to hang him out to dry."

"There's something going on but I can't talk about it yet."

"Is that right? Well maybe you'll have to talk about it if Brett gets back here and finds that one of your lot has been going through his confidential documents."

"What do you mean?"

"The locks on his filing cabinet were forced. There are only three potential candidates for that. The cops who'd have no motive for a document search and their warrant doesn't cover it anyway, and the same applies to the Feebies, so I wonder who that leaves."

"We didn't authorize that; it could have been anyone."

"I haven't been burgled as far as I know, so it can only have happened while your team was here, which I happen to know was while I was away."

"How could you know that?"

"Because this is me you're talking to, and because you haven't denied it."

"Look, Saffie, I don't know who did it, or even if it really was someone from the agency, but I had nothing to do with it."

"Well unless you've got anything useful to say, you need to piss off. I'm tired and I want to go to bed."

"What happened to your leg?"

"As you already know because I told the Feebies this morning, I fell off a horse. Goodnight, and don't bother to call again unless you've got something useful to say."

She could tell he was pissed as he stormed out the door, but she didn't care. Certain that whatever was behind what was happening, it had nothing to do with either Brett or her, and equally sure that if they tried to make either of them the fall guy for it, she wasn't going to make it easy for them.

Climbing into bed that night was one of the most satisfying things she'd done for more than a week, and she hoped that she'd get the sleep she desperately needed.

Chapter 17

Her leg was stiff when she woke the next day but the pain was mildly improved. She showered and changed the dressing on her wound. On a normal day at that time she'd be going for a run, but that would be out of the question for a week or two, for security reasons apart from her injury.

She had a late breakfast and took the key to her seven-year-old BMW X5 and drove to the nearest gun store less than ten minutes away. She'd been there before but doubted they'd recognize her.

Her handgun of choice was the same as Brett's, the HK45. It was one of the most popular handguns in America and needless to say they had plenty in stock, but she wanted the modified version with barrel extension to accept a suppressor. The store was a responsible place and although they had the version she wanted they were reluctant to sell her a suppressor until she revealed her agency badge. Normally, gun control laws would have made her wait twenty-four hours to take the firearm away, but her CIA status allowed them to waive that.

When she returned to the house, she pulled through the gate behind Linda.

"You're early," she said, climbing out of the car at the same time as her friend.

"Your call intrigued me, so I got my deputy to do the survey that I'd planned," Linda said as they hugged. "What's up?"

"If you want to join me in a walk around the garden I'll tell you before you start."

"Sure. Why are you limping?"

"I'll explain while we walk."

Linda Baker was a forty-year-old African American with a PhD in electronic engineering from MIT. She'd been at the agency when Saffie had first started, they'd worked together on several ops and they'd become good friends. She was highly respected and regarded as one of the best in her trade, but after an op went badly wrong, the agent involved had blamed her, and she wasn't supported by others in the agency. Linda was so pissed off she threw her badge at her supervisor and told him to stuff it. She now ran a very successful business providing electronic and digital security services in DC, Virginia, West Virginia, Maryland, and North Carolina.

"This is so good of you to come out like this Linda. I know that you must be really busy."

"Nonsense, I'm never too busy to help a friend. I've got good people to take the wheel when I go out in the field to get my hands dirty. Just tell me your story."

It took more than twenty minutes for Saffie to pour her heart out, telling her friend as much as she dared and probably more than she should. Not one normally given to tearful spells she choked up more than once in the telling.

"For fucks sake Saff, they must be a mole in there somewhere or someone trying to cover their ass."

"Those were my thoughts, and I think whoever it is, is trying to pin something on Brett."

"Let me do a sweep before we talk again. Have you got someone to look over your security system since all this started?"

"Not yet, been too busy."

"I can get my guys over to do it if it helps. Mates rates."

"That would be fantastic, but I don't want just an overhaul. I need a complete upgrade. What's more I don't want any discounts, the assholes who've been doing this will be paying."

"Have you checked your video recordings since you got back?"

"Not yet, too many things on my mind."

"Let's have a look before I start."

It took only moments to see that the video cameras had been turned off by someone on the evening of the day that she made her trip to Richmond. The Covid face-masked culprit was caught on camera at the control box moments before the screen went blank.

The two women looked at each other with furious expressions that didn't bode well for whoever the perpetrator was, should he or she be caught. When Linda saw the video of Ben's abduction she was incandescent. She beckoned Saffie outside.

"That's it, no stone unturned and every possible precaution from now on. You don't mess with a colleague's kids, that's a line nobody crosses. In your business if you can't rely on your fellow agents to have your six, and by that I include your family then the whole organization is a house of cards. Leave it with me."

Saffron went back inside to put on a pot of coffee. A few minutes later Linda came back inside. "I've got my best two engineers on their way: they'll be here in thirty minutes. Your security system will be up and running by the end of the day." She showed Saffie a note that read, 'As you suggest, we'll be doing quite a bit more than a repair.' Saffie raised her eyebrows and smiled.

She felt helpless as Linda went around doing a sweep for bugs, so she called Brett.

"Evening sweetheart," he said when he answered, "Or morning where you are."

"Hello darling how are you?"

"I still feel like shit, but I'm improving. At least I think so. I've still got a bit of an infection, but they think it's under control. They've given me some crutches and they're going to fly me back to the States, leaving in about an hour."

"How are you travelling?"

"Scheduled flight to Frankfurt. Transfer to Ramstein, military transport to Andrews, then chopper to Walter Reed Hospital, Bethesda."

"What the Hell, why? Are you worse than you've been telling me?"

"No, that's no bullshit I promise, HoS here is telling me that they think I've suffered enough, and the journey would be bad for my injury."

"Since when did the company start worrying about agents suffering enough?"

"Maybe they're feeling guilty."

"That'd be a first too. So you're not coming home yet?"

"Another few days I guess."

"I'll try and visit you."

"I'd really like that."

Linda interrupted her to show her a note saying she'd found something she needed to see.

"I'm sorry sweetheart, I've got someone here sorting out our alarm system at the moment and they've hit a problem. I've got to go."

"Okay darling, I'll let you know I'm back as soon as I can."

Linda summoned her with a hooked finger, took her on a tour of the house pointing out hidden listening devices and tiny cameras in almost every room, including her shower room. Most of the cameras were in addition to those from her own system. Then they went back outside.

"I hadn't realized that it was Brett you were speaking to or I'd have waited."

"Don't worry about it. Tell me what you think."

"Someone, or some people are really trying to do a number on you. It looks as if there are two people or groups of people involved. My guess is that the bugs on your desk and the landline are cop kit - the equip.m. ent is standard issue, good but not top of the range; and only cops would bother to put bugs on a landline these days; nobody uses them, and none of it is FBI equip.m. ent."

"What about the rest of the stuff?"

"Very good quality imported equip.m. ent, expensive, and sophisticated. It remains radio silent most of the time but it's motion activated and then it comes to life. It has two flaws; short battery life and limited range, so whoever it is that's listening, has a base somewhere nearby."

Saffie was furious, "These bastards are going to suffer when I find out who they are!"

"The question is what do you want to do about it."

"I know what I'd like to do, but what do you suggest?"

"You could leave the cops' stuff where it is if you want. If you move it, it will only give them grounds for suspicion. They're on a tight budget so they've only bugged the study and would have found it hard to get a warrant to do more. You know what and where it is so you can work it into your day, and even feed them info that you want them to have if that's what you want. The other guys are way out of order; no judge would have granted permission to put cameras in your bathroom without probable cause. The right to privacy isn't in the constitution but it's established law covered under numerous acts and precedents, so when the time comes you can nail them."

"When I nail them, it won't be in a court room. Is there any way to pinpoint their base from here?"

"I've already done it. It's in your neighbor's house; her garage would be my guess."

"Bitch."

"Don't be too harsh; dollars to donuts she's been fed a line that they're trying to catch the people who took your Ben."

"So what should I do?"

"First of all you need to kill the cameras in your bedroom and bathroom. I can do that without giving too much away by obscuring or refocusing the lenses if you decide to leave the others.

"I could jam the signals, although that could have unfortunate side effects for other electronic equip.m. ent in the area. But my favorite would be for you to go round there and have a quiet word in their ear, in the inimitable way you've done with some of their fellow conspirators in recent days."

"They'll know that I'm on to them."

"It would be my guess they'll get the idea in a day or two anyway, but it's up to you."

"Great, wait here."

She went back inside and took her new gun from its packaging, stripped it, made sure it was in order, put it back together and loaded it. After tucking it into her belt behind her back, she marched out the gate and up the ungated drive of her neighbor's house.

She rang the doorbell and waited, there was a short spell of yapping from a small dog, cut short by a mild rebuke of a woman's voice before her neighbor came to the door.

"Mrs. Hamilton?"

"Hello, Mrs. Price, isn't it? So nice to meet you at last," the smartly dressed woman in her late sixties said. "All this time and we've never spoken. That's terrible isn't it? Please come in."

"Lovely to meet you too, and it's just Saffron, or Saffie for short."

"And Clara for me likewise. What can I do for you?"

"I believe that someone is conducting an illegal surveillance of my home from your property."

The elderly woman looked shocked, "B-but it's the FBI, it can't be illegal surely?"

"Did they show you any ID or give you a card?"

"He said he'd run out of cards, but he did show me a badge."

"How closely did you examine it?"

"Well, not too closely I admit, but then you don't, do you?"

"This is my card, and this is my badge; please feel free to examine them as closely as you wish."

The woman nervously took the items and looked at them incredulously, "You're in the CIA?"

"That's right, as is my husband, and for obvious reasons we'd be grateful if that could stay between ourselves."

"Of course. Then who's the man that's been working in my garage?"

"He's an imposter, that much I know. As for who he really is, that's what I need to find out."

"But how can you be sure he's not who he says he is?"

"Because he's been filming me in the shower."

The woman was horrified, "What! The filthy bastard. Excuse my language."

"I've said much worse in the last few days Clara, believe me. Is he there now?"

"He went home for a shower and a change of clothes; said he'd be back about three."

"Would you mind if me and my electronics expert took a look at his equip.m. ent in the meantime?"

"No, please do."

Saffie selected the number from her recent calls list, "Hi Linda, could you join us so we can take a look at this guy's kit together?"

Two minutes later, Linda joined them in Clara's garage. "Okay, give me a few minutes to play."

She looked over the equip.m. ent, which included a laptop computer.

"Is he using your Wi-Fi?" she asked.

"Yes, he said it wouldn't affect my bandwidth. I don't know what that means."

"I wouldn't worry about it. Would you mind if I used it as well for the next few minutes?"

"Not at all. I'll just fetch the card with the code."

While she was away Saffie asked, "Will you be able to get into it?"

"Oh yes, once you've got the control box serial number, they're not difficult to hack. I just need to download a piece of software first."

Clara returned and handed over the card, Linda typed the passkey into her own laptop and handed it back.

"Give this a minute to download and install, then we'll see what we can see."

When it was done, Linda asked Saffie to read the serial number off the back of the surveillance control box to her, and then a few seconds later they were viewing the hallway of Saffie's house as one of Linda's engineers walked past. Then one by one Linda scrolled through the various camera views throughout the house. One shot was of a room she didn't recognize.

"Those are the live shots," Linda explained. "What I can't see until I can get into his computer is what he's recorded and what he's transmitting to anyone else, nor who that might be."

"Where was that last one? It wasn't in my house," Saffie asked.

Saffie glanced at Clara, who was looking ashen-faced.

"I think it's the en-suite shower room in my second bedroom. My granddaughter is using it at the moment; she's only thirteen."

"Thanks Linda, I'll let you get on with what you were doing now. I'll give you a call when I need help again if that's okay."

"What are you going to do about it?" her distraught neighbor asked.

"Leave it to me Clara. He'll be suitably admonished and out of your hair before the end of the day. Let's have a cup of coffee while we wait for him to return."

The flustered woman led the way to her kitchen and wordlessly started her coffeemaker.

"What did he say his name was?"

"Special Agent Harvey. What am I going to tell Samantha and her mom?"

"I suggest nothing for the moment, not until I've had time to find out what he's doing with the videos. There's no point in unnecessarily distressing them. If he's keeping them to himself as his own personal jerk off vids it's one thing, and they probably don't need to know, but if he's selling them on, then we'll need to bring in the cops."

"Oh my God, do you mean he could be putting them on the Internet?"

"It's possible, but let's not jump to conclusions."

"I think I need something stronger than this coffee; can I get something for you Saffie?"

"Thanks, but I'm on painkillers at the moment."

She disappeared and returned holding a crystal glass with a generous shot or two of what smelled like bourbon in it.

Clara asked Saffie about the kidnapping and her limp, and she replied giving as little away as she could. It passed the time.

Chapter 18

When the doorbell rang, the dog somewhere in the house yapped a few times, but Clara went white.

"Oh God he's here."

"Leave it to me Clara," Saffie said taking the gun from her belt. It was clear that Clara hadn't spotted it before.

"Oh my goodness, you've got a gun."

"Clara I'm a CIA agent; it sort of goes with the job. Go sit down somewhere and finish your drink. I'll let you know when we're leaving."

Saffie went to the door and waited for Harvey to ring a second time, snatched it open and thrust her gun in his face.

"Special Agent Harvey I believe. Please come in. You've taken such an interest in me; I thought it was time I introduced myself."

The man stammered his way through protests and threats about Federal agents, but it was clear his heart wasn't in it, and he was terrified. She grabbed his shirt, dragged him inside and closed the door.

"Let's go through to your little workstation in the garage and we can have a bit of a chat." She prodded him ahead of her with the gun, "Take a seat and hand me your IDs, both of them."

He handed them over.

"Are you armed?"

"N-no."

"I hope that's true because there will be consequences if you're lying." She looked at the fake badge. It was one you might buy from a theatrical supplier for film or TV work. His own wallet revealed he was Harvey Wallace, an alarm systems and closed-circuit TV security specialist from Springfield.

"Are you licensed to do security work?"

"Y-Yes," he stammered.

"Well, not for much longer. Do you know who I am?"

"Saffron Price."

"That's right, but do you know what I am?"

"He said you were a suspect in a baby-farming case."

She showed him her own ID. "Can you see now how this could be a problem for you?"

"Oh God, I had no idea."

"Who hired you to do this work?"

"He gave his name as Lopez; he's a Special Agent in the FBI and he gave me $10,000 up front and told me I'd get another ten when the job was complete."

"What did he look like?"

"About five ten, glasses, thin face, dark hair and a little bit fat."

"Could the hair have been a wig?"

"Maybe, I don't know."

"Anything else?"

"I can't think of anything."

"What about any idiosyncrasies; a twitch or a limp?"

"He did have an odd cough, sort of squeaky."

"So how are you sending Lopez this footage?"

"It's saved to a directory in my cloud, and I've given him access to it."

"So can he just watch recordings, or does he have access to live footage?"

"Just recordings."

"Okay, time for me to bring in an expert of my own." She called Linda who came straight back. "Give my colleague the passcode for your laptop Mr. Wallace."

The man hesitated at first, but it took very little persuasion to convince him in the end. Linda spent the next five minutes examining the contents of Wallace's computer, and then looked up at him.

"My, my Mr. Wallace, you've been a busy boy, haven't you?"

"What's he been up to?"

"For starters, whoever this Lopez is, he has live access to all the cameras in your house via this control box, except the one in yours and Clara's shower rooms, but access to the recordings of them from Wallace's cloud as well if he's clever about it."

"Lying to a federal agent is a felony, Mr. Wallace. I thought you would have known that."

"That's only the start I'm afraid," Linda continued. "It appears he has feeds from about twenty houses, and his recordings show he has a particular interest in young teenage girls' showers and bedrooms His cloud has multiple directories of voyeuristic video of young women and girls, including one of you I'm afraid. I've only looked at a few but some of them are quite graphic."

Wallace was sweating now.

"Can you see who he's been sharing them with?"

"As far as I can tell, Lopez is the only person who has accessed this feed, and whoever he is, has also viewed Mrs. Hamilton's granddaughter and similar videos several times."

"Is there any way to identify who and where this Lopez is, from this end?"

"There may be, but I need to spend a bit of time on it and perhaps get some help."

"So now the question is what to do about this whole nasty business, Mr. Wallace? Obviously from the point of view about my own personal privacy I'd prefer to sit on it and say nothing more about it, but things may have gone too far for that. What's more, I'm not sure that you've fully grasped the extent of the trouble you're in. Mr. Wallace, you've committed a laundry list of felonies that would have made Al Capone blush. Impersonating a federal agent in order to commit a crime, lying to a federal agent, exposing a CIA agent to a foreign power, multiple counts of creating indecent images of a child, multiple counts of transmitting indecent images of a child over the Internet, to name just a few. Add to those, several offences under the Espionage Act and others that alone attract sentences of up to twenty years in federal prison; you could end up in chokey for life."

"Espionage, f-foreign power?"

"Who do you think this Lopez is working for?"

"I really thought I was doing something good, helping out the FBI." A puddle of urine appeared beneath the chair, and he was shaking.

"Even if I were to allow that, there's still the multiple instances of offences against children, so I can't let this slip I'm afraid. I think if we erase everything relating to the espionage, Clara's daughter, and me of course, and leave everything else where it is, that way he can still be justifiably punished for the disgusting offences against innocent women and children, and we can hold back on the treason to make sure that he doesn't mention anything he's seen or heard about what goes on in my house to another living soul. He'll still go to prison of course but if he's lucky he won't get life."

"I like the way you think. How about I grant full access to his cloud to the Virginia State Police, and we can decide where to go from there. I can keep a copy of all the espionage stuff; that way you can still resurrect it if he doesn't do what you tell him."

"Good plan; let's go with that. What do you think, Mr. Wallace?"

He sobbed an agreement.

"One problem could be if Lopez has retained copies of any of this," Linda remarked.

"When I find out who he is, I think I can deal with that. Given what I already know, I doubt he'd be the sort of person to get drawn into the distribution of child pornography; the risks of exposure of his other activities would be too great."

Linda typed away at Wallace's laptop, "Okay I've sent the link to the cops from his own email address, with a confession to his activities. What now?"

"If you could remove that camera from Mrs. Hamilton's shower room before we leave, Mr. Wallace can drive us all round to my house, and we can continue our discussion there."

Saffie assured Clara that there would no appearances of her granddaughter anywhere on the Internet, and that Wallace would be going to prison for a very long time. Ten minutes later they marched Wallace into Saffie's garage after having made a $5,000 contribution to Samantha's college fund from Saffie's account via Clara's.

Chapter 19

Once back at Saffie's, she ordered him to sit on a chair and duct taped his ankles.

"Wh-what's happening?"

"Sorry Harvey, did you think it was all over? Not at all. We still have a few things we need to clear up, and I'm going to record your responses on my laptop. I hope you don't mind, although I guess it doesn't really matter if you do."

She set her iPad on the work bench so both of them would be in shot.

"Before we begin I should warn you that you have the right to remain silent. Anything you say can and will be used against you in a court of law. Do you understand?"

"Y-yes."

"Mr. Wallace, we've established that, at the behest of someone calling himself Lopez and posing as an FBI agent, you illegally set about installing cameras and listening devices throughout my house including my shower room; is that right?"

"Yes."

"And that you failed to examine Lopez's credentials beforehand."

"Yes."

"And you didn't ask to see a warrant authorizing it?"

"N-no."

"And Lopez paid you an advance of $10,000 cash for these services, with a promise of a further $10,000 when the job was complete."

"That's right."

"How did you get into my house?"

"Lopez let me in."

"When and how."

"It was the evening after the kidnapping; he told me you were in Richmond and couldn't be there."

"I see, so he already knew the code for the door lock?"

"Yes, he said you'd given it to him."

"Did you fit all these devices on your own or did you have help?"

"On my own; they're wireless so installation is straightforward."

"Was it his idea to film me in the shower or your own?"

"Mine."

"What was Lopez doing while you were fitting all this equip.m. ent?"

"Mostly he was going through the filing cabinet in the study."

"And how long did all this take?"

"I was finished in an hour, and he told me to leave, said he still had things to do and he'd close the door when he left. He gave me that fake FBI ID and told me how to fool the old lady next door into letting me use her garage as a listening post."

"So you didn't think that a man paying you $10,000 cash for a simple job, and telling you how to impersonate a federal agent was a little bit suspicious?"

"I guess I did, yes."

"And you thought while you were about it why not make a video of her pretty little granddaughter in the shower?"

"Y-yes."

"How did you install it? You can't have convinced Mrs. Hamilton that you had any legitimate reason to go anywhere inside her house."

"She and her granddaughter went out together and left the door into the house from the garage unlocked for me to use the toilet."

Saffie paused the recording when Linda came in to ask if she had a spare laptop she could borrow.

"Use Ben's if it's good enough; it's quite old, but there'll be nothing too important on it and I've promised him a new one anyway."

Starting the recording again, she asked, "Where were we? Yes, so this business of you being a pervert is just a hobby is it? You don't use it to earn money?"

"N-no."

"Are you sure? Because if you're lying, all bets stay on the table."

"No, I absolutely promise."

"What's your point of contact for this Lopez guy?"

"He gave me a contact number - it's in my cell phone. I haven't called it. He said to only call if there was a problem."

"But you won't be needing to call it now, will you?"

"N-no."

"Because?"

"He's a foreign spy?"

"That's right. Okay then Harvey, that'll do for now." She ended the recording, then opened his laptop again. "Now's the time where you begin to make recompense for your crimes."

"What do you mean?"

"Well I've already paid out $5,000 on your behalf to compensate the poor girl next door who you raped with your eyes. I've had to employ a team of engineers to spend a whole day trying to rectify what you've done, and now I've had to hand over my son's laptop computer. Then of course there's all those other girls, whose names I'll never know, I think you should demonstrate your remorse by making a donation to a charity that helps girls falling victim to the type of disgusting crimes you've been committing. That would be the least you could do, don't you think? Let's have a look at your bank account shall we?"

"What are you doing?"

"Saving you the trouble of doing it yourself. Yes here we are, Wells Fargo, I see you've bookmarked their online banking page, and you've got it to remember your account ID, that's helpful, all we need now is your password."

"You can't do this, it's against the law."

"You mean like that list of treasonous offenses under the Espionage Act we spoke of earlier? I seem to remember us agreeing not to mention them for the time being."

He gave her his password, and she discovered he had three accounts at the bank.

"Right then Harvey, we'll say $20,000 for everything that my alarm engineers have had to do today, another $1000, for my son's laptop, plus the $5,000 you owe me, and we'll round it up to $30,000 to cover additional expenses. That just about clears your checking account, so I'll need to transfer some from your deposit account, it's got plenty in it, so that's handy. Prevent Child Abuse America is a good worthwhile organization; how much to really demonstrate the depth of your remorse do you think? There's a little over three hundred grand in there at the moment; how about a round quarter million?"

"You'll bankrupt me."

"Nonsense, there's still your investment account; there's enough in there to pay your lawyer, and you won't be spending a lot in prison will you?"

Linda came back into the garage, "Right then, my guys have tied everything up so I'll send them off unless you've got anything else, Saffie."

"No, I'm good, thanks."

"My guys also removed the stuff the cops installed because I hadn't told them not to. I told them not to bother putting it back because the boys in blue will know that you've found it by now."

"That's fine."

"Did I mention my guys found a tracker on your car?"

"No. Do you know anything about that Mr. Wallace?"

"I don't do vehicle tracking. Anyway you were in Richmond when I was here, and neither of us came into the garage."

"Are you sure?"

"Yes, I asked Lopez if he wanted a camera in here. He told me not to bother because he didn't have the key."

"What are you going to do with this piece of shit, Saffie?" Linda asked.

"Harvey and I are going to have a final little chat then I'm going to let him go home. I expect he's tired. Let me see you out."

When they were standing by Linda's car, Saffie asked, "Let me know as soon as you can if you discover anything about Lopez's location from Wallace's laptop. There is one other thing, but I don't know if it's something you can do."

"What's that?"

She explained about the burner phone that Hevil had been using to contact Lopez, "There's a telephone number on it that was used in Ukraine to contact Lopez. I need to find out as much as I can about that."

"It isn't something I can do myself in another country, but I might know somebody from my days in the company that can help out. I expect it will be expensive."

"I'm not worried about the cost, but how much are we talking about?"

"I can't be sure, possibly as much as five or six grand."

"Go for it. Would you prefer cash?"

"Not for the alarm work etcetera I'll invoice you for that. But if you can pay for the other stuff by cash that would be helpful. What about the phone that Wallace was supposed to use to call Lopez, do you want me to look at that?"

"You can take a look, but I suspect the number will just be of another burner that's never been used. Wait there while I fetch the other phone and your money."

Saffie went inside and collected the money from what she'd accumulated during her trip to Ukraine.

"There's $8,000 there. If it isn't enough, let me know."

Linda's engineers had bought all Wallace's equip.m. ent back from Clara's house and put it in their van. They were going to allow him to keep his laptop, having deleted the videos of Saffie and Clara's teenage granddaughter.

Linda turned to her, "There's something really dangerous going on here, Saffie. You need to be very careful."

"I will be. Just make sure you charge me full whack for this today though, including any extras. Wallace is paying, and I shall be exacting full recompense from anybody else that's had a hand in this."

They hugged and Linda got back in her car and drove away.

Saffie went back inside to release Wallace. "Just remember, any attempt to erase anything from your PC or cloud will constitute a breach of faith and force me to reconsider the espionage issues."

She handed him his laptop, followed him to his car and watched him drive away.

Before going back inside she called Mary, "Is that the candy store?"

"Oh God Saffie, thank God you called."

"What's happened?"

"Two guys tried to break in here last night; they were trying to take Ben again."

"What the fuck! How did you stop them?"

"I didn't, Rusty did. It was about two in the morning, he'd been to a club with Lacey, and just before she dropped him at the end of the drive they saw the car turn off its lights and pull into the drive. He hurried to see what was happening; two guys got out and left their doors open and the engine running. They spent time picking the lock on my front door, and that gave Rusty time to grab his gun. When he came after them, he saw them climbing the stairs and challenged them. One tried to fire at him but Rusty shot him dead - the other one dropped his gun and put his hands up."

"How could you be sure they were there for Ben?"

"One of them had cable ties and duct tape on him. He told the cops they'd been paid to grab him. They asked about you and Brett. I didn't know what to tell them. I'd sent you a text, but you didn't reply, so I hoped it was okay just to say I thought you were both out of the country."

"I didn't get your message, I'm so sorry Mary. What with everything else that's going on, I must have missed it. What number did you text?'

"The last number you called me on."

"Shit, I've been using so many burners lately, I must have called you using the wrong one. Is Ben okay?"

"He must be the most resilient kid I've ever known; he was a bit subdued this morning after the cops left, but he's spent the day with Rusty who he thinks is Wyatt Earp reborn."

"What did you tell the cops?"

"I'm afraid I had to tell them that you were in the CIA and that was why I thought you might be out of the country. They didn't believe me at first, but Ben went apeshit at them and told them we didn't lie and it was the second time someone had tried to kidnap him in a week. He's got some balls that kid of yours; he stood his ground and eventually they called the cops in your area who confirmed it."

"What about the second guy, you say he's talking?"

"Like a parrot from what they're saying. They're couple of small-time crooks, well known locally apparently, and they were paid to do it. I don't know the details of what he's told them though. How is Brett; have you heard?"

"He's been found, but he's wounded, and he's been in hospital in Kyiv for a couple of days, but he should be on his way home as we speak. Can I speak to Ben in a moment, but before I do, can you get Rusty or someone to check out the Wrangler and see if they can find a tracker on it?"

"I'll do that now, the two of them are just outside."

There was a short pause before Ben came on the line, *"Mom?"*

"Ben my darling, how are you?"

"I'm okay Mom. Rusty's been teaching me to drive the tractor; he put blocks on the pedals, and I sit between his legs."

"Wow! What about that stuff last night though?"

"I was frightened when it happened, but Mary and Rusty have helped me understand. They told me that the guys were the dumbest crooks ever and the dead guy was lucky he didn't shoot his own foot off. And that if they were the only crooks the guy who paid them could afford, then I was safe."

"I'm going to try to come and get you tomorrow."

"What about Dad?"

"He's on his way home; his leg is hurt but it sounds like he'll be fine. He said he can't wait to see you, but soccer may be off the agenda for a few weeks."

They chatted for a few more minutes until Mary took the phone back.

"You were right, there was a tracker. Rusty took it off. Is that okay?"

"That's great. I'm coming to collect Ben tomorrow if I can.

"Won't you want to see Brett?"

"Yes, but if they're keeping him in hospital, I might come to you first."

"Okay."

Chapter 20

When she ended the call with Mary, she was shedding tears of anger and stress at all the things happening to her family. They needed to be together but some people were conspiring to harm them, and she didn't understand why.

Despite the painkillers she poured herself a large scotch, sat in the lounge and thought through all that had happened, starting with Brett's disappearance.

He'd been held captive for two or three weeks without being interrogated so it was as if he were being held hostage for ransom, and yet no ransom demands had been made.

Then there was the attempt to abduct Ben. Once again it was made to appear as some sort of ransom exercise. It failed but only by chance and ineptitude, and yet there had been a lot of effort put into preparation including recruiting a guy from the alarm company.

Somehow at some point both her cars had been fitted with trackers early enough in whatever was happening for them to track her to Richmond and use the time to get into the house and install sophisticated surveillance equip.m. ent. Whoever Lopez was had acquired the entry code for her door lock; only the FBI and CIA had that.

They'd tracked the Wrangler to Harrisonburg, and yet waited days before making a second attempt at taking Ben. She supposed that it must have taken that time to set it up.

One thing that intrigued her was that at every stage, the foot soldiers had been at best poor professionals, such as Hevil and Wallace, and at worst buffoons with guns like the b-list drug dealers in Richmond and the lowlifes at Mary's farm the previous night. Even so the main mover was throwing a lot of money at it, both in Ukraine and in the States. Using small time crooks suggested to her that it was probably a single person at the head of it all attempting to insulate himself because it had no official sanction, but that didn't help her identify him.

In Saffie's assessment, it could only be someone in Brett's section at Langley, and the chief suspects were Radwell and Felix. If that turned out to be the case it could only mean they'd gone rogue and were trying to cover their backs. Even that didn't seem to make complete sense though; where was the money coming from?

As she thought through the various events one by one, trying to pick out any little thing that could give her a link to Lopez, the Englishman Jenkins popped into her mind. Remembering the pathetic man pleading for a fuck made her smile for a moment, but then she thought through the detail again. He'd made a lot of fuss about the money and how he couldn't afford it, and yet barely protested about the destruction of his driving license and passport; that didn't make sense. On his own, in a foreign country without clothes or money, the one thing he'd need above all else was his passport, if it were genuine that is. Maybe he had another ID and the documents were in his room. Could he have been connected in some way, and if so, how? She couldn't think how he could have been a key player.

She tried contacting Pearmain again, but he wasn't picking up, so she sent a text. '*Need info, hope you can help.*' She didn't expect an answer, and even if she did get one, it wouldn't be immediate.

Saffie returned to thinking about her two chief suspects. If either of them were really Lopez, it would mean they'd been out of the country at least once in the last three weeks. She tried to think of some way she could prove that, but there was now no-one in Langley she could trust enough to; A. get the right answer, and B. give her the information.

Following the money was a principle that usually held good in investigations and a lot of it had been splashing around in this one. As anyone involved in covert ops knows, there are always times when handlers can't or won't come up with finance to complete a task in hand. To prepare for this, most field agents unofficially relocated any loose bad guys' cash and squirreled it away to cover them, should the need arise. She doubted that either Radwell or Felix would be an exception; both she and Brett were guilty of it, her Hanrahan account being a case in point. She didn't know enough about the operational history of either of Brett's handlers to be able to judge how big a cache they could have accumulated, but what would motivate them to splash it on this illegal operation?

She went to bed without resolving anything, and a troubled night didn't help her mood when she awoke the next day. So, when Detective Sergeant Wolski rang the bell at seven-thirty while she was eating her breakfast, she wasn't very welcoming.

She saw his face on the new entry phone screen that Linda had installed and pressed the button for him to talk. "What do you want?" she demanded.

"Ms. Price, we need to talk."

"What about?"

"The abduction and attempted abduction of your son to start."

"Yes, of course, sorry. Come in." She pressed the button to open the gate, and opened the door to let him in when he climbed from his car, alone.

"Thank you for seeing me Ms. Price. I'm sure you must be extremely distressed about all that's happened."

"Yes, I am, and I'm sorry for snapping at you just now."

"This isn't an official visit at the moment, Ma'am. I'm just confused by the events of the last week, and I was hoping you might be able to enlighten me."

"You can't be more confused than I am, but please tell me what you want to know. If I can, I'll tell you."

"This part of the country is awash with federal agencies of all varieties and I've worked around here for the best part of ten years now. Inevitably in that time I've crossed paths with residents from most of the agencies who've stepped the wrong side of law or been a victim of criminality. However, this is the first time where the victim of crime has been a CIA agent and at the same time the agency has been obstructive in their support of one of their own."

"I'm as surprised as you are, Sergeant."

"Why do you think that is?"

"I shouldn't say this but fuck it I'm past caring. I believe that someone inside Langley is trying to pin something on either myself or my husband."

"That's why I'm here, because I'm beginning to think the same thing."

"Okay, Sergeant, I'll play. Tell me what you think, why you think it, and then I'll try to throw some light on it for you."

"This is off the record, okay? I've dealt with the FBI on joint investigations dozens of times, and it's no secret that relations between them and the cops frequently aren't great, so I expect them to behave like assholes. This time it's weird, because although they're being tight-lipped about a lot of what I think they know, they appear to be being as helpful as they can, but they're being fucked over by the CIA. This is particularly odd because you're one of the CIA's own and obviously the victim. You'd think they'd welcome as much help as they can get. In this country the Agency doesn't have the level of logistical resources that us and the feds have, let alone the authority to use them."

Saffie took a deep breath, "I'm not sure that I fully accept your assessment of the FBI's behaviour, but I agree with your general point. As you say, the agency doesn't give much away, and has very little standing inside the country, so they shouldn't be directly involved in any part of the investigation into Ben's abduction, yet I keep seeing their fingerprints on everything."

"Can you be more specific?"

"First of all, the FBI have seemingly done next to fuck all to discover who's responsible for Ben's abduction other than imply that I was responsible for his rescue. For example they haven't employed any significant resources of their own. Even after the second attempt they haven't bothered to contact me or the farm where he was staying. No disrespect to the police, but normally by this time in an investigation, they'd have completely taken over and told the cops to bug out. All that suggests to me that they're having pressure put on them, and the only people that could do that are the CIA.

"Next, somebody gave the entry code for my home to people who used it to install sophisticated surveillance equip.m. ent like cameras, listening devices, and landline phone bugs installed throughout the house."

"That could have been the FBI."

"They didn't have a warrant and there were cameras filming me in the shower. I don't think so. The guy who installed them was told he was working for the Feebies but was given nothing to prove it other than a fake ID, and he was paid in cash."

"How did you find this out?"

"Sergeant, I know that investigation is a police job, but you're not the only people with those skills."

"I'm guessing you used detection devices to discover the surveillance equip.m. ent."

"That's correct."

"So how did you identify who put them there?"

"I asked an electronics expert friend of mine to find him, turned out he was operating out of my neighbor's garage."

"And you just politely asked him who paid him, and he gave you the information just like that?"

"This is off the record right?"

"Of course."

"I used methods of persuasion not normally available to the police or other law enforcement agencies in this country, but I didn't use violence."

"Would it still be possible to charge him?"

"I think you'll find that as an act of contrition, he sent an email to the Virginia State police yesterday afternoon confessing to a long list of crimes. He also made a substantial contribution to a child abuse charity which he hoped would help him atone for his offences,"

"What did he do?"

"Impersonated a federal agent in order to commit a crime, committed acts that could expose a CIA agent to a foreign power, multiple counts of creating indecent images of a child, and transmitting them over the Internet, plus a number of other offences under the Espionage Act."

"They're all felonies, he could go away for years."

"I undertook not to report him for the Espionage Act offences."

"That seems odd, given it's your husband that might have been put at risk."

"Nothing I've promised would prevent them from bringing charges at some time in the future, although I suspect they'll be too embarrassed."

"Is it reasonable to assume that you haven't suspended your own investigation then?" he asked.

"Perfectly reasonable, what if I asked the same question about yours in favor of the FBI?"

"You better believe it. As things stand at the moment, and notwithstanding the shenanigans of federal agencies, at least six men are dead and a number of others have serious injuries as a direct result of people with felonious intent against you and your family, and until we're officially told hands off by people further up the chain, we'll continue looking for answers."

"Did you say six men dead?"

"One upstairs here, one at the farm in Harrisonburg, and four in Richmond."

"I wasn't aware the guys in Richmond had died. I was just told they'd been shot."

"Indications are that they'd trodden on some rival toes, and they decided to finish the job."

"It's good news to hear you're still on the case, Sergeant."

"Never good news for people who step the wrong side of the law if we catch them Ms. Price," he wryly remarked.

"Good point." She smiled.

"Thank you for your time, I won't keep you any longer."

"Glad to have been of help, Sergeant. Let me know when you want your listening devices back."

He smiled, shook his head, and left.

As soon as he'd gone she looked up the number for the Walter Reed Memorial Hospital and called. "Good morning, I'm enquiring about my husband, Brett Price.He was to be transferred to your hospital today."

"Let me check our system ma'am, what was it you said your husband's name was, Brett Price?" There was a pause, *"I'm sorry ma'am there's nobody on our system with that name. Perhaps the transfer will be later in the day."*

"Okay thank you."

It was still early; maybe the flight had been delayed. She called Felix. He didn't pick up, so she called Radwell with the same result. 'Assholes', she thought.

Chapter 21

Saffie put her gun and few things in an overnight bag and was thinking about calling a cab to take her to Harrisonburg to collect Ben when the gate bell rang again. A glance at the new entry phone screen, revealed a car containing Special Agents Ramirez and Burns. She pressed the button to open the gate, and put a pot of coffee on.

When Ramirez knocked on the open door, she called telling them to come in.

"Good morning agents, what can I do for you?"

"You can tell us where you went to on the morning after your son was abducted," Ramirez said.

"Certainly. I went to consult some former colleagues, to ask them if they could help in finding him."

"Who were these former colleagues?"

"Nice try agent, Ramirez, but if I were to tell you I'd be guilty of a felony."

"I'm quite certain the CIA would make an exception in this case."

"Are you? Have they told you that? Would you like to identify the agents?"

"We could get a subpoena to force you to cooperate."

"Yes you could, but as that would force me to go to the press with my suspicions about the bureau's collusion with a foreign agent operating inside the CIA, I doubt either the FBI or the agency itself are ready for that. What's the problem anyway? My son is now safe, and I'm told that the perpetrators are dead? This is beginning to sound a bit like sour grapes. Have you got your panties in a twist because somebody did your job for you?"

"As you reminded us the other day Ms. Price, this isn't the wild west," Burns said. "We can't have vigilantes summarily handing out punishment for alleged crimes. We have a court system to administer justice."

"Is that what these people did, whoever they are; summarily punished my son's kidnappers? Did they tell you that? I heard that rival gangsters were suspected of killing them."

"Not exactly, but the evidence suggests it."

"Fine. While you're paying attention to suggestions, did you think about applying some thought to finding out who the bastards are behind these abduction attempts, and who's initiating it all? The last I heard, you haven't even visited my friend's farm to discover what happened."

"We're under the impression that there's probably a connection to your missing husband. Investigating that, is a CIA responsibility."

"You're right, but now that my husband has been found, perhaps your two organizations could put your heads together and work towards putting the asshole instigating all this behind bars."

"Mr. Price has been found? When did this happen?"

"Dear God give me strength; haven't you been speaking to them at all?"

"We haven't found them very helpful."

"You shock me. Listen to me, I'm damned certain that whoever is behind this is either an agent inside Langley or is being fed information by someone who is. They know things about me, that only someone who knows me personally or who has access to personal information about me can know."

"Would you care to expand on that?"

"After you and the cops had searched my house on the morning following the kidnap, someone used the door entry code to unlock my front door, disable my security cameras, and install sophisticated listening and video surveillance equip.m. ent throughout my home including my shower room."

"How did you discover that?"

"Because I'm not stupid, Agent Burns. I suspected that you would or the cops plant bugs. The cops did; but what I found wasn't theirs. It's all been removed now, and I'm now pretty confident that it wasn't the FBI either."

"Anything else?"

"Yes, both mine and my husband's cars had been fitted with trackers. That must have happened sometime before I left that day, so I guess it's possible that you could have had it done, although I doubt that too. But the issue is that the only way they could have found out where my son was being looked after was by that tracker, and thereby allowing the second attempt to kidnap my son to take place."

"You could have been followed, traced through cell phone usage, or had your journey tracked via license plate recognition," Ramirez suggested.

"Any or all of those things would involve collusion with people in law enforcement, but do you really think I wouldn't have taken steps to prevent them."

"You slipped up by missing the trackers though Ms. Price," Burns said with a smirk.

"Yes I did, didn't I, but that just proves my point, doesn't it?"

"Okay then Ms. Price we'll leave you for now, and we'll revisit the information exchange with the CIA. But I reiterate my caution against unilaterally acting against criminals. The consequences can be severe."

"Point taken, Agent Ramirez."

By the time the gate had closed behind them she was already on the phone to Walter Reed Hospital where she ended up speaking to the same operator she'd spoken to earlier.

"Oh yes Mrs. Price. After you called earlier I had a few spare moments and I asked about your husband. It seems that he was to have been transferred here during the night, but the admission was cancelled at the last minute."

"Can you tell who was responsible for the cancellation?"

"Yes, it was Air Force Colonel Dr Mark Foster of Andrews Air Force Military Hospital."

"Thank you very much, you've been very helpful."

'What the fuck is going on?' she asked herself, and she tried calling the cell phone Brett had been using but only received an electronic voice telling her that the number was not available.

Next, she looked up the number for Andrews, and was put through to the hospital straightaway.

"Good morning, I understand that my husband Brett is a patient in your hospital, my name is Mrs. Saffron Price."

"One moment Ma'am."

The line went quiet for a long time, and she began to think she'd been cut off when a man answered.

"Staff Sergeant Errol Spence speaking, how can I help you Ma'am?"

"I'm trying to locate my husband, and I've been given reason to believe he may be a patient in your hospital."

"That's correct Ma'am, Mr. Price was admitted at oh-five hundred this morning."

"Is he okay?"

"Yes Ma'am, I believe he's been medically assessed, and he is expected to make a full recovery. He remains under medical observation."

"Can I speak to him?"

"I'm afraid that won't be possible, Ma'am."

"Why not?"

"Your husband is under arrest, Ma'am."

"WHAT!?"

"He is being held for questioning by agents from the Department of Homeland Security."

"What for?"

"I'm not at liberty to say more, Ma'am. I'm sorry."

She ended the call and gripped the phone so tightly she was in danger of crushing it.

The ball of hatred that had been building in her chest again restricted her breathing and it took several minutes before she calmed down enough to try calling Felix Carter and Karl Radwell. Whilst it was still not nine-thirty, both should be at their desks; she wasn't surprised when neither answered their phones.

"Enough!" she shouted, and picked up her purse, grabbed her keys and went out the door. She collected herself enough to secure her home before she drove out the gate, but it took every ounce of determination to stay within the speed limits on the way to her destination.

Chapter 22

Even though she was well known by most of the security guards, she was stopped as usual at the barrier entrance to the CIA headquarters known as the George Bush Center for Intelligence. It was too late to get the best pick of parking spaces, but she found a spot and marched toward the buildings. On this occasion her destination wasn't to be the suite of offices for the team she was attached to. Instead she headed to the building that housed the very senior echelons of America's intelligence community. Once again her identity was confirmed, this time not only using her badge, but by handprint and facial recognition.

"Who are you here to see, Ms. Price?" the uniformed female guard asked.

"Deputy Director of Operations, Patryk Wilkanowicz."

"Do you have an appointment?"

"No."

"Then I doubt..."

"It's a matter of national security, so ask."

The guard's partner raised his eyebrows, picked up a phone, dialed a number, and spoke a few sentences.

"The DDO's assistant says you have to go through the usual channels."

"Tell him I have evidence of infiltration of our East European operations by a foreign power."

The guy spoke into the handset again, and there was a long pause before he looked at her, "Okay they say you can go up. Take the elevator to the..."

"I know where it is."

She handed over her gun before walking through the archway metal detector, submitted to a scan with a security wand, and a search of her purse before being patted down by the female guard.

When the elevator door opened on the top floor she was met by yet another guard and accompanied to the DDO's suite of rooms When the door closed behind her, Walt Bannerman, the DDO's gatekeeper lounged in his chair facing away and continued to read a document.

"This had better be good Price or you'll find yourself out of a job." He was already hostile, and she didn't understand why, but then he always was an asshole. He swiveled his chair to face her, "Give me a summary of your suspicions, and I'll see if the DDO can fit you in."

"You know why I'm here, or I wouldn't be standing here. I'm not going through the detail with you so that you can unilaterally decide to kick this back to the very people I'm concerned about. I need to see the DDO; is he in?"

"He's very busy I doubt he'll have time..."

At that moment, the door that connected Bannerman's office to the DDO's opened and its occupier spotted her.

"Saffron, great to see you. How are you doing?"

"Pretty shit if I'm honest, Sir. How about you?"

"The same if truth were known. What are you doing up here?"

"I've got some information indicating that our East European team have been infiltrated and I'm being given the run around."

"Come through. Hold my calls for the next hour will you, Walt?"

"But Sir, you've a meeting with the Director of Financial Services in ten minutes."

"Reschedule."

He ushered her into the room and closed the door behind him. "Take a seat Saffie," he told her, pointing to one of four leather armchairs around a coffee table. He went to a side table, poured two cups of coffee, and placed one in front of her. "Now, tell me your concerns."

Over the following half hour, she told her former operational handler a broad brush synopsis of everything that happened. They'd worked closely together for three years and she knew she didn't need to be coy with him.

Wilkanowicz listened intently, occasionally asking questions.

"And now you say that Brett is being held at Andrews under arrest by Homeland?"

"That's what they've told me. Are you telling me that you didn't know about any of this Patryk?"

"Nothing at all."

"I was told you authorised a Level One."

"I did authorize a Level One for an agent that had gone dark without notice, but that happens more often than you would think. I didn't have any detail and I didn't hear any more. I assumed the issue had been resolved."

"So you heard nothing about going to Level Two?"

"No, I'm sorry."

"Wouldn't you have expected to?"

"If it's what it looks like, yes I would, but none of the things you've told me add up. There's no consistency; some of them even appear self-defeating. It's like someone is dropping chaff to distract from something else."

"But is there anything you can do though, Patryk?"

"I can't intervene in a Homeland investigation, Saffron, but I can certainly make some enquiries within the agency."

"Thank you, I've been going out of my mind."

"In the meantime I suggest you keep a low profile. Go be with your son, try to avoid taking executive action unless it's completely unavoidable, and keep your phone on."

As the elevator descended, she thought about what the DDO had told her. She wasn't a hundred percent confident that he'd given her the whole truth, but in their business that would be the norm. Nonetheless she hoped that the relationship and mutual trust they'd developed by working closely together for those three years was strong enough that he wouldn't have lied.

The CIA headquarters was one of the few places in the world where they checked the contents of your bags and pockets as carefully on your way out as they did on your way in. She nodded to one or two colleagues enduring the same indignities as other officials while she patiently allowed the same two security officers go through their rituals.

They returned her gun and she walked out the door almost bumping into Felix Carter.

"Saffie, what are you doing here?"

"Fuck off Felix."

"Look, I'm sorry but it's all out of my hands now."

"Like I say, fuck off, but remember this. If it turns out you had a hand in any of it, I'll hunt you down like a rabid dog and kill you." She turned and walked away leaving the man convinced she'd meant every word.

As she drove towards the car park exit a blue Model X Tesla with tinted windows cut across her front causing her to brake harshly. She wasn't in the mood to tolerate assholes on the road, and she blasted whoever it was with her horn. They took no notice. Following the guy to the exit she noticed a V-shaped dent in the rear fender of the expensive car. She knew it was childish, but she smiled grimly.

She drove home with a resolve to do exactly what the DDO had suggested, or at least give that appearance.

She garaged the BMW but before she went inside she ran the bug detector over her purse and wasn't surprised when it furiously beeped as soon as she turned it on. She emptied her purse and at first found nothing, and there was still nothing as she passed the wand over each item until she came to her wallet. Probably like many people these days, her wallet contained a lot of things, even some that had passed their usefulness. She removed it all and the offending article was revealed to be masquerading as a loyalty card for a supermarket chain that she hadn't used since a food poisoning incident three years earlier. Except for one or two items that belonged in the trash, she put it all back in the wallet including the tracker.

Unsurprisingly she found another tracker on her car, although a more discreet one this time, and a listening device behind the grab handle above one of the rear doors. She left those where they were as well.

After a visit to the gun safe for a few extra things, she packed another bag, bigger and this time with a lot more clothes for herself and for Ben. Then she called a cab.

She poured the last of the breakfast coffee into a cup, grimaced at the over-cooked bitter taste and looked around her home, wondering when she'd be back.

The cab arrived and the driver was delighted when she said she needed to be driven to Harrisonburg and would be happy to pay cash.

Chapter 23

On route she called Mary to let her know she was on her way but gave nothing away about the latest develop.m. ents.

It was only twelve-thirty when the cab dropped her outside the house, the driver unloaded her bags and waited whilst she counted out his fare. She'd expected somebody to meet her, but there was no sign of anybody, not even when she knocked on the open door.

She pressed the doorbell that also sounded a big bell on the side of the hay barn. "Mary," she called, "Ben."

When there was still no reply she began to panic and went inside to look, there was a broken porcelain mixing bowl on the kitchen floor, its contents splashed across the floor, and up the legs of a chair. She took her gun from her purse and began a cautious search of the building, but there was still no sign of Mary or her son. Running from the house she began to look through the outbuildings calling their names, even that of the dog. Finally the dog appeared from somewhere, panting and wagging its tail.

Eventually she realized that she hadn't checked the old house or the Sanders' farm buildings. The old house was locked but looking back down the length of the long drive, in the distance she saw a girl speaking into a cell phone. The girl was about to get into a car outside the Sanders' residence on the far side of the road. Painfully, she ran to catch her before she drove away.

"Lacey, Lacey!" she shouted, until her throat hurt, and she began to cough. Coughing and limping she finally attracted the young girl's attention. Lacey closed her car door and Saffie breathlessly walked to meet her.

"Saffron? What's up?"

"They're gone, everybody's gone!"

"They're probably over in the ten-acre meadow. The bull busted the fence again this morning and he's been trying to have his wicked way with Mary's new heifers. They're not ready for breeding yet or something, but Old Fred doesn't care. Rusty rushed over there about an hour ago."

"Oh for fuck's sake, after all that's been going on, I thought something else had happened."

"I doubt it, there's about eight of them over there, including three on ATVs and three on horseback. If you hang around a bit I expect they'll be back soon. What happened to your leg?"

"Got a bit of a stick injury, long story."

"Let me drop you back at the house, I'm just on my way out."

"Would you? Thanks a lot. You've changed a bit since I last saw you," Saffie observed as they climbed into her small AWD pickup.

"I guess that happens when you don't see someone for fourteen years."

"Is that how long it is? God I feel old now."

"Your Ben is a great kid, isn't he?"

"Yeah, I think so," she said smiling, her pulse returning to normal.

She said goodbye to Lacey just as Mary drove into the yard on an ATV with Ben on the back.

"Mom!" her son shouted, "We've been doing a roundup."

"Wow! That sounds like fun. Come and give me a hug."

"Old Fred broke the fence and was trying to bonk the wrong cows. So we had to herd him back to his own field and move the cows."

"Hi Mary."

"Hi Saff, sorry about that. Minor emergency, couple of new hands moved some heifers into the wrong field and Old Fred couldn't resist. That enormous beast would've crushed those little things; wrong breed."

"I confess I was more than a bit worried when I arrived and found the place deserted, and a broken mixing bowl on the kitchen floor."

"What! Gwyneth was that you up at the table again, you naughty girl." The dog looked up at her, furiously wagging its tail and appearing proud of itself. "That was going to be a cake for later."

"Cake? Have you been spoiling my Ben?"

"He earned it; he's been working hard around the farm all week."

They went inside the house, and Mary began clearing up the broken mixing bowl and its contents.

"You can use the same room as before. How long are you staying this time?"

"Until I can go and collect Brett, if that's okay."

"Is Dad okay Mom? Is he hurt real bad?"

"No, I don't think so sweetheart. They just need to be sure they've got the infection under control I expect. Come and tell me everything you've been up to while I unpack."

The young boy excitedly related all the things that he'd been doing around the farm over the previous days. Saffie had been grateful that he'd had some separation and distraction from the dangerous and horrific events happening around her, but the second kidnap attempt could have undone all that good.

"As you've enjoyed it so much, perhaps Mary would let you come again during other school vacations."

"That would be awesome Mom, but I'm still a bit scared, I've never seen you carry a gun all the time before."

"I hope it won't be for much longer, darling. Just until the FBI have caught the person responsible for hiring the men that abducted you."

"I don't understand why it's happening though."

"I'm really sorry, Ben my darling, but I haven't been entirely honest with you. Your dad was being held hostage by some people who wanted him to tell them things. When he wouldn't say what they wanted they took you thinking that they could use you to force him to talk. He's free now, so there's nothing to worry about anymore."

"Is that a taser gun?" he asked, pointing into the smaller of the two bags.

She hadn't wanted him to see some of the other things she'd packed but she'd left the top of the bag open. 'God I'm getting careless,' she thought. "Yes it is, I just bought it as a precaution."

"I didn't know you had one of those."

"Well it's not something that you leave lying around. Listen darling, Daddy and I have kept a lot of things secret from you because we thought it was safer for you not to know, but now that you do, you mustn't talk about them with other people; nobody at all. Do you understand; it's very important?"

"I know Mom. What about you rescuing me though?"

"I should have talked this through with you before, but it is very, very important that you don't speak about my involvement in that to anybody at all, even the police. I had to break a lot of laws to rescue you, and if the police were to find out it was me, it's possible I could go to prison. If they ask, just tell them that a woman you'd never seen before rescued you, drove you here and left you at the end of the drive."

"Is it against the law to lie to the police?"

"Not really. What did you tell them before?"

"Mary told them I was too upset to talk about it the first time. Then when they left, me and Mary talked about it together.

"We really ought to have talked about what happened when I found you in Richmond."

"Mary talked about that. If the FBI ask me about it, can I just tell them that I take the fifth?'"

She laughed, "I guess that would work. Let's go downstairs and join Mary shall we?"

When they returned to the kitchen, Mary had cleared up the mess and was preparing a pot roast for the evening meal.

"I hope you're not interrupting your work to act as hosts to us."

"Not particularly. I've invited Rusty to eat with us this evening. I thought it would be nice for you to get to know him better, especially after his intervention the other night."

"Can I go and help Rusty mend the fence now Mom?"

"As long as you don't get in the way."

"He'll be fine, Saffie," Mary assured her.

Chapter 24

When Ben had gone, Mary grilled Saffie for an update on what was going on.

"I hardly know where to begin Mary. Ben is back in the country, and medically I think he's well enough to be discharged from hospital, but he's been arrested by Homeland."

"What the fuck?"

"Precisely my reaction. I don't know what he's been accused of because they're not letting me speak to him at the moment."

"I don't know Brett that well, but there's one thing I do know, and that is that you wouldn't still be married to him if there was any likelihood he'd act against this country's interests."

"You've got that right, but that's not everything. At some point in the twenty-four hours after Ben's abduction, sophisticated listening and video surveillance equip.m. ent was installed throughout my house."

"Couldn't that have been the police or the FBI?"

"I know how agencies like this work, and the way whoever went about this pretty much rules out a legitimate organization. The guy who did it was paid in cash; that wouldn't happen. Not only that, but he also put a camera in my shower room. No judge would authorize a warrant allowing that. I caught the guy who did it and he told me that the man who paid him gave his name as Lopez, the same as the guy who paid the hostage takers who captured Brett in Ukraine."

"Why would he do that - use the same name in two countries, especially when it's obviously a false one?"

"Exactly, and like so many of the things that have been happening, it doesn't add up."

"Is there anything you can do though?"

"I can't be sure how much good it will do yet, but I've gone over the heads of my suspects and stirred the mud. That's a start, but I've another trick or two up my sleeve. I might wait until I see what their next move is before I decide what to do."

Ben came in from the fields after Rusty had driven to their supplier for more fencing materials.

At about three o'clock Ramirez and Burns turned up in a sedan, followed by a detective from Dayton PD in a department SUV. Mary went out to meet them while Saffie listened in from the door.

"Good afternoon, Ma'am, I'm Special Agent Ramirez. This is Special Agent Burns. We're from the Langley office of the FBI. I believe you've met Detective Sergeant Hendryx. We'd like to ask some questions about the home invasion the other night."

"Sure, come inside," Mary said.

Saffie greeted them, "Good afternoon agents, we meet again."

"I seem to recall you complaining that we hadn't made enough effort to find out what happened here."

"I'm not criticizing, Agent. In fact I'm grateful that you were paying attention; few others are."

"We're here to talk to Miss Riley, and Mr. Pickett."

"We'll leave you to it. Ben, why don't you show me what you've been doing?"

Mother and son walked outside, and Ben led them around the fence line that skirted Old Fred's enclosure to the field where he'd demolished the fence. Rusty was already back, finishing what they'd started earlier.

"Afternoon Rusty, I think I owe you a huge debt of gratitude for the way you stepped in the other night, thank you."

"No thanks necessary, Ma'am. It's just what you do, isn't it."

"It's just Saffie, and no it isn't what just anybody would do. It was extremely courageous, and it would be inexcusable for me not to acknowledge that."

"You're welcome. You've got a great kid there."

"I hear you've been turning him into a farmhand. How's he shaping up?"

"Another couple of weeks we'll have him rounding up cattle on an ATV."

Ben looked back and forth between them wearing a proud grin, "Mom says I can come back in my next vacation if Aunt Mary says it's okay, Rusty."

"Then you better get yourself a helmet; those quads can be as temperamental as a young colt sometimes."

"Can we do that, Mom?"

"I don't see why not. The feds and cops are at the house at the moment Rusty, and I think they'll want a word before they leave."

"I'm just about finished here; I'll make my way back via the yard and see what they want."

"Before you go, what did you do with the tracker you took off my Wrangler?"

"Nothing yet, I was going to put it on a sales rep's car, but I haven't got round to it."

"Just a thought, why not put it on the feds' sedan, if you get a chance before they go?"

"I like the way you think. I'll do just that."

Rusty got in his pickup and drove away, leaving Saffie and Ben to wander around.

"Mary said that you and she used to do stuff like this here when you were kids, Mom."

"Yeah, Mary and I spent hours fooling around on the farm, along with Lacey's cousin. He was older than us, but we were the only kids around and we had great fun together. We had chores to do as well though."

"What did Grandpa Walden do?"

"He was the Virginia State Commissioner for Land Management."

"That sounds important."

"It was, but it meant he was kept very busy and after my mom had her accident she didn't cope well. I had to spend a lot of time being looked after by other people, and Mary's mom and dad did most of that."

"I really liked Grandpa; he was always making jokes and singing. I miss him."

"Me too, but he'd be proud of how you're turning out, and of the way you've dealt with everything that's happened lately. Grandpa was in the marines and he used to put a lot of stock in personal courage. You've been absolutely amazing; most eight-year-olds would have buckled. I'm so sorry that I've had to keep leaving you, but I'm glad you've finally had the chance to get to know Mary."

"Mary told me that you're not allowed to tell anybody about the things you're doing to help Dad."

"That's right, and it's probably not over yet, but if I do have to go away again, I think you'll be safer here than anywhere else. Some of the people involved in your kidnap and your dad's hostage taking may be in the FBI or CIA, so at the moment I don't trust anybody. I'm making my own enquiries to find out who they are, and when I find out I'm going to make them wish they'd never heard our name."

"I get a bit scared when you say things like that, Mom."

"I know sweetheart but wait until I tell your dad how brave you've been. He'll be glowing with pride."

They made their way back to the house and got there just as Rusty was coming out.

"You're joining us for dinner tonight, I gather," Saffie said.

"Sure, I just gotta go home and wash up, but I think I'll do that other little chore we spoke about first." He winked and walked away.

When they were inside, Burns approached her. "We'd like a word with Ben now if that's okay."

"Can you use the living room?" Mary asked, "I need to finish getting our evening meal ready.

"That should be okay. Are you ready Ben?" Burns asked.

"I guess," he replied.

"We won't be long; we don't need you for this Ms. Price."

"I bet you don't, Agent Burns, but you're getting me anyway."

"Ben is just a witness; he's not suspected of a crime."

"Maybe not, but your organization is, so you can forget any notions you have about interviewing my son without me present."

"What the Hell does that mean?" Burns asked.

"Until I've eliminated the FBI from any involvement in the incidents over the last week or two, it remains under suspicion as far as I'm concerned."

"Very well. Let's get started," Ramirez interrupted, failing to disguise a small smile.

Ben had been looking from one to the other throughout the exchange and was surprised to see how easily his mom put the federal agents in their place.

Saffie and her son seated themselves on a sofa while Ramirez took a nearby armchair. Burns and Hendryx remained standing.

"Ben, you're not in any trouble, we just need to learn as much as we can about what happened the night those men took you. Is that okay?"

"Sure. I guess," he added.

"I'm going to record what you say, is that okay?"

Ben looked at his mom who nodded and answered that it wasn't a problem.

"Can I get a copy of that recording, Special Agent Ramirez?" Hendryx asked.

"I'll get my office to send you a transcript. That okay?"

"I guess so. Thanks."

"Ben, can we start by you telling me in your own words what happened, with as much detail as you can. I might interrupt from time to time to ask questions if that's okay."

"Okay I guess. I was asleep and the first I knew was someone put a hand over my mouth and told me not to make a noise or he'd kill me."

"Was he wearing gloves?"

"Yes, rubber ones, like the CSI people wear. Then he dragged me out of bed and told me to put my clothes on. I'd have shouted for my mom, but there was another man at the door with a gun. That's when I heard Mom shout to the other guy to drop his gun. He didn't though, and Mom shot him. It was horrible, there was blood all over, I'm glad it was dark and I couldn't see it very well.

"The first man took me out of the room and held me in front of him so Mom couldn't shoot him as well. Then another man came up the stairs behind us and he told her to drop her gun, and that she was stupid because no-one was supposed to get hurt. I think she must have done what he said because then we started to go down the stairs backwards with the man holding me between us and Mom.

"The third man kept his gun pointing at Mom until we were out of the front door. He dragged me into the back of a car and the man put sticky tape over my mouth and eyes. I think that's when Mom shot the third man; I heard him scream. The car drove away fast, and I heard two more shots outside the ca. I guess that was Mom. The man who was shot - they called him Fly - he kept cursing because of the pain, and cos he'd dropped his gun."

"Did you see their faces?"

"They were all wearing masks."

"What happened next?"

"The one who was driving - they called him Blue Boy - started cursing because Mom had shot one of the tires and the car kept swerving from side to side every time we went round a bend. The one in the back used the tape to tie my hands together. He was called Rack. It wasn't far, but we stopped, and they put me in the back of another car, and we drove again for ages."

Burns interrupted, "What did they talk about?"

"Mostly it was Fly cursing Mom for shooting him, and someone they called Scratchy for being a dumb 'C' word for not tying Mom up before they grabbed me. I guess Scratchy was the one that Mom shot. Rack kept asking when they'd get paid, and Blue Boy was worried that someone called Sab would find out after Scratchy got wasted."

"Is that all they said?"

"I can't tell you much more because Mom would ground me until I'm twenty-five if I said the real words, but that's most of it."

"Did they take you straight to where they held you without stopping?"

"Yes, but I couldn't see anything. When we got there they threw me on a smelly bed and tied my legs up the same as my hands."

"What happened then?"

"Nothing ;I laid there for hours. I could hear them arguing in another room. The one called Fly kept asking the others to get him a doctor, but they refused because they were worried that the doctor would call the police. In the end I heard one of them say that Rack was going to get a doctor there anyway, and that he'd threaten to kill him if he didn't come. That's when the lady came to rescue me."

"Tell us about the lady Ben."

"She was about five nine and a hundred and ninety pounds, short black hair and dark skin like she might be part African-American."

"Did she have an accent?"

"Yes, she sounded a bit Latino."

"Did she tell you her name?"

"I asked who she was and she said to call her 'Lady' and that she was just somebody who didn't like gangsters."

"Was that all she said?"

"She told me that she didn't want to talk, but she was taking me to a friend of my Mom's where I'd be safe."

"What happened when you got there?"

"She dropped me at the end of the drive and waited while I walked up to the house. Aunt Mary saw me coming and came to meet me."

"Are you sure you're telling us the truth Ben? Did you know that it's a felony offence to lie to the FBI?"

"Whoa, you can hold on right there Agent Burns. My son is a minor and he's the victim here. As far as I can see he's been very helpful until now. But if you're going to be alluding to felony charges, this interview ends right now."

"There won't be any charges, Ms. Price." Ramirez stepped in, "Have you got anything else you'd like to tell us though Ben?"

"The place where they took me was real smelly, but the lady who rescued me wore very strong perfume, it smelled like my old teacher, Mrs. Grantham, used to wear."

"Ms. Price?"

"Delia Grantham was English, and she usually wore Lavender perfume. She passed last year."

"Okay Ben, thank you. You've been very helpful. Perhaps you could join Miss Riley in the kitchen while we have a quick word with your Mom."

Saffie smiled and nodded to her son and he left them to it.

"Care to explain how this 'Lady' just happened to know where to find your childhood friend, and how she came to be expecting him Ms. Price?"

"It's quite simple really, Agent Ramirez. Lady was probably one of the former colleagues that I called for help in identifying the bastards who'd taken my son. I'd said once he was found, I'd get him to stay here until I'd found out who was behind all this. The original plan was for whoever located him or identified the culprits to contact me so that I could tell you. As it happened 'Lady' located Ben much quicker than anyone anticipated and probably didn't feel comfortable leaving him where he was while you got a warrant. So, as I would have expected from any of my former colleagues, she took executive action. From the little you've told me, and what else has happened since, it looks like she luckily made the right decision."

"Very lucky indeed, Ms. Price. Thank you, we'll be in touch."

She followed them to the door and watched their sedan drive away, with Hendryx behind them.

Chapter 25

"Ben have you developed a skill for story-telling that I didn't know about?" she asked her son. "Your English teacher will be pleased."

"What do you mean, Mom?"

"A five foot nine inch African-American with a Latino accent wearing lavender perfume. Where did that come from?"

"Mary told me that if the cops asked me about who rescued me and how I got there then I needed to have a story ready, so we kind of invented one. The cops didn't ask me so I just used that story for the FBI. You're not cross are you?"

"Of course not, but I want it to be known that I do 'not' weigh a hundred and ninety pounds."

They all thought that was funny.

"I need to make some calls before dinner. I hope nobody minds."

She went outside and called Felix.

"Saffie."

"Well?"

"I can't tell you anymore..."

She hung up. After staring thoughtfully at her phone for a moment she dialed another number, "Linda, it's Saffie."

"Saffie, great timing I've just got off the phone from my Eastern European friend. He's sent me some information about the number on that burner. There's quite a lot more than you might expect. He's nothing if not thorough. He only charged me four grand in the end, and I think you'll find it's worth every cent, although I don't know how much of it connects to what's happening to you."

"That's fantastic Linda, I'll text you an email address to send it to."

"There's more. My other friend found the current physical location of the guy that was watching that footage from your house. He said it wasn't easy."

"Go on, let me have it."

"It's in Mclean, Waverly Way."

"Do you want to say that again."

Linda read the address again, "*Do you recognize it then?*"

"Yes I do. Shit, it throws a new light on this whole thing."

"Do you need to be worried about it?"

"Yes, very worried, and you might want to tell your friend to take care now."

"Oh God, that sort of worried."

"That's right. Thank you though, Linda. What you've just told me; it may well be the difference between catastrophe and salvation."

When she closed the call she stopped to think before rejoining the others. The ramifications of what she'd just learned could be enormous and meant she'd need to plan carefully before she made her next move.

The last thing she did was turn on the burner she'd used to text Pearmain. There was a message, which had been sent an hour ago, it read, '*Text back tomorrow 0700 hours EDT using new number. I'll do what I can.*'

She didn't reply. She wouldn't have been expected to. When she joined the others she did her best to display a carefree appearance, but Mary's expression showed that she'd failed.

Mary's cooking was first class, a skill she'd never mastered herself. Rusty proved himself a very entertaining dinner guest, a great conversationalist, always ready with a witty remark or anecdote and yet still a good listener.

"So what's your background Rusty?"

"Me, oh nothing too glamorous. I was raised in California. Mom and Dad ran a hardware store in a small town outside Bakersfield. Did okay at school and college. Got a year into an MS course in mechanical engineering at UCLA, switched to electrical engineering. Then before my final year I took a job on a cattle ranch to earn some cash, loved it and never went back."

"What did your folks have to say about that?"

"Mom was upset, but Dad said that if it was what I wanted, and I enjoyed it then I should go for it. Since then I've worked on cattle ranches in half the states of the union. I've been here four years now, just about the longest I've stayed anywhere."

"So why Rusty? That's a name normally reserved for redheads."

"My true name is Ruben Levi. At my first ranch I was given the job of cleaning some woodworking tools and putting them back in the workshop, but I was called away to help with an ornery mare and forgot to go back. After two days of torrential rain I found them starting to go rusty. The foreman went crazy and made me clean them up rather than drive into town with the other guys, so I became Rusty Ruben and it stuck."

"A Jewish cowboy? Can't be many of them about."

"That's true enough, but I don't follow religion so I guess it's irrelevant. What about you?"

"Neither Brett nor I are religious and we're not raising Ben to be either. We're not atheists we just don't follow any particular religious dogma, although I guess we're nominally Christians."

"Mom does karate, don't you, Mom?"

"Strictly speaking what I do isn't karate. It doesn't have a name, and doesn't have a belt system. It incorporates some aspects of different disciplines like defendu, krav maga, MCMAP, and some karate. It's not regulated because it's dangerous and not for self-defense."

"What does that mean, *not for self-defense*?" Rusty asked.

"It means it includes moves designed to maim or kill."

"Bloody Hell, Saff, I had no idea," Mary said. "I guess I shouldn't be surprised - you always were tough. I remember when Lacey's cousin, Gabe, misread the signals and tried it on, she gave him a bloody nose and a black eye, and he was four years older than us."

"So if this system doesn't have a name, isn't regulated, and it's not for self-defense, what's it for and how do you train? Does it have rules?"

"It's a special forces system. I don't go to a dojo regularly; I just drop into group fight nights from time to time. Brett used to do it as well, but he's been out of the country too much these days. The only rules are, it's one on one unless otherwise agreed; and don't leave your opponent dead or with a permanent injury."

"Jesus."

"In reality, it's more civilized than that most of the time. The only time it gets out of hand is if one of us has a personal grievance against their opponent."

"Who decide who wins?"

"Nobody, it stops after three minutes or when three observers raise their hands to say it's enough."

"Are their other women?" Mary asked.

"A couple of former special ops girls."

"Do you ever get hurt?"

"I had my nose broken a couple of times. I thought you'd have noticed."

"I did; you told me that you'd stepped on a rake."

Saffie smiled.

"I'll have to watch my step around you then," Rusty remarked.

"The only people that are at risk from me are those that endanger me, the people I love, or my country."

"What are you going to do to find out who took Ben? From what I've learned about you, you're not the sort to just let it drop. Those assholes from the FBI today don't seem to be in too much of a rush to find out and I'm not the only one to think so."

"Just a minute before you say any more." Saffie left the room and returned a few minutes later with the bug detector and waved it under the table and throughout the kitchen while everybody else looked on with astonished expressions. She didn't find anything.

"What do you mean not the only one to think so?"

"That Sergeant Hendryx, he seemed to think they're just treading water."

"That's my impression too. But you're right, I'm not just going to roll over and take it, although I might do my best to let them think I have, whilst also doing my best to throw some spanners in their works. There are some things going on that I can't talk about, and I might not be successful. Nonetheless, whatever the success of my efforts, when this is over you can bet on a whole truck load of cow shit hitting the helicopter rotor."

"Mom," Ben admonished.

"I know, and I'm sorry, but you're likely to hear me say a whole worse and a whole lot more often in the coming days, so you'll need to get used to a side of your mom that you didn't know existed."

"You're not saying very much about yourself, Mary," Rusty observed.

"Me? I'm just a simple country girl; there's not much to say. I was lucky to inherit this farm, and I've been lucky to come through on top of the game after all the ups and downs that go with this way of life. Anyway,

I've been listening to you two reveal more about yourselves around this table than you've told me in the entire time I've known either of you. What do you think Ben?"

"I've found out more about my mom and dad in the last week than I did in the last eight years."

"Does that worry you though, sweetheart?" Saffie asked.

"I'm worried about Dad because I think there's something going on that you still haven't told me. And I'm worried about you, because you keep doing dangerous things, but I am proud of you and of Dad."

"That's a pretty smart kid you got there, Saffie," Mary told her.

"And he ain't a bad ranch-hand either," Rusty added. "Anyway folks I'm going to catch an early night. I've got to go to the Shenandoah Market first thing in the morning. Thanks for the meal Mary, and thank you all for your company; it's been a good evening."

"L'chaim," Saffie said, raising her glass.

He smiled. "And mazel tov to you."

Chapter 26

Saffie had set her alarm for six-thirty but was awake long before it buzzed. The address in McClean that Linda's contact had uncovered had deeply shocked her at first, but the more she thought about it, the more she felt that might it make sense of other things. She showered, dressed, and was making coffee before her host joined her in the kitchen.

"Are you going to be busy today?" Mary asked.

"Possibly. I've a call to make, and then I've a lengthy email to absorb before I can decide what to do next."

"I saw your face after you made those calls last night. Something's wrong isn't it; something else I mean."

"I found something out that I hadn't anticipated and it's put a completely new complexion on things. I'll need to review my strategy is all."

"Just who is it you're fighting here, Saffie?"

"If I'm right, somebody I'd never considered I'd ever have to fight. The problem is I don't know what his intentions are, nor what his motive might be?"

"How do you mean?"

"Is it me he's after or is it Brett? Are we the targets, or are we just collateral damage in something much larger?"

"Jesus, Saff! This is frightening."

"Yes, it is," Saffie said, as she stepped outside to call Pearmain. She was just in time to see Rusty emerge from the old house.

"Rusty, could you do me a small favor while you're out and pick up a couple of cheap burners?" She handed him two $100 bills.

"No problem. I may not be back until mid-afternoon though."

"That's okay. I'm just getting through them quite quickly lately."

He waved and said goodbye and she began to compose a long text to Pearmain about Jenkins. After reading it through she sent it, not optimistic she'd get a reply at all, let alone soon.

She was pouring herself a fresh cup of coffee and the burner she'd just used buzzed with an incoming message. It said, '*This the guy?*' There was an ID photo of a man attached. A poor picture but there was no doubt in her mind that it was the man she knew as Nigel Jenkins.

She texted straight back to confirm that it was the right man and seconds later, the phone rang, she answered without speaking at first.

'Wind velocity?'

"Fourteen."

'You should have killed that arsehole when you had the chance.'

"Who is he?"

'His real name is Norman Johnson; he's a Brit, or claims to be; his father was English, his mother is Ukrainian. Studied languages at Essex University and then was recruited to MI6 in 1998. He served for about eighteen months before being sacked, officially for using his position for pecuniary advantage. There was more to it than that though; he raped a diplomat's daughter in Warsaw, and there was suspicion that he was cozying up to a Ukrainian agent, and in those days the relationship between our countries wasn't what it is now. Since then he's become a source of information for anybody in the intelligence community who's happy to pay; what we in the UK call an info-whore. Calls himself White Angel. Personally, I wouldn't listen to anything he told me without an endorsement from the Pope.'

"So you think he was a plant?"

'He's a lascivious bastard, so it's just possible that he saw an attractive woman and just wanted in your knickers without knowing who you were, but it's too much of a coincidence for my taste. The thing about him is, he's arrogant and it's not beyond the bounds of possibility that whatever else is going on, he thought he could sleep with you, milk you for information and recruit you for a source.'

"It doesn't explain how he knew who I was though. Where do his parents live now?"

'His father died ten years ago and his mother moved back to Ukraine. She lives in Pavlohrad about three hours from Slovyansk. I think that's where he bases himself most of the time.'

"Do you think she knows what he does to make a living?"

'Almost certainly.'

"Thanks Pearmain. I'll try not to trouble you again."

'No trouble, you're welcome to that sort of background info anytime. I'm getting the sense that your problems haven't improved.'

"Worse if anything."

'I'll keep my ear to the ground, and if I hear anything I'll text this number, so keep it live.' He hung up.

After breakfast, Saffie spent two hours poring through the information in the email that Linda's friend had uncovered from Hevil's phone. Whoever Linda's guy was, he must have some amazing skills and access to sources US cops could only dream about. She guessed he must be in the intelligence community himself.

Hevil had spoken to a whole list of people from that burner phone, and Saffie couldn't imagine Lopez being very happy about that.

The most interesting and astonishing set of information though was what had been unearthed about the number listed as 'Lopez'. The phone had only received calls from five other numbers and made calls to only three.

With one exception the received calls were all from unlisted cell phones, most likely burners all in random locations in the Donetsk oblast. The single other call had been triangulated to a cell phone located in or very close to the US Embassy in Kyiv.

He'd received a number of brief unintelligible texts. However one from whoever it was in Kyiv read, '*White Angel, this one might be a problem, she's dangerous.*' The message had a photo attachment. She opened the file; it was her own CIA ID photo, and it had been forwarded to another number. The text had been sent while she was in the air on her way from Baltimore.

She sat back aghast at what she'd just seen. The implications were enormous; someone inside the intelligence services of the CIA knew she was on her way to Ukraine and identified her to a rogue intelligence agent. The other thing it meant was that, if Johnson was Lopez as the message suggested, unless he'd been in the States in the days before Ben's abduction, then there was more than one 'Lopez'.

When she looked at the list of calls made, two were to Hevil's burner, the third was to a landline in Ukraine located in Pavlohrad. There was no way that could be a coincidence.

She had to decide whether or not to stir the pot now by letting Johnson know that she was onto him or hold back until she could use the information to maximum effect. In the end she postponed the decision at least until Rusty returned with the burners.

Could Johnson have got into the US using a different ID without being spotted at an airport? It was possible, but she asked herself if he'd need another identity - he had no reason to believe that she or the CIA knew he was involved in this.

Using her authority as an agency analyst she logged onto the immigration data to see what if anything she could learn. It was likely that her use of the system would flag her up to Homeland, but she didn't think that they were the enemy in this case. Although she might have to answer questions as to why she needed the information.

Her search revealed no record of Johnson, or anybody matching his parameters entering the country during the two weeks prior to Ben's abduction. Astonishingly Johnson himself was recorded entering the country on a direct flight from Kyiv to Baltimore/Washington Airport two days earlier. She needed to flush him out.

Hoping that she wasn't exploiting her friendship with Linda, she called her number."

"Hi, Saffie. Was that stuff any use to you?"

"Useful? Oh yes, definitely useful, possibly even game changing. I can't thank you enough, but that's not why I called."

"What else can I do for you?"

"Would your Eastern European friend be able to get any information about calls being made and received from that landline in Pavlohrad?"

"I expect so, but I doubt he'd do it in real time. He may be able to report calls over a given period like a conventional telephone bill. Not sure how much he'd charge though; shouldn't be too expensive."

"Of course, money's not a problem. I'll text you the dates. I need to kick the hornet nest. Can you add it to what I owe you?"

"No problem, I'll see what he can do. I'll call back when I've got an answer."

She texted Pearmain again. *'FYI, I'm pretty certain that I've identified Johnson as Lopez in Ukraine but not the same person as the guy operating in US also calling himself Lopez. Johnson arrived in US a day after my return.'*

Sitting at her laptop she stared in thought at the screen for a minute or two, 'I need to learn more about this asshole,' she thought.

Then she looked online for Essex University Alumni lists for 1998. Inevitably there was a login process. Hacking wasn't her best skill and it took her some time to find it, but eventually she found a way in. Essex was a fair sized university by UK standards, and it looked as if three or four thousand students graduated each year for various higher and lower degrees. Johnson was a common name, but nonetheless she imagined a search for N. Johnson should be straightforward, but the only N. Johnson it revealed was Natalie.

She'd been typing unsuccessfully on the keyboard for two hours when Ben called her through to the kitchen for lunch.

"What have you been up to?" Mary asked. "You've been working like a Trojan all morning. How's it going?"

"Okay I guess. I keep making breakthroughs and then coming up with another brick wall."

"Ben took you a coffee an hour ago and you haven't touched it."

"I'm sorry I get so focused sometimes that I zone out."

"You were the same in between semesters when we were at uni. I seem to remember that even after you graduated and you were talking about going for a PhD, you couldn't tear yourself away."

"What's a PhD?" Ben asked.

"It stands for doctor of philosophy."

"You were going to be a doctor?"

"No, it's just a degree - the next step up from a masters."

"But you didn't do it?"

"No, I couldn't decide what I wanted to do with it in the end, so I took some time out and spent a year in Ukraine. When I came back I was recruited by... Jesus, of course that's the answer."

"Just switch off long enough to eat and drink something will you. Ben and I finally finished making that cake."

"Okay, thank you, you're right, a few minutes' rest won't hurt."

The other two could see that her mind was elsewhere from her vacant expression and vague contributions to the conversation. So Mary asked her if she'd enjoyed the mock turtle and dodo soup. When she replied that it was lovely the others burst into laughter.

"Eh? What's so funny?"

"Never mind, just go and finish what you were doing."

When Saffron graduated, she'd taken a year out before starting with the agency. The chances were that Johnson did the same thing. She repeated the exercise of looking for him in the class of '97 and was frustrated when she got the same result. She tried the same thing for '96 and found him straightaway.

The next stage of the process was to identify someone who graduated at the same time as he did, someone who knew him enough to reveal something that might provoke a response. The list showed the subjects of the graduates so she clipped and pasted it into an Excel spreadsheet and filtered out all those without language-related degrees. It still left more than thirty people.

After stopping to think about where to go next, she remembered her own graduation; the ceremony, the picnic with her family members and fellow graduates, the popping of champagne corks, the evening celebrations, and the obligatory graduation photo. Hers had sat in her parents' living room even after her mom's death.

Photographs would be the answer to the next step. Returning to the Essex uni website she looked for a link to an alumnus society and easily found one. Once again there was a member logon process, this time more difficult to find a way around. She was about ready to give up when she resorted to the old favorite used by hackers since the very first days of hacking and showed the home page in HTML. Every web designer would have been schooled to weed out any security detail that could be revealed using this rudimentary method on day one of web school.

There were pages and pages of code but she eliminated much of it by jumping through sections which had no security implications. She did a number of straightforward searches for key words such as 'login', 'password', 'ID', 'PIN', 'code' and 'membership number' without results.

"What're you doing, Mom?"

"I'm hoping that somewhere in all this gobbledygook is something that will help me find a way into this website."

"Do you mean like a passkey something like that?"

"Passkey! That's worth a try."

Seconds later she'd found six references to 'passkey', including in one line which didn't seem to serve any function, but it included the characters n1y@w/rodk@B.

"Ben Price, even if I didn't love you to pieces already, then I love you even more now." She grabbed his head and kissed him a dozen times.

"Moommm!"

"Sorry, are you getting too big for a kiss from your mom?"

"What does it mean though, Mom?"

"Watch." She dropped out of the HTML view and typed 'B@kdor' into Member Name box and then 'W@y1n' into the Password box, pressed Enter and the Members home page opened.

"That's clever, Mom, but what now?"

"I'm going to look through the photos of the year the guy I'm looking for graduated. Then I'm going to do a photo search for them elsewhere on the net."

"But you don't know what he looks like do you?"

"I do, and I have a photo, but I need to find some who knows something about him back in the day to force his hand."

"How do you know what he looks like though?"

"I'd rather not explain that I'm afraid, but it's not important."

"Can I watch you?"

"Sure, but it might be boring."

Needless to say Johnson wasn't a member but she hoped it wouldn't matter; she only wanted to find someone who knew him. Of the thirty or so language students who graduated that year only nineteen were members and as she predicted, Johnson wasn't one of them. Only four of the rest had posted group photographs and there was nobody in any of them that looked anything like Johnson. She sighed in exasperation.

"What now, Mom?"

"A long process of identification and phone calls."

All nineteen had put their photo on the site and one by one she did a photo search followed by viewing the Facebook pages that allowed public access until she got to the seventh in the list, Frances Fletcher. She looked at the photograph again more carefully a second time. "For fuck's sake, I don't believe it!"

"Mom!"

"Sorry sweetheart, but I think I've just had the most extraordinary piece of luck. What time is it?"

"About four-thirty."

She quickly looked up the number for Virginia State University and called. "Would it be possible to speak to Professor Frances Broadman?"

"Who's speaking please?"

"Saffron Waldon; I'm a former student."

"I'll see if she's free."

There was a pause of about two minutes while they played several bars of '*The Arrival of the Queen of Sheba*' on a loop.

"Saffron. What a lovely surprise. How are you? What did you end up doing, I heard you didn't progress through to do that PhD; a shame, you'd have breezed it."

"I got made an offer that I couldn't refuse, by a government department, a sort of investigative role."

"Say no more. I think I can read between the lines. What can I do for you?"

"You're going to be surprised when I ask, but I'm hoping you can tell me something about one of your fellow alumni at Essex Uni."

"Okay, I don't know how much help I can be it's nearly twenty-three years ago. Who is it you want to know about?"

"A guy called Norman Johnson."

"Oh God that's a name I hoped I'd never hear again. What's the bastard done now?"

"I can't talk about it I'm afraid, but his name has arisen in an enquiry, and we need to take a closer look at him."

"So you don't know about what happened with Johnson and me?"

"No I'm sorry, can you talk about it?"

"I guess I could, after all this time. He raped me."

"Oh shit, I'm sorry. I don't want to drag up that sort of memory."

"No, it's okay Saffie, I'm on top of it now. They didn't have enough proof to nail him at the time and he was never prosecuted. I found my way through it but the same can't

be said about my friend Jo. She was never the same. She spent most of the last twenty years in and out of therapy and committed suicide two years ago."

"Bastard. What was Jo's full name?"

"Jocelyn Travers."

"Fran you don't know how much help you've been, although I can't tell you any more about it I'm afraid. But if I have my way, Johnson will be going out of harm's way for a very long time."

"Don't worry about it, Saffie. Where are you living these days?"

"Dunn Loring, up near Langley."

"Very nice, expensive up that way."

"Where are you?"

"Jason and I have accommodation on campus now we're both senior academics. It would be nice to get together and share a bottle of wine one day."

"I'd like that Fran. Maybe when I've put this thing to bed I'll give you another call."

She sat back with a satisfied smile.

"Who was that Mom?"

"One of my tutors from uni."

"Have you found out what you wanted then?"

"Yes Ben, I think I have."

Mother and son walked through to the kitchen.

"Well you've been ensconced in my dining room most of the day. I hope you've got something to show for it," Mary said in a mock critical manner.

"Yes I have, and thanks in no small part to my son here, and a massive piece of luck."

"Maybe you can tell me something about it over dinner which will be ready in about half an hour if you want to go wash up."

Dinner was once again an amazing meal.

"Do you cook like this every day, Mary, when you haven't got guests?"

"No, it never seems worth it just for me, but Rusty comes over once or twice a week. I love cooking, and as you've seen, he's great company."

"Where is he tonight?"

"It's Saturday; it would be my guess he'll be in town with Lacey."

"Do you think he and she might..."

"No, I doubt it. I think he might be up for it, but she's gonna be a highflyer that one. I can't see her settling for a life down on the farm. He left those burner phones for you by the way."

"There is a bit of an age difference."

"Lacey was just a high school kid when he first arrived, and she set her cap for him right away. He was great with her, just like he's been with Ben, but he wouldn't have anything to do with her outside work hours until she was sixteen. Then one night before she went off for her freshman year she crept into the old house after dark and laid it all out for him. Poor guy never stood a chance."

"You said he plays the field."

"That's right, and so does she. I think she saw him as a challenge. I doubt he was her first."

Chapter 27

Saffie suspected it would be another crucial day. Although unsure how it would pan out, at least she had something to go on.

She called Felix even before she took her shower, "Any news?"

"Homeland aren't saying anything, I'm sorry."

"Whose decision was it to put Brett on that op?"

"We were short of field agents and the op was urgent, but I don't know who made the final decision."

"So who was involved, you, Radwell, the DDO, or someone else."

"Not me, way above my pay grade."

"You can tell whoever you like that if they haven't charged Brett or released him by 1700 today I'll go public and instruct a lawyer to sue for wrongful arrest and detention."

"For fucks sake, Saffie, you'll end up under arrest yourself."

"Homeland has got a lot of powers, but it can't cancel the constitution. My arrest would infringe my rights under the first amendment, and Brett's continued detainment already infringes his rights under the fifth, and given his injury, possibly the eighth."

"But revealing Brett's status as a CIA agent would be a felony."

"Someone in the agency has already done that, so if they want to go into court with that I'm up for it."

"Homeland has special powers..."

"DHS's whole raison d'etre is to prevent terrorist attacks within the United States, so unless someone is accusing Brett of planning some kind of domestic terrorism, it's bullshit. I'd like to see them argue that in court against all the evidence I've gathered."

"What do you mean?"

"Like I'm going to tell you."

"You can't..."

"Goodbye Felix, remember seventeen hundred hours." She ended the call confident that she'd set a cat among the pigeons, exactly what she wanted to do.

She left it until 10 a.m. before taking the Wrangler and telling Ben and Mary that she'd probably be out for the day. Before she left the farm, she took the tracker out of her wallet, and typed some words for someone else to read.

She drove to Charlottesville and waited in the parking lot outside McDonalds waiting for a suitable youngster to come out. Leaning against the hood of her car, she didn't have to wait long until a kid about seventeen years old appeared clutching a paper bag and a soda.

"Hi," she said, as he walked by; "How would you like to earn yourself a hundred bucks and the price of a replacement for whatever is in that bag if it gets cold."

"Oh yeah right. What's the con?" he skeptically replied.

"No con. You wouldn't have to move from where you're standing, and you'd be on your way in a few minutes."

"Is this some kind of TV gotcha thing?"

She showed him her badge. "All I need you to do is make a call on this phone and read this to the woman who answers."

"Is this illegal?"

"Nope. This is me trying to set up a meeting with an FBI agent without her knowing who she's meeting until she gets there. If I make the call she'll recognize my voice."

"You ain't gonna kill her are you?"

"Kid, if I wanted to kill her, I'm not likely to identify myself to you first and then arrange a meeting in a public place am I?"

"Okay then but I want the money up front."

She handed him a couple of fifties.

"Is this like a secret or something?"

"No you can tell anybody you like about it, if that's what you want. You can even take a photo of my license plate, but not of me."

She took the bag and drink from him, rested them on the hood of her car, and handed him the burner with the note she'd prepared earlier.

"Call the only number in the contact list, put it on speaker and read from the sheet."

He did as she'd asked. "Hello, am I speaking to Special Agent Ramirez of the FBI?"

"Yes. How did you get this number?"

"It doesn't matter, I have an urgent message to read to you, it's not from me. Please listen carefully. I won't repeat it."

"Go ahead."

"I have evidence about the recent abduction of a child in Dunn Loring. If you want to hear it, then the sender of this message will meet you at the public basketball court in Booker T. Washington Park in Charlottesville in one and a half hours. Come alone."

"What if I can't get there in time?"

"Then you'll be too late."

Saffie signaled him to cut the call.

"It's not long enou..."

"Well done, kid. Here's another fifty. Thanks a lot."

"The boy grinned and picked up his food bag and drink. "Thanks Lady."

"Have a good day," she told him. Then turned the phone off and got back in her car.

She looked up a diner on her own phone, drove there and parked up. The restaurant was busy, but she was lucky to find a table as a family vacated it and ordered coffee while the waitress cleared their plates and wiped the table.

She sat reading a free local paper left behind by the last family.

"Is it okay if I sit with you?"

A man in cargo pants and olive drab t-shirt with a 101st Airborne insignia on the chest was stood by her table. Both garments looked as if they were right out of the packaging. Looking around she saw all the other tables were taken.

"Okay," she said and continued to read, thinking, 'Fake vet if ever I've seen one.'

"So why is a beautiful woman like you having to eat alone on a lovely Sunday like this?" the guy said.

"Because I choose to," she replied, without looking up.

"Seems a shame."

"I'm happy with the arrangement."

"Why don't you let me try to persuade you otherwise? My name's Chad."

"I'm not interested, Chad, but thanks anyway."

"But you haven't even given me a chance."

The waitress bought her a cup and poured her a coffee, "What can I get you, Ma'am?"

"I'll take whatever is the vegetarian option and could you keep my coffee topped up."

"Today's veggie options are grilled cheese sandwich with caramelized onions and pineapple, or crispy cornmeal and pepita onion rings."

"Sounds great, I'll take both."

"Good choices, I'll take the same," the guy piped up. "So are you completely vegetarian or do you swing both ways, if you get my drift?"

"If that's supposed to be some sort of euphemism, I'm not amused."

"Oh come on, I thought it was quite funny."

Saffie leant forward, encouraging him to do the same. "I've made it clear that I don't want your company so if you don't fuck off in the next two minutes, I'll get the cops in here and have you arrested for harassment. Are we clear now?"

The waitress passed the table again. Saffie called her over, "Can you find this man another table? He's bothering me?"

"There's another table by the door that's free now, Sir."

Chad stood up, obviously well and truly pissed off and walked to the other table.

"Sorry about that, Ma'am."

"No problem. Is he a local?"

"Yes, I'm afraid so."

The food came, it was really good, and she took her time eating it. When she'd finished eating she left money on the table with a good tip and made to leave.

As she passed the wannabe soldier, he said, "So are you a dyke? You never did say."

"I don't know," she said in a loud voice, "Am I a lesbian, you ask. Well, until now I've never considered being lesbian, but if a fake veteran soldier like you is the best the straight fraternity has to offer then it might be worth giving it a try. I hope there no real members of US Airborne in here. They might take offence seeing someone who's never worn uniform in his life wearing their insignia."

"I have worn uniform," he protested.

"What for? School crossing patrol?"

She walked out the door as several of the other occupants of the diner burst into laughter.

Chapter 28

Before leaving, Saffie had put on a summer dress belonging to Mary and pinned her hair up. Now she checked her watch, donned a baseball cap and sunglasses and left the car a few streets from the park.

Getting to the rendezvous in time from where she lived in Haymarket would be a struggle for Ramirez, but that was the point. Saffie wanted this meeting to be just the two of them and she didn't want to give the agent time to set up surveillance. Ramirez would have had to tell her bosses where she was going of course, but Saffie needed the conversation to be off the record and in private if possible.

On a fine Sunday in mid-summer the park was inevitably busy with families supporting their kids playing softball or basketball and others with picnics. Saffie settled herself on a bench within sight of the basketball courts and waited.

Ten minutes after the appointed deadline Ramirez appeared looking flustered and stood apart from the groups of sporting spectators and looked around. Saffie waited another minute or two before casually walking as if to pass the agent six feet away, then at the last second stepped sideways toward her.

"Do you want to do this here or go for coffee, Agent Ramirez?"

"What the Hell are you playing at, Ms. Price?"

"I needed to speak to you, and only you. Hopefully off the record for the time being."

"I can't guarantee that."

"I don't expect you to yet, but I'm hoping you'll change your mind once I've told some of what I have to say."

"I'll give you ten minutes to tell me what the fuck you want. If I'm not convinced I'll tell my colleagues where I am."

"Fine, although I'm sure they're already on their way."

"First tell me why it's me you're trusting with this so-called evidence."

"First because I no longer know who I can trust in my own agency; and second, because I think that I can trust you. I hope I'm not wrong."

"As long as you're not trying to feed me a load of bullshit to lead me off the scent or break the law then you can trust me."

"Okay, but I don't want you to record this."

"Oh come on, you're making this very difficult for me."

"You haven't had time to get a warrant and get wired so any recording without my permission would be inadmissible anyway. You could of course have an open line to Burns or someone else, which would also be inadmissible, especially as I've just told you I don't want it. I appreciate that it's difficult for you, but I can assure you that this is much harder for me."

"Alright, but this better be good."

For the next fifteen minutes without giving hard evidence, Saffie began to give Ramirez a summary of everything, even intimating that she'd freed Ben from the crooks in Richmond, flown to Ukraine, rescued Brett from the gangsters in Slovyansk, and gave her more detail about the attempt to film and record her in her own home.

Ramirez allowed her to continue uninterrupted for about ten minutes before calling her colleagues and telling them to back off. From then on apart from an occasional question, she allowed Saffie to say her piece.

"That was astonishing, Ms. Price, but what do you expect me to do about any of it? You've all but admitted to dozens of crimes in this country and abroad. Although personally I understand your motives, other than arrest you and set about trying to prove what you've told me, I'm powerless."

"Be honest, I haven't told you much that you hadn't already suspected, apart from the business in Ukraine perhaps. There isn't much you can do with it because I haven't told you the most important bits."

"There's more?"

"Oh yes, a whole lot more, and although I know about it, there are people in positions to prevent me doing anything about it. Nonetheless, I don't want you to do anything about what I tell you next either. I just need someone to know about it in case something happens to me."

"How can I do anything without any record of what you tell me?"

"First, because in spite of your promise not to record me, I'd be astonished if you hadn't, and second I've kept a detailed account of everything, including recordings, videos, photographs, and scans. I update it daily, and it will be published after my unexplained disappearance or death."

"So what's the bit you haven't told me yet?"

"You already know that my husband is a field agent with the CIA, as was I when the two of us met. We're both foreign language graduates; my qualifications when recruited were the Slavic languages of Polish, Russian and Ukrainian, while Brett's were more the Germanic and Scandinavian. Although we served together once or twice, most of our professional lives we've worked apart. That's for the very important reasons that as an agent abroad you have to know your area, know the people, have excellent command of the languages, know the politics and people, but most importantly know the players in the intelligence community. Also it's essential not to be influenced in what you do by what's happening with people close to you.

"Brett predominantly worked in Germany, Denmark, Austria, and Switzerland. Then, more than three months ago he was inexplicably sent on an op to the Ukraine, a country where he'd never worked before. Almost four weeks ago, without warning, all communications from him ceased. Karl Radwell his handler and his family liaison officer, Felix Carter, kept that secret from me for more than two weeks. It wasn't until the evening before Ben was abducted that Carter came to me and admitted that they'd lost contact with him for a fortnight before they even started to seriously look for him. Since then I've been given conflicting reports about the sequence of events that followed.

"You know about all the events that happened next. It was far too much of a coincidence that the abduction and Brett's disappearance weren't connected in some way and yet the agency were and still are feeding me bullshit. I had no faith in law enforcement being able to do their jobs if they weren't being given all the information, therefore I intervened and recovered my son and put him in a place of safety.

"By that time I was also certain I was being lied to about my husband, so acting on information I gained from former contacts from when I was an agent in the country, I flew to Ukraine and with resources they helped me acquire, I did in twenty-four hours what the combined resources of the entire CIA had failed to do for almost three weeks - I located and freed my husband. If I were able to do that having been out of the game for eight years, it's inconceivable that the CIA couldn't have done so much sooner if they'd been allowed to. When I found him Brett had been shot after refusing to cooperate with his captors, he'd been given no medical treatment and had a serious infection. I informed the US Embassy of his whereabouts and flew back to America.

"Brett spent several days in a Ukrainian hospital, before he was flown home, but instead of being taken to a medical facility for further treatment as they'd told me he would be, he was arrested by agents from the Department of Homeland Security and has been kept incommunicado ever since in contravention of his constitutional rights. In protest about his treatment I went to Patryk Wilkanowicz, the Deputy Director of Operations of the CIA who denied any knowledge of the events, in spite of my having been told that he was aware and had authorised the search for my husband. Using clandestine investigation techniques, I've since acquired information that indicates that the DDO, or someone very close to him, not only knows about what's been happening but could even be responsible for it."

"Hey, hold on there, you're talking about treason by the country's most senior intelligence officer!"

"Now you're getting the idea."

"What the fuck do you expect me to do about that?"

"As I see it, you have two choices. You could take everything I've told you and what you've recorded and run with it. That would involve you charging me for all the offences I've hinted that I might have committed, me being imprisoned, and my child being deprived of yet another parent. Of course that way the investigation would be taken completely out of your hands, cause a scandal on a biblical scale, with the agency interfering at every opportunity, and potentially allowing the real culprit to escape the net I'm trying to put around him. On the other hand you could do nothing, leave me to continue my investigations under the radar so that I can reveal who's responsible for everything in a way that leaves them nowhere to go."

"So you're suggesting I do nothing?"

"This is just me letting you know what's going on so that you can factor it into your investigations. I'll be continuing my own enquiries, and I'll be taking whatever actions that situations dictate."

"If you break domestic law, you'll be arrested and charged just like anybody else."

"Exactly as I would expect."

"You're a very devious woman, Ms. Price.

"You better believe it, Agent Ramirez," Saffie told her. "Sorry to spoil your Sunday. Have a safe journey home."

"How did you calculate how long it would take me to get here?"

"Just Google."

"So you must have known where I live."

"I guess I must have." She stood up and walked away, leaving the Special Agent speechless.

Chapter 29

Driving back to Mary's she felt satisfied with her day's work, although unsure where to go next.

She drove back into the farmyard just before four, and immediately turned her own phone back on. It started beeping seconds later. Looking at the screen, Felix had called three times and there were three messages.

She called Felix back as she walked inside the house.

"Where have you been?"

"Never mind, have you got any news?"

"Brett is being released this evening."

"About time. With or without conditions?"

"Without; he's been cleared."

"Do I have to collect him?"

"No, I will. I'll bring him to your house in Dunn Loring."

"What time? I'm in Harrisonburg at the moment."

"About nine p.m. I expect."

"Fine."

"Is that all you've got to say?"

"I hope you're not expecting me to thank you. And don't you or anybody else go thinking this is over because it isn't."

"Saffie, there are things at play here that you don't know about..."

"That's what I'm talking about, so until I do know about them it won't be over, ever. See you at nine." She cut him off.

"Your mom doesn't pull any punches does she, Ben." Her phone had been on speaker, and they'd been listening.

"Is Dad really coming home?!

"He better be sweetheart, or I'll start a firestorm like they didn't know was possible."

"You'd better get some grub inside you then. How about a good ole American favorite - ham, eggs, and beans with a few fries?"

"Sounds fantastic."

Checking the rest of the messages, one was from Ramirez that read, '*Okay. For the time being I'll go with option 2 and see what pans out, but if you're screwing with me your ass is mine.*"

The second was from Felix asking her to call him ASAP, and the last was from Brett telling her he'd be home tonight.

"We'd better go pack. We need to be home before your dad because he won't be able to get in - the entry codes have all been changed."

After the meal Saffie and Ben said an emotional farewell that included many grateful thanks and a promise to be back as soon as possible. The two climbed into the Wrangler and began their journey home, but not before she'd removed the false license plates.

It was eight-fifteen when they pulled through the gates to their home, and in spite of her rush to get on, she garaged the car. They grabbed their things, went inside, and Ben rushed up to his room, while Saffie, tried to straighten things around their home that she'd hastily abandoned a day or two earlier, although she couldn't have explained why; Brett wasn't houseproud.

She was excited about seeing her husband again. Apart from those few minutes in that dark Ukrainian farmhouse, she hadn't seen him for the best part of five months.

"Mom, they've taken my laptop," Ben said, interrupting her thoughts.

"I'm sorry sweetheart, that's my fault. I was in a hurry and I needed a spare one. I was going to get you a new one anyway wasn't I; I've just been too busy. Was there anything on it that you needed?"

"No; it's all in the cloud, I just wondered where it had gone."

Saffie had left the gate and front door open so when they heard the crunch of tires on the gravel they hurried to the door expecting to see Felix's car with Brett inside, but instead were three cars full of what could only have been some sort of law enforcement agents. A small hatchback pulled up behind them, and two confused looking women got out.

"Mrs. Saffron Price?" one asked, flashing his badge. "My name is Randolph T. Garfield; I'm an Intelligence Officer with the Department of Justice. I need you to come with us."

"What the Hell for?"

"You need to answer some questions."

"That's fair enough, I'll answer them here."

"We'd prefer you to answer them at our offices in Harrisonburg."

"Well it isn't convenient. I'm alone with my eight-year-old son."

"We've made arrangements for your son to be temporarily taken into care by Fairfax County Child Protective Services."

"You'll have also arranged a court order authorizing that then."

"We can do that if necessary."

"It is necessary, because if you remove that child from me against my wishes it would be unlawful, and tantamount to abduction. As he has been already traumatized by being abducted once and been the subject of a second attempt in the last week it would be an act of extreme cruelty to repeat the exercise."

"Ma'am, can we discuss this inside?"

"Do you have a warrant?"

"No, but we could get one."

"Well I suggest you do that, and as you've given me no indication as to why you want to question me, it leads me to suspect that all this is yet another part of the campaign of harassment currently underway by the telephone directory of government agencies that have been trying to destroy the lives of everybody in my family. So far, we've had the CIA, FBI, DHS, and the police. Who's next? ATF, the Department of Agriculture, Department for the Environment, or National Fish and Wildlife?"

Another car pulled into the drive and Felix stepped out followed by her gaunt looking husband with a crutch.

"What's going on here?" Brett asked, as he limped between the crowd of men in dark suits and two women who'd been looking on in bewilderment.

"Hello, darling. Welcome home. This is just the latest in the series of people being sent by our employers to intimidate us out of revealing that there's a mole from a hostile nation working inside the nation's intelligence services."

Brett turned to face Garfield. "Whoever you are, you can fuck off and leave us in peace."

"Very well, Mrs. Price, but we still need to speak to you."

"Fine, but you're not coming in this house without a warrant, and you're not removing our child. If you want to speak to me, call and arrange a convenient time and place, and I'll be there, but you should know that it will be in the presence of my lawyer. Also you'll need to give me advance notice of what you want to talk about so I can bring copies of any relevant material."

"Very well, Mrs. Price." He turned and ushered his entourage away, and there followed a kind of motorized Viennese waltz of maneuvering cars until only Felix's SUV remained.

"What are you waiting for Felix?" she said.

"I thought..."

"Well you thought wrong. Until you're prepared to talk about the shit you've been involved in trying to bring this family down, you're not welcome in this house. Now fuck off. I want to shut the gate." She slammed the door and watched the entry phone monitor to see him get in his car do a three-point turn and drive off the property.

"Jesus, Saffie, what was all that about?"

"When you've hugged your son and given me a proper kiss I'll tell you."

Brett turned to Ben, "I can't pick you up just yet pal, my leg's still quite wobbly but there's nothing stopping me giving you a big hug. Come here."

Ben sobbed and squeezed his dad for a long time, then looked up, "You've been gone such a long time Dad. I've missed you so much."

"I know buddy, and I'm really sorry I haven't been able to keep in touch, but the company is having such a tough time out there at the moment."

"The CIA you mean."

Brett looked at Saffie with a raised eyebrow.

"I'm sorry darling, but you don't know half of what's been happening here. I had no choice but to tell him."

"Never mind, Ben's a smart kid. You'd have worked it out soon enough, anyway, wouldn't you eh?" His son smiled, and he pulled his wife to him.

Their kiss was long, and their hug was tight, both their eyes full as they stood back and looked at each other.

"Do you mind if I sit down for a bit? My leg's aching like Hell, and I need some pain killers."

"Where do you want to sit, in the lounge or the kitchen?"

"Kitchen I think because I need something to eat as well."

"Didn't they feed you?"

"Not since breakfast."

"What do you want to eat?"

"A couple of eggs with some toast would be great."

"Can I get it?" Ben cried out enthusiastically.

"What, you cook now?"

"Mary taught me how to make my breakfast."

"Is that where you've been, up at the farm?"

"You've got a lot of catching up to do. I gather that the assholes haven't told you anything then?"

"To be fair I was out of it for most of the time in Kyiv. Then as soon as I got back they started treating me as if I were somehow responsible for what's been happening, without even telling me what it was. Then Homeland arrested me and questioned me for two days. Eventually I told them to fuck off, I wasn't going to answer any more questions."

"You and Mom are doing a lot of cursing lately."

Brett laughed, "I'm sorry son, but when you're surrounded by idiots and people trying to do you harm it's difficult not to get provoked. It doesn't mean it's okay for you to join in though."

Ben made his dad egg on toast, and Saffie asked Brett to talk about his mission in Ukraine.

"The agency had lost three East European field agents within a year; they were certain that there was a mole. They decided to send some fresh blood in without any connections to the existing team to try ferret the traitor out."

"And then?"

"Just as I thought I was getting somewhere, I was picked up by Hevil's mob and kept hostage until I was rescued by someone. I was in a bad way by that time, dehydrated, my wound was infected, I had a fever, and they hadn't fed me for four or five days. I was delirious, hallucinating and I didn't know what was going on, at one time I thought it was you."

"It was me, sweetheart?"

"Why didn't they tell me?"

"They didn't know, that's why?"

"Tell me now."

Saffie began to tell the tale, this time leaving nothing out except the worst details of how she dealt with the gangsters in Slovyansk. Both Brett and Ben thought her treatment of Jenkins was hilarious, but Brett was concerned to learn that he was now in America.

Brett thought it all through as he ate. "Are you thinking what I am?"

"That the US Lopez is Wilkanowicz or his agent trying to muddy the waters so that he can find a way out of whatever trouble he's in? Yes. Tell me about the breakthrough you had just before you were taken."

"I'd identified a guy who I was pretty sure was passing info back and forth."

"Did he have a name?"

"Only a cover name - *Wolf*."

Saffie pulled up the photo of Johnson on her phone, "Is this the man?"

"That's him. Is that Johnson?"

"Yes, AKA Jenkins, AKA Lopez. Not such a leap when you think about it. I looked up the name Lopez in means 'Son of Lope', Lope itself is a Spanish word deriving from the Latin lupus, meaning wolf."

They moved their discussion to the lounge where it would be more comfortable for Brett's leg, and they continued talking until late. It was only then that Brett noticed that Ben had fallen asleep.

"Why are you limping?" Brett asked her after she'd woken their son and chased him up to bed.

Saffie told him a little more detail about events in the workshop.

"They always used to tell me that people shouldn't get in your way when things got tough, but Jesus darling, I can't believe you did all that on your own."

"An old acquaintance from back in the day helped a lot by providing a car, money, gun, and information, I wouldn't have even been able to get started if it weren't for him. Then Hevil and his gang weren't exactly Mensa contenders. They behaved like complete amateurs, half-stoned, and of course I had a lot of luck."

Brett thought about what she'd told him. "Why do you think the mole is using such a hotchpotch of bumbling incompetents?"

"My guess would be he can't afford to bring anybody else in without exposing either himself or his purpose. An operation this size with professionals would be massively expensive and would leave a trail back to him. Did Homeland ever say why they were questioning you?"

"Eventually they said I was suspected of being involved in the January 6th insurrection."

"Bullshit. We were at Senator Ruben's ranch in California, and we'd been there since before New Year's."

"When they eventually told me what the problem was, that's what I told them. Come to bed, sweetheart," he said. "We can talk more in the morning."

Saffie was still trying to piece things together in her mind, as she'd climbed in beside Brett.

Chapter 30

Saffie slept shallowly and awoke almost as tired as she had been before going to bed. Somewhere on the edge of her consciousness she'd spotted an inconsistency and it was still hovering elusively at the back of her brain as she showered that morning. She was still thinking about it as she came back to the bedroom.

Brett was sitting on the side of the bed removing the dressing from his wound, allowing her to see it for the first time.

"Oh God Brett, that's awful. Why didn't you say how bad it was?"

"I didn't want to worry you."

"They told me that you were expected to make a full recovery."

"Who told you that?"

"He said his name was Staff Sergeant Spence."

"Like he would know; he's US Air Force Security, not a medic."

"It's not a straightforward bullet wound, is it?"

"It was point blank. I tried fighting back when they took me. Two of them were trying to hold me, but I broke free and grabbed the wrist of one of them and in the struggle it went off. I'm not sure if it was intentional or not. The bullet tore a big chunk of muscle away and the muzzle flash burned the wound. In the hospital they had to cut more of the muscle away. The surgeon told me that I'd probably always have some sort of limp, but I'd get most of my functionality back. I doubt I'll be playing squash or tennis again though."

"You need to have that leg looked at by someone you're confident is on your side."

"Good point. I'll call Dr. Hirani tomorrow," he agreed.

"Time for us to invest in that gym we've been talking about."

"You're right. What about your own injury?" he asked, nodding at the waterproof dressing on her leg.

"It's still painful sometimes, but it's improving, and it should heal okay and just leave a small scar. You won't be going back on field duty again with that though, so your income will drop."

"If everything you told me last night turns out to be true, then I won't be working for the company anyway, even if they'd allow me. It's an unwritten covenant that they're supposed to have our backs. What chance do any of us have if the very generals sending us into battle are consorting with the enemy to harm us? As for income, I think we both know that we could earn far more in the private sector."

"I'm glad you said that, because that's how I feel. I'd already decided to quit after this is over. Do you need help in the shower?"

He refused her offer so she went to get them something to eat, looking in on Ben on the way. He was still fast asleep but he was a huge fan of pancakes and bacon for breakfast, and she thought that the smell would soon chase him out of bed.

Brett joined her in the kitchen and took a seat. "You were very restless last night," he said.

"Sorry, did I wake you?"

"No, I got up to take some Tylenol. They gave me Zapain but I'm not putting any more of that opioid shit in my body unless I have to. I'll just work through it."

"I hope you're hungry. I've made a double batch of pancakes today."

"Hungry? I could eat a horse and its rider."

Ben appeared at the door, rubbing his eyes, and took a seat at the table without speaking.

"I didn't think you'd be long joining us. Are you still tired, sweetheart?"

"Yes, but I want to spend time with Dad." He took a swig of OJ, caught his breath, and coughed. "Can we..." He started to say and coughed again.

"That's it!"

"That's what?" Brett asked.

"The cough, Johnson in Ukraine, and Lopez in the US were both reported to have a squeaky cough, but as they can't be the same person, it begs the question, why do they have the same idiosyncrasy."

"Just part of the disguise I guess, trying to convince you that it's the same man."

"When he was Jenkins, he showed no signs of a cough."

"So if Johnson isn't the man with the real cough, then the US Lopez must be. If either of them are."

"True, and it's puzzling, but at the moment I don't know if it tells us anything."

"Did Wilkanowicz have a cough when you were with him?"

"Not that I could tell and I was with him for over an hour. Have you been debriefed by ops yet?"

"Not yet, the Homeland guys wouldn't let anyone near me except medics, and they were reluctant to do that."

"Did Homeland give you any indication of what you were being held for?"

"No, apart from that insurrection bullshit, and I'm not sure they even believed whatever it was themselves. It never felt like their hearts were in it, like they were just being assholes because that's what they do."

"Why don't you see if you can get to see a doc about that leg today instead of leaving it until tomorrow, then perhaps we go somewhere for a meal."

"What about those DoJ guys?"

"They can await my convenience, because I can be an asshole for the very same reason as them; how did you put it, they were, *just being assholes because that's how they operate*?"

"You're not an asshole."

"I can be when I'm fucked around."

"Don't you expect them to follow it up?"

"I have no idea, but if they truly believed I'd committed an offense that called for their intervention, they wouldn't have been so easy to chase away last night. It's all part of the chaff that Lopez is throwing down to distract us and whoever else away from him. I expect they'll call sometime."

Brett called their MD and explained his injury. The doctor listened to what Brett told him and rang back fifteen minutes later having arranged an appointment for him with a reconstructive surgeon later in the morning. It was at the same hospital where Saffie had been treated.

"Who makes the next move I wonder." Saffie had asked as they waited for the doctor to call back.

"It depends on whether Lopez thinks you're out of leads I guess."

"If we drop you off at the hospital, Ben and I will go and sort him out a new laptop. Is that okay? You can call me when you're ready to be picked up."

Before they left home Saffie added Brett and Ben's palm print to the security system and got them to memorize the codes.

At the hospital Saffie parked up, intending to go inside but Brett insisted he'd be okay on his own.

It didn't take long to choose the replacement laptop and Saffie and Ben were soon at the checkout with it and a few other things when her phone rang. She handed over her card and answered, putting it on speaker, "Hello?"

"Mrs. Price, this is Intelligence Officer Garfield, Department of Justice. Your interview will be at our office in Richmond at three p.m. this afternoon."

"I doubt it."

"What do you mean?"

"Because I won't be there."

"Are you being deliberately difficult, Mrs. Price?"

"No, are you?"

"You asked me to tell you when and where the interview would be held; that's what I'm doing."

"Just a minute I'm paying for something in a store. Thank you, could you help carry it to my car while I finish this conversation? Thank you."

Saffie and Ben led the way to the car,

"Where were we? Yes that's right. Officer Garfield, what I asked, was for you to call and arrange a convenient time and place for a meeting, and when it happened it would be in the presence of my lawyer. I also told you that I would need advance notice of what you want to talk about so I can bring copies of any relevant material. Instead of that, you've tried to ambush me at short notice and expect me to make a four hour return journey to answer questions on a subject that you haven't yet told me. That venue isn't convenient, and what's more you haven't given me the opportunity to talk to my attorney nor gather any relevant material. So if anybody is being difficult in this Officer Garfield, it's you."

"Thank you, young man, have a good day," she said, handing the store guy a ten. "Now, my attorney is Franklyn Cohen of Chesham, Chesham and Adelstein. They're in Arlington - look them up. That will be all for today; I'm busy," and she ended the call.

"That's very brave, Mom, the way you talk to these important people."

"Ben, a lot of these people are a great deal less important than they like to believe they are."

They were just getting in the car when they heard a young boy's voice, "Hi Ben." They turned to see his friend Josh coming toward them with his father.

"Hi Josh. What's up?"

"Dad's just bought me a PS4 for my birthday."

"Awesome, but I thought your birthday was next month."

"It is, but Dad said he might have to be away for work, so he bought it early."

The two boys went into a huddle discussing the merits of the PS4 compared with other games consoles on the market.

"How are things Saffron?" Josh's father, Bridger Davis asked. She knew him vaguely from Langley; she thought he'd been attached to the same section as Brett at one time but not any longer.

"Pretty fraught to be honest."

"How's Brett, I heard he's back?"

Her phone buzzed with an incoming call from Brett, with the traffic noise she put it on speaker, "Sorry, just a minute."

'I'm going to be a bit longer than I thought; they want me to have a scan. Why don't you and Ben go home and I'll catch a cab back when I'm finished.'

"Don't worry about the cab, we'll come and sit with you while you wait. We can order in a Chinese for tonight and eat out another time."

"Sorry Bridger. You were asking about Brett. He's a bit worse for wear but I think he'll be okay."

"Look we just decided to go see a movie, how would young Ben like to join us?"

"That's very kind. Would you like that, Ben?"

"Yes please, Mom."

She gave him a $50 bill and told him to get Josh some popcorn and a drink. "Thanks Bridger."

"No problem, I'll bring him back later."

Suddenly she was on her own again and at a loss what to do. Then she thought, 'Sod it, I'll just go and sit with Brett while he's waiting for his scan like I said.'

Chapter 31

Climbing back in her car, she watched Bridger drive past with the two boys in the back. Bridger was on the phone. Other than hands-free, she wasn't a big fan of cell phone use when driving, especially with kids in the car. She started the engine and followed him toward the exit; he went one way and she the other. It was less than two miles to the hospital.

As she slowed for the lights at Washington and Glebe they changed in time to allow the two cars ahead of her to drive through without stopping. She followed on behind.

When the battered pickup, travelling at more than 40 m.p.h., slammed into her driver's door, she had no warning. Had she been wearing her seat belt the instant inflation of the airbags might have done more to stun her. As it was the side airbag cushioned the impact against her left side enough to avoid the worst of the collision, as it was designed to do. Thrown almost into the passenger footwell, she managed to remain conscious and spatially aware. Gathering her thoughts, she realized that other than a new pain in her left hip and the wound in her left thigh she didn't think she'd been severely injured.

Seconds later she heard gunshots; sounds that she hadn't expected to hear in daytime in any busy street so close to the nation's capital. The thump of bullets into the car made her grab for her purse that had fallen beside her. Pulling her gun she quickly glanced out the window and saw the gunman take one last shot and run for a Lexus sedan waiting with the passenger door open.

Throwing the passenger door open she leapt from the car and, taking a two-handed grip of her gun, shouted, "Federal Agent, stop where you are and drop the gun!"

Instead of doing what she ordered, he turned and lifted his weapon.

Saffie fired two quick shots and the man fell to the ground. Shifting her aim to the driver of the Lexus she hoped she'd made her intent clear. The driver of the pickup ran past her and attempted to jump in the back of the sedan but the car was already moving too fast and directly toward her. After two more shots she threw herself out of its path before it collided with her BMW. She instantly regretted her instinctive reaction; the man would almost certainly have vital information; if she'd killed him it would have been lost.

Leaping to her feet she ran to the driver's door, her gun held ready, but it was obvious it wouldn't be needed, the left side of the man's head was missing. She immediately scanned the area for the pickup driver, but he was nowhere to be seen.

Turning to look at her car she was sure of one thing; that it wouldn't be going anywhere again except on the back of a low-loader.

For an area where there would normally be a clamor of midday traffic noise, the silence that followed was eerie. Inevitably though, it wasn't long before the sound of police sirens split the air.

Saffie waited until the first police cruiser skidded to a halt, then dropped the gun, stepped away from it and held her hands in the air.

The first cop jumped from the car, "Lay face down on the floor, hands behind your head and cross your ankles."

There was no question that she'd argue, and neither did she protest when he cuffed her.

"I'm a federal agent, my ID is in my purse in the BMW. The whole thing will have been recorded on street cams, and no doubt there are at least a dozen witnesses. The pickup rammed me from the left as I was crossing on green, the Lexus came from the right and stopped, a guy got out, started firing at me and I shot him. Then the Lexus driver drove right at me, I fired at him and he crashed into my Beamer. The driver of the pickup got away."

By the time she'd finished giving her full account, three more cruisers had arrived, the traffic had built up and a crowd of rubberneckers had gathered. She was soon allowed to stand, but only long enough to be ushered into the back of a police car.

Four hours later, after answering a lot of questions, most of them more than once, her account had been verified by street cameras, and several eyewitnesses. She was handed her purse back, although not her gun. They also gave her the bags of things she'd bought from the computer store before allowing her to leave.

She dialed Brett's number wondering what he must be thinking.

"Hi darling."

"What the fuck Saffie? Did you get caught up in that gunfight in Arlington today?"

"Yeah, sorry. Did Ben get back okay?"

"Bridger just dropped him off. Are you okay?"

"I guess. My hip and thigh hurt like a bastard but other than that I'm fine. I'll get a cab and be home in about half an hour."

She called ahead to let Brett know she was near, and the gate opened as her cab approached. He and Ben came out to meet her. She handed the bags from the computer store to Ben, and in spite of a limp even more pronounced than earlier in the day, she led the way inside with a determined expression on her face.

"Are you okay, Mom?"

"I'm fine. It was some crooks escaping from a crime scene who jumped the lights. I happened to get in the way." She said it with an attempt at a reassuring smile.

"We were frightened you might have been shot."

"I'm sure somebody would have told you if I had been. Why don't you take your new computer up to your room while I have a talk to Dad? It should be ready to go once you've logged onto the Wi-Fi, but you know how to do that, don't you?"

"Of course I do."

When Ben had excitedly rushed upstairs, Saffie stormed into the lounge and poured herself a large Jack Daniels. "Whoever's behind this is going to die. Ben was supposed to be in the car with me. They were lying in wait for me, so must have had some idea where I was going and which route I was going to take."

"Maybe there was another tracker on your car?"

"There is a tracker on it and in my wallet but I don't see how it could have told them where I was headed or what route I was taking."

"What about a tail?"

"It's not out of the question, but since all this began I've been hyper-careful, and how would a tail have been able to be in front of me without prior knowledge?"

"Why was Bridger at the store? That's a pretty spooky coincidence isn't it?"

"Josh said they were there to get him an early birthday present because Bridger was going to be away for the real one next month."

"Why would he have to be away for work? Bridger's job doesn't involve field work."

"Maybe a course or something," Saffie speculated. "You're not thinking that he could have set me up are you?"

"Just considering it as a possibility. The route you were taking to hospital was the shortest and most direct, a reverse of the same one you would have taken after dropping me off. Is that right?"

"Yes."

They looked at each other as they thought through the same processes. At that point he hushed her and led her through to the garage. "Is there any way that Bridger could have known where you were going next?"

She stopped to think about it. "I was with him when you called to say you were going to be delayed. I had you on speaker, so yes he could have known. What's more he was on the phone as he turned out of the car park, and he'd have seen which direction I turned."

"Let's think this through. If we say for the sake of discussion that Bridger did somehow set you up, does that make him involved in everything else?"

"I don't know. He works in the Logistics section nowadays. There's no connection between what either of us do and what he does."

Brett called Ben and in the normal manner of an eight-year-old, he thundered down the stairs to join them. "What's up Dad?"

They ushered him into the garage.

"When you got in the car with Josh and his dad today, do you remember Bridger using his phone?"

"Yes, he said to be quiet while he made a call."

"Do you remember anything he said?"

"Nothing important. He asked the person what they were going to do and if this would be the end of it. Then he just said, 'North' and hung up."

"Thank you, sweetheart," Saffie said.

"Do you think Josh's dad had something to do with what happened today then?"

"We're just eliminating people, that's all. How are you getting on with your new computer?"

"It's awesomely fast, Mom, and it's got Windows 11, which is a bit different, but otherwise much the same as the old one, thank you."

"You're welcome, sweetheart."

He ran back upstairs.

"If that means what it sounds like, it's possible he was coerced, and may even not have known what was intended," Brett pointed out.

"If that's true, then we need to find out what sort of leverage somebody has over him."

"Is it possible that we've somehow been bugged again?"

"I guess it's possible, but I don't see how," she told him.

"Neither of us are likely to be able to investigate him inside Langley at the moment. Perhaps we could start by looking elsewhere. What do we know about his family?"

"His wife is called Brooke. I've only met her a couple of times when I've taken Josh home or she's returned Ben here, and once at a parent-teacher meeting. She has an accent that I can't place. Josh is their only kid."

"Extended family?"

"I think his mother and sister live in Oakton. I remember her saying that she'd had to look after his mom when the sister was in hospital for a minor op, and they were quite close."

"Hostages maybe?"

"Possible. But we need to think about this before we do anything," she said, as they walked back inside. "In the meantime, tell me how you got on at the hospital."

"There isn't any surgery that they can do that will make any significant difference. She told me that the wound was healing well, and the hospital in Kyiv had done a good job. It's never going to be a hundred percent, but if I start stretching it as much as I can bear until I can stand long enough to do regular exercise then I should get most functionality back. She's going to arrange some physiotherapy. How's your side?"

Saffie loosened her pants, pushed them down to her knees and lifted her t-shirt. The bruises around the stick injury were as angry as ever, but the new ones on her hip and side were only just beginning.

"Jesus, Saffie, you're a tough SOB, and that's for sure. Most people would be in hospital with an injury like that."

"Make that a DOB. It ain't so bad; a week or two and it'll be fine. We get pretty beat up on fight night sometimes don't we?"

"I'm going to make enquiries about that gym in the morning, but I'll start with a treadmill."

As they were eating their evening meal Saffie said to Ben, "I didn't give you your other present today, did I?"

"What other present Mom? It's not my birthday."

"It's not a birthday present; it's a reward for being such a brave and supportive son."

"What is it?"

"It's in that box over there next to the coffee maker."

Ben rushed over to pick it up. "It's a cell phone! Thank you Mom, and you Dad."

"I'll help you set it up after dinner."

"You always said I couldn't have one until I was ten."

"Sometimes things change, and as you keep telling me, you're getting big now."

Later that evening she called Linda.

"That was quick," her friend said.

"What do you mean?"

"I just sent you an email with that other stuff you asked for."

"Fantastic, Linda, that's great."

"It took a bit longer because he's been very busy, but I think you'll be happy with the result. He went a bit beyond your instructions so there's a lot of stuff."

"Amazing, I'll get stuck into that first thing tomorrow. Do I owe you any money?"

"Yes I'm afraid so. Only another thousand though if that's okay, but there's no hurry, so if you want to pay me in cash again that would be alright."

"Actually that might be useful. We'll need to get together soon."

"Did you see that Wallace has been arrested?"

"No, I've been a bit busy. I've another question. This work the guy in Ukraine has done - do you know anybody here in the States who does the same sort of thing?"

"I do, but she's completely under the radar and a bit of an oddball. She won't take instructions by phone or electronically and she only takes payment in cash. She's not expensive, but she only accepts commissions for what she considers worthy causes."

"That's weird."

"She says it's her little battle against the dark arts of the state. You'll like her. I'll send you her details in another email."

"What was that about?" Brett asked.

"You'll remember Linda Baker; she's been helping me out," Saffie replied.

Chapter 32

"I'm going out," Saffie told Brett as he came out of their shower room, "I doubt I'll be long, but you and Ben can go ahead and take breakfast without me."

"Where are you going at this ungodly hour?"

"Meeting up with a friend of Linda's."

Having left the tracker from her wallet at home, she climbed in the Wrangler and set the GPS for the Silver Diner, just a few minutes away. It was only six-fifty when she arrived and the old-style American diner was still closed so she turned the engine off and waited watching the door.

A knock on the passenger window startled her and she turned to see a young girl with pink hair and multiple piercings in her ears, eyebrows, and nose grinning at her. She looked no older than nineteen. Saffie lowered the window. "Are you Mad Mom?" she was asked.

"I'm bloody furious, you must be Patsy Cline."

"I am today."

"Climb in," Saffie told her and unlocked the door. "So how do we do this?"

"First you tell me your story; then I decide if I want to help. You need to be very convincing."

Saffie proceeded to tell her an abridged version of all that had happened and Patsy listened carefully without interrupting.

"So I'm guessing you're some sort of spook, is that right?"

"That's right."

"So why do you need my help?"

"Because it's one or more other spooks that are doing this to me. And if it were only me I'd deal with it, but they've gone after my family, shot my husband, abducted my son, and yesterday they tried to kill me when my son was supposed to be in the car."

"Okay, I'm convinced, what is it you want me to do?"

Saffie handed Patsy a Post-it note, "This is the cellphone number of my son's friend. I'm hoping that his father's number will be on there, and he's the one I'm interested in."

"Hey, this isn't some kinda love affair thing is it?"

"No, it isn't. I'm reasonably certain that he set me up for yesterday's assassination attempt. I don't know why. He's a work colleague of sorts although we've never worked closely together. I suspect he's being coerced, and I need to find out who he's been speaking to."

"Is that all?"

"Well for the time being, yes."

"I don't like doing revisits."

"I think this is just a small part of what's going on. How much do you want for this?"

"Call it five hundred."

"Five hundred? I'd have thought at least four times that."

"If it's more complicated than I expect I may ask for more. I'll send it to the email Linda gave me okay?"

"That's great, how long will it take?"

"This afternoon okay?"

"What? As soon as that?"

"If I get stuck in a tutorial, maybe tonight or tomorrow morning latest."

After counting out five $100 bills, Saffie added two more.

"Just five hundred, then if you're happy with what I do you can think about a tip. But you can buy me breakfast if you want."

"Deal."

Patsy ordered a huge breakfast while Saffie chose an egg and bacon muffin.

"You're a strange one."

"If you're trying to figure out what makes me tick, don't bother. I'm just a kid trying to work her way through college. I don't want to wait table, flip burgers, or wash cars so I'm doing something I'm good at."

"But you're charging peanuts, and you could be making a fortune."

"If I charged big money, people would start flagging me up to the boys in blue. I'm earning all I need to get me through to graduation without busting my ass. It's enough."

"Okay, I get it, I think. I admire your ethic. Can I drop you off?"

"No thanks."

As she reversed the Jeep into the garage, Brett came through from the house, without his crutch but limping heavily. He waited for her to get out.

"We need to do some shopping."

"How do you mean? We normally do our grocery shop online."

"I don't mean for food. We need to replace the Beamer, and at the moment we're without a handgun between us. Given everything that's been going on around us lately I don't think that's a situation we should maintain."

"I get your point, but we do have some guns; apart from the shotguns and your dad's assault rifle I mean."

"Where from?"

"Your spare is in the gun safe in the trunk along with the ones I confiscated from the gangsters in Richmond."

"If they're connected to a crime then we'd have a lot of questions to answer if we used them."

"That's true, so perhaps a visit to the gun store for me before we go to find a new Beamer eh?"

The stop at the gun store was quick. They were served by the same guy as on her last visit and he didn't ask to see her badge. Walking out of the shop, Ben asked, "What happens when you get your other guns back, Mom?"

"Mom can sell them back to the shop or keep them as spares," Brett told him.

Just as they climbed in the car, Saffie's cellphone rang. It was her supervising agent. "Meredith, what can I do for you?"

"I need you to come into the office right away."

"Whatever for?"

"I think it would be best if we discussed it in my office."

"Care to tell me what it's about?"

"Like I say it would be better face to face."

"It's not a great time right now," she said, already having an idea. "As you should know, I'm on sick leave myself with an injury, my husband is recovering from a serious gunshot wound acquired in the line of duty, and I have an eight-year-old son to look after. So, unless you can tell me why you need me in your office so urgently, it will have to wait."

"You're being suspended."

"I see. Am I allowed to know why."

"You abused your position."

"What the Hell are you talking about?"

"You attempted to detain someone and fired your weapon claiming federal authority."

"You're kidding right? Some guys attempt to kill me, failed on the first and second attempt, then when they try to escape, instead of shooting them dead straightaway, I try to stop them getting away but I'm forced to shoot them just to stay alive, and you're suspending me?"

"You know the rules Saffron. It's out of my hands. I can tell you more when you come in."

"I'm too busy, you'll have to wait."

"You need to hand in your gun and your badge."

"As you ought to know, my gun is my own, but if you want my badge in such a hurry, you'll have to come and collect it, because like I say, I'm busy. If there's nothing else, have a nice day."

"If you're not careful you'll end up being fired."

"Which is, I suspect, what the assholes behind all this want anyway, so why not cut to the chase, and just do it. I'd quite enjoy standing up and giving my account in open court about how the CIA attempts to have its own agents killed."

"I don't know what you're talking about."

"No, you don't. Bye for now Meredith."

Brett laughed. "They're getting desperate now. Where are we going car shopping?"

"Let's try that place on the Lee Highway. It's close and they always seem to have a good range of stock."

Chapter 33

An hour and a half later they were on their way home having just paid $55,000 for a one-year-old all-wheel drive BMW X5 to be home delivered by the end of the day and fitted with a gun safe.

"Are we really rich, Mom?"

"Why do you ask?"

"Because you just spent all that money on a car and nearly a thousand dollars at the gun store on top of my new laptop and cellphone."

"We're not megarich but I guess we are quite wealthy by a lot of people's standards. We've both held good jobs for a long time, and I inherited a lot from Grandpa Walden," Saffie explained. "Having said that, a big chunk of the cost of that car will be covered by the insurance on the one that was wrecked yesterday, your computer was paid for by the guy whose fault it was you needed one, and the guns will be paid for by the bastards who're giving us all this crap, although they don't know it yet."

As soon as they were home Saffie went straight to the study and tried to access the immigration database again to discover if Bridger Davis had travelled to Ukraine in the last few weeks. Unsurprisingly they'd removed her authorization. She explained what she'd been trying to do to Brett and he attempted to do it with the same result.

"Understandable I suppose," Brett remarked, "But I think I might have a way round that."

"How's that?"

"You're not the only one with connected friends you know. Give me a minute." He logged on to his own laptop and looked something up, then dialed a number on his phone.

"Heinrich?...It's Rider....I'm good thanks, you?...That's good....No, not in the immediate future....I need a favor. For reasons I don't want to talk about at the moment, I need to find something out about a fellow yank and I don't want anybody to know that I'm looking....I want to know if he's travelled to Ukraine in the last month....Chances are he'd have changed flights at Frankfurt and or Cologne....Bridger Davis....What, right now? That would be fantastic, thanks." Saffie watched as Brett waited.

"That was quick....He did? Really?...That's really helpful, Heinrich, thanks, I owe you one."

He sighed. "Bridger made two trips to Ukraine in the last two months. Four weeks ago BWI to Kyiv via Cologne he returned ninety-six hours later. The second ten days ago BWI to Kryvyi Rih returning via Frankfurt after forty-two hours."

"Got him," Saffie said.

"What now though?"

"One of two options. Either we challenge Bridger or look into him a bit deeper."

"Are we agreed that the most likely scenario is that somebody has got something on Bridger?" Brett said.

"Sure."

"If we confront him now it won't help him get out from under and it won't help us move forward right? And we haven't got enough to nail him."

"Right, so we dig deeper. Where do we start?"

"You seem to know him better than me. What do you think?"

"How about we pay his mom and sister a welfare visit?"

He smiled, knowing that it's what she'd been aiming at all along. "Tomorrow morning then, we need to spend time with Ben."

"How about we go for that meal we missed out on yesterday and see what comes up?

"Great idea," he said and shouted upstairs. "Ben you want to go out to eat?"

"Yeah! Can we go to that new Taco place? Francine at school said it was really nice."

"Sure. We're leaving in twenty minutes."

"What are we going to do with Ben if we're going to Oakton?" Saffie asked.

"We can decide that in the morning. Let's go eat first. I'm hungry," Brett said decisively. "You ready Ben?"

"Just coming."

"What have you been doing?" Saffie asked.

"Just chatting to Josh on my phone. Can he come over tomorrow? His Mom's not well and his Dad's got to work?"

"Sure, I guess that would be okay. Dad will be here, but I've got to go out for a while. What's wrong with his mom?"

"He says she keeps having anxiety attacks, whatever they are."

"I think it's a kind of depression. That sort of thing makes it difficult to cope sometimes. It will be good for Josh to spend an hour or two out of the house and it'll give his mom a break."

The Taco restaurant wasn't crowded so they were offered a table as soon as they arrived. They placed their orders and Brett took Ben to the bathroom which was upstairs. While she was waiting Saffie picked up a newspaper left by a previous customer.

The main story was of the collapse of a twelve-story beachfront condominium in Florida - sixty-four people were confirmed dead with over a hundred unaccounted for. The Covid pandemic was also dominating with statistics and conflicting claims about the effectiveness of vaccines. At the bottom of the front page was a small piece, '*CIA Agent in Arlington Shootout – Two Dead, See Page 3*'. She turned the page. There was a picture of the three wrecked vehicles with cops speaking to a woman that she knew was her, but few others would recognize, if only for the chemical dust from the airbags still covering her face.

She read the report and thought, 'Oh well, could have been worse. At least they've got the facts right. That's a first.' She folded the paper and laid it to one side as the boys returned.

"So what's happening in the morning then, Ben?" Brett asked.

"I said we'd pick Josh up about nine. Is that okay?"

"Sure, I can pick him up before I go out," Saffie said.

"He wants me to help him set up his new PlayStation before we come back here to ours. He doesn't know how to do it; he's never owned one before."

"That's okay, there's no emergency for my chores tomorrow."

By the time they arrived home from the restaurant Patsy's email had arrived in the inbox of her anonymous email account. She made her apologies to Brett and Ben and disappeared into the study to read it.

Surprised at the detail in the comprehensive and professionally presented report, Saffie settled down to read and absorb the implications.

For somebody with a career in the intelligence industry, Bridger Davis had made a catalogue of what can only be described as schoolboy security errors. By recovering the numbers of the calls and messages to and from Bridger's personal cell phone, Patsy had identified his wife's cell phone, and from that discovered he'd used a burner to call her. That was the phone where Patsy had uncovered the motherlode. Bridger had used it to call his home, wife, and son. He'd then used that same burner to call several other numbers including whoever was in charge of the team that had attempted to assassinate her. Patsy's hack revealed an undeleted text thread with the guy who was obviously his controller, *Wolf*.

'SP is becoming a problem, and we need to discourage any further interference. I'll take care of the details but I need you to coordinate. I'll send instructions, keep this phone turned on, charged, and close by.'

Then the following day, the day of the assassination attempt:

'She's taking Rider to the Virginia Hosp, on George Mason Drive and going from there to buy the boy a laptop, probably at Staples. I need you to engineer a spontaneous meeting and find out where she's going next. Call me on 703 503 4356 as soon as you know – SP will leave home soon. Don't fuck up.'

'What are you going to do?'

'Not your concern, just do your job, or...'

Then later that day:

'Today's attempt failed. Remain on standby.'

There was a single call to the unlisted number referred to but several calls to and from Wolf going back three weeks and a single text five weeks earlier. That read, '*Cometh the hour, cometh the man. Your hour will be soon.*'

Patsy said she'd tried to get more from Wolf and Davis's burners prior to that first text without success and she speculated that it was the first time either had been used, and that Davis had been alerted to activate his by other means.

However, the phone used by the attempted killer had called four other unlisted numbers she suspected were burners.

Saffie tried to absorb the enormity of what she'd just read. Someone was still able to hear what was being said inside her house. She printed the relevant page and walked through to the lounge where Ben and Brett were watching a baseball game on the TV. She waited until Brett looked up and nodded her head to summon him out of the room. He stood up and followed her to the kitchen.

Handing him the sheet of paper she said, "I was thinking of trying this recipe tomorrow. What do you think?"

He quickly read it then looked at her with astonishment. Before he could say anything she put her finger to her lips and pointed to her phone and to the pocket where he kept his own.

He nodded and took the pen reserved for writing shopping lists and wrote on the paper, '*Yours, mine, or both?*' "It looks great sweetheart. Have you got all the ingredients?"

She wrote, '*Yours I think but we can't take any chances.*' "Most I think, I'll have a look. I can always nip out to the supermarket first thing."

"You're already going out to pick up Josh. I can go to the supermarket while you're out and get anything you need." He wrote, '*And see if you're being followed.*'

"Are you sure your leg is good enough to drive?"

"Sure, it's my left leg. It should be fine."

"Go and watch the game with Ben. I'll bring us a snack and a drink. Beer okay for you?"

"Great thanks, sweetheart."

Throughout the rest of the day and evening they maintained the charade, pretending they had no idea they could be overheard.

Fortunately, Ben didn't spot the charade.

Chapter 34

They'd both left their smart phones downstairs when they went to bed; they hadn't wanted anybody listening in while they made love for the first time in more than four months. One of Saffie's burner phones provided an alarm for them to ensure they were awake.

After their showers and before they went down for breakfast they decided on their plan of action and then continued playacting through breakfast. Ben continued to be completely oblivious that anything was happening.

At eight-forty Brett said, "I'm going to Giant now darling; I want to do some reading up on gym equip.m. ent while you're out. Is it just fresh garlic and cilantro you need?"

"That's all my love."

Leaving his phone on the side he went into the garage and taking the BMW he drove out through the gate and parked a few streets away on the route to Davis's house. They had no idea whether Bridger would be at home but had agreed plans to deal with either of the possibilities.

Saffie was reasonably confident that her phone had not been hacked but was taking no chances and took it with her when they left to pick up Josh in case her location was being tracked. She maintained a consistent chat with Ben hoping to distract his attention when they passed Brett in the new car. Thankfully he didn't spot it.

A gardener was digging a rose bed as she drove onto the drive. He smiled and nodded as she passed, and she responded with her own smile and a wave. Before they walked to the door of the luxurious Davis house, Saffie left her smartphone in the car, taking only a burner inside. When she rang the bell, Josh's mother opened the door with Josh by her side. She looked pale and drawn, and didn't speak at first.

"Hi Brooke," Saffie cheerily said. "I gather that Ben is going to give Josh a hand with his PlayStation before we leave. Is it okay if I come in and wait?"

"I guess," she said, still revealing the remnants of an East European accent.

"Give us a chance to get to know each other a bit better eh?"

"I guess."

She led them into the lounge.

"Has Bridger left for work?"

"No, he's in the study at the moment."

Her burner phone buzzed with an incoming text from Brett, she glanced at the screen, '*Black Dodge Durango 50yds from the drive to your right. One person inside.*'

"You've not been well I understand. How are you today?"

"Okay, I guess."

"That's good. It's difficult for the partners of company agents sometimes, especially when they have to go away for long periods."

"Bridger doesn't have to go away; he's based here at Langley."

"I thought that must have changed. Someone from my team mentioned he was sure he'd seen him in Kyiv several weeks ago. He normally has such an eye for detail. Unusual for him to make a mistake like that."

"He might have had to go somewhere briefly without telling me the destination."

"That must be it, and the same when he was seen at Frankfurt disembarking from an inbound flight from Ukraine ten days ago as well I expect. You have a lovely house; have you lived here long?"

"We bought it five years ago."

"Where did you live before?"

"Mount Daniel."

"Oh not far then. Brett and I had a rental in Bluemont, but we moved to Dunn Loring when it was time for Ben to start school. We were lucky; my dad gave us the money for the deposit. Property around here is so expensive don't you think?"

"Because it's so close to the capital I guess."

"You're right of course."

"Do you have family close by?"

"My mother and sister live in Oakton."

"Really, that's nice. I remember you telling me that Bridger's mother and sister live there too, don't they?"

"Er yes they do; of course I meant to say that..."

"Hello Saffron," Bridger said from the doorway.

"Oh hi, Bridger. Brooke and I were just having a chat while the boys were sorting out that PlayStation thing."

Saffie could see he was uncomfortable, but she thought she might be onto something. "Brooke was just telling me about her sister and mother living in Oakton, or was it yours Bridger, I forget?"

"It's Brooke's. Look Brooke's not been well lately. It might be best if we let her rest for a bit."

"Yes of course. Sorry, Brooke, it was very insensitive of me. Perhaps we could go somewhere to chat then, Bridger. There was something I wanted to run past you."

"Come into the study then. What do you want to talk about."

"I wanted you to run your eyes over this." She handed him another printout of what she'd shown Brett the day before, but with additional instructions in a larger bold font added above.

'Don't speak, just take any phones you have on you out of the room and put them somewhere that anyone listening-in won't be able to overhear anything we say. Then come straight back here and close the door. I'll run a bug detector over this room, then we can talk.'

He went white and she thought for a moment that he was going to faint. The scan with the bug detector produced nothing, but when he returned to the room she was holding her gun.

"Wh-what are you going to do? I can explain..."

"Just shut the fuck up, Bridger. Shut the door and sit down," she told him as she set her iPad on the desk with him in the frame. "If you were about to say you can explain, you bet your fucking miserable treacherous life you're going to explain, but if you think you can excuse what you've done you can think again. The day before yesterday you took part in a conspiracy to have me killed. You're colluding with an agent of a foreign power in an operation that's led to the deaths of at least three CIA agents overseas. Your life as an agent in the CIA is over. Whether you get away without the death penalty may entirely depend upon what you do next; in particular, what you tell me during the next few minutes."

Davis was crying, "I never intended..."

"Forget it, just tell me everything, right from the beginning."

For the next hour or more he told her an extraordinary tale of entrap.m. ent that had begun with a misstep ten years earlier. In a brief and unsuccessful career as a field agent whilst on an op in Moldova he met Brooke, a language student from Chisinau - at the time her name was Bettina. They fell for each other, but after the op had fallen apart he was sent home. Instead of going through official channels to get her a visa to join him in the States, and chance a possible refusal, he made the stupid decision to talk someone inside US Customs and Border Protection (CBP) into getting her a fake ID.

The problem he had was that most of those types of semi-official fake ID sources are quickly discovered and immediately shut down by CBP. On this occasion when a CIA agent was flagged up as involved, it was reported to Langley. Someone there, probably Wolf, whoever he was, asked them not to do anything.

Brooke, as she became, travelled to the US and they thought they'd gotten away with it. However, she missed her divorced mother and young sister so much, she threatened to return to her home country. Not being able to bear the thought of being without her, Bridger chose to add to his list of felonies by using the same source to get fake IDs for her mother and sister.

Saffie knew that Wolf should have at the very least limited what Bridger had access to from that point and had everything he was doing monitored, in case this was an attempt to turn him by another country. The only logical explanation for Wolf's failure to do that was to keep Bridger as his own personal sleeper, his fallback fall guy for use if he was at risk of exposure himself.

Without exposing his own identity, he was approached by someone claiming to be an agent from Professional Standards and acting on behalf of the DDO. He told Davis that if he'd act as his personal whistleblower by reporting every transgression, wrongdoing, peccadillo, and deviation from the rules by the people in his section, his immigration rule-breaking would remain unreported. Over the next few years, that's exactly what he did.

If the fake IDs were the extent of his crimes, it might have been worth his while putting his hands up as soon as he was told to start committing crimes. However, unbeknownst to him at first, Wolf had laid a bear trap that cut off any hope of any easy way out. A bank account had been opened in the name of Brooke's mother with Bridger as one of the signatories. Periodical payments of significant amounts of money had been paid into the account by Langley appearing to have been authorised by Davis. Several small withdrawals were also made seemingly by him as well. It had been happening for more than two years before Davis discovered it. By this time he was being directly *handled* remotely by Wolf. Having told him about the account, Wolf convinced him that it was a reward for all the good work he'd been doing.

At this point in the tale, Saffie thought that Davis must be the dumbest secret agent that the agency had ever recruited. Instead of leaving the money untouched and owning up, he began to spend it. Much of the cost of their luxurious home had been paid for with that money.

The first sign that things were going to get really serious was when out of the blue, he was ordered by his boss to fly to Kyiv with a confidential file to pass to an agent working out of the Embassy. Except the agent he was to meet wasn't working out of the embassy at all; it was White Angelor Johnson as Saffie knew him to be. Before he flew out, Wolf instructed him that while he was there he was to travel to Slovyansk with Johnson and assist him to recruit a gang of criminals and pay them $10,000 from his mother-in-law's account to do something on the agency's behalf. Then if it was completed satisfactorily within four days, he was to pay them a further ten thousand via Johnson. However, after the first stage was completed he received instructions from Langley ordering him to return home immediately and the second $10,000 was never paid. Wolf assured him that the payment would be made by another agent, but it never happened.

"Did you know that the job was to kidnap Brett?"

"Not until it was too late. We went to a nightclub in Slovyansk and White Angel showed me a photo of the gangster Novak Hevil and waited outside whilst I went in to speak to the gangster and persuade him to speak to White Angel who I was to call Lopez. It wasn't until the conversation between them started that I realized what the job was."

"Did you learn anything more about Lopez?"

"He was a slimy little man. When I protested about what we'd just done, he told me to shut up. He said that I was now complicit in the abduction of a CIA agent, and if I reported it, Wolf could readily implicate me. Then he told me that Hevil had already killed one agent on Wolf's orders and so I could easily be associated with that too."

Davis explained that the second journey to Ukraine was made when guilt drove him to fly to Ukraine on his own accord and attempt to pay off the gangster so they'd release Brett. Wolf intervened and under threat of exposure, ordered him home before he was able to do it. The day after he returned Ben was abducted.

While Bridger had been talking Brett had sent another text. '*Our friend in the black car has been taken away by the boys and girls in blue.*'

She texted back, 'I'm nearly done here, go and *buy us two new smart phones and we'll see you at home when we're finished.*'

"Right then, Bridger, tell me about the cough."

"I don't know what that was about. Wolf told me to instruct White Angel how he was to disguise himself for the meeting with the gangster. Padding under his shirt and in his pants, a wig, and glasses. And he said it was important that he should use a squeaky cough every so often.

"Were you there when they arranged the kidnapping?"

"Yes but I was told not to interfere."

"Do you have any idea who Wolf is?"

"No, he must be someone high up at Langley I've always thought it was Patryk Wilkanowicz but I really don't know. I've been too scared to try and find out."

"Okay then, Bridger, this is what happens now. For the immediate future you're going to carry on exactly as you were before. If you want to have any chance at all of avoiding death row you won't tell anyone about this conversation, especially not Wolf. My best advice is not to even tell your wife; she looks about ready to crack up as it is. If she wants to know what we've been talking about, tell her that I was pouring my heart out to you and asking if you could think of anybody at Langley who could be behind what's been happening to my family. Tell Wolf the same thing if he asks."

"What's going to happen to me and my family?"

"If you tell Wolf that you've been uncovered, the likelihood is that he'll have you all whacked and try to blame it on me or Brett."

"Oh God, how long much longer can this go on for?"

"Until I've found out who Wolf is," she told him. "I've a pretty good idea already but I don't have quite enough proof. Do you still want me to take Josh back with us?

"Yes please. I'll have to go into the office now; I'm late already."
"Are you ready to go boys?" Saffie called up the stairs.

Chapter 35

When she turned her phone back on there were three missed calls and a voice message from her lawyer. She didn't respond, but turned it off, removed the SIM, put it in the new phone and called him back.

"Franklyn, sorry I missed you; things have been manic. I'm guessing you've had a call from the DoJ."

"Yes, they're going crazy, say you're being obstructive, and are threatening to have you arrested."

"Interesting; did they give you any indication what they might want to arrest me for?"

"They were being very evasive but were intimating federal crimes."

"This should be interesting then because I have evidence of a whole catalogue of federal crimes being committed by someone in the CIA, and they sure as Hell weren't committed by me. I need to talk this through with you before we sit down with them."

"Exactly what I was about to say, I've made an appointment for them to interview you here at four p.m. Can you get here by two?"

"Sure, but you might find you need to clear some space on your desk once you've heard what I've got to say."

"This sounds like it's going to be quite costly for you?"

"Oh yes. But I won't be the one settling the bill."

Brett had been preparing some lunch for them all while she was on the phone.

"Do you think Franklyn would be happy to act for both of us?"

"If he thinks he's going to get paid twice, he'll bite your hand off. Tell me how you managed to get the cops to take the Durango guy away."

"I made an anonymous call and told them I'd seen him fitting a suppressor to a gun."

"That was a bit specific. What if he doesn't have a suppressor?"

"He had one alright. I watched him screw it on his gun;" Brett explained. "What's most interesting is, he didn't follow you; he was already there."

She thought about that. "Any idea who he is?"

"You'll never guess."

"Go on."

"Remember John Atkinson."

"From West European Section - left about three years ago. He hadn't even been with us long."

"That's right, but he didn't leave. He's now with Professional Standards section."

"Shit, if he's spun the cops a good enough story, he could be back on the streets in no time."

"That's right, so you'd better keep an eye out for him when you're out this afternoon."

"Let's let them hear where I'm going to be. That will give me a better chance of catching him out."

He knew better than to try to dissuade her when she had that expression on her face. They both knew that he'd do exactly the same thing if their situations were reversed.

Before restarting their conversation, they temporarily swapped the SIMs back into the suspect phones and turned them on.

"I'll take the Beamer this afternoon, sweetheart if that's okay," she said.

"Where are you off to?"

"I've an appointment with Franklyn at his office, before seeing the assholes from the DoJ."

"I can't figure what the Hell they think you might have done that the Feebies or the cops can't deal with."

"Me neither, but we'll see. I'll leave straight after lunch."

"What time's your appointment with Franklyn?"

"Two o'clock, but the DoJ aren't due until four."

"Remember you haven't changed your E-Z Pass to the new car yet."

"I'll just take the toll-free route."

Taking the last of her sandwich with her, she left for the appointment with the lawyer. She'd chosen to take the BMW because it had front and rear dashcam and it would be good to have a video record if anything did happen. The toll free route was longer but with less traffic it would be easier to spot a tail if there was one.

It didn't take long; she'd travelled less than a mile when a Jeep Cherokee pulled out behind her. She slowed and looked in her rear view. 'Well, well, we meet again,' she said to herself as Nigel Jenkins, AKA Norman Johnson, revealed himself behind the wheel. As she sped up again and watched him gather pace behind her she almost missed seeing the Durango pull out in front of her.

'Shit, two of them!'

They were approaching the bridge on Idylwood Road where it crossed Highway 267. There would be no houses on either side and no likely pedestrian witnesses, and Johnson was closing up. Taking her gun from her open purse on the passenger seat beside her, she awkwardly cocked it under her arm and laid it in her lap. Then without slowing down or giving any indication of what she was about to do, she hung a sharp left hand turn into the last but one turn before the bridge, cutting across the path of a truck travelling in the opposite direction.

She ignored the blast from the truck's airhorn and slowed to see what action Johnson and Atkinson would take. Never having been along that street before she had no idea where it led, but at the end of the short road she could see she had three choices, left, right or straight ahead. Ahead was signed as a dead end, ruling that out; and for no particular reason, she chose left into a street running parallel with Idylwood. At the last second, as she turned she spotted Johnson hurriedly turning off Idylwood to follow her, having had to reverse to do so.

Seconds later she realized her big mistake; she was heading into another dead end. At the next junction she threw the car into a one-eighty and accelerated back the way she'd come just as Johnson's Cherokee emerged. He made an attempt to block her path but she swung the wheel so her car mounted the curb and passed in front of him and across the front lawn of a house. Throwing the wheel right to get on the road again she knew that at the road's end she'd have no choice but to turn right back toward Idylwood Road.

Inevitably Atkinson's huge Dodge pulled out of her intended route, the huge vehicle blocking the road. As it stopped, a left arm came out of the open window holding a gun. It must have been only nanoseconds before he pulled the trigger and the same before she threw her wheel right. She mounted the curb to pass behind him and his bullet missed her own car and hit Johnson's coming up behind.

With her own window open and the gun already cocked in her hand, she fired off three rapid shots. She was sure she'd hit him with at least one but had no time to assess the effect before bringing the car back under control. Making a split second decision not to stop, she continued back toward Idylwood Road then left again across the bridge, with no sign of anybody following.

Her heart was racing, pumping adrenalin through her body and she was breathing rapidly. She knew she needed to calm down or she'd be in danger of an accident. Pulling into the lot of a Tennis Club she parked out of sight of the street and turned the engine off while she waited to gather her equilibrium. Her shell casings were on the road, but she wasn't concerned about that. It wasn't long before she began to hear the sirens of approaching police and other emergency vehicles.

After giving herself ten minutes, she started the car and continued her journey to her attorney's office. She had no idea how badly Atkinson might have been hit, or even if he was still alive, nor what had happened to Johnson. Worst of all, she didn't know if her face or license plate had been caught on camera. There was no question that when the time was right she'd have to give her account of what happened but she hoped not yet.

She turned on the car radio, and soon there were breaking news reports of another street shooting incident not far from the one just days before. As she drove, more information was added to the reports. One man had a serious gunshot wound and was receiving treatment at the scene before transportation to hospital.

A reporter said that a witness had reported that there had been three cars involved, but two had fled the scene, one with a bullet hole in the windscreen. Interviews with witnesses didn't throw much light on what had happened for the listeners. One had identified the car with the damaged windscreen as a new looking Jeep Cherokee. Another complained that her mailbox had been hit by a bullet and it had been lucky that her husband hadn't been collecting the post, and she didn't understand because theirs was a quiet neighborhood, and nothing like it had ever happened before.

By the time she reached Franklyn's office the reports had become more detailed but none had identified the make of the third car or that the driver was female.

She took the memory card from the dashcam and walked into the building.

Chapter 36

"Saffron, how lovely to see you again. It's been far too long," Franklyn greeted her.

"You might not be saying that after I leave."

"Not a property deal then?"

"Not quite," she said. "Before we start, can you get someone to make copies of what's on this memory card, one for your records and one for me on a thumb drive. If you have a spare replacement, that would be helpful too. You'll be wanting to watch it yourself in a minute."

"No problem." He called his PA in, gave her the card and instructions. "So do you want to tell me what the issue is?"

"This is huge, and when I say that I mean that it may be so big that you may not want to deal with it, at least not alone."

"I see, well if we're to be done before Garfield and co get here, you'd better tell me all about it then. Can I record it?"

"No problem, in fact I'd prefer you did. I need as much of this to be indisputably from my mouth as possible."

Franklyn turned his laptop so that it focused on his client and she began.

Staring into space the whole time, it took her almost an hour and forty minutes to tell the whole unexpurgated tale. In most cases Franklyn would have had to interrupt with questions, but Saffie was candid and unambiguous throughout, leaving little room for doubt or need for further explanation. When she was finished, she turned to her attorney to see his reaction.

Franklyn puffed his cheeks as he breathed out a huge breath. "Well you did say it was going to be big, and you were right in saying I might not want to do it alone. The question is whether or not I bring one of the partners or hand it off to a firm more used to going up against the agencies of the state."

"I'd prefer if you could keep it in-house if possible. I know you, and I know your firm; I have confidence in you."

"Fine, then that's what we'll do unless the situation dictates otherwise. The question now is what advice I can give you for the immediate future

- about the events of this afternoon I mean," he said, "Of course, about that incident earlier, I should advise that I pick up the phone and call the police to make an appointment for you to hand yourself in, but I suspect that's not what you want."

"No, definitely not. Doing that will prevent me from continuing my investigation and I am so close to finding out who's not only behind what's been happening to me and my family, but also responsible for the deaths of at least three American intelligence agents, and of passing information to a foreign power."

He called his PA, "Beth, there was a shooting incident in Falls Church this afternoon. Can you give me any idea what's happening about it...You have? Tell me...Okay that's great...Tell them to wait...We won't be long. Could you keep monitoring that story?"

"I gather Garfield is here then."

"That's right. Before we go to meet them, Beth tells me that the police are looking for the drivers of two cars, one who probably has some sort of wound, and their car has been found abandoned with blood stains."

"That'll be Johnson."

"They say they don't have any information about the third car or its driver at the moment, but one TV station is already speculating about a connection with the incident the other day."

"That's good in a way. It will keep people asking questions. Did they say what was happening to Atkinson?"

"We'll talk again when Garfield's gone. Are you ready?"

"Sure. This should be interesting."

He led her through to a conference room with a table big enough to seat twenty, where Garfield and two others were already seated.

"Mr. Garfield, Franklyn Cohen," he said offering his hand. "I'm so sorry to keep you waiting but you've caught us in the middle of some important moments in Ms. Price's life, and it would have been very difficult to interrupt."

"Never mind let's get on now we're all here," the DoJ official gruffly replied, without introducing his assistants.

"We'll be recording this, Mr. Garfield," Franklyn said, pointing at a camera on the wall at the end of the room, its little red light already flashing."

"I'm not comfortable with that."

"That's a pity, because without that recording this meeting cannot proceed. We'll be happy to provide you with a copy."

"Very well then, can we begin?"

They all took their seats, Garfield and his two assistants along one side of the table, and Franklyn with Saffie on the other."

"Mrs. Price, can you tell me what you were doing on the tenth of June this year?"

"No."

"What do you mean, no?"

"As in no I can't tell you because I don't remember, and no, as in I wouldn't tell you even if I did because you still haven't told me what this is all about."

"We've received information that indicates you've been involved in paramilitary activities against the government of another country."

"I see. Do you want to expand on that?"

"The accusation is that you engaged in a firefight against members of another country's intelligence services which resulted in the deaths of six of their agents."

"That's interesting. Which country's intelligence service, and where did this firefight take place?"

"The Russian Federal Secret Service, and it occurred in the city of Slovyansk, in Ukraine."

"Who was I allegedly operating with when I brought about this remarkable military defeat on the world's most highly trained intelligence service?"

"The information we received was that you were operating on your own."

"Mr. Garfield," Franklyn interrupted, "Do you have any evidence of any of this, or is this only an allegation from an as yet unnamed individual?"

"There was an anonymous letter delivered to the US Embassy in Kyiv. It made very specific allegations, and even named the deceased."

"Is my client alleged to be the aggressor in this supposed firefight?"

"Her name was mentioned but the details weren't clear."

"And has the Russian Embassy made a complaint?"

"Well no, not yet."

"And as this firefight is supposed to have taken place inside Ukrainian territory, I imagine you'll have received confirmation that it took place, a complaint from the Ukrainian government that it was an American citizen involved, and evidence that my client was the American concerned other than an unsubstantiated anonymous allegation."

"No but..."

"Let me get this straight. You've received an anonymous accusation that a US citizen who may or may not be my client, committed an act of war against a foreign power in the territory of a third country. You've no confirmation that the incident actually took place from either the alleged offended country or the country in which the incident was supposed to have happened. Have I got that right?"

"Yes," Garfield blushed.

Franklyn rubbed a hand over his face in exasperation. "Mr. Garfield you may have a lot of time to spend on nonsense like this, but I can I assure you that I don't, and neither does my client."

"I was obliged to ask the question, Mr. Cohen. It is a serious accusation."

"Fine, but shall we let this be the last we hear about it?"

"Thank you for your time, and you Mrs. Price."

The three shook hands with Saffie and Franklyn and made their departure.

"I suspect they wanted to go through that even less than we did," Franklyn remarked.

"It was just more flak to distract me from everything else they've been doing, but this afternoon was serious. They were out to kill me, and I only survived by chance. I must be getting really close, because, Atkinson, the shooter they sent today would be an important asset and to risk exposing him means whoever it is must be getting really worried about me."

"Which makes them all the more dangerous. Tell me who you think it is."

"CIA Deputy Director of Operations, Patryk Wilkanowicz, or someone close enough to him to make a telephone call from where he lives."

"Oy vey, Saffron, pick a hard one, why don't you? What are you going to do next?"

"Continue where I left off. He must be running out of assets now. One way or another I've neutralized three today."

"I'm going to speak to my fellow partner Aaron Slivovitz if that's okay. He's had some experience of going up against the FBI."

"If your PA has got that memory card and thumb drive I asked for, I'll be off."

"I was going to tell you to be careful, but from everything you've told me in the last three hours, I think it might be a waste of breath."

"Franklyn, they came after my husband and child. These bastards are going down, one way or another."

In the car she put the replacement memory card in the dashcam.

Driving home she didn't expect another attempt so soon after the last one but she was taking no chances and kept an active eye on her rear view.

Choosing to take the quick route home via I-66 she was pulling into her drive in a very short time. Unharmed to her great relief.

Chapter 37

She entered the house via the door from the garage and was greeted by Ben and Brett, both looking very worried.

"What's up?"

"What's up, you're asking what's up? What the Hell do you think is up? You go out and get yourself in a gunfight for the second time in almost as many days and you don't bother to call us and tell us that you're okay, then you don't answer your phone. And now you want us to tell you what's up."

"I'm sorry, sweetheart. I'm not hurt. I didn't think that you'd know that I was involved. Then I had to go through everything with Franklyn, and after that there was that pompous asshole Garfield to sort out. Franklyn's PA said they didn't know who the other driver was. I thought it would be okay."

"The TV guy said one of the drivers was wounded. Didn't it occur to you that as far as we were concerned YOU might have been the other driver?"

"Now you mention it, it was kinda dumb. Sorry."

"Why didn't you answer your phone?"

"I turned all my phones off when I went into the meeting with Franklyn, in case they'd been hacked."

"Come here you crazy woman, I love you," he said. They hugged and kissed.

"We were really scared, Mom."

"I'm so sorry, my darling. I'll try to be more thoughtful in the future."

As she tightly hugged her son she spotted another young boy's head peer around the door. "Hi Josh, you're still here."

"Bridger called and asked if Josh could sleep over," Brett told her.

"Well of course he can," she said. "You're always welcome here Josh, you know that. What are we going to do for dinner though? Are you going to make one of your culinary masterpieces Brett, or shall we order in."

"Well seeing as we've got a guest I think we should make it a pizza night don't you, Ben?"

"Yay, pizza!" he shouted. Josh just smiled weakly.

Brett called and ordered a selection of pies with side dishes. While they waited, the boys went upstairs, and Saffie pulled Brett to one side. "What's happening with Josh? Anything else we should worry about?"

"I honestly don't know. Bridger called about an hour ago and said he was taking Brooke to the hospital because she keeps fainting."

"That sounds like horseshit to me. If someone faints you might call a doctor, you wouldn't go to the hospital. Given what happened this morning it's kinda weird they want him to stay over, don't you think."

"One of us should go over there and check it out."

"Best if we leave it until tomorrow I think. Before that I'm going to do some stirring of my own."

Using the one remaining Ukrainian burner that she had left, she dialed the number for Johnson's mother that Linda's friend had acquired and speaking in Ukrainian she said, "Mrs. Johnson, my name is Rebecca Ferguson, I'm an administrative assistant with the British Embassy in Kyiv. I've been asked to pass on some information."

"What is it? Is it about my son, Norman?"

"Yes it is I'm afraid."

"Has he been hurt?"

"I'm terribly sorry to have to inform you that Norman has been seriously wounded in a shooting incident in Virginia, USA."

"What happened?"

"I don't know the details, but I understand he has been admitted to the Walter Reed Hospital, Bethesda, Washington. The police are at his bedside waiting to question him in relation to the incident. Your son has asked that we pass on the message that his phones were taken in the attack and you shouldn't take calls from any of them."

"Oh God."

"I'm sorry to be the bearer of bad tidings. If we can be of any further assistance please don't hesitate to contact me." She ended the call before the woman had chance to reply.

Saffie handed Brett the phone, "What I need you to do is call Johnson and... No wait, I've got a better idea." She took the phone back and typed a text, '*I regret to inform you that your mother has been seriously hurt when a car deliberately ran her down in the street. Sorry to be the bearer of bad tidings. Friends of Jocelyn Travers.'* Then pressed send.

She showed him what she'd sent.

"Who's Jocelyn Travers?"

"One of his rape victims while he was at uni. She committed suicide two years ago after a lifetime of depression."

"I hope I never get on your wrong side," he said. "You can't be sure that either of them will believe what we've told them. What good will it do?"

"Unnerve him I hope."

That was when the gate bell rang.

"That's too quick to be the pizzas," Brett said.

Saffie looked at the entry phone screen and saw it was Ramirez, and it looked like she was alone. She pressed the button for the gate, opened the front door and waited for her to get out of her car. "Good evening, Agent Ramirez."

"Good evening. I wonder if we could have another little talk."

"No problem; come in." The three of them walked through to the study. "Is this going to be another one of our on/off the record informal talks that you're not going to record but probably will anyway?"

"If that's what you prefer."

"Okay have a seat and tell me how I can help."

Ramirez began, "You've probably heard, there was another shooting incident quite close to here this afternoon."

"So I gather. It's all getting a bit close to home now."

"Did you know that one of your colleagues was seriously injured in the incident?"

"That's awful. No I didn't hear that. What's their name?"

"John Atkinson."

"I don't know him personally although I've heard the name. Is he going to be okay?"

"He was shot in the chest; I understand the bullet punctured his right lung. He's had surgery and is expected to survive but he's lost the lung, and his employment opportunities will be severely restricted from now on."

"That's terrible. Has he been able to identify the shooter?"

"At the moment he's not really fit to be interviewed but he's said that he's invoking his right to silence."

"That's odd if he's the victim. Are the CIA offering any help?"

"They say they're unable to comment at the moment."

"This all sounds very controversial," Brett said. "I remember John Atkinson. I think he's now with the agency's Professional Standards section, like your Internal Affairs."

"Really, that's interesting. There was another man hurt in the shooting; we believe he was shot by Atkinson."

"Who was that?"

"Unfortunately, he fled the scene. He abandoned his vehicle five miles away and car-jacked another."

"Have you got a description?" Brett asked.

Ramirez went ahead and read out the description that the driver of the car-jacked SUV had given.

"Was it him that shot Atkinson do you think?"

"At the moment we can't be sure because there was a third car involved, as yet unidentified."

"That description is remarkably close to someone who I suspect of being involved in Brett's kidnapping in Ukraine," Saffie said.

"That's interesting, do you want to tell me more?"

"His name is Norman Johnson. He's a former British MI6 agent gone rogue."

"Could he be in the USA?"

"We've no way of knowing. I'm currently suspended, and Brett is still on sick leave or we could probably tell you."

"Suspended, what for?"

"Exceeding my authority by defending myself in that shooting incident in Arlington apparently."

"I'll never understand spooks," she replied. "So you can't shed any light on today's shooting then."

"I'm afraid not."

"Would it surprise you to know that Atkinson was arrested earlier in the day very close to here - Sandberg Street?"

"That's interesting. As I expect you already know, another of our colleagues, Bridger Davis, lives along that street."

"Actually, we didn't know that."

"I hope Bridger's not in any trouble; his wife hasn't been well. His son is upstairs with Ben right now because Bridger was taking his wife to hospital. Any further advance on the investigation into our son's abduction, Agent Ramirez?"

"Very little I'm afraid. In the absence of any other evidence, we're starting to believe your suggestion that whoever was responsible for arranging it, works inside the George Bush Center. We're trying to get enough leverage to force them to open up about it."

"You won't get any argument from us about that," Saffie said.

"Haven't you anything you want to say about any of this, Mr. Price?"

"Agent Ramirez, I was out of the country when the abductions took place, so I have little I can add. Everything that's happened since has only involved my wife, and she's quite capable of passing on any relevant information to you without my help."

The gate bell rang again. "That will be our pizzas," Brett said.

She gave a knowing smile. "I'll leave you to your meal then."

Brett opened the gate and allowed the agent out at the same time as the pizza delivery girl came in."

Brett closed the door holding the pizza boxes and bag of extras. "You know she'll be round the Davis's before the evening is out, don't you?"

"Saves us the bother then, doesn't it?"

They'd finished eating when Saffie's cell phone rang. "Special Agent Ramirez?" she said and took the phone through to the kitchen.

"What's going on, Ms. Price? There's no sign of Davis or his wife at their home, and we've spoken to all the hospitals within reasonable travelling distance and none of them have heard of Brooke Davis."

"I can't explain that; all I know is that their son is here to stay the night because they asked us to look after him."

When she returned to the table, Brett was serving ice cream to the boys.

"I have to go to Oakton first thing tomorrow, Brett. Can I leave the boys with you until Bridger picks Josh up?"

"You don't have to do all this by yourself you know."

"I know, but at the moment, out of the two of us, I'm the fittest. Not only that, you and Ben have got some catching up to do. There is something you can do later though," she said and winked.

They cleared away the detritus of their meal, and the boys asked to watch *Olympus Has Fallen* again.

"You'll wear the DVD out soon, Ben. You must have watched it ten times already."

"It's an awesome movie though, Mom."

"Okay then, let's all watch it together."

"I take it your trip to Oakton is to visit Brooke's mom and sister," Brett said, as they prepared for bed.

"That's right, but via the Davis home first for a quick look around."

Chapter 38

At 5.30 a.m. Saffie left home wearing the black outfit she'd bought in Baltimore and took the Wrangler. It was still an hour before sunrise and there were very few other cars about.

Parking in the street, away from the nearest streetlamp, she slipped on a pair of nitrile gloves and approached the Davis's home with her silenced gun in her belt. Confident that she hadn't been followed from home, and seeing no evidence of anyone who could observe, she rolled the ski-mask over her face and swiftly walked to the front door, knocked, and rang the bell.

Unsurprised when there was no response she walked a circuit around the large two-storey home. The three car garage was detached and a glance through a window revealed two cars inside. She'd only ever seen them use two vehicles - a red Honda Civic, normally driven by Brooke and Bridger's huge Chrysler 300, that Saffie had always thought was a bit ostentatious. Both were still there.

Trying all the windows as she went and without any realistic expectation that one might have been unlocked, she was astonished to find one of the double doors leading from the deck into a sunroom slightly ajar. This made no sense. Why would they have gone out and left the place unlocked, and why hadn't the FBI spotted it? For Bridger Davis, a man whose job it was to think of every possibility in an emerging security situation to make such a stupid mistake was absurd. It was possible that the Feebies were holding off to get a warrant, but Ramirez had been there the night before, and she'd have done what Saffie was doing now even without one. Someone had been inside since.

She had no wish to trigger an intruder alarm, but she knew where the control box was; she'd spotted it when she visited the day before. Saffie was confident in her ability to reach the box, see if it were set, and if it were, make her escape before police or security arrived, so she pulled her silenced handgun from her belt and opened the door. It took seconds to confirm the alarm was off so she decided to take the opportunity to look around.

There seemed little point in trying to see what she was doing by the light from her phone so she turned the lights on in each room as she looked around and off again when she left. At first, it all looked perfectly normal and she left everything as she found it. Then, opening the study door, she could see that the room had been ripped apart by somebody searching very thoroughly. Having no idea what they'd been looking for, and confident that if it had been there, the likelihood was that they'd have taken it, there was no point in looking herself. She left the room as she'd found it and completed her tour of the first floor before heading to the second.

From the head of the stairs she could see that the door of almost every room was fully open. In what she imagined was the master bedroom suite, it looked as if it had been searched as thoroughly as the study, but a half-packed suitcase lay open on the bed.

In another room, which by the posters on the wall was obviously Josh's, the treasured PS4 console lay still connected on the floor in front of the TV. There was no evidence of either a search or packing to leave.

Saffie saw little point in searching further. They had clearly made a hurried departure, whether of their own accord or not was another matter.

As she left the room and turned toward the stairs, she heard someone very close by, attempt to smother a squeaky involuntary cough. She spun towards it lifting her gun, but before she knew what had happened, she took a hit her very hard on the head with a heavy object. If she hadn't been in mid-turn there was little doubt that the blow would at the very least have knocked her unconscious. However, her lightning reactions had moved her head sufficiently from her attacker's aim that the blow skidded off the side of her head and hit her left shoulder.

The ski-mask had helped cushion the blow, but she was still stunned, although not so much that she couldn't try to bring her gun to bear on the place where she thought her assailant had been. She fired and heard the simultaneous phut of the shot and a short exclamation of pain.

Whoever her assailant was, they didn't wait around for her to fire again but ran off down the stairs emitting another squeaky cough. By the time that she'd completely regained her senses and followed down the stairs, her assailant had fled through the sunroom, leaving the doors swinging behind them. She heard a car in the street start up and with a screech of spinning tires drive away at speed.

She turned the sunroom light on again, rolled up the ski-mask, and put her hand up to her head. It came away with a smear of blood but nothing more. Her head hurt, and so did her shoulder, but she knew that whoever her attacker had been, they'd be long gone by now.

Returning to the first floor she found the weapon laying on the floor, a faux bronze art nouveau figurine of a near-naked woman gracefully holding a crystal globe. If it had caught her where it had been aimed she'd be dead. She checked to see if there were any of her blood on it, wiped it with her t-shirt in case and placed it back on the Doric column-like plinth from where it had no doubt been taken. Whatever part of the attacker she'd hit when she fired had clearly not caused a wound that bled a great deal because there was no sign of anybody else's blood. She picked up her shell casing and returned to the ground floor.

After turning off all the lights, and pushing the door closed behind her she made her way back to the car. Before setting off for Oakton she unscrewed the suppressor and put it in the glove box, removed the ski-mask and changed her t-shirt for something more befitting a visit to a colleague's parent.

The GPS said the journey to the remote dead-end road to the west of Oakton would take less than twenty minutes, meaning that she'd arrive before seven, far too early to claim she was making a casual call. A Google search found her a chicken grill restaurant not far from her destination that would be open for dine-in or drive through.

The short journey was long enough for her to reflect on how close she'd been to either discovering the owner of that cough or dying. Annoyed at the first but relieved by the second, and not one to be overly introspective about things like that, she mentally shrugged it off. Driving to the grill, she went inside and ordered an egg and bacon muffin, and a Greek yoghurt, with coffee.

The restaurant was busy with men and women on their way to work, and she hoped she wouldn't be bothered by any more eating-place Casanovas, imagining that a few smart words and an offer to pay for her meal was going to get them laid. As it turned out the only people asking to share her table were a mother and her young daughter.

She tucked into the food telling herself that she needed to stop eating all this fast food.

Once again she availed herself of a free newspaper to read an account of the previous day's attack. Accurate details were scant, but in normal journalistic fashion they'd filled the gaps with conjecture and ill-informed reports from self-proclaimed witnesses.

"You've got blood in your hair," the girl said, pointing, "and on the neck of your t-shirt."

"I banged my head earlier today."

"You should go to the hospital."

"It isn't serious. I think it'll be fine."

"Mommy's taking me to the hospital in Baltimore cos I've got a 'tuner' in my brain and I'm going to have an operation."

The mother rested her hand on the girl's arm, "The lady doesn't want to know about our problems Brittany."

"Not at all. Brittany's problems are a great deal more interesting and far more important than mine. When will your operation be, Brittany?"

"Tomorrow. I'm not allowed to eat after breakfast so Mommy brought me here for strawberry pancakes and ice cream."

"I've got a little boy about your age. His name is Ben, and when I get home I'm going to tell him about the brave little girl called Brittany that I met at the grill. I've got to go now but I want to wish you good luck for tomorrow." She handed the girl's mother a hundred dollar bill. "Mommy, please buy Brittany a little present from Ben."

"You can't do that Miss, it's too much."

"I took that money from somebody who tried to kill my husband. I think if a little of it goes to give a small girl a few minutes pleasure that would be a good thing. I hope it all goes well tomorrow."

She stood up to leave, gave a $50 bill to the waitress and said to pay for Brittany and her mom's meal as well as her own and keep the change.

It was ten before eight when she got back to the car, after pausing to decide how to make her next move.

It took only a few minutes to find the road where Brooke's mother and sister lived. Using Google Earth Saffie had been able to see there were only two houses on the road. What she wasn't sure about was which one was the Davis relatives' home. When she'd questioned Josh he'd only been able to give the name of the road.

The area was predominantly woodland, and the road led up quite a steep hill with a long sweeping right hand bend. On Google Earth the house at the end appeared to be two storey; but before that, on the left-hand side of the bend and set back from the road, was a smaller, single-storey building facing down the hill.

She drove up the road until the small house came into view then stopped. Quickly, she reversed out of sight and backed in amongst the trees. It would make sense if with only two residents the smaller house would be theirs.

Leaving the car where it was she walked through the trees on the opposite side to the small building. As she drew closer she spotted an old, battered and very large pickup truck. It appeared to be the only vehicle at the house, making it unlikely to be the home of an old lady requiring care and her daughter.

Cutting the bend by going through the trees, she approached the bigger of the two houses from the side. A small hatchback was parked out front with a large Mercedes Sprinter van reversed alongside it. It was light by this time and impossible to tell whereabouts people inside might be, so she knew she needed to get closer to learn more.

Dodging between trees and crouching in the undergrowth, she managed to get within twenty feet of the side of the house without being seen. The closest window seemed to be to a kitchen, and at first she couldn't see anyone.

As she watched a young woman about twenty-five years old came into the room carrying some dishes and stood facing the window at what was probably the sink. It appeared as though the woman, who Saffie assumed was Brooke's sister, had started to wash dishes, when a man about thirty with dark stubble but hair dyed silver-blond came up behind her, grabbed her breasts and nuzzled her neck with a lascivious grin. It was obvious to Saffie that his advances weren't welcome as she tried to shrug him off, then saw her grimace with pain as he tightly squeezed her breasts until she tearfully submitted.

Making her way further around the building she could see that the kitchen area opened into a large open plan room used for living and dining. From her vantage point behind some tall ostrich ferns, she could see right through to the front door. Bridger and Brooke were seated around one end of the table and an extremely overweight man sat at the other with his back to her.

Saffie thought that if there were only two, and she could develop a workable strategy, tackling them on her own might be a realistic proposition. She knew that to do that, she'd need a better idea of the building's layout so she continued her circuit of the house without crossing the front. The prolific growth of the ferns made scouting the area whilst staying unseen relatively easy, but unfortunately it produced nothing useful in terms of an intervention plan.

Returning to a position where she could observe what was happening in the big room as well as some of the kitchen area she saw that none of the occupants had moved but the Davis family members were both looking extremely distressed. There was an open window and although she was unable to make out the words, Bridger was pleading for something. Brooke was crying and Bridger hugged her to him for comfort. It was clear he was equally upset. At that moment Brooke's eyes met Saffie's who quickly put a finger to her lips. Brooke made a tearful but barely perceptible nod in acknowledgement.

Hearing a sudden scream of pain from the woman in the kitchen Saffie hurried to where she could see what was happening in both rooms at the same time. The woman was bent over the sink with her skirt above her waist. The blond man's pants were around his knees and he was raping her. Out of the corner of her eye she saw Bridger make to stand until the fat man casually placed a gun on the table.

There was no way on earth that Saffie could allow what was happening to continue, so she crossed to the kitchen side door. It had a clear glass window, so she could be seen, but praying it wasn't locked, she turned the handle and pulled it silently toward her. Thankfully the door opened, and she aimed and shot the man through the ear, spinning swiftly toward the main room, and firing twice more, felling the fat man as he reached to lift his own gun from the table.

"There's another one upstairs!" Bridger shouted, grabbing the fat man's gun.

"You women, outside and hide in the trees until we call you. Now!" Saffie shouted.

She strode to the bottom of the stairs and cautiously looked up. Seeing nothing she called, 'Your buddies are both dead, so if you want to stay alive you'd better drop your weapon and come down now. If I have to come up there to get you, I won't be taking prisoners.

"Dasha, are you okay?" Bridger called.

"Bastard man, he climb out window," an old woman shouted back.

Saffie and Bridger rushed to the front door to see the third man had jumped in the Sprinter, and it had already started to move when Bridger ran to the driver's door and shot him through the glass. The van continued to move down the incline in a straight line into the trees across the road.

The two of them hurried after it to ensure the guy didn't escape, but with her injured leg Saffie lagged behind. Halfway across the road she was knocked sideways to the floor when a bullet struck her upper arm.

Bridger spun in the direction of the shot and began firing randomly in the direction the shot had come from, but without any idea of his target, his gun soon clicked on an empty chamber. The gunman whoever he was, emerged limping from the trees and jumped into a small anonymous looking sedan and drove away at speed, causing an approaching pickup truck to swerve out of his way.

"Saffron, are you okay?"

"No I'm not okay, fuck you; I've been shot and it fucking hurts. Get some police and medics here quick. Is the driver of that truck dead?"

"Yes."

"Then help me up and get me a towel or something to hold on this wound."

The driver of the pickup jumped out and helped Saffie stand. "I called the cops, what the fuck happened?"

"We'll need medics as well," Bridger told him.

The guy took his phone out and dialed 911 a second time.

Chapter 39

On a seat under the porch and holding a tea towel against the wound, Saffie waited with Jake the pickup driver, while Bridger rounded up his family.

Brooke and her sister Anastasia came as soon as he called, but it took some effort to get Dasha to join them from the first floor, fear of the stairlift adding to her mobility problems They'd only just managed to get her seated on a chair outside when the first police cruiser arrived.

This Fairfax County PD crew seemed to be about as efficient as any that Saffie had encountered. They didn't cuff her because of her wound, although they did restrain Bridger after he pointed out the weapon on the floor at his feet.

One of the first patrol officers attempted to question her but she interrupted. "I'm sorry officer; I'm really not trying to be difficult but firstly I'm in a great deal of pain here; and secondly I ought to tell you that this incident is very likely related to the shooting at my house ten days ago."

"Which shooting was that Ma'am?"

"In Dunn Loring. Your Detective Sergeant Wolski was dealing with it; you might want to give him a call."

"Are you that CIA woman?"

"I'm afraid so. Mr. Davis here is also in the agency."

"Shit in a bucket; Wolski won't like this," the second cop said. "The feds are going to be all over this."

Neither cop got to say very much more before they were lambasted in very loud half English and half Moldovan by Dasha. The fierce tirade was barely intelligible but left listeners no doubt that she was accusing them of harassing the woman who'd saved them from the 'bastard murdering rapists' that had been holding them hostage for hours. They were rescued by the arrival of the Fire and Rescue Department medics who took Saffie into the back of their ambulance to treat her wound.

Luckily, in spite of the pain, the injury was less severe than she'd first thought. The bullet hadn't penetrated her arm but had taken a chunk of flesh from about three inches below her shoulder leaving a wound about half an inch wide and two inches long. The paramedics tried to persuade her to go to hospital, but she refused.

"It needs surgery," one told her.

"I'm too busy for surgery."

Wolski arrived and asked if she was conducting her own personal war against the gangster fraternity of Virginia. Apparently the dead men's prints had been scanned, and they all had long records for involvement in drugs, violence, and gang activity. When she explained that the incident had yet another connection with the agency, he rolled his eyes and asked if he should be surprised.

Ramirez and Burns arrived soon after. At first they ignored her and spoke to Wolski before the three of them went inside to see the crime scene.

Jake, who turned out to be the guy who lived in the small house further down the hill, described all he'd heard and seen to the patrol officers. He told them he'd been climbing into his truck when he heard the first shots, dialed 911 and drove to see what was happening. The escaping gunman had driven him off the road.

Having given his preliminary statement he asked if he could leave to go to work, but with some of Saffie's blood on his clothes he was told to stay until he'd been swabbed by CSI and interviewed by detectives.

"I need all you four at the police station to be interviewed on tape," Ramirez told Saffie and the Davises, "And I don't want any arguments from you, Ms. Price. I'm pissed off with this. Everywhere you go you leave a trail of dead bodies."

"I'm not arguing, Agent Ramirez. I'm as eager for this to stop as you are. Before we go though, can you get someone to fetch my purse from my car and lock it?"

Wolski called one of the patrol officers over, Saffie handed him her key and told him where to find it. In the end he moved it to stand beside the house, before returning both keys and purse.

They allowed her to call Brett before they left, but she wasn't looking forward to his reaction.

"Hi, darling, how's it going?" he answered.

"Not fantastic to be honest."

"What's up?"

"Hit a bit of a snag. I'm going to be quite a while getting back."

"What's happened?"

"A bit of gunplay at Brooke's mom's house."

"Shit, anybody hurt?"

"Three bad guys got to finish the day early and won't be bad guying anymore. I got a bit of a scrape and I probably won't be driving for a day or two. Do you think you could get a cab up here to collect the car and come back via Vienna cop station to collect me?"

"What about Josh?"

"We might need to hang on to him for a bit. I don't know what's happening yet, but the Davises will be at the cop shop with me. It might be good to give Franklyn a call and give him the heads up about what's happening."

"What is happening?"

"A TV van just turned up so I guess there'll be something on the news, but what I mean is if you could call him and ask him to have somebody on standby just in case. Gotta go now they're taking us all to the police station."

A police minivan arrived to transport the four of them. Dasha treated them to loud protests about their innocence, how she thought America was supposed to be a free country, and that she wouldn't say a word without a lawyer.

They were interviewed individually except Dasha, who insisted that Brooke be with her, but as she'd expected, Saffie was made to wait until last. The problem for Ramirez was that it gave time for Franklyn to get there before they got started.

They gave her a few minutes to consult with Franklyn and against his advice she told him that she wanted to make a full statement. Then, as soon as the formalities were over, Ramirez asked, "Ms. Price, can you give me one reason why I shouldn't arrest you for murder?"

"One very good reason would be that I haven't murdered anyone."

"Since the night your son was abducted, gunfights involving injury and death have followed you around Virginia like a bad smell. To our knowledge you personally are responsible for at least six deaths by gunfire."

"Five."

"Why only five?"

"I only killed two today, two when I was attacked in Arlington, and one in my home on the night my son was abducted."

"Three people died today."

"I only shot two of them, both in commission of felonies and to prevent further injury to innocent parties. Bridger Davis shot the driver of the van."

"That's not what he said."

"You'll have evidence of that other than a statement of someone with a motive to lie then. You'll have a bullet from my 9mm HK45 in his body, rather than a .44 from the Smith and Wesson he'd taken from the hostage takers?"

"We haven't got a ballistics report back just yet."

"Well until you do, I suggest that you withhold judgement about who shot the van driver. I've undertaken to give you a full statement of what happened today, and then unless you have substantive evidence of a crime that I've committed, I'm going to leave. I believe my husband and child are waiting outside. Furthermore, if you have ideas of releasing Mr. Davis, you might want to hang fire on that. I have evidence of him passing information to a foreign power that people further up the food chain in the bureau might want to put to him. I think he's a flight risk."

"I'll need to see that evidence."

"And you will. Just as soon as I've made my statement, and I have clearance from the CIA."

She interrupted the interview to ask Burns to see that Davis didn't leave. He returned to say he'd been too late.

Saffie gave a full description of the day's events leaving nothing out.

Franklyn stepped in. "If there's nothing else, Agent Ramirez, my client has given a full account of her actions during the day. She's tired and in pain. Perhaps you can concentrate your energies on trying to find out who the gunman was who shot her, who was behind the previous attempt on her life, and who abducted her son. I believe that she's told you about the indications that the culprit is inside the CIA and if you feel unable to penetrate their renowned wall of inscrutability then perhaps you should push this further up the ladder."

"Very well, Ms. Price, we'll leave this for now."

"One last thing though, Agent Ramirez," Saffie said, "the cops have now got three guns that belong to me. Could you have a word with them and get them to return at least one of them? Buying weapons for self-protection is becoming very expensive."

When she and Franklyn were outside the building, the lawyer turned to her. "You're playing a very dangerous game, Saffron. My advice is to go back in there now and tell them everything you know."

"If I did that, much of what I know to be true wouldn't be considered evidence by a district attorney much less a federal one, my suspension would become a dismissal, and one day one of these assassination attempts would be successful."

"Was today another assassination attempt do you think?"

"Not in the normally accepted use of the word. It was far too random to have been planned, but it was definitely an attempt to put me out of business. Hitting a moving target from that distance with a handgun would be a lucky shot even for an expert. I think that the cougher may have followed me from the Davis residence, took the opportunity to take a shot when it arose and got lucky or unlucky depending on how you look at it."

"You could ask for witness protection."

"They'd only normally consider that for potential witnesses in a trial, and as yet they don't even have anyone to indict. Not only that, but I also don't see why I should have to go into hiding because the country has a traitor operating in the highest tiers of our intelligence services. Wherever they might put me, or wherever I chose to hide, he'd find me and have me whacked. Whoever he is he needs to be out of harm's way, before I'm safe."

"He? Do you know who it is for sure?"

"As I told you before, I'm pretty confident I do, but I still can't be absolutely certain. The list of candidates is very short and they're all male."

Chapter 40

Brett had seen them leave the building and got out of the car to meet them. Seeing Saffie's bandaged arm in a sling horrified him. "What the Hell, Saffie?"

"Seems my adversary isn't quite as good a shot as he'd like to be."

"This isn't a time for joking, Saff."

"I know but we must be getting close if he's this determined to stop me."

"Talk some sense into her will you, Franklyn."

"I've already tried. I was hoping you'd have better luck."

"Thanks, Franklyn," she said.

"I didn't do anything in the end."

"No doubt you'll bill me for it anyway."

"You bet your life I will."

They shook hands and the lawyer climbed into his enormous Mercedes, waved, and drove away.

Saffie turned to Brett. "Is that Josh in the car with you?"

"Yes, I caught Bridger as they came out of the building. He was about to get into a cab with Brooke and I guess it was her mother and sister. He asked me if we could keep Josh with us for another day or two before he got in the cab and drove off without speaking to him."

"Jesus wept, what's the matter with the asshole?"

"Josh is really upset."

"I suppose I'm not that surprised. I think Bridger might be making a dash for the hills. He tried to blame the killing of the unarmed van driver on me. He must have known it would be easily disproven."

As they got into the Wrangler, Saffie turned to Josh. "Hey buddy, looks like we get to have you for another couple of days. That's good, don't you think, Ben?"

"Yeah it's great we can play *Call of Duty* right through to the end. We never get time to do that. Josh is really good at that."

"Hey, here's an idea. How about we get Ben one of those PS4 things like yours and a couple of other games; then you can really have a good time?"

"You'd get me a PS4! Really Mom? You always tell me I spend too much time on Dad's Xbox 360."

"Dad and I think that you've been such a brave boy lately, and so grown up you deserve to be spoiled a little. It won't mean that I won't curtail your use of it if you let it take over your life, especially after school starts."

"I don't want to go to Staples today, darling, we've got too much to talk about," Brett complained.

"We can order it online when we get back."

Ben was excited by the prospect of the new games console and tried to engage Josh, but his friend remained very subdued.

Once inside their home, Saffie took Josh aside. "Josh, I know this is all very confusing for you but your dad has got a lot of problems right now, and I don't yet know how it's all gonna pan out for him. I want you to know that you're welcome here for as long as it takes. You can continue to share with Ben or you can have your own room if you prefer."

"Mom and Dad didn't even speak to me. They just got in the cab and drove off."

"I'm not sure why they did that at the moment but as soon as I know more I'll tell you, I promise."

"Why were you at Dasha's house today?"

"Because I went to your home and I saw that someone had broken in. I wanted to make sure your Mom and Dad were safe. I was worried. Why don't you sit down with Ben and make a list of what he needs to go with this PS4 thing, so I know what to order?"

Brett had listened to what she'd said. "If he's in the wind, we have no idea how long it will be before he's found."

"Two things to say about that; firstly by the time he's caught they'll have established that he was the one that shot the van driver and they'll bring charges for that. Brooke, Dasha and Anastasia's immigration status will have been gone through in minute detail and I suspect they'll be detained as well. Bridger is unlikely to see the outside of a prison cell for twenty years at least. For the time being Josh is safe here amongst friends and until the authorities decide what happens to him, this is the best place for him."

"You're right, I know you are, and I agree. It's just very worrying is all."

"Can you get me a couple of Tylex, this arm hurts like a bastard and Tylenol just aren't gonna do it."

Ben and Josh came running back in with a list of what they wanted.

"Brett, can you order that stuff for me, charge it to my account."

"There's a place on the Lee Highway that has it all in stock. He says he'll match Staples' prices and do same-day home delivery to here if you call and order before three p.m. ," Ben told them.

"How do you know all that?"

"I called them."

"Didn't want to give me time to change my mind eh?"

"No, I just wanted..."

"I was only joshing."

"Thanks, Mom. I love you."

They disappeared trying to decide which game to play first.

"I'm going to have a lie down, Brett. Do you mind?"

"No you go ahead, sweetheart."

It was almost eight o'clock when Brett woke her to ask if she wanted something to eat.

"Yes please, with another couple of Tylex as a starter."

As they ate, Saffie asked, "Do we know anyone who could find out who might have had treatment for an open wound on their left lower leg in the last twenty-four hours?"

"Why?"

"Because I'm pretty sure that the guy that hit me over the head in the Davis's house was wounded in our struggle, and the guy that shot me this morning was limping on his left leg."

"If it's a gunshot wound he wouldn't be likely to go to a hospital would he?"

"I guess not."

"We still think it's someone high up in Langley don't we?"

"Of course."

"Then why don't I try to find out who on the top floor is either absent from there today or who's limping?"

"Do you know anybody up there likely to tell you?"

"Sort of, but I'll need to be canny about how I go about it. Give me a minute while I look up a number I haven't called for years. This is a bit of a gamble so bear with me."

She followed him through to the study, while the boys attempted to disappear upstairs. "Hey, you two, what about loading the dishwasher?"

In the study Brett found the number he'd been looking for. "Cammie? It's Brett, Brett Price. How are you?"

"A bit flummoxed to be honest, getting a call from you after all these years. If you're hoping to take up where we left off, you're out of luck. I'm a married woman again now."

"I'm pretty well spoken for as well these days. It's a bit cheeky - I'm looking for a small favor."

"As long as you don't want me to disclose any national secrets or interfere in anything I'll consider it."

"Somebody in Langley is trying to set my wife and I up for something we're not involved in. The list of potential culprits is pretty short, but we've managed to narrow it down to someone on the top floor."

"I can't get involved in any investigations Brett."

"I know that Cammie; that's not what I want. We know that whoever it is was away from the office today. We're just trying to narrow it down."

"That's easy, if it's one the big swinging dicks you're after, there were only three out the whole day today. Wilkanowicz, Roy Scott, and Joni Collins."

"Joni Collins? Who's that?"

"The new Director of Digital Innovation."

"Okay, thanks that's really helpful Cammie. Thank you, I owe you one."

"Well if this husband doesn't work out I might have to call you on that one."

"Was that Camilla Blumenthal? I didn't know you two had had a thing going."

"It was before we met on that first op together. We just went out a few times that's all."

"I'm not sure how it helps that much though. I expected Wilkanowicz to be amongst them, but it's not proof of anything in itself, unless he has a limp next time he's seen. I think we can rule out the Collins woman; she was brought in from the Department for the Environment and she's only been in post for two months."

"What about Roy Scott, Director of Analysis?" he asked.

"A possibility I suppose, but why? He's my ultimate boss, and he hasn't bothered to touch base with me since this began which in itself begs questions, but he always was an insensitive asshole with zero people skills."

"This is only the first stage though; I couldn't ask Camilla too many questions without giving too much away. Tomorrow I'll try to find out if either of them have a limp, or where they are if they're not in the office."

Chapter 41

At nine fifteen the following day, Saffie's phone rang. "Meredith, what can I do for you?"

"You still haven't come to the office to hand in your badge."

"That's right."

"Why not?"

"I thought I explained. I have an injury and so has my husband. If you want my badge you're welcome to come and collect it."

"You're being obstructive."

"I'll tell you what's obstructive shall I? When one of the principal officers in the organization you work for attempts to have you charged with offences that have blatantly been committed by others. Or when that doesn't work, sends lowlife gangsters to assassinate you. All this because they don't want to be exposed for the foreign agents that they are."

"Don't be absurd."

"How would you know, you're little more than a copy typist promoted beyond her competence."

"There's no call for insolence."

"I tried to speak to Roy Scott yesterday to have it out with him, but he wouldn't take my calls."

"Roy is in the UK with Patryk Wilkanowicz. They're at a NATO meeting of intelligence heads. They'll be there until the end of the week."

"If they'd told me that yesterday it would have helped. I'll try again next week. If he'll see me, I'll drop off my badge while I'm there."

"You can't use it while you're..."

She ended the call knowing that it would enrage her. "Shit! Where does that leave us?"

"Just because Wilkanowicz says he went to the UK, doesn't necessarily mean either that he did, or that he stayed there," Brett mooted.

"That's true, but it still doesn't confirm anything either way."

"The boys will wear that game console out if they keep going at it like this; they were up at six o'clock on it this morning," he told her.

"While Josh is coming to terms with things I think we should give them a bit of a free rein. It's not as if we're in a position to do anything else with them at the moment."

"Okay I guess," he sighed.

"Is there any way we can find any more about Atkinson's involvement?" she asked, changing the subject.

"I've been trying to think about that, but I don't know anybody in Professional Standards; not that they'd talk even if I did."

"What about from before he was transferred there?"

Brett thought about that. "He was in the FBI before he came to us."

"That's an unusual career path."

"I guess his investigative history helped getting him the spot in PS."

"I'm not ready to reveal my involvement in that fracas with him to Ramirez just yet, Is there anyone else we know in the Feebies who might be able to ask a few pertinent questions?"

"The only Fed that I knew was Faye Barossa, but she quit about three years ago. I think she's working as a PI in Seattle now."

"Do you think she'll talk to us?"

"Worth a try I suppose, if I can find her number."

"Is she another one of your conquests?" she asked with a grin.

"I did ask her out once, but it turned out she's gay."

There were nineteen private investigation companies listed in and around Seattle. It took him half an hour to narrow the list down to sixteen possibles, but it was still only 7 a.m. there, too early to start calling. At noon he began, most of them answered congenially and then became unhelpful when they heard he was looking for one of the opposition. On the ninth call he got lucky.

"FA and CA PI, how can I help?" a female voice answered.

"I'm trying to track down..."

"I'm sorry sir but we don't do missing persons."

"You misunderstand me, I'm looking for Faye Barossa. This is a personal call."

"I do apologize sir would you give me your name, and I'll see if she's free."

A few moments later Faye came on the line.

"Brett Price; that's a name I didn't expect to hear again. How are you?"

"I'll get by, and you?"

"I'm good thanks; a married woman now. I go by Faye Abney nowadays. That was my other half you were just speaking to."

"Congratulations, I'm really pleased for you."

"What can I do for you?"

"Do you remember a guy called John Atkinson from when you were in the Feebies?"

"Now that's a name I'm unlikely to forget. Why do you ask?"

"I'm trying to learn a bit more about him. His name has cropped up in connection with something here in Virginia."

"He's an asshole, and I'm pretty sure he's crooked. He was in the same team as me for a while, and a big investigation into child trafficking went toes up when a raid failed. We knew they'd been tipped off, and Atkinson was widely suspected to be the culprit. Nothing was ever proven but they forced him to resign."

"So you didn't know that he's been working for the company."

"What? How the Hell did that happen?"

"It gets worse; he's in our Professional Standards Department."

"For fucks sake!"

"Do you know any more about what happened to him after he quit?"

"I heard he went to work for Woolfe Northwater."

"That military contractor; the one mixed up in the arms for drugs scandal in Afghanistan?"

"That's the one, but that's all I can tell you I'm afraid. If I think of anything else, can I call you on this number?"

"That would be great, thanks, Faye; that's a big help."

He turned to Saffie. "Wolf, it's that name again."

"It's spelled differently but worth looking into, because it would be a freaking big coincidence if it wasn't."

"How do we get a list of the investors I wonder?" he asked.

"That's my job but typing one-handed is going to slow me down."

"Can I help?"

"Maybe. Let's give it a try."

They went to the study and went to Saffie's desk and booted up her laptop. She was about to tell him what to do next when she hesitated.

"No wait." Then she went to the bottom of the stairs and called up. "Ben, are you using your new PC at the moment?"

"No, Mom."

"Would you mind if we borrowed it for a couple of hours?"

"Of course not, I'll bring it down. Shall I bring the power cable?"

"Yes, please."

"Why Ben's PC and not yours?" Brett asked.

"First because, they may have hacked mine, or yours too for that matter, and second because it's faster."

As soon as they booted it up they logged on using Ben's account. "Right first go to the Companies Register and look to see which country Woolfe Northwater are registered in. I doubt it will be this one."

As she'd expected Brett wasn't as quick navigating between screens and finding his way around websites as she was, but that wasn't his main skill set but they quickly established that the company was registered in South Africa, originally just under the name Northwater. Their main offices were in Arlington. Its portfolio listed operations in South America, Iraq, Syria, Afghanistan, and contracts with the NSA and CIA, but there were no indications about when those ops were conducted. They changed their name to Woolfe Northwater after a big investment in 2018.

Their most recent published accounts indicated that they were still active and had significant income in spite of the 'drugs for arms' affair but gave no detail how they were making the money. Looking back through previous years accounts, showed that the scandal had caused little more than a blip in their earnings.

The list of current directors took some time to locate. The chairman was a Gideon van Riebeek. Google listed him as a South African businessman and former director of De Beers diamond mining company and one of its subsidiaries. With a net worth of $1.7 billion he ranked as the twelfth richest person in South Africa in 2020.

There were only three names on the board that either of them recognized, Tammy Warren, Lindsey Johnson, and Mitch Cassidy, all little known current senators. They had to do individual searches for each of the others to learn more about them. Unsurprisingly, most turned out to be people with obscene amounts of wealth appearing impressively high on various rich lists, having acquired their wealth in a variety of ways. However, there were two where no information was readily available - Remy Raymond and Wilfred Bauer. Inevitably there were plenty of people with those names, but none of them appeared likely to be the ones on the board of a multi-billion dollar military contracting company.

"I wonder if we could take a look at their offices in Arlington," Brett asked.

"Can we leave it until tomorrow? This arm is hurting like a bastard, and I'm more than a little tired."

"Why don't you take a couple of Tylex and lie down for a bit?"

"I think I will, but like you, I'm wary of opioids, I guess a couple a day for a day or two probably won't hurt. I'll take one now and another before bed."

"Good choice. I'll carry on looking for an hour or two."

"Thanks," she said.

Four hours later Ben nudged her awake. "Dad says dinner will be in about fifteen minutes, Mom."

"Okay, sweetheart, I'll be right down."

Brett had conjured up a chicken curry out of the ingredients they had in the cupboards and it was delicious. Even Josh enjoyed it, and he'd never eaten curry before. After ice cream for dessert the boys cleared the dishes allowing Brett to lead Saffie into the study to talk about his findings.

"Northwater aren't listed on the stock exchanges. They have a suite in an expensive anonymous looking office building on Crystal Drive; looks as if they've taken the whole third floor. Their AGM is the day after tomorrow, but it's not a public event, so I'm guessing it will be in their offices."

"Maybe we could do a stakeout. We might be able to put some faces to those last two names," she suggested.

"It wouldn't be easy. There must be hundreds of people going in and out of that building, some arriving by cab, others by car as well as pedestrians."

"Our guys aren't gonna be arriving on foot are they? They'll be in limos or top of the range cars."

"True. How about one of us stakes out the front entrance, for the limo travelers, and the other the car park? What about the boys though?"

"Maybe we could find something for them to do for a couple of hours. What time is the AGM?"

"Two p.m."

"That's good. By that time most of the workers will have had their lunch and be back at their desks. We won't need to stay there for the whole day will we? Just say from about one-thirty until two-thirty."

"Where could we take them that we could be confident of being safe though?"

"Google *kids activities Arlington.*"

Brett soon had a list, but most of them were either for toddlers or young accompanied kids."

"What about that one, the kids stage school. Maybe they'll be worth a try," she suggested. "Let me give them a call."

After a few minutes on the phone she'd found them places on a stage-set painting course. Initially they'd told her that all the places were full but when she offered to donate $1,000 to their support fund they decided they had space after all.

"That has to be the most expensive creche in the world," Brett laughed.

They gave up for the day, told the boys to give the PlayStation a break and all watched a Disney movie together before bed.

Chapter 42

"How's the arm this morning?" Brett asked, seeing Saffie sitting on the side of the bed when he woke.

"A little easier today I think, but not good enough to put that thing to use," she told him, nodding at his morning glory. "How's your leg?"

"It's been less painful overnight."

After breakfast, the boys decided to go into the garden and play softball catch, leaving the adults to continue their research into Woolfe Northwater.

It was Brett who was the first to make some sort of breakthrough by discovering that Remy Raymond, the board member they'd been searching for, was actually Raimond Remy, a Canadian heavy metal mining billionaire. He was a reclusive individual who'd managed to avoid the cameras in spite of unproven allegations of participation in child sex trafficking. The speculations about his involvement began after it became known that his name had appeared in Jeffrey Epstein's black book, and he'd been a three time visitor to the private resort in the Virgin Islands.

In 2017 the scandal resulted in Remy's resignation from three boards. His subsequent sale of shares in their companies caused big fluctuations on the Canadian stock market for several weeks. For some time there was speculation about where he'd re-invest the money. The Financial Times of Canada later that year disclosed that he'd moved most of his assets into arms and military supplies.

"What year was it that Atkinson moved from the Feds to Northwater?" Saffie asked.

"From what Faye said it must have been about 2016/17. Are you thinking that Atkinson may have been put in place as an asset?"

"It crossed my mind. If that were the case it would suggest that Remy is some kind of hostile asset himself and explain where the money is coming from to fund this crap."

"Even if that's true, we're not going to be able to prove it using Google, are we?"

"No, but we might be able to look closer at Atkinson."

"I'm going to call Ramirez," Saffie said.

Calling from the same burner that she'd had the kid in Charlottesville call Ramirez from, she dialed the Special Agent's number.

"Is that you Ms. Price?"

"Yes, I wondered if you were free for coffee."

"Would this be another one of those non-meetings?"

"So much less formal don't you think?"

"Where do you suggest?"

"I thought a little bistro table on our deck would be nice; the weather is fine, and driving is still a little uncomfortable for me at the moment."

"Okay, I'll be with you in half an hour."

"Dress casual," Saffie replied and ended the call.

She went outside to call the boys who'd decided to change games to soccer after the softball had disappeared into Clara's garden.

"Boys, we've got Special Agent Ramirez coming shortly, and we're going to have coffee on the deck. Would you mind restricting your game to the end of the garden or finding something to do inside while she's here?"

"Okay, Mom. We'll go and play Fortnite in my room when she gets here."

The gate bell announcing Ramirez's arrival rang ten minutes earlier than expected.

"Agent Ramirez, thank you for joining us," Saffie welcomed the agent.

"I wanted to speak to you anyway, so I hope we can make this meeting worthwhile for both of us."

Saffie led her through to the deck, Brett followed with a tray and poured the coffees as they took chairs around the little table.

The boys spotted them and stopped kicking the ball to go inside.

"Thanks boys," she said. "Ben, before you go upstairs could you grab my iPad from the study and bring it to me."

"Is that the Davis boy?" Ramirez asked.

"Yes, we're keeping him with us for a while."

"So when they made a break for it, they didn't take the kid?"

"That's right. They just asked us to hang onto him for another couple of nights. In fact they didn't even say goodbye to him."

"So we're only looking for four people not five."

"I'm afraid so."

"Did they give you any idea when they'd be back?"

"None at all, but if you'd like my best guess, it won't be until they're arrested."

Ben brought the tablet, handed it over and went back inside.

"So you think they've abandoned him?"

"That would be my guess. It makes sense in one way. If they're caught the three women are all likely to be deported, and Bridger will be lucky if he sees the outside of a prison cell for twenty years. Josh is an American citizen by birth and I guess they assumed he'd be better off here."

"It was Davis I wanted to speak about. Can you give me any more detail about what made him run?

"Yes, a great deal more detail. I'll provide you with video of him confessing to treason. I might have handed it over before, but I wasn't sure if I could use it to learn the identity of Lopez AKA Wolf as I've now learned. I apologize for that."

Saffie played the video.

"Jesus and Holy Mary mother of God," Ramirez said when it had finished playing. "You're right, you should have handed that over earlier; that shooting incident in Oakton needn't have happened if you had."

"True, but I had no way of knowing that they were about to be abducted, or even that they had been, until I got there that morning, and by that time I was left with no choice but to intervene."

"How did you learn what was in those texts between him and Wolf?"

"Let's just say that someone I know has some unusual skills."

"I'll accept that for now, but it remains to be seen if my bosses will when this plays out. What are you going to do about the boy?"

"For the time being we're happy for Josh to stay here, providing the authorities will allow that to continue," Brett said. "Everything has been traumatic for both him and Ben, and their friendship will help them cope."

"Why did you ask to see me?"

"First because I thought you needed to see that video, although I still hope you might hang fire before using it. Secondly I was hoping you could do a little background research for me."

"Depends on what it is?"

"Well it may be that you've already done this for your own investigations. We think we need to know more about Atkinson. This is what we know so far. We know that he was an FBI agent for a brief period, and quit under a cloud. We know that after that he spent a short time with a private military contractor called Woolfe Northwater, before somehow finding his way into the agency. His previous history should have barred him from even being considered for a post in any capacity, let alone being fast-tracked into Professional Standards."

"We didn't know anything about his time in Northwater, but we haven't finished looking into him yet. Is there a connection between the Wolf on that recording and Woolfe Northwater?"

"That's what we're thinking. It's too much of a coincidence otherwise."

"What do you want to know?"

"We want to know about John Atkinson, before he joined the FBI."

"What do you think that will tell you? Is he that important in this saga?"

"We're not yet in a position to prove it, but we believe he has been placed in the agency as an asset, and this whole thing is being financed by a foreign power via one of the Directors of Woolfe Northwater."

"Are you sure you're not just seeing reds under the bed?"

"Do I strike you as a conspiracy theorist? I've been a CIA agent for twelve years, four of them as a field agent, Brett for sixteen on the front line. Do you think we'd have been here this long and stayed alive if we didn't have some idea how these things work? We're as certain as we can be that there's a foreign agent inside the George Bush Center, and he has had at least one, probably two people working for him. Bridger Davis was one; we believe that Atkinson is another. Davis has until now been a sleeper, of no real value, just a useful idiot for when the moment arises, but Atkinson is a whole new ball game."

"I can't sit on this any longer Saffron; it's far too big. I'll need to leapfrog a few people and go to the top."

"I understand, but in the meantime can you tell me all you do know about Atkinson, and whatever more you can find out?" Saffie asked.

"Atkinson wasn't his birthname, we know that. The real John Atkinson with that birth date died when he was twelve days old, and his parents were killed in a car wreck three months later. The man we call Atkinson was raised in a small village called Sainte-Agathe in Quebec. The couple that raised him took the names of his parents. The father and mother worked at a small provincial golf club - he ran the shop and she worked in the club bar. The boy was privately educated, took a degree in Political Science at Fordham, and joined New York State Police straight from uni. He was uplifted to Criminal Investigation after only a year. Four years later he joined the FBI. Very little more is known so far."

"What have you done with that information?"

"As yet nothing. Because of the security implications they've restricted the team to just me and Burns since day one; it was our plan to take it upstairs tomorrow."

"Okay. Do you know who owns the golf club?" Brett asked.

"No, is it material?"

"It could be. It might explain how the parents got their cover in the first place. We have our suspicions who it might be, or a short list at least."

"Where are you next going with your investigations?" Ramirez asked.

"We're trying to learn more about Woolfe Northwater, it looks as if they were the conduit through which Atkinson became embedded in the agency."

"Have you told me everything that you know now?

"Not everything, no."

"If what you've told me so far turns out to be true, then you're putting yourselves in a lot of danger."

"We're already in a lot of danger," Brett told her. "They've hired low-life gangsters to abduct our son twice, abducted me, in effect abandoned me to my death, and attempted to kill my wife three times."

"Three times? I only know of two."

"Use your imagination, Agent Ramirez."

She didn't comment, she just told them, "Burns and I are booked in to see the Bureau Deputy Director at ten tomorrow."

"How do you think she'll react?"

"First, she'll roast our asses for not taking it to her sooner, then she'll tell us we'll be lucky to walk away with our badges. But she's a tough pragmatic SoB and she'll listen. Difficult to predict whether she'll run with it, or march straight into Wilkanowicz's office with half a dozen agents. My guess is she'll put the whole thing through the wringer before she decides. If that's the case it'll give you another few days to tie up whatever it is you're trying to do."

"What's Burns saying about this?" Brett asked.

"He thinks Saffron here is up to her neck in something; he just doesn't know what, how or why. If James had his way, you'd both be behind bars for obstructing justice. I've restrained him until now, but he's the one who insisting on pushing it all upstairs, and I can't think of any more reasons not to."

"Good to know."

Saffie Bluetoothed the video file to Ramirez's phone before they watched her drive out the gate.

"Phew, that went better than expected."

"She's right though, you're sailing very close to the wind, and it's you that's at risk. If they come after me they'll expose themselves for everything that happened in Ukraine, but you they could expose for all you've done here in the States."

"I know you wouldn't expect me to back down to that sort of intimidation; you know me better than that."

"I'm worried on Ben's behalf as well."

"I know that. I've bent a lot of rules, but if they put me on trial for defending myself and my family against traitors, convicted criminals, and my own employers they'll risk exposing themselves for the vindictive incompetents they are. I won't stay quiet; I'll make Julian Assange and Edward Snowden appear mute."

Chapter 43

"Do you know where my Mom and Dad are Mrs. Price?" Josh asked her, as she mixed batter for their breakfast waffles. Brett and Ben hadn't finished showering.

"I wish I could say yes Josh, but at the moment I can't."

"I don't understand why they ran away and left me."

"I know one thing for sure, and that is that they left you here because they thought that this would be the safest place for you for the time being," she told him. "Your dad has done some pretty dumb things and he knows that he's in trouble. Running away isn't going to solve his problems, and sooner rather than later the police will catch him, and we can all find out what your mom and dad's plans are for you. In the meantime I'll just repeat what I said to you before; Ben, Brett and I enjoy your company and you're welcome in this house for as long as necessary."

"I wet the bed last night."

"Well we won't worry too much about that will we?"

"I'm really sorry."

"Hey, these things happen; don't worry about it; we'll keep it just between you and me eh? Have a seat, and I'll serve you up some nice hot waffles. How many would you like to begin with?"

Brett and Ben joined them, but Josh was still subdued. Sensing his mood Brett announced, "Hey boys, we didn't tell you did we? We've arranged a fun outing for you both this afternoon."

"What is it?"

"Learning how to paint scenery for the stage. What do you think?"

"We don't know anything about that?"

"That's the point though, a few hours doing something you've never done before. It won't matter if you find you're no good at it, but you might find you're budding Leonardos. Either way it should be fun."

"What if we get paint all over our clothes Mom?"

"I think they'll provide smocks, but if you wear your old clothes it won't matter too much."

"My clothes are still at home."

"If you give me a list of what you want, I'll ask if I can have access to your house to collect you some clothes."

"Can't I go with you?"

"At the moment, I think it's best if you don't go to the house until we're sure it's safe. I was attacked when I went before."

Saffie texted Ramirez, who immediately replied saying that the FBI had finished with the place, and as long as she could gain entry without breaking in, it would be okay with them.

"Have you got a key for the house, Josh?"

"I left it at home, but I know where Mom keeps a spare key in the yard."

"Really, where's that?"

"Behind the garage there's a black box that looks like it's for rat poison but it isn't, it's a sort of key safe. There are keys for the house and garage in there. To get into it you have to push the lid down and press the buttons on either side at the same time."

"That's clever, thanks."

Brett looked concerned, "Will you be okay to drive?"

"My arm's a lot less painful today. As long as I keep my movement to the minimum I should be okay."

For no particular reason Saffie took the Wrangler. It was her first day without the sling, and her arm didn't like the big movements when steering sharp corners, but it was bearable. She drove slowly to be sure of spotting a tail if there was one but saw nothing.

She reversed up to the front door then walked around to the back of the garage. There were two seemingly identical rat poison boxes, and the nearest one proved to be just that, the lid wouldn't open without a special key, just like the ones she had in her own yard. The second though was subtly different, it was screwed to the wall, and it opened exactly as Josh had described. Inside was a bunch of three keys. She took them out and was about to close the lid when she spotted two four figure numbers on a card stuck to its underside. She guessed that one was the alarm code but had no idea what the other might be. Before closing the lid she took a picture of the card in case the cops had somehow set the alarm.

The keys opened the front door without difficulty. The alarm hadn't been set, but using the first of the two numbers she set it and unset it again to be sure that she was right about the number. She'd had no intention of doing anything other than collecting the things for Josh as she'd said to Ramirez, but in the end she couldn't resist a daylight look around before she began.

The only thing that aroused her curiosity was an open safe in the master bedroom closet. It was empty. At first she assumed that the second number must have been for that, but a closer look revealed the lock was a dial type numbered 1 to 100. The safe door was open and whatever had once been inside had been removed.

It took her less than fifteen minutes to find a suitable case and pack enough of Josh's clothes and shoes. It wasn't worth bringing the games console, as they had one of their own, but she packed the four games that lay alongside it as they were different to the ones they'd bought for Ben. It was a struggle getting the heavy case down the stairs with the wound in her arm and her leg injury still painful because the banister rail was on the wrong side for her injuries. She succeeded in the end and lifted it one-handed into the trunk of the car.

After locking the front door she was about to replace the keys in the rat box, when she passed the side pedestrian door to the garage and decided to take a look. One of the keys on the bunch opened the door without difficulty and it was immediately obvious that it had been searched. Cupboards above and below the workbench had been left open, and so had the trunk of the Chrysler.

At one end of the workbench was a large, tall cabinet. The open door revealed an array of garden tools and brooms, which she almost dismissed until she remembered seeing a small shed which was where you would normally expect garden equipment to be stored. With a second look she saw that none of the tools looked as if they'd ever been used and remembering seeing the gardener using a spade. She'd not seen a truck in which he might have brought his own tools. It made her curious.

After removing all the tools she looked closely at the bottom of the cabinet. At first glance there was nothing unusual to see; the base was the same height from the garage floor as all the other cabinets below the workbench. An attempt to lift the front of the base failed at first, but when she pressed down on the back there was a click and the front hinged up to reveal a safe set into the floor. Using the second of the four figure codes, the digital lock allowed her to lift the heavy lid off. She was more than a little surprised at what she found.

Saffie had seen floor safe's before, but this one was bigger, much bigger, and it was almost full of money, a great deal of it. There were bundles and bundles of $100 bills each worth $10,000. On top of them was a thumb drive, not one of the tiny ones with huge capacity currently available, but an old one about the size of a school eraser with a capacity of 2 gigabytes. She slipped it into her pocket and looked for something to put some of Davis's ill-gotten gains in.

On the bench was a tool bag filled with yet more tools looking as if they'd never been used. She emptied it out and began to fill it with bundles of notes. She realized there must be more than half a million dollars there, too much for her to readily hide at home so she put some back, in the end taking twenty-five bundles, locked the safe, replaced the tools and carried the bag to her car. Then she remembered the three guns she'd taken from the gangsters in Richmond that were still locked in the Wranglers capacious gun safe. Quickly returning to the garage she reopened the safe and put the three guns inside.

'That'll confuse them if they ever do a ballistics search on them,' she thought, smiling to herself. Then, after putting everything back as she'd found it, she locked the garage, and replaced the keys.

There was no sign of a tail on her drive home. When she got there she reversed into the garage and Brett came through from the house to meet her.

"Why did you bother garaging it? We're going out again in an hour?"

"I wanted to unload it."

"How much did you bring back for God's sake?"

"Just the two bags. Call the boys to get the big one and they can take the contents upstairs a little at a time. You can help me decide what to do with the small bag."

He called the boys and then asked, "What's in the small one?"

"Compensation," she said with a grin.

He opened the bag and quickly closed it again as the boys joined them. They lifted the suitcase out of the trunk, and the youngsters wheeled it through to the hallway and began decanting the contents to the bedroom that Josh had chosen the night before.

"So talk to me about this compensation," he said.

"I discovered a safe that the feebies had overlooked and inside was a lot of money and this," she said, holding up the thumb drive. "It occurred to me that one way or another we've spent a great deal of our own money dealing with various aspects of the fallout from whatever this is. We don't know whether we'll ever be able to get compensation from the bastard that started this. Even if we win this war, the chances of the CIA refunding it all are close to zero, and if we lose we're going to have to spend a great deal more on lawyers. So I liberated some of the Russian dollars that Davis has been hoarding."

Brett smiled and shook his head, "We still need to find somewhere to put it."

"I know but it will have to wait until we get back from the Northwater AGM. Would you mind driving this afternoon. I need to use my sling again for a while?"

Brett called upstairs, "We're leaving in fifteen minutes, so if you haven't finished with the clothes yet, you should get changed right now and finish when we get back."

They eventually arrived at the bottom of the stairs after twenty minutes, and were quickly herded into the BMW. The car was out of the gate by eleven forty-five.

"We haven't had lunch," Ben complained.

"We're stopping at a burger bar on the way, so if you can quickly give me some idea what you want I can order ahead and you can eat in the car," Saffie told them.

They couldn't decide, so Saffie decided for them, and ordered cheeseburgers and Mountain Dew all round. When they arrived at the theatre she was thankful for the moistened wipes that the restaurant had provided, and she had to spend five minutes cleaning them of ketchup before she could take them inside.

Brett waited in the car while Saffie handed them over to the theatre staff. The course tutor and theatre director came out to meet them, both wanting to express their gratitude for the generous donation she'd made and attempted to persuade her to become a patron. Saffie fobbed them off with a smile and a promise to give it careful consideration, then she said goodbye to the boys with a promise to pick them up at five o'clock."

Chapter 44

Brett had swapped places with her a hundred yards from the building and walked to the coffee franchise on the first floor of the building. In the coffee shop he took up station near a window where he could observe the comings and goings to the front doors of the office block.

Saffie's hopes of parking in the basement car park were almost dashed when she was refused entry because she didn't have a pass. But after she convinced the parking guy at the other end of a speaker that she was there to buy membership of the basement health club he allowed her two hours parking in an unused space.

She knew her movements would be observed on security cameras so she made great play of seeking out the health club entrance. In the reception she was greeted by a beefy nineteen-year-old in a polo shirt, training pants and expensive sneakers who insisted on giving her a tour of the facilities. She knew she didn't have much time and in the end she bought a day pass and told him she'd be back later.

As she made her way back to the car she noticed that some bays were marked with the name of the company that leased them. It didn't take long to locate the bays allocated to Northwater; the letters *WN* were stenciled on the floor. Three were in use, but there were nine empty ones. Conscious that she could still be seen she surreptitiously took pictures of the three license plates, spotting that one of them was the blue Model X Tesla with the damaged rear fender that had carved her up in the Langley car park.

'Shit,' she thought, 'missed him.'

Back in her car where she could observe the entry ramp she sat there until past the time when the meeting was to have started. She was about to get out of the car and take one last look at the Northwater parking places, when an old guy in a security uniform knocked on the window.

"Excuse me Ma'am. I allowed you to use the parking space so you could use the health club. I've been watching you and apart from ten minutes inside you've just sat in the car. I'm going to have to ask you to leave."

"Sorry about that. I did buy a day pass, look." She showed him the card. "Then I felt a bit faint from my injured arm."

"Well if you're feeling better now, I suggest you leave." There were plenty of free spaces, so she didn't see why it mattered, but decided it wasn't worth arguing.

"Yes, of course. Thank you though."

She didn't think there would have been anything else to learn by hanging around, unless she waited until the meeting was over, and she couldn't afford the time to do that. Starting the engine, she pushed the lever into drive and drove towards the exit ramp waving to the security guy.

Brett had been similarly prompted to leave after not buying enough coffee. It was still only three-fifteen, far too early to pick the boys up.

"It's not worth going home. Can we go and park up somewhere. I can do some research on the phone. Did you find out anything?"

"There were six limos of varying sizes dropping off and I think I've got reasonable pictures of all their passengers," he said. "What we do with them is the next problem."

"Let me speak to Linda; she might be able to help."

Ten minutes later they'd forwarded their photos to Linda from both their phones.

"What will Linda be able to do with the pictures? I know she should be able to identify the owners of the three cars in the car park; that'll be more useful than the photos I expect."

"She's going to get one of her contacts to run the photos through facial recognition."

"There are six of them; can't that take days?"

"Things are quicker these days and if you restrict the search parameters it abbreviates the process. These are prominent people. I expect they'll have a noticeable presence on the Internet and a lot of photographs that will shorten the process as well."

"We can't be sure what we'll learn from knowing who's on the board and finding out what they look like."

"It might tell us if someone isn't who they say they are - if say they're using other identities elsewhere."

Her phone buzzed. "That was quick Linda...Okay, which ones?...Okay. Which car doesn't associate with a driver?...So who does?...Okay, thanks

Linda. How much did she charge you?...That's very reasonable, make sure you add that to what I owe you....Speak soon."

"What was all that about?" he asked.

"The two cars that her friend was able to associate with owners belonged to Tammy Warren and Mitch Cassidy. The one car she couldn't link to an individual was registered to Woolfe Northwater. Perhaps it was Lindsey Johnson."

"No, I don't think so; he was one of those that I saw roll up in a stretch limo."

"That's useful but in itself not the most interesting thing I learned today. The day I went to Langley to have it out with Wilkanowicz, that car cut me up in the car park. So it means that someone on the board at Northwater either works at or has access to Langley."

"What car does Wilkanowicz drive?"

"The only times I've seen him in vehicles in recent years is when he's being driven by his bodyguard in a company Range Rover, but that doesn't mean he couldn't use his own car from time to time. To be honest I rarely see him anyway."

They discussed what they'd learned as they whiled away the time before collecting the boys. At four-fifteen her phone pinged announcing an email. Linda's other friend had put a name to every face arriving in luxury vehicles, which were presumably there for the Northwater AGM.

All six names had significant recognizable Internet presence except one, Auguste Laurent. There was only one picture of him on the web, from when he was identified in a Quebec local paper as the philanthropist who saved a small provincial golf course from closure, by buying it.

"Bingo!" she said. "Laurent is either Remy Raimond or Wilfred Bauer - process of elimination."

"Remy Raimond is a French name; my betting would be with him."

"Mine too. One more phone call before we collect the boys." She selected a number from her phone and called, "Clara, it's Saffron from next door. I wonder if I can ask a favor....Do you have a safe?...You do. Would you allow me to use it for a while? The FBI broke into ours while I was away and damaged the lock....No that wouldn't matter at all. I'll pop round later if it's convenient. You're very kind, thank you."

"So the safe place for your ill-gotten gains is our neighbor's safe. What if she gets nosey and can't resist taking a look?"

"It's an old-fashioned gun safe in her garage, they brought it with them from their last home and it's key operated. I saw it when we were dealing with Wallace. She just told me that she's only got one key, because her husband had the other one with him when he died in a plane crash on a hunting trip in Alaska."

Chapter 45

Brett waited in the car again while Saffie collected the boys. When they climbed back in the car they were buzzing.

"Did you have a good time then boys?"

"It was awesome, Dad," Ben told him.

"How about you, Josh?"

"It was good fun, Mr. Price. Thank you."

"Josh is really good at it; he painted a tree with some flowers and a rabbit at the bottom. He had to stand on a ladder to do the top of the tree."

"Are you good at art then Josh?"

"I guess. I've always liked drawing."

"You should have said and I could have picked up your drawing stuff from the house this morning. I doubt they'll let me go again, but we can get you some more if you tell me what you want."

"Would you do that?"

"Sure."

"My dad said that art was a girl's subject."

"Well not wanting to damage your father's image in your eyes any more than it is already, but that's crap. The best art in the world in all its forms have been created by both sexes. Michelangelo and da Vinci didn't seem to think it was just for girls."

"We need to replenish the cupboards and if we order online it won't get here until the day after tomorrow; do you want to stop at *Giant* on the way home?" Brett asked.

"Sure, why not? Are you okay with that boys?"

"Can we pick what we want for dinner tonight?"

Saffie laughed. "I guess so. Will you be okay with your leg walking around that huge store, sweetheart?"

"I guess if I push the cart it will give me something to lean on if I get tired."

They parked as close to the store's front door as possible and the boys ran to grab a cart. It was a long time since Saffie had taken Ben to the store for a major shop. He was very helpful but she'd forgotten about his penchant for wanting to experiment with new foodstuffs. It often took a lot of persuasion to rein him in, but she loved his enthusiasm, and Josh seemed just as keen.

Brett was browsing the herbs and spices when Ben joined him with a new variety of Cheerios. Saffie was still in the fresh meat section,

"Dad, I think we're being followed," Ben whispered to him. "There's two of them."

"Okay. Try not to look at them but describe them to me."

"One of them is about the same height as you and he's wearing a plaid shirt, denim pants and a camouflage cap like you and Mom wear when we go hiking. He's behind you. The other one is bald, about Mom's height wearing a green hoodie, grey training pants and black sneakers."

"Really good descriptions, Ben. Well done. Where's Josh?"

"Josh is trying to watch what the bald one does; he's following Mom."

"Can you go and find him and not let these guys see that they've been spotted if you can. Then tell Mom what you told me. We're not in any danger."

He chose a few things from the rack and threw them in the cart before turning toward the other side of the aisle. As he turned he saw the plaid shirt guy trying to look as if he was closely examining the range of cooking sauces. The guy had cop written all over him.

Saffie and the boys caught up with him as he put a box of laundry capsules in the cart. She put five packs of meat and a sharp kitchen knife in the cart.

"That little thing won't be much use as a weapon."

"I don't want it for a weapon." She turned to the boys. "Ben, when we're at the checkout I want you two boys to go and wait outside the door. When we come out I want you to watch for those two guys to follow us out, see what car they get in, then join us at our own. Can you do that?"

"Sure, Mom."

It was nearly six p.m. by this time and the after-work busy period was well underway making the checkout queues long, but the boys remembered what they'd been asked. They'd spotted the tails, each carrying a basket with only one or two items, both hovering near the express checkout tills, trying to time their exits with Saffie and Brett's. As her husband paid for their shopping, Saffie struggled trying to remove the packaging from the knife without being seen by others nearby. The knife was on a card enclosed with transparent plastic and then shrink wrapped for safety. Thankfully, her fight with the packaging succeeded and they made their way to the door, spotting the two cops hurrying to pay for their own bits and pieces.

They ignored the boys at the door and made their way to their car. Brett and Saffie were only halfway through decanting their purchases into the trunk when the boys joined them.

"They're in a dirty white F150. It's not new, about two rows over. It's got a Virginia license plate KGV-5561."

"Wow, you two are very thorough," Saffie told them. "Carry on ignoring them even when we're in the car.

"What's your plan?" Brett asked.

"Go to leave just as you would normally, except slow enough to give them time to tag on behind. Ideally they'll allow another car or two to fall in between us. But I'm going to drop out before we get to the front of the queue."

Brett followed her instructions, while Saffie watched in the vanity mirror as the Ford fell in behind two cars back. When there was only one car in front of them, Saffie jumped out and ran back to the cops' car, stabbed the knife into both front and rear nearside tires and hurried back to their car. She was back in the passenger seat, and Brett was driving away with barely a pause.

"That was fun," Brett remarked.

"Who were they?" Josh asked.

"I'm pretty sure they were cops."

"But you'll get into trouble for that won't you?"

"If the cops wanted to know where we were or where we were going, they only had to ask."

"But what if they are cops?"

"We only have our instinct to tell us they were cops and we've had catalogs of bad guys trying to do all sorts of things to us in the last two weeks; they can see how their actions could so easily be misinterpreted."

"Perhaps they didn't expect us to notice them."

"No disrespect to you two, but if they were spotted by two eight-year-old boys they must be pretty dumb cops. How did you spot them by the way?" Saffie asked.

"It was Josh spotted the one with the green hoodie first."

"He kept turning up in the same aisle as Mrs. Price and she wasn't going in a particular pattern like you were. Then, after I told Ben, he started watching out as well and he saw the other man."

"That was pretty smart thinking boys."

"My mom was always telling me to be on the lookout for paedophiles, but she never said how to recognize them," Josh explained.

"When we get home, I need you to help Brett unload the trunk, while I go round to our neighbor. Is that okay?"

It didn't take many minutes for Saffie to carry the bag of cash next door and unload it into the old gun safe. She was soon back in her own house helping put the groceries where they belonged.

"How's your arm?" Brett asked.

"Better than yesterday, but I wouldn't complain if it hurt less. What about your leg?"

"Same, I guess."

Brett produced a Moroccan dish for dinner which Josh took some persuading to eat because he didn't like the smell. In the end he ate some and decided he liked it.

The boys were given permission to spend the evening on the PlayStation while the adults sat in the living room with a bottle of wine trying to decide where to go next with their investigation.

As they prepared for bed, Brett turned to Saffie, "How do you think those cops picked us up at the supermarket?"

"Probably that tracker in my wallet."

"If that's right, it means that someone in Langley is pulling strings in the cops."

"I know," she replied. "Shall we have a look what's on that thumb drive I found in the safe?"

In the end what they discovered was a Word document that contained a much more detailed confession to the one that Davis had made to Saffie, much of it attempting to excuse or justify his actions. It was relatively up to date, and when she checked, she saw that the file had been created the day before. There were also two voice recordings of telephone conversations with Wolf, which didn't in themselves help identify him but might at some point be useful for voice recognition.

Chapter 46

As they dressed the following morning, both adults reported that their injuries appeared to be getting marginally less painful although both still had restricted movements in their affected limbs.

Ben asked if he could cook egg on toast with bacon for everybody. Saffie agreed as long as he allowed her to supervise.

They had barely finished eating and were deciding what to do with the day when the gate bell rang. Saffie went to the entry phone and saw Sergeant Wolski so she pressed the button to open the gates. When she opened the door she was surprised to see two cruisers follow the detective's car through the gate. Wolski climbed out with a uniformed cop who she immediately recognised as one of the goons in the supermarket, the one in the hoodie.

The cruisers both discharged uniformed patrol officers, the drivers pulled their handguns, their partners were holding pump action shotguns, and all six were wearing body armor.

"What the Hell Wolski, are you expecting a war or something?"

"Saffron Price, I'm arresting you for the murder of Jamal Skillet. You have the right to remain silent. Anything you say can and will be used against you in a court of law. You have the right to speak to an attorney, and to have an attorney present during any questioning. If you cannot afford an attorney, one will be provided for you. Do you understand?"

"No, I don't. Who the Hell is Jamal Skillet?"

Hoodie man stepped behind her and roughly wrenched her arms behind her.

"Ouch. Fuck you asshole, I've got a bullet wound in my arm."

"Yeah, well this is me not giving a shit. Cocksure bitch."

"Control this asshole, Wolski," Brett angrily told him. "My wife isn't resisting. Everything he just said and did was recorded on video and when the time comes, we'll be sure to use it when we lodge a complaint. If she's anyway harmed or her wounds are exacerbated by his brutality, he personally and Fairfax County Police in general will find themselves at the wrong end of a lawsuit."

"Reel it in Larsen," Wolski ordered. "Mason make sure she's clean then you and Jackson put her in the car."

The female patrol officer patted her down, and they manhandled her out of the door.

"Mom!" Ben pleaded.

The two cops roughly shoved her into the back of a cruiser. Saffie decided to say nothing more, but in the end she had to ask. "Hey, where the Hell are you taking me?"

"You'll find out soon enough."

The cop in the passenger seat was the guy in the plaid shirt from the day before.

"What, was that too challenging a question for you?"

"Listen you mouthy bitch, we get enough crap from feds trampling all over us when we're trying to do our job, so I'm all out of shits to give if you ain't happy with your treatment. If you want me to make your stay with us even more unpleasant then just keep flapping your jaw."

"Drive carefully; you don't want to get a flat. I mean you wouldn't want to get stranded halfway to your destination. I heard that can get embarrassing in your profession."

He turned and grinned, "You do like to live dangerously don't you?"

"So I'm told."

If this were normal, she would have expected to be taken to Fairfax City, or Vienna police stations but that clearly wasn't happening; it looked more like Mclean. Mclean was a district headquarters. Maybe they were upping the ante.

When they arrived they led her into the custody suite, and a sergeant behind a raised desk in reception looked up. "This the spook, Jackson?" he asked.

"That's right Sarge, a mouthy bitch."

"Put her in number twelve."

"Don't I get to call my lawyer?" she asked.

"In good time."

"Aren't you going to book me in? I mean you'll be wanting to record this for your custody records, won't you?"

"My custody records will say whatever I want them to say."

Jackson jerked her injured arm deliberately harshly but she was expecting it and she gritted her teeth not to cry out. The cell was the last one along the corridor. Larsen the second cop, opened it without speaking and Jackson shoved her inside and closed the door.

"Hey what about the cuffs?"

Jackson looked though the hatch and grinned. "Suck it up."

"Fuck you," she replied.

The tiny cell was for four people; bunk beds with plastic-covered mattresses were on either side and it stank of stale body odor, vomit, and urine. Just inside the door, behind a half height wall was a filthy stainless steel toilet pan with an equally filthy basin beside it.

Two women were already in there both looking stoned on either drink or drugs. Neither registered her arrival. One was lying on a bottom bunk moaning, her head hanging over the side, and there was a puddle of vomit on the floor beneath her head. The second woman sat on the opposite bunk, swaying and staring into space.

There were comings and goings from the other cells, shouts, protests, pleas of innocence and cries for help over the next hours. Most involved some sort of interaction with police officers, but nobody came near cell twelve.

It must have been at least five hours before another female officer came to look through the hatch, by that time both the other women had sobered some, not that it improved their appeal as cellmates.

"You gonna get someone to take these cuffs off me, or would you prefer me to bring charges of maltreating a prisoner in custody?"

"How long have you been in here?"

"I don't know what time it is now, but it was nine-twenty-five on the custody clock when they wheeled me in. And both these women should have been given medical supervision in that time but nobody has even opened the hatch until now."

The officer called the custody sergeant. When he arrived it was a different one than before, and he removed the cuffs before giving her a bucket and mop to clean up the vomit while they supervised. When she finished, she handed the bucket to the Sergeant. "I didn't catch your name Sergeant."

"Flores."

"Sergeant Flores, do you think you could ask someone to tell me what the fuck I'm doing here, call my lawyer, and arrange something for us all to eat and drink. If someone could get me some painkillers too it would be great."

"Haven't you been interviewed yet?" the woman asked.

"No. I was arrested without a warrant, told it was for murdering someone called Jamal Skillet who I've never heard of, given no information about when and where this crime was supposed to have taken place, then shoved in here so roughly that the gunshot wound on my arm has started to bleed again."

"The custody record says you were only brought in an hour ago."

"Big surprise, the custody sergeant bragged how he could make the records say whatever he wanted."

"Who brought you in?"

"I was arrested at my home in Dunn Loring by Detective Sergeant Wolski, with five other officers."

"Six of them?"

"The two who drove me here were called Larsen and Jackson if that helps. No doubt you'll have video record of all parts of the custody suite, which should have recorded my arrival."

"Okay, I'll look into this. In the meantime Walker get Mrs. Price something to eat. I'll arrange to process and discharge these other two; apparently they were only here to sober up."

Twenty minutes later both the two junkies had gone and Walker had brought Saffie a sandwich and a bottle of water.

But for the wound in her arm, she might have fallen asleep, so when Flores opened the hatch later she asked, "Any chance of those painkillers sometime soon? My wound is hurting like a bastard after your colleague jerking it around."

"Wound?"

She turned her arm toward him, revealing the blood on her sleeve, "I have a gunshot wound on my left arm. Is there nothing in your custody record about that either?"

"Look I'm having problems finding out what's going on. I can't find any record of a murder victim of that name, Wolski's gone off duty and won't answer my calls."

"Did you look at the security video from nine this morning?"

"That's another problem; the video was turned off at eight o'clock."

"What about speaking to the custody sergeant that was on duty, or the two grunts that brought me in?"

"They've all gone off duty."

"What time?"

"At ten."

"So who did you take over from?"

"A standby sergeant from Vienna."

"Do you want to explain how I know the name of two officers on duty at nine-twenty-five who went off duty at ten, if I wasn't brought in until - what time does it say in the log, Sergeant Flores?"

"Two, that's when I took over and you weren't even on the board then. You're right something is very wrong here, but I can't release you until I know what's happening."

"What about my lawyer?"

"The custody record says he was called when you were bought in."

"And his name, the lawyer that they called?"

"The public defender."

"Since when did anybody get a public defender before they're charged?"

"Shit! Do you have a lawyer?"

"Shit indeed. Yes I do, he's name is Franklyn Cohen of Chesham, Chesham and Adelstein. Nobody bothered to ask before."

"I'll contact him straightaway."

"And don't forget the painkillers," she called after him as he closed the cell door.

Flores returned half an hour later. "We're really not supposed to give out pharmaceuticals, but here are a couple of Tylenol from my locker."

"Thanks Sarge, much appreciated."

"Your lawyer told me that you're a CIA agent. Is that right?"

"That's right."

"He's been trying to find out where you were taken since ten o'clock this morning. It didn't sound like I need to be one of the cops involved in this when he finds out what went wrong?"

"You'd better believe it. When will he be here?"

"About an hour I guess, he was with a senator in the Capitol when I called. I've never heard of anything like this," he told her. "You're taking this very calmly if you don't mind me saying."

"Sergeant, in the last two weeks or so my son has had two abduction attempts at gunpoint, one was successful, another not so much; my house has been burgled, there have been three attempts on my life, my husband has been shot, and now I've been falsely arrested for a murder that didn't happen. If I didn't take it calmly I'd be in the funny farm by now."

"You must be the spook involved in that shooting in Arlington."

"That's right."

Half an hour later she heard a commotion out in the custody suite before the cell door opened and a Police Captain in uniform was standing there with Larsen and Jackson. Sergeant Flores was to one side looking furious.

"You two cuff her and get her out of here before her fucking lawyer gets here." the captain barked.

The two grinning goons didn't need asking twice. They took great pleasure in causing her as much pain as possible as they dragged her out of the cell. As they passed through the custody reception Flores came up behind her. "I'm going to find out what the Hell is going on here."

"Get out of the way Flores," the unnamed Captain ordered.

There was no further delay and they bundled her out to a waiting police cruiser.

The journey was over very quickly and she immediately recognized where she was, the County Detention Centre. The barriers across the entrance lowered themselves into the ground and the car bumped twice as it drove across them.

Roughly dragged out and pushed ahead of them by the two thugs, they went through a rudimentary identification process before she was ushered into a small room where Jackson roughly pushed her face against the wall.

"We have a way of dealing with mouthy whores," he said as he spun her to face him and squeezed her left breast as he pressed himself against her.

"I guess a pussy like you needs to have a woman restrained if he wants half a chance of getting laid."

He grinned as Larsen's hand grabbed her crotch.

"If you two don't take your perverted hands off me, I'll make you regret it."

"We're just conducting a routine search," Larsen said.

Their smiles didn't last long, because she drew her head back and head-butted Jackson as hard as she could. Unfortunately, her blow hadn't been as damaging as she'd have liked, but it was enough to force him to let go, grab his bleeding nose, and stagger back barely able to see.

Saffie pulled her right hand from behind her and chopped Larsen in the side of his neck. He fell to the floor with one side of his body partially paralyzed. Then holding out the handcuffs, "This what you were looking for Officer Larsen?"

Instinctively he went to reach for a gun that wasn't there, forgetting in the moment that firearms weren't allowed inside the jail and they'd been taken from them on their way in. He then found himself helpless to defend himself from the series of well-aimed debilitating blows that followed. Using just her right hand and her feet Saffie left him cringing in the corner before swinging to face Jackson and releasing as powerful a kick to his crotch as she'd ever used on any opponent. The cop screamed and fell to the floor holding his balls. She turned back to Larsen who was trying to stand on an uncooperative leg whilst cradling a broken arm with the other.

"Stay down unless you want some more," she told him.

The whole fracas had taken less than a minute, but before the crooked cop could reply, two burly prison deputies burst in with batons raised.

"Your friends seem to have hurt themselves," she told them.

"Stand against the wall. Now!" one of them yelled.

She did as he'd ordered. "I'm not dangerous unless you plan to sexually assault me like those two assholes who shouldn't even have been in here. I know you need to search me and I'll cooperate if it's done by a woman without men present."

"How did you get the cuffs off?" one of them asked.

Saffie shrugged. "I guess they didn't put them on properly." In truth Flores had slipped her a key when he'd sidled up to her in the custody reception as she'd been taken out to the cruiser.

"If you give us any more trouble we'll beat you until you're black and blue. You got that?"

"Like I say, if you don't sexually assault me then I won't be any trouble. In the meantime you might want to get these two sex attackers some medical help, and if you've got any video of what went on in here you might want to make sure it's saved, because I will be pursuing a complaint."

She knew she'd ultimately have to submit to an intimate search, but the two female guards who'd been given the task had clearly been told what had happened to the cops and dealt with it as perfunctorily as they could get away with. She was given an orange jumpsuit with *VADC* stenciled on the back and a pair of flip flops. Then they cuffed her in front for a change, handed her a blanket, two pairs of prison panties and two sanitary towels.

"Am I going to get to see my lawyer any time soon?" she asked.

"Not our department," one of them dispassionately replied as they led her through a series of locked doors and eventually into a group cell housing about twenty other women. "Find a spare bed, if you can," he said.

"I won't be here that long."

"You think?"

Her arrival sparked an outbreak of comment and curious looks from the other women.

Searching for an unoccupied bunk, she wandered through the other women trying to appear nonchalant at their hostile expressions. For the most part they stepped aside and allowed her to pass, but one or two jostled her.

A bottom bunk, about as far from the door as possible appeared free so she dropped the blanket on it.

From some of the remarks by other prisoners she realized that this wasn't a short-term holding cell, but a remand unit for prisoners refused bail and awaiting trial. That was when she began to be concerned.

The objectionable noise and smells of the jail had moved to the back of her mind as she laid back attempting to focus on what was happening.

"You the cop?"

She lifted her head to see a grossly overweight woman about five feet eleven tall.

"No."

"That's not what I heard."

"You're misinformed then; perhaps you should check your sources."

Three other women gathered around her.

"I don't believe you."

"That's your prerogative of course."

"Fancy words, the sort of words that a cop would use."

"You must be talking to a rare variety of cop then that's all I can say, most that I come across can barely string two words together in a coherent sentence."

"There you go again, fancy words."

"No seriously, which cops are you speaking to? I was only brought in about ninety minutes ago. I put the two street cops that brought me here in hospital so it must be one of the more senior ones, perhaps you're a C.I. or maybe just a grass."

Other women had started to gather around now.

"Yeah Crystal, who was it told you she's a cop?" A woman with a blue Mohican asked, one of her original henchwomen,.

"I got my sources."

"I think you just made my point, Crystal," Saffie told her. "Anyway, as I told you, your pet cop got it wrong. I'm not a cop, I'm a martial arts instructor and I got a beef with a police captain. I guess he's the guy you're talking to."

"You a rat, Crystal?" Mohican asked.

"Fuck off whore."

A clamor of loud angry female criminals voices began, resulting in Crystal punching Mohican and knocking her to the floor. In the full-blown fight that developed Crystal was outnumbered, and eventually the huge woman was overcome and forced to the floor. When four guards with batons burst through the door, another woman was on top of her pulling her hair with one hand and punching her with the other. It took only a few brutal applications of the batons to the arms and thighs of inmates to restore some sort of order.

"Get on your beds, all of you now, and you D'Arcy," he said, pointing his baton at the woman who'd straddled Crystal.

"Get her out of here; she a snitch," D'Arcy snarled.

A chorus of agreement followed by a chant of, "Ditch the snitch bitch" repeated over and over, each time louder than the last. In the end the guard who appeared to be in charge told two others to take Crystal out for her own protection. That was followed by triumphant jeers from the other inmates.

The senior guard turned to Saffie. "Listen to me you uppity bitch, if I find out that you were behind that, you'll be finding yourself on the wrong end of my baton, d'yer hear me?"

"I didn't catch your name officer."

"Deputy Adams."

"Well, Deputy Adams, whilst I'm grateful for your intervention, but when you examine the footage of what happened just now I'm sure you'll find that I wasn't even involved. However, if as I suspect, you find that the cameras have been turned off, it might be beneficial for you to ask who and why someone did that just at the time a disturbance was about to break out."

The Deputy thought for a moment, then turned away without speaking.

For the next hour or two Saffie lay on the bed, trying to think despite the throbbing pain in her arm. The other prisoners largely avoided her, too consumed with discussions of how being locked up with Crystal might affect their case if she were a snitch. On the few occasions they spoke to or about her they'd taken to calling her Cynthia after the martial arts film star Cynthia Rothrock. She did nothing to correct them.

The evening meal came and went, providing very little sustenance to Saffie, but hunger pains were the least of her worries. She was more concerned about what was happening at home. Brett would be kicking up a storm, raising Hell with every contact that he could, and threatening everybody with retribution. Ben would be worried sick, and she was worried what would happen to Josh; even in his short stay under their roof he'd endeared himself to her, and she was anxious for his future.

She'd now reconciled herself to the fact that nothing would now be going to happen until the morning at the earliest, and when the lights dimmed to their nighttime setting she settled down to sleep.

"Hey Cynthia," the girl in the lower bunk next to her whispered.

"What's up?"

"I don't know if you're really what or who you say you are, because that sounded like some real clever shit you pulled on Crystal, but she's a seriously nasty bitch so I don't care. You need to know that she's still got friends in here, so you need to watch your ass."

"Okay, thanks." It was no surprise for Saffie to hear that. Neither was it any comfort to have it confirmed.

The noise in the big room of snoring and groaning women talking in their sleep and others getting out of bed to use the john were constant, but in the end she slept.

She had no idea of the time when she felt a hand around the throat. A voice whispered, "Okay bitch, get outta bed now and be fucking quiet or I'll slit your nose down the middle."

There were three of them altogether. The girl holding her throat with her left hand was holding a shank close to her eye with the other. The other two stood at the end of the bed looking nervous.

"Okay, where are we going?"

"For a little walk but keep your voice down."

"What for? I'm tired. I don't want to go for a walk," Saffie replied at normal speaking volume.

"I'll slice your eye out if you don't."

"A moment ago you were going to cut my nose; now it's my eye. You don't seem too sure of yourself." Her voice was starting to get louder.

"It won't matter to you when you're dead, bitch."

"So now you're going to kill me. Actually I think that's what you've got planned anyway, so I'll stay here if it's all the same."

"So I'll kill you here."

"What in full view of those cameras? I don't think so."

"The cameras have been turned off."

"I guess those little blinking red lights are just for show then."

The woman momentarily loosened her grip on Saffie's throat to look into the high corners of the room where there was no blinking light. The distraction wasn't much but it gave her enough time to grab the wrist of the hand holding the shank with her good hand and use her other to hit the pressure point on the side of the woman's neck. She hadn't hit her hard enough to kill her, but the blow had sent a shock to her carotid artery causing her to faint. Twisting the wrist, the shank fell to the floor, allowing Saffie to stand and pick it up. The other two women were too shocked to intervene.

"It's very late; you two must be tired. Why don't you go try and catch up on your sleep."

"What're you gonna do to Billie-Jean?"

"Nothing as long as she tells me who put her up to this. We're just gonna have a little chat that's all. Before you go though, you do realize that whoever you think you've been working for, you're probably wrong. It'll be the same crooked cop that set Crystal up to do it, and if you thought that you'd get a free pass for it, you can forget it. They'd laugh as you sat in the electric chair."

They turned and sheepishly went back to their beds.

"Okay Billie-Jean, did you hear all of that?"

She nodded.

"You've been pretty damn stupid, haven't you."

"Bitch."

"I may be a bitch, but I'm not a cop, and I'm no threat to anybody in here unless they become a threat to me. Right now you seem to be a threat to me and I'm the one with the blade, so unless you want me to kill you, you'd better start telling me who gave you this shank, and who put you up to this."

"Then it'd be you in the chair, 'cept there ain't no death penalty in Virginia no more."

"True in most cases but there are exceptions, such as murder by a prisoner confined in a state or local correctional facility, or of a law-enforcement officer, or an employee of the state or of the federal government. But it's worth you knowing I could kill you and most coroners would think it was a natural death."

"I knew you were a cop."

"I'm not a cop, I'm an agent in the CIA, and I'm in here because there are people who want me dead and are prepared to set you up to do it."

"It was one of the prison guards."

"What was his name?"

"Art Stewart."

"What did he promise you?"

"He said he could arrange for my kid to visit me when I go down."

"How long are you going to get, do you know?"

"Probably twenty years. I killed my husband."

"Did you really believe that a pissy-assed prison deputy has the pull to fix something like that?"

"I just wanted any chance to see my little girl is all," she sobbed. "She's so little and so pretty. I killed her asshole father cos he was using her as a drug mule."

"Okay Billie-Jean, this is how it's going to go. If I get out of here alive, I'll get my lawyer to look into the possibility of getting a guarantee for visits by your daughter. I don't even know if that's possible, but I'll get him to find out. What's your second name?"

"It's Bates, but why would you do that?"

"Because you were being set up the same way I am. Is that a good enough reason?"

"I guess so."

"Fine now go back to bed."

Saffie settled down and tried unsuccessfully to get back to sleep.

Chapter 47

When the lights came on, the queue to use the very non-private toilet and washing facilities formed quite quickly, Saffie stoically went about her business attempting to maintain her dignity. It appeared that most of the others had given up trying.

When it was time for breakfast she joined yet another queue. At the hatch she asked the officer his name. He held his chest to the hatch and showed his name tag. It wasn't Stewart, so she passed the shank through to him.

"I found this dangerous article and didn't think it should be left lying around, could you dispose of it for me?"

The guard looked dumbstruck for a moment but took it from her and handed her what passed for breakfast - the same as every other meal, a sandwich, an apple, and small bottle of water. This wasn't a prison, and because most inmates were only there for two or three days awaiting trial, it wasn't required to provide the same level of nutrition. Taking the offering she returned to her bed to eat.

It must have been about eight-thirty when guards came to the door and called a few names, and one by one they filed forward to be cuffed and taken away to be transported to court for their hearings. Saffie tried to get one of the guards to listen to her plea that she'd been in custody for twenty-four hours and had still not been interviewed nor given access to a lawyer. The guard gave the impression that he heard similar tales every day of the week and gave hers about the same amount of credence.

Throughout the morning other prisoners were called, some returned, and new ones were admitted, most of them clearly seasoned customers of the penal system who took it all in their stride, but one girl, seemingly no more than eighteen, looked terrified. She looked lost as she searched for somewhere to settle.

"Hey, sweetheart, the top bunk here is free if you're looking for a spot."

She shuffled over.

"First time in a place like this, huh?"

"Y-yes."

"Me too."

"They put their fingers inside me, front and back."

"I know, it's horrible. Try not to think about it. What's your name?"

"Kristen Barfield."

"What happened?"

"My boyfriend stole a car and we crashed."

"That's tough. Did you know it was stolen?"

"No." She was shaking.

"What have you been charged with?"

"Grand theft auto."

"Jesus, that's excessive. Have you got a lawyer?"

"I think so, but I haven't met him yet."

"Didn't they get you one when you were interviewed?"

"They said that it would delay everything, and I'd get a PD in court."

"So it's a public defender?"

"I guess."

"Okay, would you like me to get you a proper lawyer?"

"I can't pay."

"I'll pay."

"Why would you do that. I couldn't pay you back?"

"I don't want to be paid back, and I'd do it for two reasons, first because it sounds like you've been handed a crock of shit, and second because it'll help me out?"

"How?"

"Because I've been locked up in here by a crooked cop for thirty hours without a charge and they won't let me contact my lawyer. If you insist on having your own lawyer and use mine, you can tell him that I'm in here and he can do something about it."

"Who's your lawyer?"

"His name is Franklyn Cohen of Chesham, Chesham and Adelstein. Can you remember that?"

"I think so."

"Great, but make sure you insist on them calling him, don't let them talk you into seeing someone else."

They'd eaten lunch together and spent the next hour talking when a guard called her from the door, "Your lawyer's here."

"Tell him you want to see your own lawyer. Remember, Franklyn Cohen of Chesham, Chesham and Adelstein."

She went to the door. Saffie went with her, and listened to what was being said.

"I-I want to see my own lawyer."

"Listen kid, I doubt you can afford your own lawyer's coffee bill, so stop fucking around and see the PD like everybody else."

"N-no I want my own lawyer."

"Do you even know the name of a lawyer?"

"Y-yes it's Franklyn Cohen of Chesham, Chesham and Adelstein."

The deputy laughed; the law firm was a big name in DC.

"Yeah right, like he'd be interested in your pissing little GTA."

Saffie intervened. "Deputy, I hope you're not refusing this young woman her constitutional right to have her own lawyer."

"What's it got to do with you?"

"More to the point what's it got to do with you? Which lawyer she chooses or whether or not she can pay for it, is her affair."

"Okay, but the judge won't be happy with her if she's just fucking around to waste time."

"The same can be said of you if she gets into court and tells the judge you obstructed her access to proper legal representation, especially as the cops have already done that once."

"Okay, I'll call you when he gets here, if he does."

"Now listen Kristen, it may not be Franklyn himself who comes, he may send someone else. I can't be sure, but it doesn't matter. Whoever comes will do a good job for you. You just need to tell him about me being locked up in here for a murder that hasn't happened, that I haven't been charged, I haven't been interviewed and there's been an attempt on my life. My name is Saffron Price. Can you do that?"

"Yes."

"That's it then."

Little more than an hour later the guard called Kirsten's name.

Saffie accompanied her to the door again.

"Fucking Hell, kid, your lawyers are sure anxious to see you, there are two of them."

He cuffed her and led her away. An hour later the guard called the name 'Safara Parilla'. Guessing that it was the name they'd given her, she went to the door where he cuffed her and led her to an interview room where Franklyn was waiting. The guard hovered after removing the cuffs.

"You can go now officer," Franklyn said.

"This is a dangerous woman, sir and I was concerned for your safety."

"Well you can quit being concerned right now. I'm in absolutely no danger from Ms. Price."

The guy left and closed the door.

"Well these bastards are sure out to get you, aren't they? I've been turning over every log in every federal agency and police department in Virginia, I've even been to the Capitol. That stroke you pulled with the kid was genius. The bastards had you registered here with the wrong name, but as soon as I got the call about the request for a lawyer from here I was certain it must be you that instigated it."

"What's happening about Kristen?"

"Don't worry about her. That charge is bullshit. She'll be on her way home before the end of the day, and the cop will have a formal complaint from the judge against him. One of my associates is dealing with that pro bono. I need you to tell me everything from the moment you were arrested until you walked through the door a few minutes ago."

Saffie's account took a long time because they hadn't let him bring a recording device into the prison and he was having to take notes. They'd been talking for an hour when the door opened.

"Times up I'm afraid," the guard told them.

"I suggest you turn around and walk right out of here, Deputy. This jail is in enough trouble as it is. There's likely to be charges brought against people who work here, so unless you want to add to that number..." He left it to the deputy to draw his own conclusions about what he'd say next.

He left them to it, and it took another forty minutes before she finished.

"I can't get you out of here today Saffron, but I hope to have you home by lunchtime tomorrow."

"Okay but there's one more thing I want you to do for me. There's a woman in here awaiting trial on a murder charge. Her name is Billie-Jean Bates. I promised to get someone to see if arrangements can be made for her daughter to visit her when she goes down. Can you get someone to look into that for me. I'll pay for it of course."

"Okay if that's what you want."

The guard took her back to her cell and passed the meal trolley on the way.

"Don't I get anything to eat?"

"You shouldn't have spent so much time with the lawyer."

"Another item on my list of complaints."

"Like I give a shit."

All the other inmates had returned from court and she resigned herself to another night in the cell.

"Safara, did you do anything about my visits?" Billie-Jean asked.

Saffie didn't bother to correct her. "I asked my lawyer to have one of his associates look into it, they may want to speak to you."

"That's fantastic. Thank you."

"I don't know what if anything he can do."

"How come he hasn't got you out?"

"He will, and when he does, a lot of people are going to get their asses handed to them on a plate."

"You want to watch your back though; I overheard Crystal is trying get herself put back in here."

"Thanks, Billie-Jean, that's good advice."

Saffie lay back on the bed and tried to concentrate on her next moves through the throbbing pain of her arm. The lights had dimmed and people had started to settle when the door opened. Curiosity got the better of her and she lifted her head and looked through the other bunks to see Crystal staring directly at her, wearing a vengeful expression.

Crystal chose an empty bunk opposite Saffie on the other side of the room and sat up staring at her.

"Couldn't keep away then, Crystal?"

"You better keep your eyes open tonight, Price - cos as soon as you close them I'm coming over there and slit your throat."

"I guess you'll have been chatting to that cop again."

"I'm no rat, bitch."

"No, then how come you know my real name? The jail have me registered under a false one."

The conversation had attracted the attention of the other women.

"She's a fucking snitch!" one of them shouted.

"Snitch!" Several others shouted until it developed into a chant of 'Ditch the snitch bitch', just like the day before.

Inevitably the noise attracted attention, the lights came on and the riot squad charged in, although this time there was no fight to break up.

"What the fuck is going on?"

"She's a rat and she's threatening to kill Safara," Billie-Jean called out.

The chant restarted, and in the end they conceded and moved Crystal out again.

"You better make sure she doesn't have a weapon, officer," Saffie said with a smile. "She seems like a dangerous character."

He searched the bed that Crystal had been using and found a shank.

"That shank looks suspiciously like the one that I handed to one of your colleagues this morning. You might want to ask around to find out how it found its way back into Crystal's hands. What do you think?"

He grunted and followed the others out of the room."

The women took a while to settle down, but eventually most were asleep, and Billie-Jean came and sat on the end of the bed.

"Why are they so set on killing you?"

"Because I have information that can put some very important people in jail for the rest of their lives."

"Fucking Hell!"

"Why don't you tell me why you said that to the guards about Crystal," Saffie asked. "Doesn't that make you a snitch?"

"Yeah, but I told the others what you did about getting that lawyer to help me, and they said about you helping that kid out this afternoon. They all believed Crystal's been working with the guards anyway so that sort of gives me a free ride."

Saffie laughed. "Thanks for that Billie-Jean. Good luck with those visits by the way."

She was so tired that sleep was inevitable once again in spite of the hunger.

When the lights came on and the wakeup call sounded, an uncharacteristic torpor made it difficult to force herself from bed which left her at the end of the queue for the washroom facilities. Her period was due sometime in the next day or two, and coupled with her injuries and exhaustion, it was hardly surprising she felt the way she did.

It was almost her turn to use the washroom when the door opened, two female guards stepped inside and one called, "Safara Rivanna."

Her first thoughts were, 'Jesus that's early. Well done Franklyn.' But then when they cuffed her, it registered that they were still using the false name, and she began to have doubts. They took her back to the room where she'd been told to strip when she first arrived, removed the cuffs, and gave her a bag with her own clothes. They waited while she dressed and cuffed her again.

"What the fuck is going on?"

"You're being transferred."

"Oh brother, is this jail fucked. I'm going to see to it that everybody here that colluded in this conspiracy becomes an inmate in this crooked institution, and the paymasters here are going to have a huge hole in their budget."

"Listen Rivanna, we don't have a fucking clue what you're going on about, and care even less, so just shut the fuck up and let us do our job."

They led her outside where a police cruiser waited.

This made even less sense. Prisoners weren't transferred by police, but by the Department of Corrections.

"This isn't right," she told the cop. "Where are you taking me?"

"Where we've been told to. Now just get in and shut up."

Watching out of the window she recognized most of the streets they drove along as they were all near to her home, so she was astonished when the police car drove into the lot of a cheap motel in Falls Church that she'd driven past dozens of times in the past.

"If this is some sort of hit, you should know that I won't go down without a fight."

They helped her step out of the car and led her to one of the first-floor motel rooms before removing the cuffs.

"Go inside, Mrs. Price. The door's unlocked," one of them told her.

Warily she opened the door and was stunned by what she saw.

Chapter 48

The small room seemed even smaller with the group of people standing in what little available space there was. She recognized them all; Andrea Torres, Deputy Director of the FBI, Patryk Wilkanowicz, Deputy Director of the CIA and Special Agents Ramirez and Burns.

"What the fuck Ramirez? You've sold me out?"

"Calm the fuck down and listen, Price," Torres said. "At the moment, Mr. Wilkanowicz is under arrest and you have two hours to convince me not to release him."

"If he's under arrest, why's he not in cuffs?"

"Because I said so."

"Why is he in here at all, because I'm not going to have a debate."

"Same answer. You don't like it, fucking hard luck, because those are the rules."

"Okay, but first I need some painkillers and something to eat because in the last forty-eight hours all I've been given are two sandwiches and an apple."

"Fine, but we ain't going to wait around while you go hunt down a diner. I'll have someone get something in and we start right now. Burns, get someone to arrange some painkillers for Ms. Price and some food, something that will let her eat and talk at the same time."

Burns left the room.

"What happens if I can't convince you?"

"Mr. Wilkanowicz will be free to leave."

"What about me?"

"Same answer."

"Can I ask Wilkanowicz questions?"

"That'll be Mr. Wilkanowicz to you, and yes, you can ask him questions. He's been Mirandized, so he's not obliged to answer although he's said he won't exercise his right to silence unless it threatens one of his agents overseas."

"Mr. Wilkanowicz, why was my husband sent on the mission to Ukraine when it was not a theatre he was familiar with?"

"We'd lost three field agents in the area over preceding months and we suspected that we had a mole. The indications were that the traitor was somebody local such as in the embassy or another agent. So, after discussions it was decided to send in someone from outside the team to specifically winkle out the culprit."

Burns returned with a packet of Tylenol.

"Who picked Brett and why?"

"I chose Brett, simply because he's the best agent in Europe."

"He missed two scheduled contacts before any alarm was raised and three before anybody informed me, his wife. How soon were you told something was wrong?"

"After the first missed contact I authorised a level one discreet contact, but I wasn't informed which agent they were referring to. Missed contacts are a surprisingly common occurrence and it would be rare for me to refuse a level one."

"What normally happens next?"

"I'd get a report of what happened, successful or otherwise. That didn't happen this time, and I should have investigated when I hadn't heard after twenty-four hours, but I didn't. I wasn't aware who the lost contact was, until after the discreet contact had failed and he'd missed the second scheduled one. It was at that point I discovered that Brett was the missing agent. I immediately authorised a level two search, and to go to Level three missing agent status after a further twelve hours if nothing was heard. You should have been informed after the discreet contact failed."

"What have you done about the obvious mistakes in reporting. In particular I'm asking about the personnel involved."

"I've instituted a top level investigation by Professional Standards into what happened, and who's responsible. In the meantime I've drafted in an Associate Director from the Central America team to oversee operations, and all the agents and handlers have been told they'll be moved to other duties when this investigation is complete. However, if things are as bad as they appear it's likely that some or all of them will lose their jobs, or even face charges."

"What have you discovered so far?"

"That comes under the heading of information that could endanger agents overseas."

"What exactly did the agents in Ukraine actually find?"

"I'll only say that Brett had narrowed his suspicions to two people and he was hoping to expose the actual mole when he went missing. I can't say more for the reasons I've just given."

"I want to know how the people sent to conduct the level three search discovered nothing, when I managed to locate and free him after less than twenty-four hours in the country, and I'm not even an active field agent, and haven't been for eight years."

"So you admit to conducting an illegal clandestine operation in a foreign country without authorization?" Torres sounded judgmental.

"Well it didn't look like 'authorized' illegal operations were working."

"You could have sparked an international incident."

"And the murder of American subjects wasn't going to?"

"How did you do that without resources?" Burns asked.

"I did have resources - just not from the CIA. Don't ask me to expand on that."

"Okay, carry on," Torres said.

"Thank you. Mr. Wilkanowicz, by that time you'll have known about the abduction and subsequent rescue of my son. Surely you'd have made the connection with Brett's disappearance. What did you do about it?"

"In fact, I wasn't made aware about the abduction until much later, but as soon as I learned about it I suspected possible involvement of people in the Eastern European team at Langley, and I asked for an agent from Professional Standards to investigate."

"What was the name of the agent?"

"I didn't ask for a specific agent, but it was John Atkinson who was given the job."

"And what did he report?"

"He reported back after two days that he'd found no reason to suspect any of the agents directly involved in Ukraine operations but would continue to investigate."

"Do you know why Atkinson was chosen?"

"No, it wouldn't be normal for me to have any involvement in that decision. PS is independent from my direct command."

"Why didn't you take full control of the investigations into what had been happening yourself? You must have realized that the possibility of involvement by someone working for a foreign power inside Langley was a massive threat to national security."

"You're absolutely correct but as soon as I heard that Brett had been found, I halted all operations in Ukraine. The FBI were the correct people to conduct the external investigations in the USA, and I reported my concerns to Andrea, who said that Special Agent in Charge Ramirez was already on the case who'd said she was happy to have Special Agent Burns as her wingman."

"Ms. Torres?"

"That's accurate, and I restricted the team to the two of them because of the national security implications."

"Agent Ramirez, Special agent in Charge? I don't remember you mentioning that."

"Too much of a mouthful for everyday use in my opinion. It was on my ID. Does it matter?"

"I guess not."

A knock at the door. Burns opened it for someone to pass him a pizza box, a box of twelve donuts and a tray of large coffees.

"Tell them to repeat the coffee order in an hour," Torres told him. "Carry on when you're ready Price."

"Everywhere I've turned in this I've come across an elusive character calling himself 'Lopez'. In the Ukraine he was the recruiter of the abduction gang that took my husband."

"How did you discover that, Ms. Price?"

Saffie noted the passive aggressive addition of a title to her name. "Fifth amendment. If it works for Mr. Wilkanowicz, it works for me too, right?"

"Fair enough, continue."

"Then, later in my investigations I discovered it was someone calling himself Lopez posing as an FBI agent that had hired a crooked security camera engineer to install expensive miniature surveillance cameras throughout my house."

"How did you discover that?" Torres wanted to know, "Did you spot one of the devices?"

"I'd kinda expected the cops or the FBI to bug me because that's what you do. So I started by using my own bug detector. I began the search in my study and picked up two listening devices right away, but there were two types. I didn't think it likely that both the cops and the FBI would bug me so I hired a private specialist."

"That would be Linda Baker I suppose?"

"If you say so, but it's not relevant. It's what was discovered that brought me to suspect that neither agency was responsible. Not only were there listening devices throughout the house but sophisticated expensive cameras as well. One camera had even been installed in my shower and no judge would sign a warrant agreeing to that. We discovered that the operator was conducting his operations from my neighbor's garage and I challenged him. He revealed that he was hired by someone calling himself Lopez. Under close questioning he gave a description of the guy which was remarkably close to that given by Novak Hevil, the lead character in my husband's abduction. At first that led me to believe that Lopez was able to travel freely back and forth between the US and Ukraine, not an easy journey, and not easily arranged."

"Did you manage to identify him?"

"I'll come to that because things aren't that straightforward. Anyway I confiscated the camera guy's phones so that I could have them analyzed."

"Wait a minute," Burns asked, "What did you do about this crooked camera guy?"

"I persuaded him to make a full confession of his voyeuristic offences which turned out to include numerous incidents of recording young teenage girls in their bedrooms and showers, including my neighbor's granddaughter. He agreed to make a contribution to a charity that helps victims of those kind of crimes and compensate me for my consequential losses on condition that I didn't report him for his felonies under the Espionage Act."

"What! You've no authority to grant immunity to that!" Burns exploded.

"I didn't grant immunity. I only agreed not to report him. There's nothing to stop you bringing charges. The guy's name is Harvey Wallace; the

Virginia State Police have him in custody on a long list of charges at the moment, so he won't be hard to find."

"What about the evidence?"

"Will a videoed confession, and a cloned copy of his hard drive help?"

"Carry on, Price," Torres said.

"There was one aspect of this guy's involvement that I didn't spot at first, but the timing of the camera installation and other things wasn't right. I knew that they couldn't have been installed until after my son's abduction, so I suspected that someone inside the cops, FBI or CIA had provided the entry code to my house. I ruled out the cops because I'd not given them the code, and they'd been sidelined by the FBI. At that point I trusted neither federal agency.

"I spent a long time trying to think of someone who could be the mysterious Lopez and came up with nothing, until I remembered an English guy I met in Slovyansk who told me he was called Nigel Jenkins. He propositioned me in the hotel, alleging that he thought I was a prostitute. Seemingly, at the time, I thought he couldn't have anything to do with it, and I dismissed him as just a horny travelling salesman. So I just humiliated him and sent him on his way. I still don't understand his motive for that approach.

"However, by this point my investigation into who was responsible had stalled so I decided that I needed to eliminate him as a suspect. After giving my contact in Ukraine a brief description, he identified Jenkins as a rogue British Agent called Norman Johnson. A man that I last heard you were searching for in connection with a shooting incident in Falls Church, not far from here."

"So is he Lopez?" Torres asked.

"Yes and no."

"What do you mean?"

"There's more than one Lopez - at least two."

"So what the Hell are we doing here?" Burns said. "I thought your theory was based entirely on Mr. Wilkanowicz being Lopez, and you were trying to find ways to prove it."

"Firstly, I didn't call whatever this is today, and secondly that might be how you go about investigating, Agent Burns, but not me."

"How did you conclude there's more than one then?"

"Timing. I used the agency's resources to discover if Johnson had travelled between Ukraine and the US in the previous two months. It turned out that he had, but only once and he was still here. Timing ruled him out from being the Lopez here in the USA, but not necessarily from being the one in Ukraine."

"What did you do next then Ms. Price?" Torres asked, by this time there was respect creeping into her tone.

"Using a contact of my resource in Ukraine, I had him do a detailed investigation of Hevil's mobile phones that I'd taken when I questioned him. It revealed some interesting things. First, not only that he'd been in communication with somebody either in or very close to the US Embassy in Kyiv. Second, he'd also spoken to a number I later discovered had been contacted by somebody else of interest here in the US. Up to this point all these numbers were burners, making it difficult to nail a specific person."

"Cellphone use inside US foreign embassies is jammed," Burns told her.

"Precisely, but it was useful information anyway. By this time I was as certain as it was possible to be that I was being followed here in the US because I'd discovered trackers on both my family cars, the one I'd used to transport my son to a place of safety near Harrisonburg and the one I'd left at home. They could only have been planted before I left home to find my son."

"So is that an admission to the murders of the five gangsters in Richmond then," Burns gleefully asked.

"I admit to nothing Agent Burns, except to say when I left those men, they were all still alive. Anyway, to continue where I left off, the trackers on my vehicles must have been placed before I set out for Richmond, because there was no other opportunity. But knowing this didn't help me to learn if it was someone inside Langley or someone inside the FBI."

"Why would you think it would be someone inside the FBI?" Torres asked.

"Because it was possible it could have been. There seemed to be no progress by the Bureau in discovering who was behind my son's abduction, and little interest in the second attempt either. The only way anyone could have guessed where I'd taken him was from that tracker. So at that stage I still wasn't sure.

"My trip to Langley to see Mr. Wilkanowicz was enough to narrow it down to someone there who was having me tracked."

"How?" Wilkanowicz spoke for the first time since the first few questions.

"Because while I was there, someone put a tracker inside my wallet. It might even still be there."

"Fuck!" Torres exclaimed, "Ramirez, did you collect Ms. Price's purse from her home like you were asked?"

"Yes, Ma'am."

"We need to get out of here, right now!"

At that moment someone knocked on the door.

"It'll be the coffee," Burns assured them.

Before anyone could stop him he opened the door and a hail of bullets threw him back into the room. Other than Saffie, the occupants threw themselves behind the beds, but Ramirez pulled her weapon and fired twice before her gun jammed.

Saffie had dropped to the floor behind Burns' body. She pulled this handgun from his exposed holster and shot the gunman through the head before he had time to refocus his fire.

Once again Saffie experienced the eerie silence that follows a period of intense gunfire. Then she asked, "Has anybody else been hit?"

"I have," Wilkanowicz answered.

"I've got two teams of agents, the cops and medics on the way," Torres said. "Well done Ramirez, and you Ms. Price. How bad is it Patryk?"

"It hurts like fuck, but I don't think I'm gonna die. How's Burns?"

"He's dead," Saffie confirmed.

Ramirez was trying to contact the rest of the agents that were there to prevent precisely that sort of event. "Nothing, nobody's answering. I hope to God it was a lone shooter, but we can't risk sticking our heads out until help arrives."

It was late morning so it was likely that the only other occupants of the motel were the desk clerk and cleaners, but the wailing of a woman in pain from somewhere nearby was an indication that Wilkanowicz and Burns weren't the only casualties.

Torres was tearing up sheets to stem the bleeding from Wilkanowicz's wound. He'd been lucky, the bullet had skipped across his ribcage beneath his left arm, leaving a wound about five inches long but not deep. If it had been two inches to the right, it would have been his heart.

The sounds of multiple sirens soon dominated and they were being encouraged to vacate the crime scene and relocate to Falls Church police station by its police captain and by FBI special agents alike. Wilkanowicz was refusing to go to hospital in spite of advice from paramedics and the fact he was in a lot of pain.

"No, we need to get this done. We need to finish this; we need to know. I'm as anxious to know who's behind this as everybody else. Is anybody going to tell us how many others have been hurt?"

The police Captain told them that one of the motel cleaners had been killed and one injured, three other FBI agents were dead, and a fourth seriously wounded.

"Who was the shooter, and can we be sure that he was alone?" Torres asked.

The cops weren't able to identify the gunman from his prints, but Saffie confirmed that it was Johnson. She showed them the sophisticated tracking device that had been in her wallet and a patrol officer provided a Faraday RFID protection pouch that he used for his car key to contain it before the FBI took it into evidence.

Chapter 49

In the police station they reconvened with the intention of continuing where they'd left off, despite the fact they were all still shaken by events, but Saffie refused to cooperate until she'd spoken to Brett and the boys and been given something more to eat.

Torres conceded that it wouldn't hurt to eat while they continued, so an agent was instructed to order in for the four remaining people, although Ramirez said she didn't feel like eating after seeing her partner murdered in front of her eyes an hour earlier.

Saffie's phone call to Brett was emotional for all of them, including Josh. She assured them that she was safe, that she'd be home before the end of the day; and that she hadn't been harmed any further, although the injuries on her left side had been aggravated when she dived to retrieve Burns' gun.

When they reconvened their conference, Wilkanowicz asked how the device had been planted in her wallet while she was in Langley.

"The only time the wallet was out of my hands was at the security desk in your building on the way in and again on the way out. I only decided to go there less than an hour earlier. I'd told nobody, and to plant it on my way in they'd have needed prior knowledge and instruction, so it must have happened as I left. So it follows that it could only have been ordered by someone who knew I was there. Of course that could be a whole list of people, but the most likely suspects are you Mr. Wilkanowicz, your PA, or Felix Carter. Carter 'bumped into me' as I was leaving, and it's possible that he'd seen me earlier and told the security woman to plant it. I haven't been able to investigate further because of my suspension, but also I didn't want to alert whoever that I was onto it."

"I wasn't aware you'd been suspended," Wilkanowicz claimed.

"Would you have expected to have been?" Torres asked.

"Absolutely, every time. When did that happen?"

"After the first assassination attempt."

"First attempt! How many have there been?"

"At least three."

"Tell me," he said, appearing genuinely concerned.

"The first was the incident in Arlington where I was rammed."

"I knew about that, but what else?"

"The incident in Penguin Place was next."

"So that was you?" Ramirez said. "I knew it. You were the third driver."

"That's right. Brett and I had already identified Atkinson as a player the day before. Brett spotted him watching me enter the Davis house. At first he gave him the benefit of the doubt, wondering if he was just checking us out, but when he saw him attaching a suppressor to his gun, Brett made an anonymous call to 911. They picked him up but he must have convinced the cops that he was some sort of good guy because of his job in PS and he was released.

"Later that day I spotted a car pick up my tail while I was on my way to see my lawyer. I ID'd Johnson following closely behind. Then Atkinson pulled out in front and they attempted to sandwich me. I dodged into a residential division to give them the slip but they still almost fenced me in. I was lucky, he was firing with his left hand, and so when I swerved to dodge his aim, he ended up hitting Johnson. I fired out of my open window as I passed behind him and got lucky. I'm ambidextrous so I guess my aim was better than his."

"For God's sake, Price - you've got more lives than a cat!" Ramirez exclaimed.

"When was the third time?"

"After the shooting in Oakton, that's when I picked up this gunshot wound."

"What happened in..."

Wilkanowicz interrupted, "We know who the shooters were in Arlington, and we know that Atkinson and Johnson were the shooters in Falls Church. Have you any idea who it was in Oakton?"

"My guess it was Lopez or his paymaster."

"What makes you say that?"

"Whoever it was, wasn't one of the gang that took the Davis family hostage because he was late on the scene, yet he was obviously part of the conspiracy because he fired at me on sight. That's one reason, but mostly because he was limping on his left leg."

Wilkanowicz appeared to have taken over the questioning now, "What does that mean?"

"The day before the Oakton incident, the Davis boy had been spending the day with our son at our house, but after I'd questioned Bridger about his involvement in the Arlington assassination attempt, I think he must have got cold feet and decided to run for the hills and they asked us to hang on to Josh. I think their plans were interrupted by their abduction."

"Why were they being abducted?" Torres asked.

"I suspect they were to be murdered and I was to be the person they'd pin it on."

"What's the limping guy got to do with Lopez?"

"Because that morning I'd gone to the Davis house to find out what was happening with Josh. When I got there I found the place unlocked and apparently abandoned. I went inside to have a look around. The place had been turned over, and it was obvious that they'd left in a hurry, although there was no sign that they'd been taken hostage at that time. I decided to see if they were at the grandmother's house. When I got there, I decided to make a covert approach, and after an initial recce it was obvious that Bridger and his wife were being held hostage. I'd have called it in at that point, but one of the hostage takers began to rape the young woman, so I intervened."

"Hold on a bit I'm confused," Wilkanowicz said. "What's this about Davis's involvement in the Arlington shooting?"

Saffie explained how she deduced his involvement and how she'd paid a private consultant to look at Davis's phone records and that she'd uncovered a great deal of incriminating evidence and associations with someone who called himself 'Wolf'. She went on to explain how she'd interviewed him on video and how he'd admitted everything and explained how Wolf had recruited him as a sleeper. How he'd been ordered to fly to Kyiv meet with Johnson and assist in arranging the recruitment of a gang to abduct Brett, paid for with money that Wolf had been paying into his mother's account.

Torres confirmed that she'd seen that video and asked, "How does that all link to the shooter in Oakton being Lopez."

"When I was looking around the Davis house I was jumped. I guess it was whoever had turned the place upside down. Anyway there was a struggle and my gun went off and he screamed. I'm pretty sure my shot caused him a minor injury to his left leg. I gave chase but I was dazed from where he'd hit me and he got away. Later, after the guy took the shot at me he limped away on his left leg."

"He could have been hit by one of Davis's bullets," Ramirez pointed out.

"If you'd seen the random shots that Davis was spraying around, you wouldn't say that. It would have been more likely to have hit a plane coming in to land at Dulles."

"How does that lead to him being Lopez though?"

"On its own it doesn't but coupled with another thing it does. All the descriptions of Lopez have included the same detail; he has a squeaky cough. That's relevant now because Davis was instructed to tell Johnson to fake a squeaky cough when he met with the gangsters in Slovyansk. The guy in the Davis house had a squeaky cough, and the man who recruited the security camera guy had a squeaky cough."

"That's still a pretty big leap for him to be Lopez."

"If the shooter is Wolf, he must also be Lopez."

"How do you come to that?"

"Because the name Lopez comes from lupus, the Latin word for wolf."

"Hundreds of people have names that mean something in a different language."

"I haven't finished yet; I'll join the dots before I'm done. Someone in Langley is pulling the strings. That much is certain and I'm sure as I can be that it's someone on the top floor, because only someone at the very top of the tree would have enough pulling power to make these things happen. Think about it; ordering Davis to Ukraine, getting Homeland to detain Brett at the airport and keeping him incommunicado for no reason, then reporting me to the Department of Justice for some bullshit charge.

"The abduction of my son, and the second attempt, served no purpose. There was never any attempt to demand a ransom, nor any attempt to interrogate Brett whilst in captivity. They wanted Brett out of the way because he was getting too close. They needed me to be charged with something, anything, to distract me because they knew from my reputation that I wouldn't lay down and play dead, which explains my son's abduction. Then when that didn't work and I started to get too close, they saw assassination as their only option."

"So do you now think that you know who it is?" Torres said, becoming impatient.

"Yes but I also think there's a trail that leads to Wolf's accomplice, Atkinson."

"Explain, and don't hang about getting to the point."

"Agent Ramirez, Do you want to tell Ms. Torres a bit more about Atkinson?"

"As I indicated to you earlier Ma'am, Atkinson isn't his birthname," she began. "The real child with that name and birth date died when he was twelve days old, and his parents were killed in a car wreck three months later. The man we call Atkinson was raised in Sainte-Agathe near Quebec. The father and mother worked at a small provincial golf club; and the boy ended up joining the Police straight from college.

Saffie took up the tale from where Ramirez left off. "When Atkinson left University, he did so under a cloud after twice being accused of rape, and yet somehow he was still able to join the New York State Police. From there he joined the FBI but left under yet another cloud. Next stop, he went to work for the private military contractor, Woolfe Northwater. From there he found his way into the CIA. Atkinson should never have been allowed to set foot inside Langley, let alone get a job there. His previous history should have barred him from even being considered for a post in any law enforcement agency let alone the CIA and as for being fast-tracked into professional standards, it stinks to high heaven."

"Woolfe - that name again. Are you suggesting there's a connection?" Torres asked.

"Yes."

"Why can't you just tell us what we need to know?"

"Because when I tell you I don't want to have to back track and try to fill in the background in order to convince you."

She sighed, "Okay then carry on."

"Are we agreed that whoever has been doing this is m,very powerful, and has access to a lot of money?" They all nodded, "This has been a hugely expensive operation, and as far as I can tell, apart from the money paid into Davis's mother or mother-in-law's account, it's all privately funded. That indicates that he must be very wealthy or has access to funds from a clandestine source. Brett and I decided to look a bit deeper into Woolfe

Northwater. It turns out to be a pretty shadowy private company, its shares aren't traded publicly and it's owned entirely by its board members. At its last published accounts it had a net value of fifty-three billion dollars. Its board consists of three serving and two retired US senators, a number of other extremely wealthy but little known individuals, and two people whose name we know but could find little about at the time. The two are called Remy Raimond and Wilfred Bauer.

"The day before I was arrested, Brett and I staked out Northwater's AGM to try to identify the two unknown board members by photographing them and using facial recognition. Without going into detail we concluded that Remy Raimond is actually Auguste Laurent. There was only one picture of him on the web when he was identified in the background of a photograph published in a Quebec local paper. The article it illustrated was about a 'philanthropist' who saved their small provincial village golf course from closure, by buying it. The village was Sainte-Agathe."

Torres and Ramirez gasped, Wilkanowicz remained unmoved.

"That left us with Wilfred Bauer as the final unidentified board member, except we did manage to identify his car, a blue Model X Tesla license plate UUS-9146 registered to Woolfe Northwater. That might have been the end of the trail for a while except for the fact that, on the day that I went to Langley to see Mr. Wilkanowicz, that exact same car cut me up in the car park.

"Now, returning to the shooter that escaped from Oakton, it's reasonable to assume that even for a minor gunshot wound he'd have needed medical treatment, therefore would likely to have been absent from the office on the day after the shooting. If not he'd at least have had a limp. Our enquiries revealed that nobody on the top floor had a noticeable limp that day and the only people absent were Mr. Wilkanowicz, Roy Scott, and Joni Collins. It goes without saying that Joni Collins can be ruled out because she's a woman. Roy Scott and Mr. Wilkanowicz had both allegedly been in the UK at a NATO conference all week, but there's no proof that either stayed for the whole week. Finally, the phone call that Wallace received from Lopez was made from, Waverly Way, Mclean. And Ukrainian word for Wolf is 'Wilk'. Where do you live, and what car do you drive Mr. Wilkanowicz?"

After a brief pause, Wilkanowicz nodded. "I do live in Waverly Way, at 1231, and I do have a persistent cough similar to the one you describe. It comes and goes - it's a side effect of the ACE inhibiting drugs that I take for my blood pressure. However, I don't own a car, I have a driver. I haven't driven a car for three years, not since I lost sight in my right eye after laser treatment for a cataract went wrong.

There was a momentary silence in the room, before Wilkanowicz continued. "But that's not to dismiss anything you've just explained, because it can all be attributed to another man on the top floor. My personal assistant Walt Bannerman also lives in Waverly Way, at 1251, drives a Tesla, and he's had a persistent cough since recovering from Covid. He was supposed to have been with me in the UK all that week but returned after the first day claiming health problems. I suspect after what you've just said, it was because he'd discovered that Davis was about to be exposed.

"It's my fault entirely that Brett Price's disappearance wasn't picked up sooner. I apologize for Saffron; it was unforgiveable, I can only say that everybody in that team will either lose their job or be transferred to other duties.

"I can't explain how Atkinson was recruited. It couldn't have happened without the support of someone on the top floor, logically someone in my team. It's possible that Bannerman could have lobbied for his transfer to Professional Standards with other directors on my behalf without my knowledge. That would need to be investigated. As my PA, Bannerman has control over a budget of his own, and he's been in post since before I was appointed, I don't know how much he's been paying into that account over the years, but he'd only have had to lose about two or three million over that time I guess, and I doubt that would be too difficult to hide in the scheme of things."

"If everything you suggest turns out to be true," Ramirez commented, "Then Bannerman must have latched onto the fact that the first four letters of your name meant wolf in Ukrainian and ran with it, and started using it in as many ways as he could. Clever, even if more than a little opaque."

"Bannerman must have been finally forced to sacrifice Davis as an asset not only because of Brett's investigations, but because of Saffron's courageous and relentless pursuit of the truth." Wilkanowicz continued, "After the failed assassinations and the unplanned confrontation with Saffron in the Davis house, he must have felt compelled to chance revealing himself in Oakton."

"Who audits your departmental accounts?" Torres asked.

"Mike Abbott."

"He'll need to be brought in," she said to Ramirez, "and we need to put an extra guard on Atkinson. Put out an APB on this Raimond Remy-Auguste Laurent guy."

"What about Bannerman?" Saffie asked.

"Maybe he can be turned. What do you think Patryk?" Torres asked.

"Don't even think about giving that piece of shit a pass," Saffie quickly intervened. "He's ultimately responsible for the deaths of three CIA agents, four FBI agents, and at least ten others, not counting what he's done to my family."

"Things have gone too far for that to be an option, Andrea. No he needs to be taken in, and quickly."

"You'll need to authorize that, Ma'am," Ramirez told her.

They watched while Torres spoke to somebody in FBI HQ and gave a list of instructions.

"What's happening about the Davis family?" Saffie asked.

"They were picked up last night near Rochester, New York State. They were trying to board a boat to cross Lake Ontario into Canada."

"None of the three women have legitimate IDs, but their son Josh, currently staying with my family, is a US citizen by birth."

"How happy would you be to keep him until a permanent placement can be arranged?"

"Fine, the kid's had quite enough to contend with without being shunted around between foster homes, but we're not approved to foster."

"I'm sure we can help accelerate that, if you're happy to. What about your husband? CIA field agent isn't a great job to put on an application to be a foster parent."

"Neither of us will be going back to work in Langley again. Brett's injury precludes it anyway, and I'm not fond of working for people who try to have you killed."

"That's not necessary Saffron."

"I don't care Patryk; I doubt you'll be staying much longer either."

"No I won't, I'll be handing my resignation in before the end of the week. I'm so sorry I let you down."

"Me too and maybe one day I might forgive you, but right now I'm going home."

She opened the door and looked for the exit. She found Brett and the boys in the public waiting area at the front of the station. They all hugged and exchanged kisses, but she told them that their tearful reunion would have to wait until they got home because she was still too angry.

Chapter 50

The following afternoon reports began appearing on TV news channels of the arrest of two CIA agents, naming both Atkinson and Bridger Davis. By the evening, more reports began to emerge of a missing CIA principal officer, later named as Walt Bannerman, along with rumors that a possible foreign agent had been operating inside the agency for many years.

Within forty-eight hours the previously unreported deaths of three CIA field agents in Eastern Europe were being mentioned. Bannerman was still missing and his picture was in every newspaper and on every news bulletin. Two more agents were being questioned, several more had been suspended and so had three agents inside the FBI. By the end of the week the resignation of the Deputy Director for Operations of the CIA was announced to nobody's surprise.

It hadn't been impossible to shield Josh from the publicity about his father. He frequently disappeared to his room to cry. It was going to take a long time for him to come to terms with the fact that his father was a traitor, and that he might never see the rest of his family again. Ben was upset by the effect it was having on his friend, and generally the mood in the Price household remained subdued.

Brett and Saffie discussed employing a private tutor for them to save Josh from the inevitable bullying that he'd otherwise be subjected to on his return to school.

After Saffie had been granted immunity from prosecution, the Price family adults spent hours at the George Bush Center being debriefed, sometimes by the FBI, at others by the CIA. The investigation was likely to take months or even years, and at some point they'd both have to give evidence in court.

The press and media frenzy continued without let up, and one or two had got word that Brett and Saffie were CIA employees and rung the gate bell to ask for comments before being told in no uncertain terms to go away.

It was three weeks after the motel shooting that one optimistic reporter followed Saffie to the supermarket; she'd spotted him seconds after leaving home and allowed him plenty of time to keep up. She'd recognized him from when he'd buzzed the gate bell several times over the previous week. He hurried to catch her after she got out of her car in the parking lot.

"Ms. Price, I wondered if you'd like to comment on the recent events inside the CIA."

"Are you proposing to film me and put it on TV?"

"If you're able to give us some insight into what might have happened, the public would be very interested to learn what you have to say."

"You'll know of course that revealing what goes on inside the George Bush Center could be a crime, so you'd have to let me see what you were going to broadcast."

"No problem, Saffron. Is it okay if I call you that?"

"I guess that's okay. Do you want to do it here, right now?"

"If that's okay, Saffron."

"Go ahead."

He unfolded a small tripod, clipped his phone to it and rested it on the hood of a nearby sedan, before focusing it on Saffron.

"I've never seen a tripod that small before. Can I see it?"

He handed her the phone with the tripod still attached. She took it from him, dropped it on the ground and stamped on it with her heel several times.

"Hey that's a thousand dollar phone!"

"Listen you ignorant little twat. I just saved you from twenty years in jail so shut the fuck up and piss off."

"Wh-what do you mean?"

"Exposing a CIA agent to a foreign power is a felony."

"I wasn't going to show it to a foreign power."

"What, you think they don't have TVs in other countries? Now fuck off."

She bent to pick up the mess that had once been a valuable hi tech piece of equipment so as to hand it to him but as she started to straighten something caught her eye that made her rugby tackle the reporter to the floor while grabbing for the gun in her purse. Shots began to ring out from an SUV stopped about thirty feet away, three bullets thudded into the sedan they'd been standing beside.

Saffie and the reporter had landed half hidden behind the car with just their legs exposed to the gunman.

"Pull your legs in and stay down," she ordered, as a bullet hit the ground near their feet.

Screams could be heard elsewhere in the parking lot.

Saffie crept towards the rear of the car and quickly popped her head up to see through the rear windows. The shooter was now out of his car and walking purposefully towards their position holding his gun two-handedly but swinging it from side to side searching for where she was hiding. Clearly an untrained gunman, the attacker, had enabled her to gain the advantage. With another quick glance at his position through the car windows, she moved around the rear of the car, stood, took two quick two shots and the gunman was dead before he hit the floor.

She rapidly scanned the area for collaborators and when she'd satisfied herself there were none, she rested her gun on the floor, put her foot on it and waited for the police. It didn't take long.

After going through the ritual of surrender, allowing herself to be cuffed, searched, and given a preliminary interview for the third time in far too short a period, she was made to wait for more senior officers to arrive. With no CIA ID to assist, the cops seemed to be in no hurry to move things along.

The young reporter was in tears for some time but a policewoman eventually managed to calm him down.

"Who's the shooter?" one cop asked, after failing to find an ID on the body.

"His name is Walt Bannerman; he's wanted by the FBI for treason," she told him.

"He's the asshole on the news? Jesus darling, you're gonna be a household name."

"I doubt it," she laughed. "While we're waiting, do you know what happened to Detective Sergeant Wolski after that business with the shootout at the motel?"

"Were you involved in that?"

"You could say that."

"I heard he's been busted to detective and posted to Charlottesville. He's kicking off big time; says he was framed by a Captain from Louisa."

Ramirez finally arrived with her new partner and told the cops to remove the cuffs.

"I might have guessed it would be you that brought him down. That's saved the State a whole bunch of money in court and prison costs."

"That's gun number four of mine that the cops have got. Is there any way you can persuade them to return at least one?"

"I'll speak to them. Have you heard anything about repercussions inside Langley?"

"Some; I doubt much of it will ever be made public. Radwell and Carter both lost their jobs, and Radwell may face charges. Two others have been suspended and a senior finance officer has been charged."

"There needs to be a complete review of how the section works in my opinion," Ramirez said.

"There's going to be a congressional enquiry. What's happening about the Davises?" Saffie asked, "Nobody's told us anything."

"Bridger has been charged with a list of offences under the Espionage Act; he'll probably get twenty to life. The women have all been charged with fraud and tagged by ICE for deportation. Their lawyer is trying to appeal, but my contact in CBP says their chances of success are close to zero."

"I wonder where that leaves Josh."

"My guess would be that they'll leave him with you until you tell them that you don't want him anymore. After abandoning him without even saying goodbye, Child Protective Services aren't likely to hand him over to a foreign national with a record. With his knowledge of some of the things that went on they won't be anxious to put him out there where he can spill the beans.

"We won't be asking for him to leave."

"How is he dealing with it?"

"Good days and bad days I guess."

"Did those foster papers go through okay?"

"Yeah; some people have to wait a year for that to happen."

"Don't knock it. So what now for you and Brett?"

"We've both handed in our papers, and we're negotiating severance packages. You can be damn sure we ain't going cheap. We thought we might try for PI licenses."

"Good choice."

"How was Burns's funeral?'

"Traumatic. He had three kids and his wife is pregnant again."

"That's real shit."

"Yeah."

"Okay if I do my shopping now?"

Ramirez shook her head and smiled. "Go ahead. I'll get you at home to take your full statement."

Printed in Great Britain
by Amazon

37412621R00175